The Naked Room

by Diana Hockley

Copyright © Diana Hockley 2010. All rights reserved. No part of this book may be reproduced or transmitted in any form or by any means, electronic, mechanical, including photocopying, recording, or by any information storage and retrieval system, without permission in writing from the publisher.

The Naked Room
Published by
Diana Hockley 2010
www.dianahockley.webs.com

Book layout and cover design
by Publicious Pty Ltd
www.publicious.com.au

Printed in Australia by
SOS Print and Media Sydney
www.sos.com.au

Printed in the UK, USA and Europe
by Lightning source
www.lightningsource.com

ISBN: 978-0-9775870-6-3

All characters and events in this publication are fictitious, any resemblance to real persons, living or dead, or any events past or present are purely coincidental.

Copyright © Diana Hockley 2010.

DEDICATION

For my patient husband, Andrew, who has endured hours of silent madness from me over the last three years, and for my dear friend, Pam Cairncross, who has sustained me with her support and optimism in spite of my wailing and whining. And for my sweet granddaughter, Ally, may you always be safe.

Contents

Chapter 1 In The Dark..................................1
Chapter 2 The Empty Piano.........................6
Chapter 3 Preliminary Enquiries.................11
Chapter 4 Once Upon a Father..................22
Chapter 5 Images of a Lost Child...............28
Chapter 6 God's Punishment......................41
Chapter 7 The Reckoning...........................48
Chapter 8 A Significant Decision................59
Chapter 9 Phone Call at the Witching Hour.....65
Chapter 10 It's Blood..................................72
Chapter 11 Someone Like Her....................79
Chapter 12 Secrets......................................90
Chapter 13 Sleuthing..................................97
Chapter 14 But I Did................................105
Chapter 15 Courier Mail...........................112
Chapter 16 Repercussions.........................113
Chapter 17 Retreating from the Heat........121
Chapter 18 No Fresh Flowers by Request......129
Chapter 19 A Surfeit of Old Goats.............136
Chapter 20 Hide and Seek........................145
Chapter 21 Painting by Rote.....................155
Chapter 22 Illusions..................................163
Chapter 23 The Numbers Game................165
Chapter 24 Doing Coffee..........................173
Chapter 25 On The Mountain...................183

Chapter 26 A Wedge Between Friends...........189
Chapter 27 A Precarious Position..................194
Chapter 28 Damage Control........................201
Chapter 29 Re-grouping...............................211
Chapter 30 Dark Aura..................................217
Chapter 31 Dubiety......................................220
Chapter 32 Shredding the Witnesses.............228
Chapter 33 The Weakest Link......................239
Chapter 34 The Sound of Silence..................252
Chapter 35 In The Frame.............................255
Chapter 36 Just Routine...............................264
Chapter 37 Machinations of A Ferret...........274
Chapter 38 Unwanted Goods......................281
Chapter 39 As Dusk Falls.............................291
Chapter 40 A Bit Of A Glitch......................293
Chapter 41 A Just Reward...........................297
Chapter 42 Confessions and Collectibles.......304
Chapter 43 Armageddon..............................310
Chapter 44 After Dark.................................317
Chapter 45 Aftermath..................................321
Chapter 46 Recriminations..........................328
Chapter 47 Closure......................................333
Chapter 48 Promises....................................335
Chapter 49 Coming Home..........................340
Glossary...345
Acknowledgements......................................347
About the Author..349
Celibate Mouse (sample chapter)..................353

CHAPTER 1
In The Dark

Ally

Saturday: before dawn.

My head feels like it's crammed in a vice. I force my stiff muscles to move, my fingers to unknot, then rub my hands over my bare icy arms. My feet are numb. I stare into the blackness; there's not a glimmer of light. Is it night?

I'm in a hammock or a sling of some sort, resting on a hard surface. I wrap my hands around the lengths of covered pipes and then slide them along. It feels like a camping stretcher. I can't keep my eyes open...*sleep*.

He clings to a sharp outcrop. The wind buffets him. His thin t-shirt whips up, exposes his skinny little body. A foot slips, he teeters. 'Ally! Allyeeeeeeeee! Save me!' He is torn away. Dressed in a tuxedo, he screams as he sails over the ocean, his bloodied right leg dangling...

The nightmare's back. Just when I think it's gone forever, it comes back, like a never-ending price I have to pay. I'm drenched with sweat; my heart is about to burst from my chest. Try to be calm. Slow your breathing, deep breaths. My head is pounding; my mouth is so dry, I can hear air rasping over my tongue.

It's daylight. The room spins then slows. Slim brown female legs appear beside me. I struggle to sit up as they back away. I draw up my legs. Pain hits, my knees scream as I roll hard to the right. The stretcher tilts and drops me onto the floor; my knees slam into the floorboards. I grab the woman's wrist, almost pull her off balance and drag myself halfway to my feet. She glares over the top of a surgical mask and jerks her hand away. The hatred in her eyes stuns me. As I open my mouth to shout at her, she turns and rushes out the door.

Run!

I scramble to my feet, but before I can take more than a couple of steps I slam into a man who grabs my upper arms. My legs collapse and I sag against his rock-hard body, my fingers scrabbling to hold onto the overalls he's wearing. His hot breath fans my face. The brown eyes staring coldly through the holes of his green knitted balaclava show no mercy. He's a snake primed to strike. No! His fingers dig into my flesh.

'Let me go!' My voice is a croak. I struggle weakly and reach for his hood. He twists aside and rams me back against the wall, so hard that the impact knocks the breath out of me. My chest heaves for whatever skerrick of air I can grasp, forcing a strangled moan from deep in my throat. Splinters prick the skin of my back through the thin material of my top; my bare feet fight for a foothold on the cold, wooden, floor.

His muscular body crushes mine and the woollen balaclava rasps my face as he forces my head back with his forehead. I close my eyes. He smells of lemons and garlic. His erection presses into the cleft of my legs.'

'Get away from me!'

His hand moves down. Oh no, not that! Something flashes in my face, light glinting along serrated silver. My head slams back into the wall when he slaps his hand across my mouth, blocking my nostrils. The cold edge of the blade presses under my jaw.

Freeze. I suck at the air around his palm.

'Settle down or we'll drug you again. Behave and you'll get something to eat. Carry on fighting, you get nothing. Do I make myself clear?' His voice sounds as though it's coming from the bottom of kerosene tin.

The woman returns with a small paper bag and a covered styrofoam cup, which she sets on the floor and leaves. The smell of coffee is nauseating, but I force my stomach to behave.

The man's smile stretches the wool of his balaclava. He maintains eye contact as he backs after her and whisks out, closing the door. I lunge after them but the door slams in my face. The key turns in the lock and they're gone. My hands are stinging and glowing red from pounding on the door. I press the hem of my skimpy glittering cammie to my face, quelling tears. The beading scrapes my mouth. An elf in my chest is pounding away at my heart with a hammer.

Don't panic. Deep breathe. What in God's name is happening?

My tongue sticks to the roof of my mouth. I take the lid off the cup of coffee, not stopping to savour the aroma before taking a mouthful. The warm, sweetened liquid rolls around my dry mouth, calming my mind and my stomach, relaxing my clenched muscles just a little. Is it drugged? Too late now, I've swallowed.

Steel security mesh covers a tinted window, the only source of light. The expanse of lawn below looks grey through the heavily-tinted pane. There's a tiny gap of about a centimetre under the sill. I finish the coffee and stick my fingers into the gap to try to pull the window up. Of course it won't budge. I lean back and peer through the mesh at the window frame. It's nailed shut.

I poke my fingers through the square holes in the steel, but can't reach the glass.

Rage curls inside me. I want out!

There is a line of trees and thick bush a few hundred metres away on the other side of the paddock. This place is obviously out of town, but there is nothing to tell me where it might be.

I turn my attention to the rest of the room. The bare walls are made of rough wood. The ceiling is very high, like in a tower room or attic. I can just see the outline of a manhole into the roof, but there is no way to reach it. There are vents just below the ceiling line and a wisp of air wafts through a crack between two of the floorboards. The stretcher and a portable toilet in the corner are the only other things in the room. They have left me one toilet roll.

Crying's not going to solve anything. Get control. Think. Who are they and why would they want to lock me up? If it's money they're after, a concert pianist at the beginning of her career is not a gold-mine. I'm not rich and nor is my mother. None of my friends could afford to pay a ransom, with the exception of my godmother, Georgie.

A wave of dizziness sweeps over me. I prop myself against the wall, waiting for my throbbing head to tumble off and roll around the floor. Slivers of pain shoot through my stiff muscles. I slide down to sit on the floor. Fear threatens to overwhelm me. Am I here for—are they going to rape me? Or make me a sex slave? But there's a woman involved surely she wouldn't allow that? Don't be so sure...for some reason she hates me, I saw it in her eyes. I'm sure I've never seen her before, so why on earth does she feel that way about me? I'm not sure she'd protect me. At least I'm not tied up, but are they so confident of the man's strength that they don't need to?

I've been here all night—my God, the concert! Brie, Sir James and the orchestra management surely realise I wouldn't miss a concert, or even a rehearsal. They must be looking for me by now. I feel I'm going to suffocate in here! Bloody hell, pull yourself together. That's it, slowly. Breathe into the palm of your hand. 'Get real, start acting rationally, Ally. Think. First things first...'

What time is it? My wristwatch is missing, handbag gone. Reading glasses, earrings, keys and driver's licence. Now, they have my name. Cold prickles run up my arms. Of course they know who you are. How do you think you got here? Is this a sick joke, or some kind of Pacific Orchestra ritual to initiate guest artists? Will the door suddenly open and everyone be standing there, laughing? No, it's too nasty.

Anger sweeps over me. No joke and definitely not my friends.

I bend down, pick up the paper bag and open it; two sandwiches, an egg and a ham. There's a piece of paper inserted between them. I draw it out and smooth it flat on my thigh.

The printed message is perfectly clear: You can go when you're paid for.

CHAPTER 2

The Empty Piano

Briece Mochrie

Saturday: 6.00am.

A spider popped out of a narrow crack in the ceiling and scuttled along his silken rope to grab a tiny entangled fly, then scooted back to its web and disappeared. A perfect analogy for my life—Ally snaring me, wrapping me up and then disappearing without a word on the night I planned to tell her I loved her.

What a miserable start to a shit of a day.

Scenes from a few hours before shunted like a power point presentation through my mind, my frantic search when she disappeared, the pain, and then the blow to the gut after I approached the doorman at the entrance to the club.

'Have you seen a girl with long red hair? Black skirt, sparkly top and handbag. 'I held my hand at eye-level. 'She's about so high.'

'Who are you?' he snapped, looking at me belligerently.

'Briece Mochrie, I—'

He rolled his eyes. 'Listen, Mr *"Breece Mock-ree,"* there's so many girls wandering in and out of here, I can't remember squat.' He began to turn away, and then paused. 'As a matter of fact I do remember a redhead, with hair down to there,' he placed his hand just above the curve of his arse, 'and wearing a black coat. Left with a bloke about an hour ago now, wrapped around each other like two koalas. I heard him call her Ally, so if that's your girl's name, mate, she's shot through. Didn't see any more, I was busy.' He winked. 'Dumped ya did she? Well, it happens to the best of us.'

My imagination pounced on scenes of her lying in her lover's embrace in some posh penthouse suite. His appearance was unimportant. The thought of their arms and legs tangled together, her smiling eyes as he bent over her naked body…shit.

She could have told me she wasn't interested anymore. Why agree to come back here after we'd been to the club, but then go off without a word? We both knew what it was all about. How could I be so fucking gullible? I'd never have taken Ally for a cock tease. I could've sworn she wanted me as much I wanted her. Yeah, sure.

I couldn't stay hiding in my bed like a wombat in its burrow. I threw off the bed covers and headed for the bathroom. My eyes stared back at me from the mirror like an animal in a pet shop. Fuck shaving. I ducked into the shower and turned on the tap. The cold water hit my chest, caused me to shudder. Rehearsal would start in a couple of hours.

My kitchen reminded me of last night's failure. My sister's bright table cloth, the highly polished cutlery and two wine glasses mocked me. I cleared the setting, shovelled it back into the cupboards and organised a caffeine hit. The cat bullied me until I fed her.

Then I sought refuge in my music, which normally sustains me through life's stuff-ups. My double bass stood in its case on its rack in the third bedroom cum practice room; my cello leaned against the piano. I thumped the coffee mug onto the side table and picked up the score for Elgar's Concerto in E Minor.

1.00pm.

Burning rubber along the tunnel under the concert hall worked off some of my anger, but not the dread in my belly. The machine at the car park accepted my musician's card. Once in my favourite spot at the far corner, I loaded my cello onto its trolley, pushed it to the lift and hit the button. By the time it reached the stage level, pain and embarrassment was swamped by enough rage to burn the whole fucking place down.

The depths of concert halls are the same all over the world, fuggy with conditioned air and the reek of oil-based make-up, perfume and aftershave mingled with boiled sweets. A faint clatter of dishes came from the distant canteen.

I stalked belligerently onto the stage, where eighty musicians tuned instruments, discussed yesterday's football results and argued over the cricket scores. Some rustled newspapers. The lighting and sound technicians clunked stuff high above us, and Centre staff fussed around in the gloom of the auditorium. A glittering audience, flushed with good food, wine and anticipation, would fill every seat that night.

Pam pounced on me the moment I stepped onto the stage. 'Ally's not here.'

'Not my problem. She's probably still shagging her new boyfriend.' I edged toward the other cellists. 'Give it a rest, okay?'

She persisted, her voice raised. 'No, listen to me, you Irish git, Ally would never miss a rehearsal. You know how dedicated she is. She's not answering her mobile and I can only get the machine.'

'Perhaps it's out of range. Look, stop trying to defend her.' Pam and I were going to fall out shortly.

'Damn it, Brie, she's a professional, the solo artist for

tonight, for *God's sake*! She's *never* let us down and or put her career in jeopardy. You know that.' Pam tended to scatter italics like rice at a wedding, when she was agitated.

'Look,' I said. 'We all searched for her, but the doorman told me she left with another bloke.'

'I'm not sure Ally went of her own accord. What if he was mistaken?'

'I didn't dream it. Perhaps her car broke down this morning and she couldn't get a taxi.' I was getting rattled. Somewhere deep inside me uncertainty stirred, like a carpet python waking from hibernation.

'For God's sake, it's Saturday, Brie, not a work day. Taxis are easy to get. Anyway, she'd have phoned me for a lift, if she couldn't start the car.' Pam rolled her eyes. 'And if she has a new boyfriend—which I don't believe for a moment—he would have brought her in for rehearsal!'

Michael chimed in. 'Have you spoken to her this morning?'

I whipped around. 'For God's sake, are you both mad? Of course, I haven't.' I bent down and started dragging things out of my tote bag. The tightness in my throat forced me to straighten and face them. We shared a moment of wordless dread, turned and headed for the orchestra manager, standing in the wings of the stage near the vacant piano.

Pam recounted the attempts she'd made to contact Ally. He frowned as he carefully clipped the pen into his shirt pocket. The conductor, Sir James McPherson, loomed behind us, eyebrows raised in inquiry. In a voice which sounded as though he'd eaten poison, he asked why we were at a nightclub. We described, yet again, the celebration at Traynor's after finishing the day before's recording session Ally disappeared. 'I'll go and see if I can find her,' I offered, gritting my teeth.

McPherson intervened. 'No, Briece, I need everybody here. Regardless of Ally's absence, we've got to get on with the rehearsal. John, you go.' Finished, he loped to the podium.

Fear and guilt vied each other for dominance. If only I'd listened to Pam and Michael when they suggested something might be wrong. Maybe the doorman misheard. Perhaps, it was Alice? Pam had defended Ally's integrity from the start. Why hadn't I listened, for chrissakes? I wanted to punch walls.

Sir James tapped his baton for our attention. 'Our pianist is late, so we'll begin with the Beethoven.' He stared without expression at his score for a few moments as we scuffled through our music. Whispers rustled across the stage. Jessica's laughter erupted amongst the violins. Hans, second cello seated by me, almost fell off his chair as he leaned over to whisper. 'Bet she's gone off with some lucky bastard!' He hauled his chunky body upright, laughing. Damn bloody Jess and her big mouth. Something stirred in my memory and then vanished before I could grasp it. I finished tuning up, placed my cello in position and waited for Sir James to lift his baton.

Then it hit me. Pam said Ally wore a short skirt and glittery camisole top. She hadn't mentioned the black coat the doorman described.

So, who did the coat belong to and why was it wrapped around her?

CHAPTER 3
Preliminary Enquiries

Detective Senior Sergeant Susan Prescott.

Saturday: 2.30pm.

The Ally Carpenter case came in at two o'clock. I had almost cleared my current "paperwork" and was looking forward to getting home in time to attend a much-anticipated classical concert that evening. A large masculine frame loomed in the entrance to my cubby-hole of an office.

'Yes?' I asked, without raising my eyes from the computer screen. 'Can I help you?'

'Yes, you can, Susan.'

Superintendent Courtland Greaves stepped in carrying a file, waved me to stay seated and took a chair, which creaked under his sturdy figure.

'DI Peterson's tied up with the Hetherington murder, so I've got an urgent one for you, Susan. Might not come to anything, but a young woman went missing last night at approximately eleven o'clock from Traynor's nightclub in the Valley. The AC wants her found, fast. Cleared with Peterson,' he added, referring to my immediate superior who was away for a rare weekend with his family. He laid the file on my desk. 'She only went missing last night?'

I was reluctant to put aside the folder from which I was working.

'She's an important person, a celebrity concert pianist, no less. I've actually met her at a few social events, dinners and a couple of receptions.' Greaves looked sheepish, a tinge of red beginning to show above his pristine collar. *You old rogue, you fancied her.*

'What on earth was a concert pianist doing at Traynors?'

'It's not forbidden, Susan. Young classical pianists like to have fun too. Apparently she trotted off to the ladies toilet, and then disappeared.'

'So tell me about her, and who's pushing the barrow out here? Why not give this to Missing Persons?'

'The Pacific Symphony Orchestra. Ally Carpenter is their star turn for the big concert tonight. The conductor, Sir James McPherson and one of the directors, James Kirkpatrick hounded the Commissioner to have it fast-tracked. That's why I've brought it here—well, to CIB. Technically she's not missing yet.' He leaned back, fingers steepled and peered at me over the top of his bifocals.

'Is she the one who's performing at the Concert Hall tonight?'

He nodded.

'My husband is taking me to that concert. He's been looking forward to this evening for months.' Bloody hell, couldn't the woman have chosen another night to go missing?

Greaves hauled himself to his feet. 'I don't know how they'll cover her absence if she doesn't turn up by then. It depends on whether something happened to her or if she's gone off with a boyfriend. Must say she didn't seem the type to do that, but you never can tell about young women these days.'

Would they jump to the conclusion that if a man disappeared he had run off with a girl? Of course not, but Ally Carpenter is female and automatically flighty. I grit my teeth to keep from biting him; chomping into a Superintendent is hardly a career enhancer.

Oblivious, he tootled on. 'A substitute will be obtained, of course. If you're free, attending the concert tonight'll be in the line of duty, get the feel of the orchestra.' We understood that if we found the pianist's body, then I, a Detective Senior Sergeant, wouldn't be going anywhere.

'One of her friends who was at the club last night is coming in to make a statement and look at the surveillance discs. We need to get this under way.'

'Right Sir, I'll get onto it.'

Sighing, I read the preliminary report. In my opinion, a twenty-five-year-old pianist would be most unlikely to jeopardise her career by running off with a boyfriend the night before a major concert. I clicked onto Google, brought up the girl's name and went into Wikipedia where there was a considerable amount of basic information on her childhood, mother, education and the beginning of her career. There was no mention of her latest concert round with the Pacific Symphony, so the site was not up to date. I didn't have time to search the internet for more about Ally Carpenter; I could do that later. I clicked off and went in search of assistance.

Detective Sergeant Evan Taylor, my work partner, lurks in a cubbyhole overlooking the river, amid a rat's stash of files, apple cores and scum-ringed coffee cups. He's comfortably padded, genial and deceptively lazy. My knock jerked him out of an afternoon nanny-nap. The file he was pretending to study slid off his chest onto the floor.

'Bloody hell, Susan, now look what you've done,' he

grumbled, stretching down for it.

'Courtland Greaves gave me an urgent one,' I replied, slumping into the only chair not covered in files. He made preliminary notes as I brought him up to scratch.

'I'll get over to her house and take a look. She might have lost her memory, gone for a walk and be injured somewhere. On the other hand, she could have shot through with a boyfriend. Do you want forensics on it yet?' Bloody men are all the same. Even the nicest ones can't get their minds off the sex angle.

'Not unless you find something. Organise one of the girlfriends to meet you at Carpenter's house. She may know if any clothes are missing.' I handed a sheet of paper over on which was written Pamela Miller's phone number. 'Apparently a neighbour at number six has a key, but Ms Miller's probably got one too. I'll get someone to call at Traynors and pick up all the CCTV footage from last night. Uniform will do a door knock around the club.'

We locked eyes and shared a moment of understanding. What if it's the worst case scenario? Evan got to his feet, swung his coat over his shoulder and ambled out the door after me.

Saturday: 5.00pm.

I was reading some publicity material on Ally Carpenter, when one of the team appeared.

'Susan, Ally Carpenter's friend, Pamela Miller went through her clothes and said there doesn't appear to be anything missing, except what she wore last night. Her car is still in the garage. Nothing untoward at the house. Seems to be a normal, messy young woman.' He smiled, obviously thinking of his teenage daughter's room. 'No signs of wild partying or drug use. We've sent out an all-points bulletin and the Traynor's employees were questioned. The doormen maintained she left with a man in a white car at about 10.00pm, a four-cylinder Toyota Corolla. He said the bloke called her Ally. *Oh no, what if Evan and Greaves are right?*

'Well, she's innocent until proven guilty,' I snapped. He stared at me, astonished. I softened my tone, achieving something professional. 'We can't assume anything, so expect the worst for now. The hospitals have been alerted. Her phone's not answering and her email's full. Keep trying.'

He nodded and vanished. I studied the photo of Ms Carpenter, speculating on the familiarity of her face. The telephone rang. 'Ma'am, a Mr Mochrie from the Pacific Symphony Orchestra is here to see you.'

Evan met me at the lift, and we descended to the ground floor where a covey of young female police officers and clerical staff twittered in the corridor.

'Excuse me, ladies.' They turned flushed, smiling faces to me.

'What's going on?' I asked. Someone giggled.

He slouched against the wall, around 195cm of rampant testosterone, with superbly styled, gleaming black hair and designer stubble, enhanced by smooth olive skin. Graceful and model-gorgeous, he was every parent's nightmare. *And who's going to protect him from me?*

'He's got more than his fair share of hair,' muttered follicularly-challenged Evan. I suppressed a smile. But was Briece Mochrie as careless with women's hearts as his looks might suggest?

'Mr Mochrie?' We shook hands; he had a grip like a boa constrictor. Fear lurked in his eyes—*because Ally Carpenter was missing, or because he was responsible for that?*

'Come through, please. A cup of tea for you?' He nodded and followed me into an interview room. Evan sent a probationary constable to the canteen, while we got the business of obtaining his personal details out of the way.

'When did you last see Ms Carpenter?'

'At about four o'clock yesterday afternoon. We finished cutting the final track to a recording for the Pacific Symphony and planned to celebrate at the club.' His voice reminded me of melted rum and raisin chocolate. *Tongue back in, you old fool.*

'What is her car rego?' I waited, pen poised. It would save time if he knew.

'1994 Ford Capri convertible, dark blue.' He dredged into his memory and gave us the number.

'She got a ride with Pam last night and I was going to take her home.'

That would be Pamela Miller. I made a note. 'Okay. Now, first of all, have you ever known Ally Carpenter to miss an important concert or rehearsal before this?'

'Once. A couple of years ago, apparently sh—'

'Why?' I couldn't wait for him to beat about the bush.

'Appendicitis,' he snapped.

'Well, she's obviously a reliable person. Now, Mr Mochrie, tell me what happened last night at Traynors? Take your time. We need to know everything you can remember, however insignificant.'

His account was quite straightforward, but we took him through the events of the past evening twice, focusing on his conversation with the doorman. When we finished, a constable rolled in a trolley with viewing equipment, which he positioned and plugged into the wall socket. I decided to push Mochrie a little. 'So, you didn't try to find her this morning? Go to her flat?'

'No!' he snapped, slamming his styrofoam cup onto the desk. Tea slopped over the top. I handed him a tissue to wipe it up. 'Of course not! I thought she'd gone off with someone else.' *Good grief, why would you dump this hunk?*

'And did you go home as soon as you left the club?' I asked, looking him straight in the eyes. He stared right back at me.

'Yes...er, no. I took Jessica Rallison to her place first and then I went to my flat.'

'Did you go inside with Ms Rallison before you left? For coffee or anything?'

'No, I didn't.' He reddened, clearly uncomfortable. I had him on the back foot.

I wonder what's going on there?

'Did Ms Carpenter ever talk about another man? Have you seen her talking to a persons or people you aren't acquainted with?'

He stared at me for a moment, before shaking his head. 'No, I don't recall anyone except business acquaintances. She has friends outside the orchestra, mainly from her student days, but there's really been no time for her to make any new ones, apart from neighbours perhaps. She only got back from the UK a couple of months ago. Since that time the orchestra has done an outback tour and I know she's been busy working on her programme for tonight's concert.'

I questioned him about the tour. 'Did she socialise with anyone in particular? Go to people's homes?' A yahoo bushie from out West could not be discounted.

'She went to parties and receptions, but she didn't go anywhere without people from the orchestra. *Aha, without you, I think sweetheart! Bet you didn't want to let her out of your sight. A control freak?*

Time to change tack. 'What time did you get home,

Mr Mochrie?'

He blinked. 'Around 12.30am, maybe a bit later.'

'Can anyone vouch for that?'

'No.'

'No-one?'

'Unless you can count the cat,' he replied, looking irritated.

'If it can talk, I will. Is Jessica Rallison a friend of yours? Or of Ally Carpenter?'

He wriggled. 'Both of us. I had a relationship with Jess for a short time earlier this year.' He was clearly embarrassed. *Okay, Jessica was out and may not have been happy.*

'So, you're sure you didn't call at Ally Carpenter's house on your way home? Or perhaps park outside?' I persisted.

Mochrie glared. His lips turned down at the corners. 'No, I definitely didn't go anywhere near Ally's house. I wouldn't want to!' *Jealous enough to hurt her?*

'Do you know of anyone who didn't like Ally and who might want to harm her? Or perhaps a fan who might be too devoted?'

His eyes widened. 'You mean someone she knows?'

'Maybe.'

'No. I can't think of anyone who would pull a stunt like this, and if a fan was stalking her surely we'd have known about it.' *No, you might not, and she wouldn't necessarily be aware of it either.*

I let him off the hook for the moment, closed the interview and switched off the recorder. 'Right. Now we'd like you to look at last night's CCTV from Traynor's.'

We watched the group of three friends arrive and settle at a table. Michael Whitby went toward the bar and the girls put their heads together. The music would have been head-bangingly loud; I wondered how classical musicians would be able to stand it. No one approached them. I gestured to Evan, who fast-forwarded the tape to where Whitby returned with a tray of drinks. Again we fast-forwarded to when Jessica and Ally stood up and went off together, then switched to the disc which focused on the ladies' restroom. Jessica emerged and returned to the table—

'Wait a minute! Go back, I want to look at that again—' I stabbed at the screen with my finger. Evan re-wound the disc; we watched her nod to someone she passed. 'Do you recognise anyone?' I asked the cellist.

'No. No, I don't.'

'Okay, keep it rolling.' Ally Carpenter left the restroom. She fought her way through the crowd and then someone engaged her in conversation. The dancers surged forward, obscuring her. No matter how many times we ran the section, we couldn't see who she or Jessica Rallison had spoken to. Eventually we left that one and rolled forward. Briece Mochrie arrived, sat down and talked to the group. Ally was still absent; Jessica Rallison was present, sitting between Pamela Miller and Mochrie. Whitby sat beside Pamela with an empty chair, obviously Ally Carpenter's, between himself and Mochrie.

We watched as Mochrie fought his way to the bar, stopping to speak to someone on the way whom he identified as his mechanic. He said they had talked for around twenty minutes, so we rolled the disc again. Mochrie arrived with a tray of drinks, then left in search of Ally Carpenter. The friends certainly looked genuinely anxious. Michael Whitby went toward the back of the nightclub and Mochrie headed for the entrance in a circular direction to disappear from view. He explained that he'd been talking to the doorman, then clawed his way back through the crowd and waylaid a young woman who appeared to kiss his ear. They spoke for a moment, faces close together, after which he broke free and went back to their table. I noted the angry expression on his face.

'Who was that woman?' I asked, re-winding the tape and freezing the scene.

Mochrie looked sheepish. 'I don't know. It was right after I was told Ally had gone off with another bloke, so I asked her to dance,' he admitted, 'but she said her boyfriend was with her.'

'But she kissed your ear, 'I insisted.

'No, Ms—er—sergeant Prescott. She licked my ear.' He blushed.

I wound the tape forward a little and watched the scene again. From the expression on his face, he'd been brassed off enough to grab anyone. I made no further comment, but signalled to Evan, who exchanged the disc with the one from the surveillance cameras mounted above the awnings over the entrance to the nightclub. He ran it backward and forward until he located the scene we wanted, a man supporting a woman wrapped in a black coat, as described by the bouncer.

They left the club and crossed the footpath to a light-coloured, four-cylinder Toyota Corolla, but only the backs of their heads were visible. An older woman caught up with them and held the door open for the man to shovel his companion into the back seat of the car. The doorman hadn't mentioned her. What else did he miss? It was a well-planned and executed operation—if the woman in the black coat was Ally Carpenter.

Briece Mochrie appeared to be willing himself into the screen.

'Her build looks about right, but I can't see if it's Ally.' His shoulders slumped with disappointment. Then the older woman went to step into the car after the couple.

His eyes widened and he jumped to his feet.

'The woman getting into the car with them—she's got Ally's handbag!'

CHAPTER 4

Once Upon a Father

Ally

Saturday: afternoon.

Have I slept around the clock? My mobile phone's going to be ringing until the message bank's full. The rehearsal must be over by now and my name will be mud. Surely my friends will realise something's happened to me? Brie must know I wouldn't go off without a word to anyone. Bloody hell!

You can leave when you're paid for.

Who in God's name did they expect to pay for me? A shiver runs up the back of my neck. My tormentor, he of the balaclava, has sneaked in without a sound and half-closed the door behind him.

'You total bastard!' I launch myself at him. He tries to push me away; I clamp my teeth onto his finger.

My face explodes.

I'm spread-eagled across the camp stretcher, the metal pipes biting into my back, shocked and blinded by tears. My nose throbs. Warm liquid runs down to my lip, into my mouth and oozes down my throat. The warm coppery taste sends nausea swirling in my stomach. I swipe the back of my hand across my mouth and chin, but it does nothing for the lot I'm forced to swallow. Don't give him the satisfaction of crying.

He cradles his left hand around his finger; blood seeps into his cuff and trickles down his hand. His eyes are half-closed, the energy of his anger crackles around me.

'Ally, Ally,' he croons, shaking his head. 'Why did you make me hit you? You're too valuable to us, darling, for me to damage you.' His voice is creamy smooth. As I roll slowly off the stretcher onto my knees, the tips of my fingers catch a paper plate of food sending it askew to knock over the mug of coffee beside it. A pool of liquid forms on the floor.

I attempt to stand, trying not to let him see my knickers. Loose sequins fall off my cammie and scatter on the floor. Blood drips onto my cammie top, some soaking into my skirt. He feints toward me; I back into the corner of the room. My bare feet slip in the coffee.

In a flash he's up close, stroking the side of my face and throat with his bitten finger, his breath hot on my face.

I try not to breathe as his fingers slither around the neck of my camisole, stopping to caress the fluttering pulse in my throat. They skim the top of my breasts and he moistens them with blood then draws gentle circles on my skin. My nipples harden; he smiles. The tip of one finger dips down and presses the left one, lightly. Nausea churns in my stomach. He withdraws his hand, slowly licks his finger and runs his tongue along his lower lip, smiling. Blood is seeping into the woollen stitching of his balaclava.

'Let me go...please, let me go.' Begging does not come easily to me.

'No way. You're our tickets to riches, Ally,' he whispers. 'You're not going anywhere until we get paid for you, but if you persist on fighting, we'll have to drug you again.' He moves to force me against the wall. I whip my knee up, but he twists his body sideways and it bounces harmlessly off his thigh. 'I can think of something better than drugs to calm you, sweetheart.' He chuckles and thrusts his hips at me. His crotch bulges, Scarpia to my Tosca. I understand that any further resistance will encourage him in ways I don't want to think about.

'Sweetheart, there's no way you're going anywhere until your father pays the ransom.'

What? 'My father's dead. You've mistaken me for someone else!' Relief shoots through me. *They've got the wrong person.* 'You can let me go. I promise I won't tell—' I surge forward, but he pushes me back against the wall.

'Oh no, he didn't die, Ally Carpenter. He's very much alive! I'm not going to tell you his name, but you better hope he does care what happens to you, or ...' He pulls the knife out of a sheath on his belt and carefully runs his tongue along the flat side. I match him stare for stare. His teeth flashing in the slit of the balaclava match the twinkle in his eyes. Perspiration pours down my forehead onto my cheeks. My tongue sticks to the roof of my mouth.

'We have a lot of persuasion to send him.' He slowly runs the flat of the blade over my earlobe. 'Do you need this?'

Nooooo...

Before I can fully comprehend what he has said, the door swings back and the woman comes in with food, a plastic water bottle and a towel. Now she's wearing a blue scarf over the lower half of her face. She dumps a bottle of water on the floor and tosses a towel onto the stretcher. The ferocious expression in her hazel eyes both chills and confuses me. There's something very personal in the hatred emanating from her. Why?

She slips out of the door and in seconds, returns with a mop and bucket to clean the mess on the floor.

If I can get to the broom… he blocks my access, legs splayed and hands on hips as he rocks backward and forward—Action Man.

Run for it! Now. His eyes beg me to try something. He rises on the balls of his feet, like a hunting dog ready for the chase and waggles his finger at me. Naughty, naughty. I want to punch him in the face. Claw his eyes out.

Without a word, he backs out the door, still smiling and slams it shut. The key turns in the lock, ice forms in the pit of my stomach. How many kidnap victims live to tell the tale? I don't want to know. Tremors ripple through me as I struggle to drag breath into my lungs. Blood drops off my chin onto my clothes. Stooping like an old woman, I pick up the thin towel to wipe my face.

My unknown father, who is apparently very much alive, has to pay a ransom. 'Oh, no he didn't die, Ally.' The memory of Scarpia's throaty drawl ricochets through my brain. Scarpia, the evil cop in Verdi's *Tosca*, but this one's no policeman.

I need to get my head around this. I slide down the wall and sit on the floor, reaching for the water bottle, my mother's words returning loud and clear: 'He died before we could be married, Ally. It was a terrible time. I was only eight weeks pregnant with you.'

The reality of death kicked in when I was about seven. Our cat died and I cried for days, not only for the cat but because I finally understood that he couldn't ever come back and purr in my arms. And my dad was dead too. He'd be all swollen and smelly like the cat when we found him after he went missing for days. My ten year-old voice rises into my mind: 'I wish I had a dad. Everyone else does. Why don't you get married again?'

Another memory surfaces, of packing a satchel with

essential items—doll and clothes, bananas, a bottle of water—and marching down to the wharf, where I planned to catch the ferry across to the mainland and find a father. Any reasonable, kind man would do. The ferry master refused to take me and asked the postman to cart me home. Mother was not best pleased.

I may be an adult, but my heart still aches for a father who would come to my concerts, clap proudly at the wrong places and tell everyone around him, 'That's my daughter.' Just a dad who loves me. A grainy photo lives in my wallet, a pleasant-faced man with mid-brown hair, standing beside a sports car. The accident happened when he was coming home from a rugby match, mum said. Heartbroken, she had come back to Australia and given birth to me seven months later. He was an only child and so were his parents, which put paid to my dreams of extended family. 'Leave well enough alone, Ally, the whole thing is best forgotten,' she'd commanded.

Bloody hell, it was all lies, lies and more lies. Has she deliberately kept me from my father? Or was that his choice? I know that man is telling the truth, because they wouldn't commit this monstrous crime unless there was a reasonable expectation of success. Excitement flickers deep inside me. My father isn't dead; Robert Parker is still alive. He must be in Australia, or at least nearby. Maybe in New Zealand? But what if he doesn't believe them? Tells them to get stuffed? If he does…no, don't go there.

I force the fear to the back of my mind and set to work, wetting a corner of the towel to dab the blood from my sore nose. My clothes are clammy. My stomach won't let me ignore the food, a piece of bread and butter, a small slice of cold meat cut into pieces, a tomato, and a spoonful of potato salad. At least The Cow is feeding me.

Did mother tell the wrong person who my father is? But who? Georgie? Aunt Rosalind? Even Pam? The thought slithers into my mind that one of these beloved women who comprise the only family I have may actually be involved. But I would have trusted them with my life. *You might have to, Ally.*

CHAPTER 5

Images of a Lost Child

Eloise Carpenter

Saturday: 3.00pm.

I was re-painting the laundry and had no premonition that anything was wrong when the telephone rang. My goddaughter, Pamela, spoke so fast I couldn't make sense of anything she said. 'Darling, slow down. Take a deep breath and start again.'

'Ally's missing and the police have been called in!' Fear turned her voice shrill, starting my heart pounding. I was momentarily unable to reply.

'Aunt Eloise? Are you still there?' Pam has called me "Aunt" since she learned to talk.

'Yes, yes. Give me a moment.' Dear God. The room felt drained of oxygen, my hands trembled so violently that I could barely hold the receiver. Breathe. Somehow I pulled myself together, forcing myself to speak calmly.

'What's this about a night club? Pam, slow down and tell me again.'

She repeated the message.

'What do the police say?'

'They're looking for her already because Sir James McPherson got on to some bigwig in the police force straightaway and threw his weight around.'

Thank God! I read somewhere that you couldn't report a person as missing until a certain time elapsed. My mind began to squirrel around the logistics of travelling so late in the day. 'I'm coming down to Brisbane, Pam. I hope to God Georgie's home.'

'Aunt Eloise, can you catch a flight to Brisbane? Or could you ask mum to drive you down?' Pam must be frightened; she knows how flying affects me.

I knew she would rather have her mother cope with me. 'Your mother's away for a couple of days and I don't know anyone else who'd be free at short notice,' I replied. I'm afraid of flying to the point where I am aviaphobic, but "needs must."

'I'll have to try and get a flight. But it might need to be the bus. It's so late...'

'Of course, Aunt Eloise. Let me know the ETA and where, so I can meet you.'

I slumped into a chair, incoherent thoughts skittering through my brain. *Better make a list...ring Johnny Morse and see if he can take me to the mainland on his water taxi, ring Georgie and ask her to come over. She'll feed the animals, but first of all, ring the airline. No, ring Georgie first and ask her to ring the airline. Or should I just get onto the night bus? No, ring Johnny first and find out if he can take me—no, have to ring Georgie. Oh my God, Ally. Ring Ally.*

Surely her mobile...she would answer? I had to check for myself that she was not available to answer her phone. I hit the speed dial and listened as the mobile on the other end rang six times. For a heart-stopping moment, I thought she answered, but it was message bank.

My closest friend and Ally's godmother, Georgie, arrived within ten minutes of my frantic phone call. She made me a hot drink into which she put her panacea for all ills, a heavy slug of whisky. I sipped while she organised the island taxi driver to take me to the mainland.

'Try for a seat on the overnight bus.'

'Are you sure? I thought in this case you might find it would be better to fly. They might bump someone.' My stomach did a slow roll and prickles of perspiration broke out over my body. I shook my head. 'Okay, I'll try the buslines.'

Georgie booked me a seat on the overnight coach and rang Pam to advise arrival time. She also promised to feed the animals and look after the house.

We made the bus in plenty of time. A gibbering wreck had nothing on me as I stuffed my handbag, with its cargo of precious documents, into the back pocket of the seat in front of me, then turned my mobile phone onto vibrate. I could not entertain the notion that Ally would, or could not, ring back.

Determined to retain my composure, I switched off the overhead light and pulled my travel rug up to cover my shoulders. My fellow passengers settled at odd angles, like abandoned puppets. The driver hunched over the wheel, occasionally glancing into the rear vision mirror as though to check we were all on our best behaviour.

Ally disappearing the night before a major concert performance? No way. She'd never do something as irresponsible. But what if a pervert had taken her? What if.

Images of parents in television dramas viewing a sheet-draped body rammed into my mind. 'Yes, that's my daughter.' 'Yes, that's my daughter...' 'Yes, that's my daughter.' Sometimes, the mother just—screamed.

No. No. I refused to believe it would happen to us, only someone else. Ally's mobile was her diary, her office. I groped my phone out of its pouch, shielded the glowing screen and hit speed dial. Again, Ally's sweet voice asked me to leave a message. 'Ring me. Mum.'

I slumped down in my seat, willing myself not to keep phoning. I'd fill the thing up at this rate and then I wouldn't be able to hear her voice at all. When she was a teenager, Ally never neglected to call me or send a message if she thought she would be late home or wanted to sleep over at a friend's place. Even when we rowed, she always rang and snapped where she would be. She uses Skype at least once a week. 'Mum, I'm off to Italy tomorrow, staying at...' or 'Mum, guess what? I'll be in Moscow next Thursday!' But not this time. Dear God, please, please, keep her safe.

The bus stopped and started countless times to pick up and set down travellers. Each time I jerked awake, disoriented and exhausted, to hear the driver stowing luggage under the bus, the slam of the locker door and the hiss of the main door closing. Boarding passengers scuffled past, bumping me with their wanted-on-voyage bags. I wanted to scream, 'Hurry up, for God's sake. Stop stuffing around!'

I turned on my reading light and peered at my watch. 4.00 a.m. Two hours to go. The temptation to try Ally's mobile again was overwhelming, but I restrained myself.

Images of the past slid into my brain, like old newsreels looped to repeat themselves for an ever-changing audience. Ally, looking angelic at church with a pet rat peering through her waterfall of hair, scaring the living daylights out of the uptight Women's Guild. That prank cost me a couple of sponge cakes for their next morning tea. Ally going to school for the first time, lip wobbling, eyes filling, the uniform so long that the hem sagged past her knees because I needed her to grow into the larger size. Georgie scolded me and I shortened it pretty quickly.

My newborn, squashed, red and screaming under a tuft of red Mohawk, her delicate infant neck warm and talcumed, snuffling like a baby hedgehog as she burrowed for my breast. *What if the worst... no, don't go there. Get yourself together, Eloise.* Years of what might have been fell away, my determination to put my past behind me crumbled by terrifying images of my missing daughter. The past might be about to rise up and beat me about the head with an emotional bullwhip.

In my shy way I'd craved adventure and hoped to find some in England in 1983. Flush with money inherited from my father, I headed overseas in search of self-confidence and romance. After a few months and a couple of false starts, I settled into digs with two other girls, and obtained a job at Cambridge University in England. My flatmates were noisy and outgoing in sharp contrast to my tongue-tied demeanour when meeting people for the first time. However, a number of parties after we'd been threatened with eviction, I'd found self-confidence. It was time to find romance.

I met the one whom I thought my soul mate at the Fort St George, a pub much patronised by students. Stuffed into a corner seat in The Snug, I listened to the roar of conversation all around me, while hiding from a particularly persistent youth who thought my life would be greatly enhanced by his ardour. Eager to reach the restroom without my admirer following me, I tripped over a pair of highly polished riding boots protruding from the next table and landed on the floor. Their owner bent and gallantly lifted me to my feet. I looked into his twinkling blue eyes framed with burnished brown hair and fell madly in lust.

'Women don't usually fall so hard for me!' he said, 'I need to make the most of this.'

'In your dreams,' I replied, emboldened by his appreciative gaze and shot full of newfound confidence. He let me go and I could feel his eyes on me as I sidled through the throng. He waylaid me on my way back to the table and that was the beginning of the most wonderful time in my life—until it ended in heartbreak and humiliation.

For the first time in years, I allow the memories of the six glorious months during which he cherished me in every way an average looking Australian farm girl could only dream of. When I let my guard down and became a vulnerable fool as ninety percent of women do at sometime in their life. If they're telling the truth, that is. How I managed to keep my job with my mind all over the place, I'll never know. His love gave me the confidence to blossom and courage to be myself, except around his family and friends, who regarded me as NLU, not like us.

James came from a long line of upper crust gentlemen who, somewhere along the way, had sullied their class by becoming manufacturing stalwarts. A comparatively recent ancestor gambled away most of the family shekels in the 1860's, so his heir was forced to-God forbid-go into trade. Having had to suck it up, as Ally would have said, they made a fortune and played aristocrats when it suited them. A hereditary peerage helped considerably. The pressure for James to conform by entering the family business as his brother Peter had, was immense. Failing that, as the second son, one of the forces would be a suitable occupation.

By the time I met him he had almost finished a degree in economics, but secretly yearned to take music at Trinity College. I loved to listen to him play the piano—Mozart, Beethoven, Haydn—the names at that time unfamiliar, but which tripped from Ally's tongue every day.

Memories of the morning after my pregnancy was confirmed loom in my mind. James had gone on an extensive trip to Europe, reluctantly standing in for his father on business for his family's firm which manufactured agricultural tools. We argued the night before he left when I urged him to confront his parents with his plans for a musical career.

'Eloise, it's not the right time. They need me to do this trip for them now.'

'But James, this won't be just one time. There'll be another, then another—'

Was I the only one who could see the family sucking him inexorably into the course they'd set for him? This three week trip was the thin end of the wedge. Guilty, because he would be throwing back the support given by his father, he felt he owed them some time. 'Back off, El, it's none of your affair. They're my parents and I have to handle this my way. It's the least I can do,' he'd snapped. I knew by the fleeting kiss which he had given me as he left, that he was still angry.

Yes, I had been pushy, but I thought we were close enough for me to show how I felt. Stupid, stupid. Big mistake. I sank into the depths of despair, waiting for a letter, even a postcard over the next ten days. The phone in our flat was out of order so he couldn't have called me. At that time, only a few people had mobile phones, and what they did have were the size of bricks.

Nausea roiled in my stomach for several mornings and then I realised my period was two months late. The morning after the doctor confirmed my pregnancy, I became so sick I almost staggered into the street to ask a passer-by to call an ambulance. Jemima, my flatmate at the time and James's cousin, arrived home unexpectedly, burst into the bathroom and caught me heaving over the toilet. I was a mess. My nose ran and eyes streamed from the effects of a roaring cold. After a brief but successful inquisition, she couldn't get to his parents fast enough to tell them all about it.

They arrived at our flat later that day. James's father, Sir Randall, smiled sincerely when I answered the door. Lady Margaret, the old bitch, barged past and looked around with flint-eyed scorn. They listened to my confession with great interest and then suggested they get in touch with James and tell him I was ill. Randall comforted me. 'Perhaps he'll be able to come back early,' he said, patting me on the arm. He offered to go out and ring James; naively, I accepted.

Randall hadn't been gone two minutes, before Margaret, who was no lady when it suited her, took the opportunity to vent the hatred and scorn which previously found outlet in sly put downs. *This is Eloise, our colonial friend.*

'You can't imagine we would allow our son to ruin his career by marrying a common little upstart like you? You're getting on a plane back to Australia and never contacting him again. We'll make sure of it.'

The accusations turned ugly. 'How do we know it's our son's child? Jemima swears she's seen you with other men. Jemima and her friends will soon let James know you've been playing around behind his back.'

'No, no! That's not true. It's James's baby,' I croaked.

'Who do you think he'll believe? Oh no, we've got plans for our son and they don't include you!'

Randall arrived back shaking his head in sorrow. James, he reported, was horrified by the news and needed time to come to terms with it. He suggested I return home and he would follow later when he cleared some business matters and sorted things out at Cambridge. We'd decide what to do then.

Even I, the dippy, ever-hopeful innocent, recognised the brush-off. Any confidence our relationship would recover after our argument and his ten days of silence evaporated like mist in the indescribable pain of betrayal. Ill and heartbroken, I became putty in the expert hands of his parents. I should have refused to go until I could talk to James face-to-face. But then, remembering his rejection, would coax myself into believing it had all worked out for the best, including my fairytales, carefully constructed to protect Ally—or myself.

My eyes flew open. Had my mobile vibrated? I flipped open the cover and shaded the screen. No missed calls. I forced back tears of disappointment. 'She'll be home when I get to Brisbane. It will all have been a mistake,' I told myself, clinging to a fragile control.

Perspiration prickled under my armpits. I kicked off the blanket and switched on my reading light. 5 am, with an hour left to travel. Bracing myself against the movement of the coach, I staggered to the toilet. My frightened eyes stared at me in the minuscule mirror, tangled hair falling out of its customary knot. My mouth, a blotchy red gash in the harsh light, bore testimony to every one of my forty-five years. Tears trickled down my cheeks.

As a very small child I had attended church, but only because Mother wanted to show off her extensive number of flowered hats and play the organ for the service. Incongruous, when I remember that she left my father for another man when I was five, but there in the lurching, smelly toilet cubicle of the coach, I prayed for Ally's safety, hoping God would overlook my tendency to talk to Him only when I needed something.

At the Transit Centre, I fell weeping into my goddaughter's arms. Pam stuffed me into her car and drove straight to her flat in the West End. I listened closely while she told me everything which had occurred, from the moment they realised Ally had gone missing on the Friday night.

'Aunt Eloise, you need to have a hot shower and get

into bed. If there's any news I'll wake you. You can't do anything now, you're too tired. Would you like some tea and toast?"

I nodded gratefully. There was a lot of her mother in practical Pamela. 'Yes, thank you. I'll pop into the shower first.'

When I got back to the guest bedroom I asked about the concert the night before and how they coped without Ally. Pam's face showed intense strain.

'They announced Ally was ill and got the soprano Jacqueline Mabardi in. You remember Jacq, don't you?'

'Yes, of course.' I met the gorgeous opera singer, a guest of one of the musicians, at a meet the orchestra party a few weeks previously.

'Did it go well?'

'Yes, Jacq was fabulous. She got a standing ovation at the end.'

Ever pragmatic, after a slight pause, she pre-empted my question. 'Now, Aunt Eloise, try to rest. And no, Ally didn't ring while you were in the shower, I promise you.'

She placed a pillow over my knees and balanced a tray on top. My gaze flickered around the room behind her, lighting on the china fawn I'd given Pam for her sixth birthday, a book for Christmas the year she passed her first music exam. How I wished Ally was still that young and in my protective custody. Oh God, please, where is she? As Pam turned to leave the room, a thought occurred to me. 'Do you think she might have gone home for some reason and be hiding there? Perhaps she's had a nervous breakdown ...'

She stared at me as though I lost my senses, which I had. 'What do you mean?'

'Maybe she's back at the house—'

'Aunt Eloise, I've already been there with the police late yesterday. We've rung all her other friends and our orchestra manager went over there when she didn't show up for the one o'clock rehearsal just to make sure she hadn't had a fall or gotten sick. Brie and I drove all around in the early hours of this morning and went back there several times, in case she'd gone home while we were driving. I'm so sorry,' she added, her eyes filling with tears. She came over and put her arms around me. We clung together, weeping with fear and tiredness.

Then Pam's mobile jingled madly from the kitchen. A frisson of excitement shot through me. Perhaps it was Ally? My hopes collapsed when Pam announced that Jessica wanted to borrow some sheet music. As I forced down the food, more buried memories leaped out of my Pandora's Box of a brain, relentlessly dragging me back to that dreadful day of betrayal.

James's parents, playing good cop, bad cop to perfection, got me out of England within forty-eight hours. Margaret, snarling like a mad wolf, stood guard over me to make sure I packed and wrote the right notes to my friends and workplace, while Randall went off to make arrangements for my departure. All pretence of empathy vanished along with my hopes for the future. They were like barracuda circling a goldfish.

God only knows what they told the university, but my immediate boss sent a glowing reference and work record by courier. Randall arranged for my return ticket to be upgraded to first class on the next flight available on the following day, and they gave me an international banker's draft for fifteen thousand pounds.

I spent the journey back throwing up in the toilet after I used all the sick bags available and cowering in my seat, terrified, humiliated and sweating under a blanket. Aerophobia is the bane of my existence.

The hours and then days waiting for James to call

dragged me further into despair, but always hoping that he had changed his mind and wanted us. I became increasingly desperate. The flat, emotionless voice of Directory Services advised that his phone was disconnected and the new number registered as silent. The family business office refused to accept any calls from me and the staff, at first kind, turned nasty after about the fifth time I telephoned.

University Administration wouldn't give out private phone numbers. A woman, with whom I had always enjoyed a good relationship, eventually advised me that the Dean's office had ordered that I was not to be accommodated in any way. Never mind strings: good cop Randall had yanked twine.

The so-called mutual friends we made were uncommunicative. I suspected Jemima, who was so spiteful and sly that everyone kept on her "good side," had trashed my reputation very effectively. My former flatmates moved on during the time James courted me, so it was useless trying to contact them. My letters were returned, intercepted by his parents. Heartbroken, I finally acknowledged that James was finished with me and turned my energy to building a secure future for my child.

During the last twenty-six years, I have sometimes read snippets about his career in magazines and business periodicals. Photos of him smiling at concerts, on the polo field and at the opera, wife cleaved to his side, appeared from time to time. When he was widowed ten years previously, I'd been tempted to contact him, but pride came to the fore. Why be a glutton for punishment?

I should have told Ally the truth about who he was and the circumstances of her birth, but I lied and even gave her a photo of a stranger who happened to be standing in front of a building and looked at me as I clicked the shutter. He accepted my abashed apology with charm. Later, I even made up a name for him so when the time came, it was easy to concoct a sad, dramatic story of his death to hide my humiliation and prevent her contacting James or his family. Why should they get to know her now when they hadn't wanted to before, I reasoned.

James domiciled in Brisbane, alternating between the UK and Australia attending to business interests, which included the Pacific Orchestra to which Ally was temporarily contracted. I'd written his phone number in the centre page of my address book and sometimes allowed my mind to wander into the realms of 'What if I picked up the telephone and called him? What's the worst that could happen?' He'd just hang up.

How long do the police search when someone goes missing? A week? A month? Maybe James could persuade the Commissioner of Police to make sure the search continued, or he might hire a private detective to do things the police couldn't. What I'd sowed, I had to reap, no matter the cost. Feel the fear and do it anyway.

I threw the bedcovers aside, padded to the telephone and dialled with trembling fingers before I could renege, yet again. The sound of his warm, cultured voice almost broke my nerve. I took a deep breath.

'Hello James? This is Eloise McFadden.'

CHAPTER 6

God's Punishment.

Ally

Sunday: dawn.

Let me out let me out let me out...

I'm lying halfway off the stretcher. The metal is cutting into my spine. It's an effort to haul myself against the wall, to press my aching body against the timber. A faint light comes from the window. I look around. The gaunt, bareness of the room is threatening because it appears not important enough to bother painting. By definition, the content–currently, myself–is not worth anything either. My throat hurts, bringing memories of crying and pounding on the door for what seemed like hours. I clasp my hands and wince because they are so sore.

I will get out. I'm a strong girl. I try to do some gentle stretching exercises. Have to keep supple.

Sunday. 'Bloody hell, the concert.' The words croak out of my throat, startling me. The police, my friends–are they looking for me? I'd need to be dead to dump a concert, for God's sake. I feel like something the cat dragged in then rejected. I'm freaking out. These–*people*–actually know who my father is! And the one person I thought I could trust lied.

I didn't hear the door open. How long has he–Scarpia–

been watching me?

I lunge at him, but he's no fool. He pushes me violently; my back smashes into the wall. Before I can get my breath, I slide halfway to the floor. Then he drops a newspaper onto the stretcher. I push myself up then start pacing backward and forward in a series of arcs across the corner. Must keep him away from the window.

'What's the matter? Not game to take me on?'

'I'll take you on any time, Ally!' he replies, flicking his tongue in and out of his balaclava, like a lizard.

'In your dreams.'

He chuckles. 'You're gunna find out just how much we can sell you for soon sweetheart!'

Ignore him. I pick up the paper and pretend to read the front page.

'You might need these.' He fishes my reading glasses case out of his shirt pocket and holds it out to me. Thank God. I snatch it out of his hand.

He giggles. 'Your father's gunna to have to come up with three million dollars for you!'

'Three mill–'

They're kidding themselves. Why would he pay for a daughter he's never met, especially three million dollars? Don't panic. Scarpia's mouth curls as he watches my pathetic attempt at nonchalance.

'Not so mouthy now, are we? He's got forty-eight hours from when we make the phone call tonight and you better hope he doesn't tell the police, because if we're in danger, you're in more. That's a promise.' He makes a pistol with his hand.

'It's Sunday and you're only demanding a ransom now? Of course they've told the police I'm missing. I didn't show up for the concert, for God's sake.'

'Yeah, we thought about that, but the longer we keep you outta the loop, the more likely they'll think you're being carved up. Wouldn't want to have a finger or two go missing, would we?' His voice is soft, the tone gentle. He glances down at my hands; I whip them behind my back. Oh, my God. Noooooooooo. Not my fingers. Cold seeps through my body. I feel dizzy. *He's winding you up. He wants you to go berserk, so cool it, stupid.*

He laughs, eyes twinkling in the holes of the balaclava and snatches my left hand in a vice-like grip. A twitch of his wrist and I'm forced to face him. I try to slap him, but he blocks easily.

'You're hurting me, let go!' Sweat breaks out all over my body. He pulls playfully on my fingers, singing the words in a ghastly parody of the nursery rhyme:

'This little fingy went to market, this little fingy stayed at home. And this little fingy went wee wee wee, all the way to the slaughterhouse! How're ya gunna play four-fingered, Ally?'

He wants you to cry.

His black eyes glint through the eyeholes in his balaclava, indicating his immense enjoyment of my situation. I can't let him see the effect of what he is saying is having on me. Nausea threatens to engulf me. I try for a matter-of-fact tone, tugging my hand away. He releases me and steps out of kicking range.

'The police will find me.'

'No, they won't. Not here, sweetheart. This is the last place they'll look for you, believe me,' he crows.

'For three million dollars, you wouldn't want to damage such valuable goods by–cutting me up.'

'As long as we get the money, we don't care what shape you're in if they get you back.' He beams like a satiated leopard.

The woman enters and puts something on the floor, then pauses. I feel her ferocious glare, but keep my focus on the man, remembering the suspicions which danced around my mind like demons throughout the long night. *Leave it, Ally. Don't provoke him.*

I take the option of prodding the crocodile with a stick. 'Someone had to put you up to this. Who was it a member of the orchestra?'

His eyes flicker. 'Whatever turns you on, babe, but it won't matter too much who it was in the end,' he promises, laughing at the expression on my face. My fear is obviously hilarious.

Scarpia gives me a convivial wave as they whisk out the door. Unpainted splinters of wood prick my bare skin as I lean against the wall, breathing heavily. The packet of sandwiches they left holds no interest for me right now, because all I can think about is losing a finger.

Or more.

They had to know where I would be on Friday night in order to grab me. Of course, someone helped them. I may have been pointed out innocently or did Scarpia and that cow of a female go to a concert? Is that how they identified me? But how did they know about my father? Do they know him? Or someone they know has to be privy to mum's secret. Georgie or Aunt Rosalind? They would never betray us, never. So, who else did she tell? I want to cry. Pull yourself together. Did she tell someone like a solicitor or a doctor, and did he let the cat out of the bag? This is doing my head in; I've got to let it go for now.

The paper is my only contact with reality. I should be grateful, but it's been given with the intention of taunting me.

CARPENTER CANCELS CONCERT screams the headline at the top of the main column. Apparently a disaster was averted by pianist, Lyn Donovan, who took my place for the first half of the concert. The inference is that after the massive publicity hype, the audience was let down by my non-appearance. Tears well up in my eyes. How can he? I've only missed one concert before when I had appendicitis, performed with a raging temperature–London, in the throes of pleurisy, Paris and a broken love affair.

Forget it, you drongo, and get back to work.

I'd dragged at the corner of the grill on and off most of the night trying to loosen the screws. The edge of the screen bit into my hands making them bleed and breaking my fingernails. The glass is too dark for anyone to see me from outside, but there's only a great big lawn between this building and a clump of gum trees about a hundred metres away. Exhaustion flows over me; I can't stand any longer...

Ally! Ally, come here! Jess runs in front of me, wearing a paper bag over her head. I laugh and race across the rocks, waving to the boats out at sea. We chase each other around the base of the lighthouse. Laughter drums in my ears, bounces off the sand. Screaming with excitement we run toward the rock, which rears high above the surf.

My mother stands behind me. 'I told you not to go near the Wild Pony, Ally! When will you listen to me?'

The kid hovers nearby, clasping his little hands in supplication, curly brown hair tossing in the sea breeze. 'Please don't make me, Ally! Please don't make me.'

'Cowardy, cowardy custard! Ya guts are made of mustard! Go on, I dare you to climb it!' we chant.

I pick up a boat lying in the sand nearby and start smacking him in the face—

Tears stream down my cheeks. I struggle to sit up, draw my legs to my chest and wrap my arms tightly around them. Cut the self pity, Ally. I force my hands to stretch, pushing away the withdrawal symptoms from not following my practice program. There's a saying in the music world, and it's true. If you refrain from practising one day, you will hear the lack. Two days and your colleagues will note it, but three days and your audience will too.

Two days—and how much longer will I be here? I can't bear to think about it. My cammie stinks from the dried blood. My thoughts drift like scarves floating in the wind, and a long-ago conversation pops into my head. Pam, Jess and I were sitting in a coffee shop after a lecture one afternoon when Pam asked, 'What would you do differently, if you could live your life over?' We laughed and made asinine remarks, but now the comment has relevance.

Masters Island kids were a law unto ourselves. I wish I could return to the times we had, playing pirates—old Mr Appleton's walking sticks made great swords—running races along the beach, being towed along by the ropes which we secured to our family dogs' collars. How many times have I implored God to take me back to before that time at Wild Pony Rock? The one thing I wish I could change—

That's a car starting up! I press my face against the grill but it's out of sight. Disappointment floods through me. My right forefinger is bleeding again from pulling at the mesh. No don't think about your fingers. He was just trying to frighten you.

Really.

Truly.

The mattress on the stretcher is almost as thin as a bedside mat. I pull it onto the floor and lie flat on my back, remembering when I went to yoga classes at university. Relax, close your eyes and let your mind wander …deep breaths. Go to a safe time, like when you were a child…

We island kids attended to school on the mainland,

catching the ferry early in the morning, returning late afternoon. My red hair, so beloved of old ladies, gave the townies the excuse to taunt me. 'Carrot, carrot, island parrot!' was a favourite. My reading glasses were broken so often that mother was offered a discount by the optometrist.

A safe role for me was becoming a storyteller, a court jester to the bully's monarchs. The staple literary diet of the playground became one of breathlessly gothic tales, girls in peril and dark mysterious heroes blessed with good looks, smart tongues, and libidos of gargantuan proportions. Drunk on unaccustomed popularity, I morphed into a control freak.

So many times I've wished I could go back and put my worst crime right.

If I lose a finger and my career, will it be God's punishment, and no more than I deserve?

CHAPTER 7

The Reckoning

Eloise

Sunday: 8.30am.

My God, he's forgotten who I am! Hang up, you fool. Then, he spoke quietly. Ice chips bouncing off a window pane couldn't have sounded colder.

'Eloise.'

'Yes.'

The silence seemed to go on forever, and then thank God, he responded. 'And how are you?'

'I'm well, thank you' I replied. The banality of convention confused me. He waited for me to state my business, the sound of his breathing in my ear mingling with the frantic drumbeats of my heart.

'I need to talk to you, James,' I said, 'Please would you—it's urgent, really urgent.' The silence stretched. Just as I was about to grovel, he asked, 'Are you here in Brisbane?' An almost imperceptible edge to his voice told me he was not unaffected by my call, how, I was not sure.

'Yes, I'm at my goddaughter's flat in West End. Please, can I talk to you?'

'Why? What could be so important after twenty six years that you can't tell me over the telephone? I think you showed how you felt when you left me.'

I abandoned him? I didn't understand what he meant, but I only had seconds to convince him of the seriousness of my request.

'Please, it concerns you. Something you need to know. And it's private.' I sank onto the chair beside the telephone table to prevent my legs from giving way, knowing I would crawl barefoot across broken glass if that was what it took to keep him on the line. Again, seconds ticked by before he responded.

'Tell me where you are. I'll send a car for you.'

Traumatised, I couldn't remember the street address, but then my eye fell on Pam's electricity bill. I reached over, snatched it out of the letter rack on the wall, and read it to him.

'Be ready in half an hour,' he said abruptly and hung up.

9.00am.

The passing scenery held no interest for me. I leaned back, closed my eyes and tried to rehearse my coming speech. All too soon, I feared, our reunion would end in rejection and perhaps, hatred. Conscious of his driver's occasional glances at me in the rear vision mirror, I looked resolutely out of the window, trying to present a calm facade, pressing my knees together to prevent them bouncing with agitation. Just minutes now and for the first time in twenty-six years I would set eyes on the man whom I'd expected to marry, the man who dumped me when he discovered I was pregnant and broke my heart.

My heart rate rose, as the car swept through imposing wrought-iron gates and along a tarmac driveway and came to a halt in front of the house. Stone steps led up to a door grand enough to have been the entrance to a castle, its forbidding facade seeming to reflect its owner's heart.

The chauffeur turned off the ignition, climbed out, came around the car and opened the door for me. I took a deep breath, stepped out of the car, hitched the strap of my handbag over my shoulder and tweaked my skirt to make sure it wasn't caught up behind my knees.

The castle door creaked open and James appeared in the entrance, one large square hand tucked into his pocket, the other holding the door half-open, as though he was still deciding whether to invite me in.

'Eloise.' He nodded dismissal to the chauffeur, then stood aside and gestured for me to enter, his lemony aftershave wafting into my nostrils as I passed. He scanned me from head to toe with a sweep of his eyes as I stepped inside, limbs quivering, feeling like a hunted animal.

The entrance opened into a foyer where a large landscape hung on one wall and a couple of urns of flowers graced pedestals. He grasped me impersonally by the elbow and steered me through to an octagonal office, the walls lined with bookshelves. Files and papers were stacked on a table and piled up on the floor; two armchairs rested before the fireplace. The room was comfortable without being outright messy. A black and white border collie lying on a rug grinned and flapped its tail at me. I smiled weakly down at it. At least the dog was happy to see me.

James moved behind his desk and watched, making no attempt to put me at ease. Twitters of fearful excitement scampered a mad game through my stomach. I perched on the edge of an upright chair facing him and placed my handbag on the floor beside me the silence was broken only by the ticking of a grandfather clock standing in a corner.

Twenty-six years had left their mark, but he was still

beautiful. His warm brown hair was flecked with grey and impeccably groomed, but there was no trace of the carefree lover of my youth in this intimidating man. His dark blue eyes coldly assessed my appearance.

My long-held dreams of being within touching distance of him vanished and now my carefully rehearsed speech disappeared like Scotch Mist. Jumbled thoughts wittered through my mind, moths released from a disused cupboard. Somehow I needed to tell him I'd given birth to his daughter and beg him to use what influence he could to help find Ally. This meant convincing him I hadn't betrayed him and that the child I carried was his.

'James—' my voice came out in a croak. He stood up, moved to a tray near the window on which there were tumblers and a jug of water, poured some and handed it to me. My hand shook and the glass clacked loudly against my teeth as I took a mouthful. He cleared a spot on the desk and thrust a coaster forward as I attempted to put it down again with trembling fingers.

'Let's get one thing clear, Eloise. Whatever you've come for, don't beat around the bush. I haven't the time or inclination for this.'

His mouth settled into a hard line, accentuating the grooves running down his cheeks. He didn't actually glance at his watch, but managed to give the impression that his time took precedence over my own. 'Yes, of course,' I acknowledged, glowing with embarrassment. *Whatever you do, don't cry. Remember, he was the one who bailed out.*

'My daughter is twenty-five years old. I gave birth to her after I came back from England.'

He stared at me. 'So? I know how long it is since you left me, Eloise,' he said dryly, not having twigged what I was on about.

'She's your daughter too, James,' I reminded him.

Shocked, he stared at me. 'What? What do you mean? You had my child?'

'You know I did. You dumped us, remember?' I couldn't believe this.

His eyes narrowed to slits. For a moment, he seemed to be having trouble breathing.

'But—how do I know it's mine?'

'*It's?*' I wanted to punch his handsome face, and bunched my fist before I reminded myself it would be worst thing I could do. 'How dare you even suggest for a moment she's not yours? I can arrange a DNA test.'

'You do that!' he snapped. The dog jumped up and ran to scratch at the door. James emitted a muffled exclamation, moved across to give it a reassuring caress and a gentle word before he let it out. He swung back and started pacing, slapping his hands on the backs of chairs, eyes glittering, apparently unable to find words to express what he was feeling at first.

Then the storm broke. 'After all this time, twenty-six years of silence, you decide to appear. What makes you think I give a damn? Who did you think you were? First of all, you start an argument with me just before I left on that trip. I told you to back off, but you wouldn't let it go. I came home three days early because I couldn't bear to be away from you any longer. I wanted to make up with you and what did I find?'

His voice cracked, as he mimicked someone's long-ago words. 'Eloise has returned to Australia. Eloise doesn't believe your relationship will work. No one knows where she is. How could you have done that to me? No explanation whatsoever. Not a word about being pregnant! *My God!*'

I couldn't believe my ears. Rage bubbled out of my mouth in a vitriolic stream. 'How dare you! What utter rubbish. I waited for days for you to write to me, send me a postcard—anything! Then all I get is a message. You're the one who sent me away! You didn't want me and our child! Remember?' I shouted.

He ranted on, oblivious to my interjection. Fury burst out in a stream of bitterness–and to my astonishment, pain.

He glared into my face. 'I searched for you, damn it! I found those cousins of yours out at Quilpie, but they hadn't heard from you for years. You didn't have a home in Australia, so I had no way of contacting you. None of your former employers knew where you lived and you had no other relatives to ask. I advertised in all the major Australian papers for you, but there was nothing. You didn't write to me, you just vanished into thin air. You weren't even on the electoral roll.' He threw his arms wide in a gesture of frustration.

'But you knew my old address in Australia!' I yelled, stunned beyond all belief. 'If you— tried there anyone would have told you where I was.'

He was so angry he appeared unaware I had interjected. 'Eventually I gave up and got on with my life. After all, what was the point in loving someone who thought so little of our relationship she dumped me without a word? And now you expect me to believe you had my child? *Who were you seeing behind my back, Eloise?*'

No. Not this—crap—again. I struggled to remain calm and pitched my voice low, lest I started screaming. There was no way I was going to let myself to be short-shifted again.

'Damn you, no-one. You know we were living in each other's pockets. How would I have the opportunity to be with someone else? I–loved–you.' I clenched my teeth, annunciating clearly so there wouldn't be any mistake in his mind. 'Your father told me you said I was to go back to Australia and you would follow me later, that you weren't sure whether you wanted the baby. Your parents were horrible to me, and from you? Nothing– except, of course, rejection.' I could hear my words bite with sarcasm.

'What are you talking about?' He threw me a look of contempt. 'You loved me? You took off without a word when my back was turned. That shows just how you really felt about me.' He charged over to the fireplace, snatched up the tongs and poked viciously at some crumpled paper amongst the ashes. I found a screwed-up tissue in my bag and swiped at the tears of anger and frustration spilling down my cheeks.

'You know it wasn't my choice to return to Australia. For crying out loud, James, you told me to go. You father told me you said I had to go,' I insisted.

'What do you mean I told you? I've never heard of anything so ridiculous. My father certainly didn't tell me anything. I only spoke to him about business before I got back and found you gone,' he hissed, ashen-faced. He jammed the poker back into its holder.

I jumped to my feet, sending the chair crashing onto its back.

'Your parents arranged for my ticket to be updated and marched me to the airport. If they could have put me in handcuffs, they would have. I didn't bloody dream it, you know! They said you would follow me to Australia.'

Old enough to be grandparents, we confronted each other, hands clenched like bare-knuckle fighters. Our anger rendered us shell-shocked. He picked up the chair, thumped it in place and charged back behind his desk where he sat staring silently at me as though I was an alien. His colour was returning, but his expression remained grim. 'Very well. Let's hear your version of what happened that day.'

I tried to speak, but my mouth was too dry. He reached over and poured more water into my glass. I sat straight backed, notifying James I wouldn't tolerate his bullying. Outwardly calm, I recounted the events of that terrible day, describing how his parents behaved and how they packed me back to Australia. I talked about finding work in Townsville before buying a cottage on Masters Island.

'They grabbed the opportunity to get rid of me. You were away, the phone in the house out of order and I was too ill to cope with anything.' I related my efforts to contact him, groped for my handbag and fished out the letters which had been returned to me twenty-six years previously.

He took them from me and slowly opened the top one, to read a few lines in shocked silence. Then he shuffled through the others. Not Known At This Address, Return To Sender All marked with the same message in his mother's handwriting. 'My God, El. The wasted years ... what's been done to us?' His face twisted in horror and our shared pain mirrored in each other's eyes. 'But why did you let my parents intimidate you and fool you into believing I would do such a thing? I know you were sick, but why did you listen to them? I loved you, Eloise. I would have welcomed our child.'

'Because I was so damn sick I couldn't cope with anything, let alone two horrible—' I pulled myself up, realising that I couldn't really call those two excrescences "horrible" to their son, who might actually love them.

He blinked. 'Yes, well you're a mature woman now.' He took a deep breath and wiped his hand slowly over his jaw. 'There was never any mention of a baby. My parents and Jemima swore you were two-timing me swore you left with another man. A John Faulkner.'

Anger licked my insides into a furnace. 'I've never heard of a John Faulkner, then or now.' I took a sip of much-needed water.

'You know, it always seemed too good to be true that an ordinary girl like me could attract and keep the love of a man like you. You've enjoyed the best of upbringing, English public schools and lots of money—the advantages of class. You had your pick of beautiful, well-educated women, while I was the low-class daughter of an Australian small-crops farmer. Still am. And there's nothing like the English class system for snobbery, especially all those years ago. All they thought about, and probably still do, is money, property and maintaining the stud book. Woe betide anyone who tries to get inside. Love needn't enter into the equation.' I couldn't keep the bitterness from my tone.

'Did I ever give you cause to feel that way?'

'No you didn't,' I admitted, 'but your parents, many of their friends and some of yours did, especially your cousin Jemima. I tried to tell you how they laughed behind my back, but you didn't want to see what was happening. Jemima was just waiting for the opportunity to get you for herself!'

The corners of his mouth twitched and for a fleeting moment I recognised the man with whom I had fallen in love. A sensation which I'd not felt in all the years I missed him, uncoiled inside me. I've touched this man in his most intimate places. And he has touched me.

We made eye contact; something hot arced between us for a split second before giving way to wry humour.

'No chance. First of all she is my cousin. She always was a sly cow and now she's an old one. You'll be gratified to hear she's been divorced by two husbands and looks like a Shar Pei from sunbathing in Spain.'

I was girlishly pleased to hear it.

'And what about your husband? Did he accept—the baby?'

'I never married. I changed my name to Carpenter by deed poll before my child was born.'

Refusing to allow myself to waver, I described the life I created for the two of us, confessing I spun a web of lies so tight they should have choked me. When I finished talking, he turned and stared out into the garden for a long time, before he finally faced me. I met his gaze straight on. Gesturing for me to sit in one of the armchairs, he went over to a tray on which sat a decanter of whisky and poured two shots.

'I don't suppose I can blame you for making up a story for her, it's understandable,' he acknowledged, handing me a drink.

'Are Margaret and Randall still alive?' I held hopes of them being slowly and thoroughly basted in Hell. I flicked a glance at the wall from where the framed faces of his parents gazed triumphantly down on me.

'No, mother died five years ago, father seven,' he replied. 'The conspiracy must have been organised immediately on a massive scale because, as I said, I came home early. Our employees would do what they were told, but our relatives and friends would all have to be advised of the game plan.' His expression bleak, he looked out the window onto the darkening landscape. I picked up my drink, sipped and closed my eyes, exhausted by the events and emotions of the last twenty four hours.

'I remember you said your mother left when you were a baby, your father died and relatives brought you up under sufferance. I'm sure that's why you didn't consider yourself worthy of my love and allowed my parents to destroy our future. I should have known something wasn't right, and tried harder to find you, El.' His voice seemed to come from a long way away.

God forgive me! For just a short while, I'd forgotten Ally's plight! I jumped to my feet, slopping my drink over my shirt. 'Ally's been missing since Friday night!'

'Ally?' His jaw dropped.

'Ally. Ally Carpenter, my–our–daughter!' I repeated impatiently.

'The concert pianist? Ally's *my daughter?*'

CHAPTER 8
A Significant Decision

Briece

Sunday: 9.30am.

Last night Pam rang with an idea that Ally might be nearby, though she only had a feeling to go on. She arrived shortly after midnight and we drove around the West End, shining a torch in every shadowy doorway, slowing down when we spotted a lone figure walking along the street. We must have scared a few people witless but nobody called the cops. At least we felt we were doing something.

We stopped at several cafes and pubs, then drove to Ally's place where we knocked on the door and then let ourselves in with Pam's key. We called out as we turned on the lights, hoping she had returned, gone to bed and hadn't heard us knocking. We checked the bedrooms and of course, she wasn't there. Pam tried to clean up a little, saying that Ally needed to come home to a nice house. We washed the few dishes which were sitting on the draining board and tried to cheer ourselves up.

'I just wish I'd gone to the loo with her. At least she'd still be here.' Pam looked about to cry.

'And what could you have done if you'd been with her? Stop blaming yourself, I need you to hang in there and help me.'

She looked at me sympathetically. 'Yeah, I was forgetting you were planning the Big Sex Scene on Friday night.'

I could feel myself flush. 'What do you mean?'

'Oh come on, Ally knew what you were up to. Supper indeed!' I could feel myself flushing. Pam laughed. 'Brie, you're so obvious. We all know how you feel about her, including Ally. She was looking forward to "supper" which is why I know she would never have left with those people without telling someone. We have to be strong, Brie, because I think she's in serious trouble.'

'Do you think I don't know that?' I could feel frustration and anger starting to boil inside, which wasn't fair to Pam. 'Come on, let's get out of here. I can't stand it.'

As we walked down the hallway to the front door, the house echoed abandonment with every step we took. Had I lost the one woman who might have been my soul mate? *Please God, save her save her save her...*

When I was ten years old, Mum and Dad had taken my siblings and me to a classical concert in the local town hall, where I fell irrevocably in love with the cello. I whined them into paying for lessons, at first on a piano, after which I made it my business to learn to play every instrument I could get my hands on. If rehearsal for the school orchestra started at 9am, I was there at 8. And when I wasn't with my teacher or practising, I fought for my life in the school playground, Mochrie's a poofter, but they let me live because I was good at soccer.

After I proved I was a stayer, my godmother paid for an almost new cello. Proficient at the piano, I excelled on that cello. Jazz, rock, heavy metal–I played them all, and still play jazz in The Cellar most Friday nights. But classical became my total passion. I don't get to go home to the country often. Fortunately my younger brother, Tim, is a born farmer and was only too happy to step into the breach. Mending pumps, fencing and shearing sheep is not my idea of a life's work, but I could if I had to.

Music is my career, my comfort–my link with Ally. Schubert's Impromptu in G, one of her concert pieces got a good work-out. While I played, I felt she was safe beside me. Every time the phone rang my heart jerked, thinking it might be her. Just before dawn, I crashed on my bed fully clothed and fell asleep, but not for long.

Violent hammering jerked me awake. Ally! I leapt out of bed, staggered blindly to the front door and threw it open.

My heart sank. The tiny foyer outside the door of my flat was crammed with my sisters, clutching bags of groceries. Judging by the happy expressions on their faces, they hadn't heard about Ally's disappearance. It would be up to me to tell them. I would kill for my sisters, but right then, needing time by myself, I could cheerfully have wrung their collective necks.

Exclaiming over my desperate appearance, they swept through the door in a relentless tidal wave of love and admonishments. They rooted in my refrigerator, snooped inside my cupboards, stacked tins of things into them and stocked up my freezer. I was about to tell them about Ally when the telephone rang. I had forgotten to check the answering machine; Pam's voice bellowed through.

'Brie, have you heard any news of Ally yet? The police have been here again and Aunt Eloise arrived on the bus this morning. Ring me as soon as you get this message, I've got something important to tell you!'

She hung up; my sisters gawped in horror. 'What's happened to Ally?' they shrieked, clustering around the door leading to the lounge room. I picked up the phone and hit recall. Pam answered on the first ring.

'The cops were here again, but they've gone now. I forgot to get the paper, so I don't know if it's in the news yet. But listen to this! I collected Aunt Eloise from the Transit Centre then I went to do some shopping and take a CD to Jess, so I was away a couple of hours. Aunt Eloise was supposed to be asleep, but when I got back here, she left a note'– her voice rose with excitement–' saying she's gone to see Ally's *father!*'

Stunned, I hit the speaker phone button but before I could comment, she rattled on. 'Yeah, I know. Shocked me too. He must be in Brisbane somewhere. Probably has been all along.'

'Fucking hell,' I snapped, enraged on Ally's behalf. 'Ally's father's supposed to be dead. What's going on?'

'I'm stuffed if I know,' Pam replied, 'but Ally always thought there could be more to the story. Aunt Eloise would never budge. You can tell who Ally takes after, can't you?'

'But perhaps he didn't want her? Maybe Ally's mother's been protecting her from him?' chimed in my youngest sister, Lara. 'Domestic violence.' She nodded knowingly. As a teacher, she understands how that affects families.

I thought about that for a moment. 'It doesn't matter, she should have told the truth. Even if he didn't want her, at least she'd know,' interjected Pam, having heard the suggestion.

'Well, Mrs Carpenter'll be sorry now, won't she?' I commented dryly.

'Shall I come over?' asked Pam.

'Of course,' I replied.

'And bring some pizzas, it's nearly lunchtime,' chorused the girls.

'Okay, but I'll be about an hour. Tell me what you want.'

A short discussion took place, followed by some

trawling in purses. I contributed the contents of my wallet, and then slunk into the music room. I needed time to think Friday night through again.

My mind immediately flew back to the woman carrying Ally's handbag. Ally wouldn't have let just anyone carry her bag. Did the presence of the woman mean they wouldn't hurt her? Fuck no, it didn't mean jack-shit. An icy lump settled deep in my gut. For the hundredth time, I castigated myself for my idiotic behaviour Friday night. *Ally, I'm so sorry.*

The police had questioned Michael, Pam and Jess about Friday evening. I was interviewed again, an hour before the concert was due to start, while a team of detectives questioned the other members of the orchestra.

Management, trying to hide her disappearance from the public, at least until after the concert, announced the star of the concert had been taken sick. So far they've been lucky. Either the media hadn't picked up the truth, or the police have requested a clamp down on their editors. But it was only a matter of time before her disappearance became public. Orchestra admin cautioned us not to speak to anyone, in case he–or she–is a journalist. They were pissing in the wind if they thought they could keep it under wraps for long.

Jacqueline Mabardi, the opera singer and a good friend of Ally's who was called in to perform at the last minute, wanted to know how she was. At first I was non-committal, but when she said she would phone Ally at home to see if there was any way she could help, I told her the truth.

The concert was a strain. There'd been only one opportunity to rehearse with the stand-in pianist. We were all exhausted by the time the evening programme ended and everyone melted away to their homes as fast as they could when it was over. But my thoughts wouldn't let go of the scene I'd viewed at police headquarters. Jess's apparent inability to remember who it was she nodded to at Traynors just before Ally's disappearance, didn't set right with me. She never forgets anything. *If I find anyone who has anything to do with Ally's disappearance I'll fucking kill them.*

I couldn't sit around on my arse doing nothing, so decided to carry out some investigations of my own. I owed Ally after my fucking stupid behaviour.

CHAPTER 9
Phone Call at the Witching Hour

James

Sunday: 5.00pm.

Not only had Eloise presented me with a very long ago, post-affair daughter, all the feelings I was sure were buried swirled around my mind like wasps. I pride myself on being in control at all times, but Eloise contacting me after all this time had thrown my mind into chaos.

The sound of her voice, still with the hint of the huskiness which bewitched me all those years ago, rendered me speechless. I'd longed to have her back even as I cursed over her betrayal—seeming betrayal—but wanted to reach out and touch her. And there she was, after all the lost years. Since then pain has been replaced by fury over the actions of my long-dead parents and the irrefutable proof of their responsibility for the destruction of our relationship.

I could well imagine the dreadful scenes between Eloise and my parents. My mother's strident handwriting plastered across the envelopes enclosing Eloise's letters bore testimony to what they had done. I cannot, will not, read them because of my fear that a lifetime of self-control will shatter, leaving me vulnerable, weeping. As the kids say these days, I don't "do" weakness.

My mind roamed ceaselessly back to the joy of loving

Eloise. She brought a freedom into my life which my rigid upbringing had all but stamped out. Her shyness and lack of self-esteem had been endearing after the self-assured arrogance of the girls with whom I had mixed all my life. During the short time we were together, she brought me down to earth, and showed me that giving your heart to another person did not mean losing yourself.

'You're getting too complacent, James, I think I'll find a younger model!' She laughed, teasing me for being an uptight prig. Her glowing face, rosy in the morning light surrounded by a waterfall of rich, red hair, flashed into my mind. I'd dragged her back into the bed and showed her just how much I thought of that idea. But it was a memory which I, hurt beyond words at the time, was all too anxious to forget after listening to Jemima and my parents. I understood, finally, why she found it so hard to stand up to my parents.

Now I had no heart for the music I loved or for dealing with the mountains of paperwork piled up on my desk. I sat in my armchair worshipping the Black Douglas, re-living the past in front of the flickering fire. Her face is still beautiful, skin fine and her hair bright. Her figure, still girlishly slim, is now full-breasted and womanly. Her face is so very like Ally's I wonder why I didn't see the resemblance, but the old saying, "can't see for looking" springs to mind.

'Ally Carpenter. Our daughter. My daughter, Ally.' I spoke the words aloud several times, but my voice sounded as though it belonged to someone else. Ally is a woman whom I greatly admire, but it is impossible to regard her as my flesh and blood. I need more time to assimilate the knowledge imparted to me only a few hours ago. The thought of her being held against her will by a predator and perhaps raped or tortured horrifies me, but the terror I should be experiencing as her father eludes me.

My dog, lying on the hearthrug, stirred and whined. My housekeeper, Mrs Fox, called him as she rapped the top of the dog food tin with a spoon. He looked at me hopefully but when I couldn't bring myself to respond, he settled back, dropped his head and gave me a reproachful look.

All the questions which had emotionally destroyed me in my youth were answered, and now my life has been turned upside down.

Again.

I am the parent of an adult daughter who is making a name for herself in her chosen field of expertise, one moreover in which I possess some skill. An unexpected flush of pleasure flows through me, as I realise that talent must have been passed to her through my genes. How I regret the lost years, not being to rescue her when she fell at life's hurdles, her first steps, her high school years or her first forays into dating and the world of serious study, helping guide her career. In short, being a father…

Mrs Fox's distinctive, light footsteps stopped outside the study door, followed by a quiet knock. 'Sir? Is Benji in there with you?'

I got to my feet and went to open the door. The dog slipped through and scuttled, nails clicking on the polished floor, along the passageway to the kitchen quarters.

'Yes, well, he was here,' I replied, watching his tail flick through the kitchen door. Mrs Fox gazed warily up into my face. I knew I intimidated most people, and that is how I have always preferred it.

'I'll give him his dinner and let him out for a quick run. I'm leaving bacon and egg pie for you in the microwave, Sir. You only have to heat it on high for three minutes,' she said, untying her apron with quick fingers, anxious to get back to the staff accommodation before dark.

'Yes, thank you Mrs Fox. Goodnight to you.'

I went back to my study. The wood on the fire was turning to coal. I stoked it, watching as sparks flew up the chimney, and then retrieved a log from the box beside the hearth. Flames licked gratefully, bathing the room in a comforting glow. I poured another whisky and resumed my chair.

I put my life on hold for more than two years while I searched for Eloise, but it ended in bitter memories which were, on occasions, deadened by alcohol. Eventually, I forced myself to move on and complete my degree, but I couldn't abandon the dream we'd shared. Her words of love and encouragement stayed with me in spite of my pain and anger, so in the face of my family's opposition, I went on to study music at Trinity College, Cambridge.

I can't understand how my family, the parents who supposedly loved me, could watch my life fall apart and not make any attempt to tell the truth. What sort of love was that? Even for people of their class, their actions were so viciously calculated...I wonder now how much of a part they played in my brother's choice of wife? Alison "fits," Eloise didn't. Had Peter known of the deception? If so, why didn't he tell me? Surely he would have spoken up. But I realised that the fewer people who knew, the better for the success of the conspiracy. Only my parents and Jemima would have known the truth. Our company staff would do what they were told and the university would have received a lucrative backhander.

My sisters married obediently and well and then moved to other parts of the world, perhaps with good reason. On the rare occasion when I do visit, they always appear to be happy enough. I wonder now if I was emotionally oblivious to any problems they may have had, but as I didn't enquire beyond the normal civilities, why would they confide in me? *Dear God, what else have I been blind to?*

I met my wife, Helen at a society ball and we married after a brief, traditional courtship. Her family felt she'd chosen beneath her, which is ironic when I know now my life was devastated because my parents considered Eloise beneath me.

We embarked upon a first affectionate, then friendly but sometimes hesitant relationship, the kind which eventually deteriorates into pleasant communication over the breakfast table, separate bedrooms and carefully orchestrated public appearances. These were to convince everyone and ourselves that all was well. This state of affairs continued until her death from cancer, ten years ago.

We had no children because Helen was terrified of being pregnant and giving birth. With both our family's feelings about class in mind, adoption was never on the agenda. Ironically, Peter and Alison were childless also.

Horses and dogs made up whatever gap there might have been in Helen's need for fulfilment. My music and growing collection of antiques and art pasted over the cracks in my heart. I put my desire for children, a private grief, to the back of my mind and decided to make the best of things.

During her illness we became closer than at any time in our marriage. 'Why did you marry me, Helen?' I queried, one cold winter's day toward the end of her life, as we sat in front of the fire.

'No one else asked me, James,' she replied wistfully.

I looked at her ravaged face and body, her wig slightly askew, hiding what she regarded as the shame of her baldness and twisted from a gibbet of guilt. I hadn't done her any favours by marrying her. The chips were down and when she posed the same question of me, I told her about my devastating affair with Eloise. She was silent for a few minutes, and then surprised me.

'I remember. I never actually met her, but from what I understand, she didn't appear to be the sort of girl who would betray you. I wonder if there was more to that than met the eye? Your parents always ran her down behind your back, you know.'

Her words should have sparked an idea of what might have happened, but foolishly, I didn't pick up on it. We were silent for a moment and then she asked the question I dreaded. 'Did you love me, James? At all?'

'Yes, I loved you, Helen.'

'But not the way you loved Eloise,' she replied sadly, thereby summing up the wasteland of our marriage. Regretfully, it occurred to me that if Helen had always been as loving and gentle as she was shortly before she died, our marriage may well have been successful. But it takes two, as they say, and I had not made much effort to be more affectionate and attentive.

Since Helen's death there's been no desperate urge on my part to search for a meaningful relationship. Loneliness sometimes cuts deep, but I've never been able to let go of the notion, that love such as I felt for Eloise would again end with me being abandoned.

I am not an unattractive man—I've had many women, some of whom appeared determined to make me happy and whom I might have made happy, but not for me the glitzy socialite, the trophy wife or the precious academic. A practical businesswoman may well suit, but at forty-nine years of age, I can't seem make up my mind what I want. The thought is unwelcome.

I once desired Ally Carpenter, warmed myself in the

glow of her charm and admired her unusual beauty, even allowing the thought to creep into my heart that many older, rich men make successful marriages with younger women. Therefore why not try my hand at winning her?

Fortunately, not wanting to turn a good friendship into something more, I backed away from the attraction. Although I couldn't possibly have known her relationship to me at the time, I squirm with shame at the memory of lusting, briefly, after my own child—

The insistent ringing of the telephone jolts me into the present.

I glance at the clock and realise I've been dozing for hours. A prickle of fear trickles through me. Late night calls are always the harbinger of bad news. The room is suffocatingly warm. Tears course down my cheeks. I dash them away with the back of my hand, as I stumble to the desk, turn on the table lamp and pick up the receiver.

'James—'

A muffled voice interrupts, but the meaning is clear.

'Listen to me very carefully. We have your daughter, Ally Carpenter. I've got plenty of places to dump her body if you tell the cops. I'm warning you, do that and she'll die. A pre-paid mobile phone will be delivered to you tomorrow night, along with another packet. Wait for instructions. You have forty-eight hours to find and pay the first instalment of three million dollars.'

My voice seems to come from far away, shocking me by its calm, automatic response.

'Australian or American?'

CHAPTER 10

It's Blood

Ally

Monday: early morning.

I feel so sick. I had no water last night, only coffee, but I couldn't taste anything strange. Time is meaningless, only broken up into morning and night when they come, and then it feels like an invasion of my privacy. I've been forced to make this room my own. After being trapped here, it has become my refuge. Even if an opportunity occurs and I get away, how long will be before they catch me? Where would I run? I'd be fresh kill to Scarpia's leopard. But I must try.

I'm so cold. I want to pee, but the effort to get to the loo…got to get there before they come in. I feel squashed. My arm hurts. What—there's a big bruise on the inside of my elbow with a large puncture mark. What have they done? Is that how they drugged me? No, I'd know about it.

I swing my legs awkwardly around to the floor. Uh, large, blackish-red spots on the floorboards. Blood? Has my nose bled again? It's so bunged up, I can't smell the dried blood on my top and skirt. Fear rises in my throat. I grope around the stretcher for my glasses, put them on to touch a splotch and hold my finger right against my nostril. Yes, it's blood.

I place my spectacles carefully against the wall, then sweep my hair back and start to plait it. My hands tremble, but I'm managing. Long strands fall and cling to the front of my clothes. A tug here and there and hanks come loose. A chunk of my hair has been cut just under the base of my skull.

Now I understand why my arm is sore. A man—my father, whom I do not know—will get a hank of my bloodied hair and a demand for three million dollars.

Terrific. He will be pleased.

I want to rip their throats out. How dare they keep me shut up in here? How dare they ruin my career and threaten me?

They're coming up the stairs outside. I flatten myself against the wall next to the door, ready to attack and run. As it swings open, Scarpia stops in the entrance, just out of sight. I can't get behind him.

'Fucking hell—' He lunges forward. I shove him, using every bit of my remaining strength, but it's like trying to move a telephone pole. He whirls around and grabs me by the hair, almost wrenching it out of my head and then throws me onto the floor. The hard ridges of someone's feet break my fall, biting into my back. My breath rasps as I try to suck air and roll to face them, but I am still anchored by my hair.

A shadow looms over me. The Cow swings her arm back to strike me.

The man stops her.

His boot swings toward me...my head explodes. I wrench my hair away from his grasp and curl myself into a ball, trying to protect my face as kicks land indiscriminately. I don't how long it is before I find myself alone again. Blackness envelops me. I can't open my eyes. My face stings and there's blood in my mouth. It hurts to breathe and my head is aching so badly I can't think straight. I put my hand to my face. My lungs wheeze in the silence, every breath a painful though hazy reminder of the assault.

Then it all comes back to me. I attacked him, he kept kicking me and she pulled him off. My hands. They're okay, I think. I can feel my fingers, he didn't cut them.

Now I can see light, just a little out of my left eye.

I'm so thirsty. I crawl to the wall and try to stand up.

The stretcher. Get to it.

It takes forever to drag the blanket around my body and over my head.

I can't stop shaking.

Pretend, Ally. You've got to pretend you're not terrified. Retreat into a place where they can't touch you, where the pain can't follow—the past.

My first piano was given to me by the postman's wife on Masters Island. No one else wanted it and I loved it. Mum bought me some easy correspondence lessons for my sixth birthday. Pretty soon it wasn't enough, and she had to find someone to give me proper tuition.

My time with my teacher, Mrs Minowski, feels as though it happened only yesterday. The first piece I played for her was Brahms Lullaby. 'Ally Carpenter, you will take this slowly now. Brahms did not intend it should be galloped through. You understand?'

'Yes, Mrs Minowski,' I hear myself chant.

Mrs Minowski is Polish, a dumpy, bespectacled little old woman, much given to wearing an assortment of bright clothes which smelt strongly of camphor. She sported an armful of bangles, which sent us into fits of giggles as they clattered on the ivory keys of the piano.

An old-fashioned fox fur lived around her shoulders, it's pathetic little feet clasped together with a hook made out of its own toenails. Beady little eyes glared watchfully out of its broad face, ears flattened to its skull. When

I thought no-one was watching, I would touch the wet-looking nose and apologise for the animal's indignity, repulsed by the barbarity of its artificial existence.

Mrs Minowski's music room was cluttered with sheet music, text books and half-finished glasses of water which, rumour had it, held gin.

I soon learned if I made mistakes, it would prolong my lesson and save me from the school thugs who circled like piranhas in the playground, lying in wait for the four-eyed island parrot. My teacher was not fooled for long. 'What is this, child? I know you are a pianist far advanced for your years. Today you are playing as a two-year old!'

She twirled the piano stool around so I was facing her. For a long moment we eyeballed each other, before she glanced out of the window, nodded as though satisfied of something important and spun me back again to face the keyboard. 'We will finish your lesson, and then you will play a duet with my next pupil, who you know well. Then we go together across to the classroom! This is the way it shall be from now on.' Her lips folded in a determined line. Thank you thank you thank you, God.

'Thank you, Mrs Minowski!' I sighed with relief, safe for the foreseeable future. A knock came at the door and my best friend, Pam entered, flushed and panting.

'Aha! Pamela! You are on time. Good.' She pushed me forward, beaming from ear to ear, teeth clacking as she chewed the menthol cough lozenges to which she was addicted. We fell to giggling and pushing each other. Mrs Minowski clapped her hands and admonished us to behave.

Pam got her flute out of its case and Mrs M's eyes glittered with excitement. She grabbed Pam by the sleeve of her uniform blouse and propelled her into position beside me at the keyboard.

'Now, the Lullaby. One, two, three!'

Brahms Lullaby filled the room; Mrs Minowski clasped her hands, tears welling.

'My wee ones,' she sobbed, 'so beautiful. Never have I had two so talented children at once, never! You will be famous, I know it.' I still send her my CDs when they come out and receive voluminous letters in return, which contain a great deal of advice, much of which I am grateful for.

Pam and I were accepted into the Conservatorium of Music. Our mothers leased a three-bedroom flat for us which, unbeknownst to them, had been previously occupied by two call girls. The lavish décor, an African jungle motif, should have alerted us to something untoward, but we only discovered this from the neighbours after we had lived there for a couple of weeks.

We needed another girl to help out with the rent, but despite advertising and asking around, it was about three weeks before tall, slim and self-contained Jessica Rallison, also from Townsville, stood on our doorstep. Her olive skin glowed; her long, black hair fell in a thick, glossy plait. She oozed over the threshold and sauntered through the unit, eyeing our photos, furniture and general mess.

Pam and I fluttered behind her like acolytes to a priestess, trying to resist the temptation to snatch cardigans, books and clutter and stuff it under cushions. If we had worn white robes and crawled on the floor behind her, we couldn't have grovelled any harder. All that was left was to make a sacrifice in her honour.

We designated the smallest bedroom for a third flatmate. A momentary wrinkle sullied her perfect forehead when she saw it, but her eyes gleamed when she was shown the bathroom. The call girls had obviously designed and installed it for their pleasure. It was our pride and joy too.

A deep, claw-footed tub under a shower, chequerboard tiles and faux gold fittings were complemented by a set of cupboards running the full length of the wall. These were supported by a wide bench top, with a huge mirror screwed to the wall. The full length makeup bench, inset with two deep hand basins was polished granite.

We allocated the medium-sized second bedroom, decorated with an African veldt mural with sunset waterhole scene as our music room, having coaxed our current boyfriends into helping line the walls with egg cartons to deaden the sound.

Jess hovered just inside the door. My upright piano and Pam's music stand took up most of the space on one side, a filing cabinet packed with sheet music, another full of CDs and a black vinyl collection occupied a good deal of the room.

'I could fit my stand there—' Jess pointed a contemplative finger at the only spot left. We smiled as though approved for an honour by the Queen, then bowed and scraped our way to the kitchen for coffee. A flushed glance of agreement and we invited her to move in. Jess settled in and we all mucked in together, but it wasn't long before we discovered that she was a compulsive cleaner. This was great to start with but later we felt guilty because we knew we disappointed her with our grottiness.

Jess wasn't always easy to fathom. We three could spend hours practising in our music room, sharing confidences about study and socialising—a euphemism for clubbing and hunting men, but Jess had a barrier which she seemed unable to overcome. We knew she had emotional problems left over from childhood and couldn't seem to sustain a relationship for long, but despite our support, she could never confide any worries.

A year later I won a highly prestigious competition and was offered a scholarship to study at Trinity College, Cambridge. I left for London on a bleak day in March; Pam and Jess arrived a few months later. We found, after much searching, a flat we could ill-afford and nowhere near the standard of the one we enjoyed in Brisbane. But there we lived lives which alternated between desperation and joy.

Desperation. You didn't know the meaning of the word, you idiot.

But you do now.

'Hey, wakey, wakey, Ally!' They're back. He kicks my leg, which is hanging over the edge of the stretcher. I keep my arms wrapped around my head and face to protect them. *Please God, help me.*

'Ally, right about now your dad's wonderin' how he's gunna raise that money,' Scarpia announces, joyfully. 'Bet you're the one fuck he wishes he'd never had!'

CHAPTER 11
Someone Like Her

Detective Senior Sergeant Susan Prescott

Monday: 7.30am.

The car park reeked of rubber and exhaust fumes. I almost fell over the disgusting bucket into which the smokers put their stubs. I'm sympathetic, but there's a limit. Chocolates are my addiction of choice.

A group of media were clustered in reception. 'The word must be out,' I muttered, as I scuttled across the foyer to the lift, keeping my face averted. Fortunately, they were engrossed in trying to bully the imperturbable counter staff. I breathed a sigh of relief as the doors closed. As the lift lifted me to CIB, I brooded over last night's conversation with my husband, Harry, and feeling guilty over my irritable response.

Ally Carpenter's face is startlingly familiar. He speculated endlessly during dinner and throughout the evening. 'Susan, she reminds me of someone. Where did her family come from, originally?' he asked for the umpteenth time, as we prepared for bed.

'I don't know. And if you had met someone like her, you'd remember. Now for goodness sake, go to sleep, Harry. We've both got early starts in the morning.'

His hurt expression tugged at my heart strings. I leaned over to kiss him, but at the last minute he turned his head away and my lips bounced off his ear.

'I'm sorry I snapped, love. I'll find out more about her tomorrow.'

He looked at me for a long moment, his face expressionless, then pulled the bedclothes up around his ears and turned his back, effectively shutting me out. My guilt made sleep elusive; I felt washed out and not my usual self.

Evan had already updated the whiteboard timeline documenting the movements of Ally Carpenter and her friends on Friday night. Shots from the security cameras were pinned on a separate board, beside an enlarged photo of the victim. My investigating team trickled through the door clutching their notebooks and slumped into chairs, seemingly in slow motion.

'Good morning. Is everyone here?'

A desultory chorus replied. To be fair, most of them had worked throughout the weekend, but I needed everyone on the ball. Two days and three nights since the girl was snatched; I didn't hold out much hope of finding her alive.

'Right, now let's sum up what we know so far, which is damn all. Detective Sergeant Taylor will take you through what we have so far.'

Evan stepped forward. 'First of all, the media are on the rampage and a conference will take place shortly with DI Patterson and Senior Sergeant Prescott. We've advised the management of the Pacific Orchestra to make sure their members and admin staff refrain from speaking to journalists. Hospitals and taxi companies have been checked for sightings of Ms Carpenter, and cadets are viewing CCTV footage of bus and train stations. Facial imaging didn't pan out, the features of the mob in the Toyota Corolla weren't clear.' He cast a beady eye on his nephew, DC Ben Taylor. 'What did Traynor's staff have to say?'

'Well, Sarge, the barmen don't remember her, but the doorman said she left with a man just before ten. He didn't see them get into the car, but they would have turned up to the city or onto the Storey Bridge.'

'It could just have easily headed down Brunswick to New Farm,' said Evan, frowning severely at Ben. 'Or gone up Ann Street and gone right to the western suburbs. Ma'am, over to you.'

Before I could speak, a uniformed constable handed me a message. 'Ma'am, uniform located a white Toyota Corolla sedan which fits the description of the wanted vehicle from Traynor's Friday night, abandoned in bushland at Gumdale.'

'Right, I nodded to a pair of my team. 'Off to Gumdale with you. Get forensics to go over the car. Here—' I passed the paper.

'No sign of forced entry at Miss Carpenter's house. No sign of a struggle or abduction from the premises. Her friend, Pamela Miller maintains there are no clothes missing. Her passport is still in the house as well as jewellery and medications, iPod. Her emails have been checked, Facebook and Twitter pages, but no sign of stalkers or threats. Her answering machine only has a couple of messages on it from friends who are being checked now and her mobile phone records show no calls from unknown numbers. Pamela Miller verified most of the calls, the others checked out as work related. Sergeant Taylor and I will talk to Rallison, Whitby, Miller and Briece Mochrie again. At this stage, we're going with predator snatch.'

I paused for a sip of water.

'However, the woman carrying Carpenter's handbag could suggest she knew them. But if that's the case, why didn't she tell her friends she was leaving? The one thing you should all remember is that Ally Carpenter is a mature, professional concert pianist. Sir James McPherson and James Kirkbridge from the Pacific Orchestra insist she's not given to taking days off or hysterical behaviour. The concert on Saturday night was a long-anticipated and well advertised event, which was part of a series of performances for which the Carpenter girl was contracted. She had put a lot of work into it. So it's unlikely she went off with a boyfriend, as has been suggested. Her mother has arrived in town from North Queensland and Sergeant Taylor and myself are leaving now to interview her. Right, that's all for the moment.'

The team got to their feet and trooped out of the room, muttering among themselves. Evan gathered his notebooks. 'It's not looking good,' he commented, as we buckled ourselves into the car.

'You're telling me. If we can't get anything concrete today, I'm not sure where we're going to go next. Perhaps the mother can help.'

I cast a glance around the neighbourhood while we waited a good three minutes for the door to Pamela Miller's unit to be answered. She lived in a block of four trendy faux-colonial flats behind a row of tall trees. A dog toilet nestled at the base of a collection of knee-high shrubs. The door was opened by Eloise Carpenter, a small attractive woman with terrified eyes and wild red hair, Her appearance took my breath away. I'd seen her, or someone very like her, before.

'Have you found Ally yet?' she blurted, as soon as we identified ourselves.

'No, I'm sorry, Mrs Carpenter.'

Her shoulders slumped as she turned and ushered into a comfortable, airy lounge room. Newspapers were strewn on the floor, well-stocked bookshelves lined the walls and a portly tabby cat lay belly-up, purring, on the settee. A recess revealed a small upright piano with a computer on a desk beside it. Sheet music littered the floor, a radio played soft classical music and the aroma of brewed coffee and fresh baking wafted through the air. Our noses twitched like rabbits.

'Would you like some coffee and scones?' our hostess asked. She looked poised to bolt. Why? We replied in the affirmative, trying not to sound too greedy. It felt like a long time since breakfast. She waved us to the sofa and disappeared into the kitchen.

Before Evan got halfway across the room to follow her, she returned with a loaded tray which she put on the table and proceeded to pour coffee. I had no time to snoop, so I sat and rubbed my hand over the furry tummy of the cat, which wriggled happily then wrapped its paws around my arm and bit my wrist before jumping to the floor and stalking to the kitchen. Ungrateful little shit.

Evan chewed on a generous bite of scone, swallowed and then wiped cream and jam off his lips, with a handkerchief the size of the national flag.

'First of all, Mrs Carpenter, is your husband, Ally's father, with you?' 'We were estranged before she was born, Detective Sergeant.'

'I'm sorry. That must have been very difficult for you.'

She nodded, but made no further comment on that.

'Have you had any problems with the media? Because—'

'They don't know I'm staying with Pamela, Detective, and the Orchestra has rung to assure me they're not giving out any information to the press, apart from a formal statement. They said not to speak to anyone about it, except for you of course.' She folded her lips, defensively. *Something's going on here...*

'That's good. Journalists can be very aggressive and

the longer they're out of the loop, the better.' I smiled in what I hoped was a reassuring manner and she seemed to relax, just a little.

'Mrs Carpenter, we need to ask you about Ally. We have the accounts from her friends, but we need to know her from your perspective.'

'You think she's run off, don't you?' Eloise Carpenter slapped her mug down on the tray. 'Ally is not the sort of person who would do that. She's a professional!' Her eyes brimmed. She fumbled for a tissue from the box on the coffee table, finally tearing out a handful, most of which showered to the floor.

'Mrs Carpenter–'

'Ms Carpenter,' she interrupted. 'I've never married.'

'Oh. Ms Carpenter, we are well aware Ally is a dedicated artist who would never blow-off a concert. That's why we are working on her disappearance without waiting for the stipulated time before embarking on a Missing Person's investigation.'

Eloise Carpenter, between sobs, gave us an in-depth portrait of her daughter. Once she got back to Ally in her teens, I diverted her by enquiring about the one aspect her mother hadn't yet touched upon, although we already knew the answer. It would be interesting to find out how much she had confided in her mother.

'Ms Carpenter, has Ally a boy—err—man friend? Are you sure she wouldn't go away for an impromptu holiday?' Having just conceded her reputation precluded that possibility, I felt stupid, but it had to be asked.

Again, Eloise drew herself up defensively. 'I have already told you, Ally would never miss a major concert. She is a dedicated, professional musician. She's always had a lot of friends, both men and women, Detective Senior Sergeant Prescott,' she snapped. 'She does not go away for impulsive weekends or stay out late without letting someone know.'

She glared at us defiantly, lips trembling. I reached out and gently touched her hand. 'Ms Carpenter, I am not implying otherwise. We need to know about all her friends, even though we have no reason to believe any of them had anything to do with her disappearance.' Let's not mention Madam Jessica, for now.

Eloise was mollified. 'Well, I do know she's formed a friendship with a cellist in the orchestra. Brieve or some name like that.'

'Briece Mochrie,' I supplied, 'and Pamela Miller is your god-daughter?'

Eloise nodded.

'What can you tell me about Jessica Rallison and Michael Whitby?'

She bowed her head for a moment, then looked up and snapped her posture into the ramrod position. 'They're close friends of Ally's. Ally, Pam and Jess lived together in Brisbane, and then in London when they were students at Cambridge. She has friends outside the orchestra, here and overseas and from school. I can give you their names, but I can't for the life of me see any one of them hurting Ally.'

'Do you know of anyone, perhaps a fan, who might be a little too eager to know her? We need to know as much as we can about your daughter if we're to find her.'

Her eyes widened. 'You mean a stalker? Good heavens no! And I'm sure she would have told Pam or Jess if there was one. In fact, I am sure you would know by now.'

'Her emails don't reveal any sign of inappropriate behaviour on the part of the senders. We've asked her friends and colleagues, Ms Carpenter, and they all say Ally's not mentioned anyone. What about her father, Ms

Carpenter? Is he here with you?'

'Excuse me.' She jumped up and scurried off to the kitchen with a turn of speed which took us by surprise. Obviously we'd touched on delicate territory. Just then my mobile rang; Jessica Rallison had called in sick to the orchestra admin.

Evan smirked. 'A convenience?'

'Hm. We'll pounce later. It'll be a nice surprise for her.'

We sipped our coffee and ate the last few mouthfuls of scone while we awaited Ms Carpenter's return. I scanned the room again. A scattering of photographs showed the two friends, young, smiling and gap-toothed, clutching musical instruments. A photo of Ally, Pamela Miller and Jessica Rallison, capped and gowned, waving their degrees stood beside it. Various family photos, many taken with a woman I assumed to be her mother littered Pamela Miller's bookshelves. Some included Eloise.

She returned from the kitchen, once more under control. 'I would rather not talk about Ally's father. He's dead.' Her wide-eyed innocence and direct gaze said otherwise. *You're lying. Why? Did he have something to do with Ally's disappearance?* She folded her arms across her body. Lock down time again. Evan smiled reassuringly and tried another tack.

'I'm sorry, Ms Carpenter, we didn't mean to upset you,' he said calmly, holding eye contact. 'But we may need to talk about him in the near future.' Eloise looked away first. We'd run a check on her when we got back to headquarters.

'Do you know of any problems Ally had? Any arguments or differences of opinion with the orchestra?' he continued.

She drew herself up. 'There were none that I know of. You would do better asking her friends.'

He tried another angle. 'We will, ma'am. Does she

have any religious membership? In other words, could she belong to a cult who might have taken her?'

'She doesn't belong to any church group, Detective–er–Sergeant. There was one thing though—' She hesitated. I cast an encouraging glance at her. 'Ally and Jess weren't getting on too well in London. My daughter was quite upset about it. I think it was professional jealousy on Jess's part.'

Evan and I avoided looking at each other, not wanting the mother to know we were examining Jessica Rallison's behaviour on the night in question.

'Ally went to America for a short concert series and then flew back to Australia to join the orchestra here. She came home for a week to see me and to arrange for her things to be transported to Brisbane.'

'Did you go to Ally's house after you got down here?'

'Pam took me over there, but it upset me. I couldn't bear to stay in Ally's house, so I'm staying with Pamela.'

She pressed her hand to her mouth. I touched her hand again, gently, and received a grateful, but relieved glance. I decided to explore the other avenue, perhaps the one Eloise Carpenter was afraid of and which might explain her extreme tension. 'Has anyone contacted you since Ally disappeared?' I asked.

Eloise looked puzzled, but wary. 'What do you mean?'

'Has anyone phoned you and asked for money or some favour in return for Ally's safety?'

Her eyes widened, perhaps a little too much. 'I haven't got any money to speak of, Detective Sergeant. And nor has my daughter.'

'Let me know if you think of anything which might help, something Ally may have said. And would you like to have a Family Liaison Officer stay with you while your goddaughter is not here?'

She shook her head. 'I'd rather not, but if I find I need someone I can change my mind, can't I?'

I handed over my card, at which she barely glanced, before putting it on the coffee table.

'Yes, of course. It's entirely your choice. And can you give me the names of all of her friends that you can remember, please?'

Eloise searched her memory for the names of Ally's friends, which prompted a thought.

'Ms Carpenter, where did you originally come from?'

Eloise stared at me. 'Western New South Wales, Dubbo actually. Why do you ask?'

'I feel I might have met you before, but I can't think where,' I explained with a smile.

When we reached our car, I turned back to wave, but she had shut the door.

'She was lying through her teeth, but there's nothing we can do except watch her bank accounts,' I said, as we drove away and I punched numbers into my mobile. 'Best get started on it. And I'll bet anything you like the father is not dead.'

'You reckon it's a kidnapping for ransom?'

'Hm...don't know. It can't be for money from the mother, but we'll check out her finances anyway. If the father is alive, there's no way of finding out who he is unless the mother tells us. Perhaps they're on such bad terms she can't approach him, or he's married and it's all a big secret. Unless we get proof to the contrary, we can only go with the predator snatch. We'll keep our ear to the ground and give the boys a "hurry up" on Eloise's background.'

Evan grunted, as he swerved to miss someone's burly tomcat coming home late from a hard night's hunting in the mountains, aka the park running parallel to the road.

'Yep, I agree. What's next? The violinist?'

'Yes.' I sighed. It was going to be a long day.

CHAPTER 12

Secrets

Eloise

Monday: 10.46am.

James's phone call had come just minutes before the police arrived to interview me. I picked up the receiver, answered and waited, pencil poised, ready to take a message for Pam.

'Eloise? Are you alone?' My heart almost leapt out of my chest. His voice was muffled, as though he was trying not to be overheard.

'James? James, what is it?'

'Are you alone?' The tone of his voice frightened me.

'Yes, at the moment, but—'

'Eloise, I had a phone call in the middle of the night. Ally's been kidnapped. For ransom.'

'What? *Ransom?*'

He repeated himself, carefully enunciating each word as though I were deaf. I flung out a hand, groping for the chair which Pam kept by the telephone table. It slewed sideways as I struggled to manoeuvre it into position and sat heavily.

'Yes, kidnapped.' His voice was flat and cold. 'Three million dollars. I've two days to find the first instalment.'

I was momentarily speechless and then asked, 'How do you know they've got her?'

'I received an envelope this morning, with a hank of bloodied red hair. So we need—'

The room went dark; spots danced in front of my eyes. A roaring in my head sounded like the ocean and drowned out his voice. With an enormous effort, I sucked in air and pulled myself out of it.

'Wait, James. Wait a moment. Tell me again. What *exactly* did they send?'

He took a deep breath and recounted the receipt of a hand-delivered package a few minutes previously. My mind gradually cleared as I took in what he had to say. Molten rage surged through me, rising up my throat to choke me. How dare someone take my child and threaten her life! There was only one course open to us.

'James, we have to tell the police. They'll know what to do.'

'No. No, Eloise, we can't. He said they had plenty of places to dump her body. Somehow I have to find three million dollars and I only hope it's worth it.'

I went cold all over. 'What do you mean, *you only hope it's worth it?*'

A short silence followed. 'I didn't mean that the way it sounded ... I'm sorry, Eloise.' His voice softened. 'It's a bloody nightmare. I meant I hope paying three million means Ally is safe. I'm still trying to come to terms with the fact that I actually have a daughter. And if they don't get the money, a young wo—my child, my flesh and blood—is going to die.'

I understood his terror only too well. Part of me bled for him, but the rest of me could have strangled him with my bare hands. How did he think I felt? I'm her mother, for God's sake.

'But James, do you have three million dollars?'

'Yes, but not even I can get it just like that, in cash. They—he—warned me if I tell the police ...his exact words were, 'do and she'll die.' There'll be another phone call in 48 hours with instructions on where to leave the money.'

I choked back tears, blew my nose and pulled some more tissues out of the box. They came in a rush, most of them scattering into a snowdrift around my feet.

'Eloise, who knows I'm Ally's father?'

I caught up with his train of thought. 'Only two people know. Pam's mother Rosalind Miller, and my friend Georgie Hird. But I can't imagine either of them telling anyone. Neither of those women would even think of getting involved in this. I'd stake my life on it.'

There was a short silence on the other end of the telephone before he spoke with deep conviction. 'You may have already staked Ally's life on it. One of them has betrayed your confidence.'

A chill settled deep in my stomach. 'Surely not?'

'If only two people know then one of them has *definitely* told someone, perhaps quite innocently. Think about it. Now, I've got to get to the city and start working on organising the money.' He sucked in a deep breath. 'What are you doing now?'

'I'm waiting for the police to come and interview me—'

He cut in. 'Eloise, whatever you do, don't tell them about this. I'll take care of it. Look, ring me on my mobile as soon as they've gone. We'll meet somewhere after I've been to the city, but we're going to have to be careful. If the police get wind of this, they'll take over and it could be disastrous. We *must* do it the kidnapper's way, at least for the time being.'

Reluctantly, I agreed to keep quiet and promised to ring him when the police left. It was only after he hung up, I realised someone was knocking on the front door, but for how long I couldn't say. I gave my eyes a final wipe, bent down, gathered up as many sodden tissues as I could in one swoop, stuffed them into the kitchen tidy and headed for the front door.

Ally's life depended on my ability to tamp down my anger and lie to the police..

After the two officers left, I shut the door and leaned against it, exhausted. Had I pulled it off? The woman detective's eyes were everywhere.

Secrets. The police deal with secrets every day of the week. God help me, if those two even suspected something so terrible had happened that I want to sit on the floor and scream like the madwoman I have become. They were just waiting for me to fall into their trap.

Needing to keep busy, I started cleaning the bathroom; Pam had always been messy. As I wiped the toothpaste and soap scum off the side of the basin and binned the make-up-splattered tissues scattered on the vanity top, I realised nothing had changed. The cat's litter tray was first out and then I settled in to clean the room. Every breath I took, every swirl of the scrubber, was a blow delivered to the faceless thugs who had my child. Long before I got to the end of my task, I had broken the handle of the brush. It was even more satisfying to grind the steel wool into the tiles, stand-ins for evil flesh. By the time it was finished, I was mentally and emotionally exhausted.

For nearly an hour the police had watched my every move. I forced myself to behave naturally without revealing our appalling predicament by so much as a blink. I almost lost it once when they asked about Ally's father, but I think I fooled them. The question as they were about to leave totally threw me. And what possible relevance could my origins have on Ally's disappearance, unless they were thinking of someone from our past? No, that was ridiculous.

As soon as they left, I'd rushed to telephone James. 'Please please, God...let it be okay,' I begged.

His answering service picked up. I put the number in, cursing as the rotten thing kept trotting out its mechanical message. Perhaps he was still at the bank? Yes, of course, there would be forms to sign. Maybe he was at his stockbrokers? No, he could do that over the phone or online.

I finished cleaning the bathroom, washed up and made a sandwich which I left drying on the plate. The weather outside looked chilly, the bleakness of the park landscape opposite Pam's flat enhanced by wind-tossed trees. Perhaps a hot shower would warm me, but of course Murphy's Law struck just as I stepped under the water. The phone rang.

'Eloise?' James spoke very quietly, 'I've finished at the bank and it's not good news.'

'Oh no, what's happened?' I shivered, not only because I was wrapped in a towel with water dripping everywhere.

'Look, I need to tell you in person. You'd better come over here, so we can talk in private.' He sounded drained.

I looked at the clock. Midday. 'All right, but—'

'The car's out now but the driver can do a detour and pick you up in say, half an hour?'

It took all of the time allotted to me to finish showering, dress and leave a note for Pam. I raced down the path and dove into the car, thanking God that James could and was prepared to pay the demand.

As before, he met me at the bottom of the steps but my reception was vastly different. He rushed me up the stairs and into his study where the dog, who seemed to be a permanent resident of the room, stood up and wagged a courtly welcome. I gave him an absented minded pat, as James waved me to an armchair.

'Eloise, it's not good news. I can't get huge sums just like that. There are regulations about these things, permissions to be sought from departments who deal with large sums of money. I can get four hundred thousand available by tomorrow afternoon and that will have to be approved by the relevant authorities. I made up a story about attending a house auction and wanting to pay cash. Thank God I wasn't asked for the details. There's a Significant Transactions Report which is called up when someone attempts to withdraw a large amount, and then there's the Suspect Transaction Report.'

He looked grim. 'My stockbroker has orders to sell parcels of shares for me which will raise half a million—hopefully the market will hold—but that's going to take time too. I've arranged a line of credit, but again I can't get a huge amount in cash. They'll have to transfer it to one of my accounts. One good thing, I had two hundred and fifty thousand sitting in a deposit box at the bank. I was going to buy another car and take a trip, but changed my mind. It's illegal to keep it there, but—'

He shrugged and remained silent for a moment, before continuing. 'I have a Gullwing Mercedes and a vintage E-type Jaguar in the garage. I've rung a bloke from the club who's always wanted to buy the Jag. I've arranged for a buyer from one of the leading galleries to check out the paintings this afternoon at three o'clock. I've got prints to put in place of the ones I lend to exhibitions or when they're being cleaned. If the art world thinks I'm broke, so be it. No one's likely to be here to look too closely at them in the next few days. In the meantime, I'd like to take time away from work, but I think it's best if everything appears as much normal as possible.' He looked at me intently. 'They could very well be watching us. After all, they told us not to go to the police.'

Fear rippled through me. 'Watching...me?'

'They won't hurt either of us, Eloise. They want the money too much.' A thoughtful expression came over his face. 'You know, I can't put my finger on it, but I feel there's more to this whole thing than money. There's no way anyone but a billionaire could raise it in two days. I think someone wants us to suffer. All I can do is give them everything I can as they demand it and hope they'll release her.'

What if they didn't? What if...my chest tightened as my breath left my lungs in a whoosh. James's voice receded; my hands felt as though they had been plunged into a bucket of crushed ice.

'Eloise?'

Lights danced in front of my eyes. James held the back of my neck, quickly pushing my face down onto my knees until my faintness had passed, then helped me to the settee and tucked a rug around my icy body. Gradually my breathing returned to normal. He sat beside me, looking so tired and worried, that I hitched myself upright and leaned forward to wrap my arms protectively around him, wishing I could hold the world back.

For a moment he stiffened, but then he pulled my head against his chest and held me tightly. The one thought which kept pounding my mind, *Will my child still be alive after the forty-eight hours are up?*

CHAPTER 13
Sleuthing

Brie

Monday: 4.30pm.

The drive from the concert hall to the riverside of West End involved the usual home-bound traffic dramas, including pedestrians flinging themselves across the street in front of the traffic, but eventually I found a park outside Jess's cottage. I walked up the garden path, stepped onto the front verandah and knocked sharply. The haunting strains of a violin playing Vaughan William's Lark Ascending ceased, followed by footsteps in the hallway.

The door opened and Jess appeared dressed in jeans and sweater, her thick, black hair neatly coiled in a knot at the base of her neck. Gold hoop earrings dangled from her lobes, her feet were bare and even in the shadowed doorway, her toenails blazed with colour.

'Oh, it's you, Brie. What have you been doing?' The tone of her voice could have shrivelled the testicles of a wharfie.

'Tutoring. I heard you called in sick and wondered how you were.' I hovered determinedly on the doorstep until she shrugged in a disinterested fashion and invited me inside, sharply reminding me to remove my boots, then walked back to the kitchen leaving me to close the door.

Her cottage was a monument to IKEA. No newspapers scattered themselves recklessly across the settee and no magazines waited to lure the addicted into idle hours. A few well-behaved novels cringed in a small bookcase by the door. Pride of place was extended to several elegant pieces of sculpture. None of their friends could understand how the girls lived together in London without strangling each other. Ally is what you might call easygoing and slightly untidy; Pam lives in perpetual clutter.

The only time Jess tolerated clothes on the floor was when they were tossed there in the throes of lust, but always gave the impression that at any moment she'd leap from the bed to fold them away, giving a whole new slant to coitus interruptus. It was a wonder to me how our relationship had lasted for even a few weeks.

She took milk out of the refrigerator, placed it on the table and then pointed to a chair. I must have looked untidy leaning against the kitchen bench. She poured coffee into two white mugs and sat opposite. No biscuits were produced; I wasn't expected to linger.

'So, how are you feeling? Recovered now?' I asked, referring to her absence from rehearsals.

Jess did "disdainful" well. 'I just wanted a day off. I'm fed up with eternal speculation and gossip about Ally,' she said, with curled lip. Her obvious unconcern over Ally's disappearance sent a tingle up my spine. She frowned and I knew there wouldn't be much time for me to dredge for information. Any minute she would throw me out.

'We had the police around all day. They interviewed everyone in the orchestra.'

'Yes, I know you did. The Prescott woman was a total bitch,' she snapped. That meant Jess hadn't been able to pull the wool over the cop's eyes.

I persisted. 'So what did they ask you?'

She shifted in her chair and took a sip of coffee. 'Oh, just about Friday night again. What Ally did, who she spoke to, what time was it when I last saw her.' She smirked. 'And how was she during the day and did she have a new lover?'

'*Did* you see anyone you knew at the club?' I asked, refusing to rise to the bait.

'No, of course not.'

I wasn't deceived. Her habitual lying was one of the reasons I'd broken off our relationship and as far as I knew, Jess didn't realise I had seen the tape from Traynors.

'So, how did you feel the concert went last night?' I was anxious to keep the conversation going because I would be out on my ear any moment.

'You know it was okay, Brie, so why are you asking?' she snapped, glancing at her watch. I wasn't about to take the obvious hint.

'No news of Ally as yet,' I commented, ignoring her bad temper.

Jess compressed her lips, as she stirred her drink in silence. I waited her out. Seeing I was determined to bring up the subject, she finally capitulated.

'Well, what do you think happened to her, Brie? I can see you're dying to talk about it,' she said, lifting the mug to her mouth and watching me intently through the steam. Her lips twitched with the merest hint of a smile.

'Well, one thing's for sure, she didn't just run off. The concert was too important to her. Someone must have taken her away. It stands to reason, doesn't it?'

She remained non-committal. 'Hm, it's possible. But what if she lost her memory and just wandered off?'

'That's not likely, is it? She was excited about her big concert. There's no way she would deliberately leave.

She's hardly got dementia.' I finished, thinking of my grandmother who used to go bush after she developed Alzheimer's. My parents used to get the dogs to find her. 'Anyway, someone would have seen her wandering in a daze,' I added, cringing as I heard my placating tones. I had a right to be concerned, for fuck's sake, and Jess should have been as well. Should have been...

Her eyes narrowed. 'What happened at the police station when you went there yesterday? Did you tell the cops that on Friday night, the doorman told you she had gone off with another man?'

'Yes, but the evidence of the bouncers was more important than anything I knew. They saw her leave.' I added, keeping my eyes on my cup. 'Do you know if she was seeing any new friends?'

Jess banged her cup down hard sending coffee slopping onto the table. 'Can't bring yourself to come out and say what you really mean, Brie? If you want to know whether Ally had another man, why don't you just ask?'

'All right, was she seeing someone else?'

Her patience had run out. 'Of course she was. Look, just leave, okay? Just get out, Brie.'

My gut turned over. Ally seeing someone else? I didn't want to believe it. Jess snatched up her cup and hurled it into the sink. The handle broke off, flew across the top of the draining board and skittered to the floor. Coffee splattered up the splash board. She remained with her back to me, shoulders heaving. I waited a moment, then stood up and went over to her, trying to implement damage control. Something was very wrong. 'I'm sorry, Jess. I didn't mean to upset you.'

'Go on, Brie, just beat it, will you?'

The phone rang, cutting into the tension like a diamond chip. Her mood changed as though someone had flicked a switch; her eyes sparkled with excitement.

Obviously it was an expected call, but for a moment it appeared that she wasn't going to answer. Then as the machine prepared to kick in, she rushed over to snatch up the receiver. I wanted to find out who was phoning and what it was she didn't want me to know. I wandered to the draining board, slowly rinsed out my mug before sauntering down the hallway to the front door. Making a production out of dragging my boots on, I strained to hear snatches of the conversation.

'Yes, in a minute. Someone's here, so—' her voice dropped, —'shortly, yes. Dinner? Of course.'

I lingered as long as I dared, then slipped out the front door, making eye contact with one of her neighbours, a self-righteous type, the sort of bloke who mowed his lawn on the same day every week whether it was necessary or not. He looked me up and down, pursed his lips and nodded coolly. I jumped into my car and drove to Ally's house.

Pam had given me the front door key earlier in the afternoon with instructions to go and check whether everything was all right, water the plants and collect the mail. I'd jumped at the chance, but now I was there, I felt like an intruder.

I emptied the letter box, headed up the path and put the key in the lock. My footsteps echoed throughout the house, making me want to tiptoe as I walked down the long hallway. Her open bedroom door revealed the bed unmade, clothes scattered across it after the search. Some of the cupboards were open, drawers with her possessions spilling out. The police search?

The smell of her perfume lingered, bringing memories of days sitting in country parks, surrounded by carefully tended gardens, lying by a river, dragonflies buzzing. And hearing Ally's soft laughter and gazing at her full, sweetly curved lips over which I spent many sleepless nights.

For the first time in my adult life, I actually yearned to be one of a couple. Me, the "slider out of relationships, the "wolf who walks by himself." Realisation sprang into my mind. I'm so lonely. My gut wrenched. Ally would never two-time me. Jess was "stirring" the pot which my mind had become.

I put the mail on her desk in her office, glancing around at the neat piles of sheet music lying beside her laptop. Pam had told me how the police had combed through her emails and hard-drive hunting for any evidence of computer a cyber-stalker or internet threats. Like all of us, Ally had Facebook and Twitter profiles and a website.

I closed the door and moved back to the lounge, a room as alike to Jess's as black to white. Well-thumbed books crammed the shelves. A large, scruffy coffee table was pushed against the wall, a mug teetering precariously on the edge. I picked it up and dumped it in the kitchen sink. My mind turned cartwheels. Was she in pain? Was she lying in a gully somewhere? What on earth would they want with a concert pianist? Or was it for something else?

My mobile vibrated hysterically in its pouch, startling me. My breath caught in my throat as I fumbled to open it.

'Brie? Any news of Ally yet?' The voice was instantly recognisable.

'No, nothing, Karen. What do you want?' My disappointment that it was my sister and not news of Ally almost overwhelmed me.

'What do I want? Brie, you can be so rude sometimes. I wanted to tell you mum has asked all of us to dinner and you have to come. It's lamb roast,' she added slyly.

'Sorry, I didn't mean to snap.'

She huffed in my ear and then apparently decided not to take umbrage. 'It's okay. I know you, Briece. You don't eat properly when you're upset. Where are you now?'

'I'm at Ally's place,' I answered testily. When Karen calls me Briece, she's set to bully me.

'What on earth are you doing there?'

'I came over to check everything's okay, right? I just want to go back to my flat, watch footy and have a beer. Besides, the cat has to be fed.'

Karen takes no prisoners. 'She can wait. Listen to me, you little shit, you still haven't spoken to mum and dad and you've not visited them for weeks! You know how mum worries about you. Now she's all upset over Ally too.'

'All right. I'll come and watch the soccer. Have a beer with dad, then.'

'You just make sure you get there.' Her voice softened. 'Brie, I know you're worried, but not eating properly won't help Ally.' On that note, she signed off.

Ally's iPod was lying on the top of the piano. I flicked idly through the menu and was startled when a glorious, powerful soprano rang out. Jacqui Mabardi singing the aria from Mozart's Zaide, accompanied by Ally on the piano, as they hammed it up at an impromptu party in this room just ten days ago. Ally had been gone three days and now, four nights. A wave of loss swept over me.

I sat down at the piano and played a few bars, trying not to let my thoughts ricochet in panic. Then a bizarre idea popped through my mind. Pam had said her Aunt Eloise was in contact with Ally's father. Maybe her disappearance had to do with him? Something he'd done— or hadn't done? Maybe he was a big-time crook! Nah, crazy. The cops would have thought of that.

I closed the lid of the piano. My stomach rumbled; Mum's lamb roast was looking good. I checked to see if the back door of the house was locked, made sure the windows throughout were still secure, closed the front door after me and tested the dead-lock.

No, Ally would not do the dirty on me. Jess was trying to wind me up and she'd succeeded.

As I walked down the front path to the car, I planned how to retrieve the bug I had planted on the underside of her kitchen table.

CHAPTER 14
But I Did

Georgie Hird

Monday: 6.00pm.

My parents were mad Parisians who had dived under hedges, blown up railways and generally lived by the skin of their teeth during World War II. When it was over they immigrated to Australia, having seen enough violence to last a lifetime. It's entirely due to them I live on Masters Island and I wouldn't change my laid-back lifestyle for the world. I can come and go as I please, stay up all night or drop everything and take off to London, Zurich—anywhere I want to go. Eloise moved to the island twenty-six years ago, she's always minded my current dog, so I have virtually no ties.

I can hear my mother's voice: 'I do wish you'd marry and have children, Georgina. Lovers won't comfort you in your old age.'

'Lovers require less maintenance than husbands, mum,' I chortled. I made the decision not to have children when I was a girl, but of course people never leave you alone, do they? When I was in my twenties there was no hassling. Mid-thirties my family and friends got restless because I was the only one in my circle not married with kids. 'Better hurry up, Georgie. You'll get too old to have babies.' Nobody realised then that biological clocks ticked our fertile lives away. We just knew you got too old to have children. But I didn't care, until one by one my friends drifted off into a haze of school camps, soccer clubs, pony club and school activities. Eventually, I found myself, with the exception of another childless stalwart—a fellow painter and close friend—standing beside me like shags on a gynaelogical rock, ovarial wings folded in contemplation of what I, certainly, had denied myself.

Painting is my only source of income, but my needs are simple. I work best in the so-called winter which we enjoy off the northern coast. Some days are windy and the sea breeze can be cold, believe it or not. My exhibition work for the first half of the year is always ready by the start of spring.

My living is my commercial work—scenes of the island, seabirds, seals, whales and of course, Wild Pony Rock and the small art gallery in our village shifts a large amount of my work.

My real love, for which I am well known, is abstracts. Ally shocked me once when she was about twelve: 'Aunt Georgie, why have you got a vagina hanging from a tree?' It's amazing how penetrating a child's voice can be in a hushed moment. It was meant to be an ear. Oh, *Ally, my precious god-daughter, what has happened to you?*

I well remember the arrival of Eloise twenty six years ago on a bright, sparkling morning in early September. Out to sea the white caps danced and black Wild Pony Rock glittered in the sun like a large, jet bead on my mother's evening gown so long ago.

I had gone down to the wharf to supervise loading my completed paintings for the trip to the mainland for an exhibition in the city gallery. I was standing with some neighbours clustered around the company office, as the ferry docked, scraping its ramp on the concrete slipway.

I noticed the small, auburn-haired woman because she had trouble getting her tyres to grip on the wet ramp as she drove off the vessel. Several men rushed gallantly forward and pushed the back of her old, green Mini, as she revved the motor. The tyres spun helplessly against the slippery surface, then grabbed. The car shot up the ramp, *les braves gens* almost landing flat on their faces.

She pulled up in the car park and came back to shyly thank them, and I heard her asking how to get to Lorne Cottage. Her knights in shining armour were tourists, so they didn't know where the place was. I stepped forward, introduced myself and invited her to follow me. The lighthouse, my home and Lorne Cottage formed a triangle which was separated from the rest of the island by lines of salt-hardy shrubs.

The cottage had been vacant for a year after the last tenants left. The stale air was suffocating. We pried open the filthy windows with a rusty screwdriver abandoned on the kitchen table. Under the mildewed dustsheets we found enough furniture for Eloise to use, but the cushions on the lounge were cosy homes in which families of mice had established themselves. Their droppings were scattered throughout the cupboards and floors. Cursory examination of the bathroom and toilet sent us reeling back to the kitchen. The one saving grace was the live telephone connection.

'You'd think the Hansens would make sure it was at least clean before they leased the place,' I said, disparagingly.

Eloise was made of sterner stuff than initial appearance suggested. 'Don't worry, Miss Hird, the rent's cheap and you won't recognise the place in a week.'

I helped her cart boxes of groceries and personal effects inside. Refusing my invitation to stay at my house until the cottage was at least habitable, and my offer of help with the cleaning, but accepting my injunction to call me "Georgie," she rang about three days later and invited me to morning tea.

Eloise gave me a tour of the now sparkling cottage, ending in the kitchen. A plate of hot scones, jam and cream and a pot of newly brewed coffee waited on the scrubbed kitchen table. My dog, Richie, promptly salivated all over Eloise's slacks, grunting his appreciation of a buttered scone and bowl of water.

'Eloise, it's beautiful,' I gushed, admiring the sparkling white cupboards, scrubbed benches and glittering Aga.

'The work kept me from thinking too much.' She smoothed her hands protectively over her aproned stomach and I realised she was pregnant. The devastation in her face prevented me from exclaiming with delight.

'Sit down, love, and tell me all about it.'

Half a box of tissues, a pot of coffee and several scones later, I knew the whole story.

'So what are you going to do, Eloise? What about your parents? Could they help you?'

She told me then that her mother had taken off with another man when she was a baby and left her with her father, a man too old to bring up a young girl. An uncle and aunt of the same vintage had taken her in after her father died. Apart from some distant cousins, she had no other family.

'But I've got a job at Doctor Williamson's office on the mainland and I'm intending to open negotiations to buy this cottage. I'd like to bring up my child here on the island. 'Where I won't get hurt,' was the unspoken message.

'Are you going to keep trying to contact James?'

'I will not give up. I need to hear from his own lips

that he doesn't want me and the baby.'

She'd spent a lot of money phoning people in England whom she thought were friends, but who hung up on her. One woman who worked with her at Cambridge, perhaps kinder—or guiltier—than the others, finally advised her that the Dean of James's School had ordered the staff not to give her any information. Evidently daddy's money and influence cast a wide net. Having exhausted every avenue, Eloise finally threw in the towel.

'That's the end of it,' she announced.

'What are you going to tell your child about him?' I asked, curiously.

'Not the truth, that's for sure.' She was silent for a moment and I could sense her mind galloping into the future. 'I shall say he died before he or she was born, before we were able to marry and that he was an only child and had no relatives. That'll keep him—or her—from searching, I hope. I may reveal the truth one day but for now ... and please, don't ever tell anyone about what I've told you?'

I had many friends, but Eloise, the daughter I denied myself, crept into my heart. "They "say it takes a village to raise a child. Eloise's other close friend, Rosalind Miller and I are Ally's godmothers. Pam, Rosalind's daughter, stayed with Eloise more often than not because her mother was a nurse who worked night shifts at the general hospital on the mainland.

In spite of the absence of fathers—Rosalind was also a single mum—I believe I'm safe in saying the girls had a wonderful childhood. When they graduated from the New South Wales Conservatory of Music, we three women stood in the university auditorium and made exhibitions of ourselves, clapping and jumping up and down with excitement. We waited with bated breath for news of their exam results and travelled to all the piano and musical competitions which the girls entered.

After the girls began to achieve some success, we ran in and out of music shops making sure their latest recordings were put in suitably prominent positions. If they weren't, we had lady-like tantrums.

Eloise almost fell to pieces last Saturday afternoon when Pam rang to tell her Ally was missing. She met me at the door, hands shaking like leaves. We held each other in terror. It was all I could do to get her organised with her bag packed, bus ticket booked and onto the water taxi.

I have tramped over to the cottage for the last three days, feeding her cats, dog and hens and checking on her three cows. The wind's been blowing something terrible up from the Wild Pony, worse than we usually get for this time of year.

And now I know Ally's been kidnapped for ransom. *Three million dollars.* Eloise swore me to secrecy. I asked if they'd been to the police, but the kidnappers threatened Ally's life if they did. She asked me if I've ever told anyone the name and whereabouts of Ally's father.

Terrified, I lied.

Sometimes I drink too much; loneliness is everything it's cracked up to be. I can abstain, often for months at a time, but sooner or later I relapse. Then came the night I have never forgotten.

I was lying in bed with my lover, delighted because he spoke about the possibility of his leaving his wife and coming to live on the island. He asked me if Eloise would sell her cottage to him. I assured him she was there to stay and he said he'd heard Ally play in a big concert once, and how much he admired her talent.

Of course, I allowed my big mouth to blab all about her and Eloise. To my shame I remember him asking where Ally's father was and my loose-lipped reply. God, I feel terrible. If I could only take back every word I said that night. I would go to the stake rather than hurt either of them, but now I have to ask myself if he told anyone. *Or does he know more than he should about what's happened to Ally?*

I see him at night or when I go to the city galleries to supervise the hangings of my paintings. He comes to the northern coast regularly, but not even Eloise knows we've been having an affair for almost two years.

Sometimes he frightens me, but I admit I am addicted to him. He has a way of looking at me out of the corner of his eyes when he's displeased and I feel a hint of danger closing in like a storm cloud, but I pretend, just for a short time, that I am loved and desirable even at my age.

I realised what I'd done after I sobered up, but it was too late. Except for that once I've not breathed a word. I begged him never to tell anyone and he vowed he would forget I ever spoke of it. When he comes tonight, I'm going to find out if he kept his promise.

CHAPTER 15
COURIER MAIL

Townsville Bulletin, 17. 11. 2010.

WELL KNOWN ARTIST FALLS TO DEATH

The body of Georgie Hird, 63, was found washed up on rocks below Wild Pony Rock on Masters Island early this morning.

It is thought Miss Hird, who was a well-known Australian painter, fell to her death sometime during the night.

Police are appealing for anyone who saw Miss Hird late on Monday afternoon or evening to come forward.

CHAPTER 16

Repercussions

Eloise

Tuesday: 7.30am.

The screaming woke me.

I hit the floor running, panic-stricken as I plunged into the kitchen, literally skidding to a halt. Pam was pointing to something in the newspaper which was spread open on the table. White-faced, her lip-sticked mouth twisted down at the corners, tears spilled down her cheeks and her mascara ran in rivulets. She looked like a clown.

I froze. No, not Ally!

She whispered slowly and carefully, as though she wasn't sure of the words needed to convey the dreadful news. 'Georgie's dead. Georgie. Is. Dead.'

'Georgie? How? What happened?'

Pam slumped into a chair. I picked up the paper, frantically searching the columns until I found it. My lips stiff with disbelief, I read the notice aloud.

It wasn't possible. Only three days ago she had shovelled me onto the bus amid exhortations to ring her the instant we had news. Shaking my head, I re-read the short paragraph, but it didn't make any more sense the second time. Georgie, my friend and sister of my heart—dead.

Pam sat like a statue, tears running down her face and dripping onto the front of her t-shirt. I felt numb. I didn't know what to do next because everything seemed to be moving in slow motion. I went to the instant hot water dispenser, checked the liquid level and turned it on. My hands jerked like a marionettes; my icy feet clung to the tiles like the suckers on a gecko's pads. My nightie flapped around my knees, reminding me that I was about to catch cold.

Get dressed.

I went to the bedroom and picked out the first garments which came to hand. Shock kept grief at bay, but deep down, my reaction was one of guilty relief that it wasn't Ally who was dead. My hands shook so badly, it took two tries to get toothpaste onto my brush. Most of it dropped into the hand basin. What was I going to do? It was all too much.

Dead. Why? The report didn't make sense. There had to have been a mistake. *Deep breaths.*

Pam was talking on the telephone when I got back to the kitchen. I busied myself making tea and toast as she told her mother everything. 'Okay, will you? Thanks, Mum.' She put the receiver down. 'Aunt Eloise, Mum got home last night. It was almost too much for her, my telling her about Ally and then Georgie...she didn't hear the news this morning. She was devastated.'

Pam's face twisted with grief. 'She said she'll get the water taxi to the island, go to your house and look after everything there for as long as it takes. She's going to ring if she gets any news today, but if not, she'll definitely call you tonight on your mobile. And you need to ring the police and tell them she's taking Rory to your house,' she finished, referring to Georgie's geriatric spaniel whom I'd promised to look after in the event of anything happening to Georgie. The laughter we shared as we made the arrangement assured me at the time that this would never happen. How many times have people said "famous last words"?

'Thank God your mother's home,' I said, opening my arms to hug Pam. We cried again, then wiped our eyes and made coffee. Pam had planned to go shopping with Jess in the city, but rang and cancelled the arrangement.

'What did she say when you told her about Georgie?' I asked.

'She was very shocked of course, but it's strange…she sounded…well, if I didn't know better, I'd say she was frightened, but why would Georgie's death scare Jess?'

Neither one of us felt like eating, but we forced down a piece of toast and gratefully drank our coffee. 'You will stay here in Brisbane, Aunt Eloise?' Pam inquired. 'You're welcome to stay with me as long as you like.'

'Thank you, dear. I appreciate the offer. Your poor mother will have to bear this on her own unfortunately. And I need to make a phone call. I'll take it outside where I can get a good signal.' I took my mobile phone off its battery charger and went out onto the balcony overlooking the back yard. James took an age to answer and when he did, I lost it again.

'Georgie. My friend, Georgie. She's dead,' I bawled.

He had to raise his voice above my sobs. 'Christ, Eloise, that's terrible. What happened?'

'She fell over a cliff on Masters Island and landed on the rocks.' Getting into an explanation about Wild Pony Rock was more than I could manage right then.

'When?' he asked urgently.

'Last night. It was in this morning's paper.'

He didn't waste time with questions. 'Are you at Pamela's unit? I'll come to you.'

'But we agreed to keep your identity a secret for the

time being,' I reminded him.

'Forget it, Eloise. It's going to come out anyway, sooner or later. I'll be there in about three-quarters of an hour,' he said briskly and hung up. I snapped the cover shut and went back inside.

'What could have possessed Georgie to go to Wild Pony Rock after dark? It's a most unlikely thing for her to do,' I mused. Suicide? Anyone less likely to do that than Georgie I've yet to meet.

Pam shook her head in bewilderment as she stacked our breakfast crockery into the dishwasher. 'I don't understand. Georgie hates Wild Pony Rock. You can't get her to go there in daylight, let alone at night. Ever since that child fell off the rock—you know, when we were twelve.' She referred to an incident which, even now haunts Ally.

Detective Senior Sergeant Prescott was my only contact in the police force and might be able to find out what had happened on the island. I ratted around in my handbag and found the card which she had given me. Was it only yesterday when she and sergeant "whatever-his-name-was," interviewed me? My heart pounded as I tapped out her phone number. If she knew the terrible secret James and I were withholding, she would be less than impressed.

Keeping my voice as steady as possible, I told her about Georgie's death—she hadn't seen the report in the paper—and asked her about finding out whether the Townsville police knew why she died. Then I told her how surprised I was by Georgie being at Wild Pony Rock.

'Have you any reason to believe it wasn't an accident?' she asked.

'No, I haven't. But Georgie loathed Wild Pony Rock. She wouldn't even go near it during the day,' I explained.

'Hm...' I could hear pages rustling.

'I've got it.' There was a moment of silence before she continued. 'I see. Well, I can certainly contact Townsville CIB. It is possible someone has come forward with information by now. I am sorry, Ms Carpenter, you've got more than enough to bear. Were you very close to this lady?'

I took a deep breath, choking back sobs. My eyes filled again. 'She is—was the closest friend I have.'

'Oh dear, that's so sad. 'Look, I'll get on to it now and phone you back. Are you still at Ms Miller's place?'

I said I was and she hung up. My legs and arms trembled; I almost tottered to a chair. Pam bustled into the room. 'Mum should be on her way to the water taxi by now. We're running out of milk and bread. We need something for lunch, some ham perhaps.'

I reached for my handbag. 'Pam, I'm giving you money for my share of the expenses—no, don't get all proud on me. You can't afford to keep another mouth and I'm very glad to be here. You're a great comfort to me.' I whipped out my purse, extracted a hundred dollars and stuffed it into Pam's reluctant hand. 'That'll help to go on with.'

'But Aunt Eloise, I earn good money—'

'So do I, Pam. Now, no more nonsense.' I glanced at the clock. 'And while you're out, the bottle shops will be open, so get a decent bottle of wine. We need it today.'

A watery smile crossed her face. 'I might get two. After all, a visitor is coming to lunch.'

She had been shocked and more than a little annoyed with me when I confessed to the deception I'd fostered all these years. But Pam is the kindest girl and readily forgave me after I told her the story of what happened before Ally was born. I hadn't, however, revealed James's identity. She was bursting with curiosity, but she would not ask questions. Unlike most children, she never hunted for birthday or Christmas presents, picked them up from under the tree or scratched at the paper. Ally and I are scratchers and shakers, but Pam saved surprises for the appropriate time. It drove us mad.

Gathering up several shopping bags tossed onto a pile of magazines by the door, she advised that she would only be ten minutes, waved and left. A few minutes later, I heard her elderly Renault start up and scoot out of the driveway.

Basil Brush, Pam's cat, twirled around my ankles. I picked him up and buried my face in his thick fur. Grief and rage swept over me again, as I clasped his portly body against me, seeking comfort. First Ally, now this. Oh Georgie, what happened? Suicide? Not in a million years.

An idea too awful to contemplate popped into my mind and refused to go away. What if she had lied to me when I talked to her on the phone? Did she tell someone who Ally's father really is, and—

When I asked her if she had ever broken her promise, she said 'No,' but in retrospect, was there an infinitesimal hesitation before she answered? The telephone rang. I unhooked the cat from my sweater and put him, protesting, into a chair.

'Ms Carpenter, I've spoken to my counterpart in Townsville, and I'm sorry to have to tell you, Miss Hird's death was not an accident,' said Susan Prescott.

'Oh my God. No, surely not…it couldn't be…' Fear made me stumble over the words.

'Suicide? No. Miss Hird was stabbed and then thrown onto the rocks below Wild Pony Rock.'

Murdered.

Cold radiated out from my stomach to slither throughout my torso and limbs. No. Unbearable pain lurked just around the corner.

'I'm so sorry to have to tell you, Ms Carpenter, and particularly over the telephone.' Again, Detective Prescott waited until my breathing slowed enough to speak. 'Do you feel able to answer a couple of questions, or would you like to talk to me later?'

'No, let's get it over with.'

'All right, if you're sure you can cope right now. You said Ms Hird would never have gone near the—Wild Pony Rock?'

'Never. She hated that rock. Several people have fallen from it over the years and she wouldn't go near it even when I was with her.'

'I see. Did Miss Hird have any enemies you know of?' she asked.

'No, I honestly can't think of anyone who didn't like her and I mean that. We've been friends since before Ally was born. She was an open, friendly person, happy to talk to everyone.' My voice broke as I remembered the warmth of Georgie's personality.

Papers rustled on her desk. 'When did you go to live on Master's Island exactly, Ms Carpenter?' Her tone sharpened, snapping me to attention.

'I can't remember the exact date, but it was September, 1984.' I replied, puzzled.

'I see. We'll leave it for now then. If you think of anything, could you please ring me here at Police Headquarters and if I'm not in, they will relay a message. I might need to get back to you again for more information.'

As we hung up, Pam staggered into the flat laden with shopping. I rushed to help her, thankful for the diversion. We put the groceries away, fed the cat yet again; we had to keep Basil's strength up somehow, when the doorbell rang. My heart leaped. I wanted to throw myself into James's arms and stay hidden until my child was safely found.

Pam went to open the door and I heard him say something. Then her voice screeched down the hallway:

'You? *You're Ally's father?*'

CHAPTER 17
Retreating from the Heat

Ally

Tuesday: before dawn.

Time is divided into light and dark. The same car comes and goes, but I've given up trying to see it. My eyes are swollen. It's hard to breathe and my face hurts so much I can hardly bear it. *Got to get out, got to get out.*

I lie in total darkness as soon as the sun goes down and have no idea what day it is. They haven't been in since yesterday afternoon. No food, only water. I try not to take more than a sip at a time and ignore my stomach's pleading. I can only see out of a corner of my left eye. I've poured a tiny amount of water onto the towel and dabbed some of the blood off my face. The front of my camisole is stiff and dry. It stinks; I stink.

The bare walls feel as though they're shuffling closer, like in the movie, Egyptian Mummy, which I saw when I was fourteen at the Saturday afternoon flicks. This woman was trapped in a tomb—she was the evil one—and the walls crushed her for her sins. Yuk. Don't think about it. 'Think about your music. It calms you down,' I tell myself.

All the times I've moaned for a bit of peace and quiet come back to haunt me. Ironic. Traffic noises, boom boxes, endless music in shopping malls...once it drove me mad, but now I would give my eye teeth to be listening to the poxy stuff. I close my eyes and clamp my lips together to keep them from trembling. Terror freezes my belly; I can hardly breathe. I can't do this.

Chopin's Etudé. I've played it thousand times and now my lips are too dry to hum the melody. My mind flits from one thing to another, like a demented moth. How long, then for—*don't even think it.*

Regrets, regrets. I try to remember the happy times in my life, like times with my friends, the concerts I've played and the awards I've won, with mum, Georgie and Aunt Rosalind leaping out of their seats, screaming and clapping their hands.

What about the times Pam, Jess and I went out clubbing, laughing like hyenas, pretending we were secretaries or nurses so the blokes wouldn't think we were too high-brow to dance with. The times we dragged each other home, half out of our minds—Pam and I almost got caught peeing in someone's front garden one night. The security lights came on outside and we fled, pulling our knickers up as we ran. A bad moment...

I remember the times on Masters Island, when mum and I would sit at home reading while the wind rocketed around our cottage or digging in the garden, planting seedlings with the cats coming along and squatting in the holes we dug. We laughed ourselves sick one time when we went mad and re-arranged our whole cottage. 'Ally, you've got muscles like spider's kneecaps!' she laughed, as we struggled with a particularly heavy piece of furniture. Why couldn't I be content with our family of two? Mum loves me and still I yearn for more. Ally, Ally, you greedy pig...

Regret surfaces in my mind, sorrow for the times I was nasty, when I could have said a kind word and didn't. The stupid choices I made years ago. Why can't I forget them? I can hear myself screeching at mum: 'You wouldn't know what it's like to be dumped!' after my first boyfriend, Larry, sauntered away with Mary Roberts, who smirked at me over her shoulder as they went. I slammed my bedroom door in mum's face while she was trying to comfort me. Perhaps my father dumped *her?*

How could I have been so mean after mum spent thousands of dollars she could ill-afford on music lessons for me, beautiful clothes which she spent hours sewing for me to wear at school piano recitals. What about the times she sat waiting while I rehearsed or played in a concert? Or when I was in my teens and needed picking up from a party on the mainland, she would stay with Aunt Rosalind, get into the car at midnight and arrive at the house where the party was held.

I remember squirming with embarrassment when my friends saw her parked out the front in pyjamas and pink fluffies. Of course, I ignored the fact that my friend's parents were doing the same. It was only my mother who looked like an idiot.

But I can't get past the fact she's obviously lied to me my whole life. Who is my father? Is he going to pay the money? What if he refuses? No, they would have done something to me by now—like kill me.

Am I really Ally Parker? My red hair comes from mum, so what do I get from him? My musical talent? I can only think about how he looks in the photo. Has mum kept in touch since I was born? How do these people know who he is to demand money from him? Who told them?

'Stop it, Ally. You may never know what happened between them. You can't allow yourself to sleep because the dreams will come.' Is the drug they're putting in my water making me hallucinate? I have to take a sip now and then to keep from getting dehydrated. I have to get strong again, in case there's another chance to get away. I want to smash their faces in and just run and run...

Memories trickle, willy-nilly, into my mind, things that happened years ago.

Calne, Wiltshire: 2004

'Now you listen here to me love, you've got to find yourself a man. Your music won't keep you warm at night, you know. You should be out dancing and enjoying life like the rest of the girls.'

'But Mrs Gordon, I'm quite content the way I am. I'm not prepared to massage their egos, or anything else for that matter.' I grin smugly as I toast myself by the fire, watching my landlady ironing the shirts which she takes in for extra money. The cat in my lap stirs, sticks out a paw and hooks a piece of wool in my sweater. We purr in unison.

I was living in a 'bed and breakfast' in Calne at the time, standing in for the music teacher of a local school who had tripped over a hockey stick on the sports ground and broken her leg. I was ready to face raging fires for my career, but unfortunately it had hit a short hiatus. After being sacked by a bloke I was mad about, I decided all men could get stuffed. Most of the ones I'd met could fill their own lunatic asylum, and Franco, a horn player with delusions of grandeur, hadn't lived up to his instrument's reputation, which would seem to be indicative of all of them.

The applause of audiences more than made up for the lonely hours spent in hotel rooms, being concertinaed into cattle class in aircraft and rehearsing in cold, bleak theatres or halls.

I lived in student digs in the UK before Pam and Jess

arrived. Firmly etched in my memory are sparsely furnished bedrooms and communal kitchens with bottles dripping HP and tomato sauce over vinyl tablecloths. If I close my eyes, I can hear the hiss of a gas heater and the smell of fish and chips at the end of the day. Please God, I will never have to go back to that way of life.

Musicians are nomadic and mostly nocturnal. Broken artistic marriages litter the concert stage like pieces of smashed glass. Perhaps one day I'll meet someone and marry him. Brie. Is he the one? I'm so lucky. I have my career, friends, mum...but is it all over? What if I can't get out of here?

I've blown my chances of getting away, but if they don't come back no one will know where I am. How would anyone know where to look? I could starve to death. If I get out of this alive I'll never, ever take anyone or anything for granted again. And treasure every day I'm given. An image flashes into my head of a dried out frog I once found under a cupboard in our cottage. Fresh waves of terror bunch in my stomach and spread outward. What if my—father—refuses to pay them?

What can I do to save myself if they get the money and abandon me? Surely mum won't stop looking for me? People go missing and then the police give up and the case is closed for years and a year...until a mummified body is found in the bush somewhere.

I can't breathe.

Calm down.

Brie. Will he forget me eventually? Like everyone except mum, Georgie and Pam and Aunt Rosalind. Jess might not care—she actually might be glad. That's an awful thing to think about one of your closest friends. But is she really my friend?

I'm so frightened. Slowly. Breathe slowly. Yoga breaths now, forget your ribs and think happy thoughts.

How did I manage to fall for a gorgeous rogue like Briece Mochrie? When I discovered he wasn't just eye-candy, I freaked out. Brie is as patient with people as he is with his work, a scary attribute when I don't want involvement right now.

'But why does he hang out with me when there are lots of younger and prettier musicians in the company?' I asked once of an older musician in the Pacific orchestra.

'You're a challenge, love. You're fun to fight with because you keep him on his toes. His groupies worship the ground he walks on. He always goes for the young chicks and you are…er…ah…' Realising where this was leading him, Patrick, a much-married man, heeded his instinct for self-preservation and trailed into silence.

'Getting on for twenty-six, Patrick?' I asked, grinning.

He smiled ruefully.

'Well, let's face it,' I went on, knowing it would get back to Brie, 'some men just aren't capable of coping with a fully grown woman.'

The side door at the theatre was often knee-deep in admirers of the younger members of the orchestra. Occasionally, because security is tight, the lads would invite girls they knew backstage and these girls would sometimes leave a keepsake for the object of their affections. The story of when Brie opened his cello case at rehearsal and found a red lace g-string tied around the end of his bow has passed into company legend. Apparently he'd been talking to someone at the time, not paying attention to what he was doing, whipped the bow out and flicked the g-string onto the conductor's podium.

'Mr Mochrie,' said Sir James McPherson—the story went—' I didn't know you cared.'

The orchestra roared.

'We didn't realise Brie still had a blush in him,' chuckled Patrick.

It wasn't until we were on the outback tour that I allowed Brie to get nearer than talking distance. When we left Brisbane, I chose a seat next to a window on the bus and was secretly pleased when he threw himself into the seat beside me.

'You can keep me amused on the way,' he announced gleefully, leaning closer than necessary. Blimey.

'In your dreams, Mochrie,' I snarled.

'What have you got against me, Ally? I'm house-trained, love animals and I'm kind to my family. I'm not bad-looking either,' he added, and winked.

I could see myself reflected in his dark blue, thickly-lashed eyes focused on my mouth. 'Oh, I don't know. I've seen better.' Liar, liar, pants on fire.

'And I wouldn't trust you as far as I could kick you,' I thought, as I turned to the window to hide the blush suffusing my breasts, creeping inexorably throughout my body. His muscular, denim-clad thigh pressed against mine and I could smell the maleness of him, clean and fresh-smelling, like a newly washed sheet drying in the sun.

As he lifted his arm to wave to someone at the front of the bus, his t-shirt rode up to expose his tanned, six-pack stomach. A thin line of silky, dark hair marched under his jeans toward his obviously well-endowed crotch. Warm twitters scudded around the centre of my femininity. I squeezed my thighs together. My breasts swelled, my nipples hardened…damn…I couldn't help watching those beautiful, strong hands, imagining them holding my…

He turned and looked down the contours of my face, coming to rest on the flushed skin at the opening of my shirt, and smirked.

I didn't want to stuff up my reputation by becoming a Mochrie groupie, but after that, he played me like a fish on the end of his line. He would retreat a little, giving me breathing room and then stare at me until I looked over the top of the piano and meet his sexy, killer smile. He'd wink or raise an eyebrow, almost causing me to lose a note.

I was ready to go to bed with him last Friday night. 'If you hadn't been kidnapped, you would have fallen right into it and he'd probably be looking for someone else by now,' I chided myself. Isn't that what they always do? Once the excitement of the chase is over? *Grow up, Ally!*

At the moment, there doesn't—didn't—seem to be enough he could do for me. My lawn mowed, the drain under the sink unblocked; I don't "do" drains. He's a farmer's son and knows how to fix things, but the times I most want to remember are when we're practising our music together, or sitting in my lounge room reading or listening to music...

What are you thinking? Marriage? Babies are not on my agenda. A couple of weeks ago, one of the clarinettists asked me to mind her three-month old son while she went to the dentist. I've never changed a nappy, let alone a pooey one, so I practically hurled. One thing's for sure, I didn't end up with any maternal urges. *You might never get the chance now to have any.*

Scarpia and the Cow burst into the room. It's barely daylight now. They're agitated, their usual air of confidence missing. Her surgical mask is slightly askew. For a split second, I think I've seen her before, but then it's gone. He makes no attempt to bait me but examines my face thoughtfully, his eyes narrowed and dangerous. Icy fear trickles through me.

Something has happened.

CHAPTER 18
No Fresh Flowers by Request

Jessica

Tuesday: 9.00am.

I sit staring into space, too frightened to move.

Pam phoned just a few minutes ago to tell me that Georgie Hird is dead. Why would Georgie go to Wild Pony Rock? And after dark? I've never been to the rock when I visited the Carpenters on Master Island. The rotten thing terrifies me.

The pulse in my throat throbs; I take deep breaths to steady myself.

I've left a piece of dry toast and a half-empty cup of cold coffee on the kitchen bench. I need to clear them away and scrub the surface. I leap to my feet, don my rubber gloves and run the hot water into the sink. I have to keep control of the fear which threatens to dismantle my very being.

Clean, clean.

It's Ally's fault. If she hadn't been so full of herself, so damn self-righteous, I would have never gotten into this mess. From the moment I first met that girl, the day I answered Pam's advertisement about sharing the flat, Ally has dominated my life. I know she doesn't realise how pathetic she makes me feel. I couldn't bear it if she knew, but not because she'd be snide. Oh no, not Ally.

She'd be so nice and understanding. Her mother loves her. She's got the mother I want.

My own is a cold, unfeeling bitch. She has never really allowed me into her life and only lets me know her when she feels like it. *Well, Mother, I no longer want to know you.*

Her favourite role is that of Mrs Lynda Rallison, solicitor and wife of Harold Rallison, architect and social climber.

She hired nannies from the moment I was born. I remember my sister sitting in her cot, wet and crying for hours while the latest nanny was off somewhere. I got into trouble for climbing up, letting the side down and trying to drag her out. I wanted to change her, but mother accused me of being jealous and attempting to hurt her. It was the pattern of my relationship with Lynda. A couple more times of trying to help my sister after that, and I got the message along with the beltings. I left Julia alone from then on and in turn was so lonely, that sometimes I wanted to die.

Mother is still as remote from me as the bird of prey she resembles. A stickler for convention, it was always, "What would the neighbours think?" if we wanted to do something even a bit out of the ordinary. As if they'd give a flying fuck what we did. But oh no, nothing must be out of place, "in case people will think I haven't brought you up properly."

'Manners, Jess, manners. Look how well your sister behaves!' she'd snarl, poking me in the middle of my back with a red claw.

It was easy once I got older and worked out how to keep out of her way, but by then she didn't seem to care whether I was there or not. So I behaved badly just so she would notice me. Even punishment was better than being ignored.

I'd steal a glance at Julia and want to hit her as she sat beside me, eyes narrowed to slits, slyly watching the world go by. Now, I understand it was my sister's way of protecting herself from our mother's carping criticism and relentless drive for social dominance. Does she share the memories which butterfly through my consciousness?

Because of the circumstances of our childhood, we're not close. I'm afraid to ask. Her answer may throw open a closet from which the bones of our family skeletons will pour out and engulf me.

Our parents actively discouraged us from bonding and I realise we've grown up like playground acquaintances, forced by the teacher to share a text book. I know that's not normal for sisters, but I don't have the skills to circumvent it even now. Julia and I were just two girls who inhabited the same house. We were sent to different schools, rarely visited each other's bedrooms or gossiped together, borrowed clothes and make-up.

Of course there were no pets in our house. I longed for a warm, furry creature to love, but I didn't dare bring any stray cats or dogs home. Once a neighbour offered Julia and me a kitten and when I asked our father if we could have it, he said, 'Bring that thing here and I'll wring its neck. Better still, I'll make you two do it.' Oh, God.

So on the rare occasions I visited friends' homes, I played with their animals, then fibbed when my parents asked what I had been doing. I'm an expert liar.

During holiday breaks and the times we flew back to Australia, I cadged invitations to Ally's or Pam's homes. My parents never made my, or Julia's friends welcome.

Music saved my life. While I was having lessons, Julia was doing her homework as though her life depended on getting it right, and it did. While I studied at the Con, Julia worked like a demon at medical school—Doctor

Julia Rallison. Even now we communicate only by Christmas card and the occasional phone call or letter.

When I was five years old, it was as though a pane of glass came between me and other people. At first I tried to shatter it, to break down the invisible barrier which prevented me from making close relationships and threatened my ability to cope with the outside world. Later, I found it a comfort and protection from emotional involvement. Oh, I knew all the methods of interaction, how to smile, giggle, flirt—all the attributes which made up the normal young girl. Inside, I was frozen, and so very, very, afraid of getting too close to anyone.

I don't remember when I first heard classical music, but one of my great-aunts gave me a violin which had been stashed in a cupboard by a long-dead relative. My father wasn't keen on hearing me learn to play it. 'For fuck's sake, Lynda, send Jessica to lessons or I'll throw that bloody thing on the dump.'

It wasn't long before I was besotted with the instrument. When I played, I escaped in a world of light. Without it, I had to confront the darkness within my frozen soul where, I was sure, dangerous ectoplasm nestled, waiting to seep into my heart and destroy me.

Nothing has changed.

I didn't have a choice in being friends with Ally. Not if I wanted to keep Pam happy and she is the sister I need. Ally is the hanger-on, the one with whom I compete for Pam's love and approval.

When I visited Masters Island, Eloise Carpenter tucked me, old as I was, under her wing, as if I were another daughter. Every chance I got, I cornered Eloise for long chats. She was endlessly patient, listening to me when I was miserable, which was pretty often. Sometimes I think she suspected my trouble, but in spite of carefully worded hints, I couldn't even confide in her.

I was the one who helped Eloise make scones, the one who went along when she walked the dogs along the cliffs, while Pam and Ally went to the only pub on the island or lay reading in the hammocks on the front verandah.

Men think I'm beautiful, but they eventually gravitate to Ally. Keeping dates away from seeing her was my main goal when we three lived together. I knew that once they met Ally, I'd be abandoned. She never bothered with them, but like leaves in the wind, they were sucked in by her personality. The only way I could compete was through music. There I could hold my own. Ally is no violinist.

But she gets me in with her charm. There are times when I would do anything for her, but deep down, I wish she'd just go away. And die. Since Ally has come back to Australia, I can hardly control myself. She's got Brie chasing after her now, and I can't even say she took him from me, because it was never going to work with us.

I can't keep my mouth shut when Ally's nearby. My venom edges around every word I utter. Dear God, what sort of a monster have I become? Sometimes I catch her looking at me, puzzled and hurt, but then I make a joke or get her a cup of coffee and hand it to her with a hug. Pam and Ally have tried to get me to open up and talk my problems through, but there is no way I can admit about my shameful secret. If I tell, it's going to diminish, to expose me. *I want to be normal, like everyone else.*

There's no way I can admit the truth about why my agent requests the bouquet which is presented to me after a concert has to be of artificial flowers. Everyone, including him, believes I'm allergic to pollen. I made Pam and Ally keep the flowers they'd receive in their bedrooms or the laundry when we were sharing rentals.

Professionally, I held my own until two years ago. I don't really know why things started to go wrong for me. Too many concerts? Too many hours in recording studios? I needed to get away from my friends, with time out to hide so no one would realise I was falling apart.

When I left London for Australia earlier this year, I held my breath until I could get safely on the plane. Then I heard Ally would be joining the Pacific Orchestra as guest artist under contract for six months and I wanted to scream.

God, I hate her so badly I can taste my own bile.

But I hate myself even more.

I am so confused and frightened. My solo career is up the creek. My CDs are selling, but only because they've recently been played on ABC Classic FM. Fortunately, the Pacific Orchestra pays well, so I can keep the roof over my head and buy myself the clothes, perfume and jewellery I deserve.

Michael Whitby is fairly attractive in a blonde sort of way and filled the gap after Brie dumped me two months into our relationship, but now he's become a nuisance. Yesterday, he overheard me talking on the phone, but he wouldn't dare tell. He knows I'd fix him with Sir James and the directors. Taking drugs means instant dismissal and Michael is hooked on a lot more than the weed.

I will not allow him to destroy me.

A few weeks ago, I met my soul mate. He thrives on playing games—dangerous games—as much as I do.

Take deep breaths and just keep cleaning.

They promised faithfully nothing's going to happen to her. I tell myself it serves Ally right for all the years I've listened to her whining.

She should be so lucky.

She didn't have a father who, from the time she was five until she was fifteen, slithered into her bedroom under cover of darkness bearing a posy of fresh flowers wrapped in cellophane, complete with gift tag, for his sweet, "princess of the night."

CHAPTER 19

A Surfeit of Old Goats

Detective Senior Sergeant Susan Prescott

Tuesday: 9.30am.

Eloise Carpenter's phone call shook me. Her daughter goes missing and one of her closest friends is murdered three nights later? Sure, I believe in the occasional coincidence, but this latest event was pushing things a little far for comfort. My team was following what clues we had, but nothing useful had come to light and the Commissioner prowled with intent.

Early this morning, footage in the news showed Masters Island, with Eloise's pretty, spacious cottage and three Scottish Highland cows tossing their horns and peering fiercely through hairy faces at the cameras. The media had made the connection between Ally Carpenter's disappearance and the murder of Georgie Hird, whose cottage and studio were shown perched near the lighthouse. I "googled" Eloise but apart from a few mentions of her as secretary of the local RSPCA and some basic stuff, most of the information was about Ally. Ally's pages were more fruitful, with snippets of her contract, program of concerts and gossip. The last entries were more hysterical, documenting her non-appearance at her concert and rife with speculation.

I sat at my desk, anxious, isolated from the necessity

of answering telephones and being constantly interrupted for decisions on other cases. At least three very well-prepared people were involved in the Carpenter case, but something about the video tugged at my memory. I picked up the telephone.

'Ben? Bring me the Traynors Night Club CCTV footage, please.'

The in-house CCTV footage for the whole of Friday evening was being scanned by a team of young, eager, police recruits to pin point the moment when the alleged abductors entered the club.

Less than a minute later, DC Taylor popped up in front of me, tape in hand.

'There's something about this which puzzles me. I need young eyes to help me out here.'

'Right, ma'am,' he replied, taking the tape out of its cover to slip it into the video player in the corner of my office. 'Any idea what we're looking for?'

'I have a feeling we've overlooked something.' I squinted through my bifocals at the whizzing images as he re-wound the tape.

'Ma'am, if you missed it, so did we,' he said gallantly.

We leaned forward as the footage slowed, stopped and then started to run. The car, its license plate angled to the ground, slid into position beside the kerb, the driver in shadow, his face hidden by the sun visor.

The man and the apparently drunken girl wrapped in the black coat, came into view, their backs to the camera. The woman behind them kept her head down and held what Briece Mochrie had identified as Ally Carpenter's handbag. She slipped ahead and held the back door open as they neared the car. The man pushed the girl a little ahead of him, almost shoved her into the rear seat and dived in after her. As he did so, there was the slightest movement, a possible other person in the back. Ally

Carpenter, if indeed it was her, would be sandwiched between two people. Not good.

The woman got into the front seat and the car pulled away, a slick, *four*-person operation, only lasting seconds.

'Hang on a moment, Ben. Run it back and try to zoom in a little. Not too much, or it'll blur.'

I leaned closer.

'Stop.'

I pointed at the hand of the man escorting the woman in the black coat. 'What do you think that is?'

'What, ma'am?'

'Is his hand painted?' I asked.

Benjamin narrowed his eyes and stared at the screen. 'No, ma'am, I think he's wearing a surgical glove. And look at the driver's hand when he brings it back onto the steering wheel. It's too white and smooth.'

Damn, how could I have missed it the first time around? Innocent people do not wear surgical gloves on a night out. Forensics would need to view this. A lot rested on whether the plan had been to target Ally or if she was chosen at random.

Remembering Eloise Carpenter's outlandish behaviour the morning Evan and I interviewed her, kidnapping for ransom had to be considered. However, though Ally Carpenter made excellent money, it was hardly enough for kidnappers to put themselves so deeply in jeopardy. Research on her relatives and friends confirmed that none of them were worth a kidnapper's while. But what if her father was alive and rich? Eloise's statement that he was dead had been unconvincing to say the least. There was no proof of his continued existence, so we had to go with the theory that if Ally Carpenter's abductor was a kinky sexual predator, time was indeed running out, if it hadn't already. Dear God, *please...protect this young woman.*

The Pacific Orchestra Board of Directors, admin-

The Naked Room

istration, cleaning staff, concert night doormen and Ally Carpenter's friends, both in and out of the musical profession, maintained there had been no indication of stalking by fans, former boyfriends or outstanding professional jealousy.

My partner, Evan, arrived.

'Got some response to the paper this morning,' he reported. 'Not a lot, but it's more than we've received so far. A couple said they thought the young woman was drunk and her family had come for her. Two callers say the car was a white Toyota Corolla, which we now know is the case and the other couldn't remember the colour, but saw the incident and dismissed it as a family matter at the time. Of course, none of them can describe the suspects.'

'Right, thanks Evan. Bring the tape to briefing, Ben.'

An officer handed me a printout of a forensics report as I reached the incident board.

'Good morning, everyone. Some updates, firstly the fingerprints on the outside of the car were no help at all, but—' I glanced at the report just handed to me, '—a strand of long red hair has been retrieved from the back seat of the abandoned car. We'll get a sample from Ally Carpenter's house and have a DNA done.' Now, something new for you.' I showed the team what we had just discovered.

'We know the gang were wearing gloves, the likelihood of getting any fingerprint matches is zilch. The car was reported missing on Friday morning in East Brisbane, wasn't there when they were going to work, left it outside the night before because they couldn't get into their driveway. A car was parked across the entrance.' I exchanged a telling glance with the members of my team.

'Has Carpenter got a boyfriend?' asked one of the

team. Predictably, the male detectives guffawed. 'Are you kidding? Did ya look at her face? Too right,' they chorused enthusiastically. My female colleagues and I rolled our eyes.

'There's to be a media conference at ten o'clock for full-blown newspaper and television coverage, appealing for people to come forward with relevant information. I am interviewing one of the directors, James Kirkbridge, at 11.30 this morning and the conductor, Sir James McPherson, late this afternoon. Ben, I want you with me for that. Any questions?'

There weren't.

A seething mass of over-excited journalists and accompanying cameramen filled a downstairs conference room. The disappearance of a celebrity is hot stuff and a welcome change from pontificating politicians.

I braced myself, smiled at DI Peterson who was to make the statement, took a deep breath and opened the door.

Tuesday : late morning.

James Kirkbridge dwarfed DC Ben Taylor and me, at well over 195cm. He herded us into the sumptuous boardroom and seated himself at the head of the table, making sure we saw him glance at his watch. As practised, power-laden theatrics it was highly skilled, but his attempt to intimidate us, futile. I have traded glares with some of the most dangerous criminals in the country. After them, Kirkbridge was chicken feed.

I fixed him with a narrow-eyed stare, allowing the silence to drag until he leaned back, crossed one leg over the other and folded his arms across his chest. I sensed, rather than saw, his foot swinging under the table. *Good, you're not as calm as you pretend, Cuddles.*

'Thank you for seeing us, Mr Kirkbridge.' As soon as we got his preliminary information out of the way, I started. 'We understand the directors mixed with the orchestra on a social level?'

He nodded.

'So, what is your relationship with Ms Carpenter?'

'I knew her as the guest pianist under contract, Senior Sergeant. As a working director, I am involved in the running of the orchestra. I help organise events, tours… it's very much a hands-on commitment. I am also a major financial sponsor and run my own business interests. I know Ms Carpenter only in that capacity.'

I watched him calmly, maintaining eye contact. He assessed me coldly for what proved to be a very long moment, before resting his elbows on the highly-polished wood and steepling his fingers. He answered my questions in note-form, in his clipped English public school accent.

'He didn't know of any religious leanings of Ms Carpenter and doubted she belonged to a cult; yes, she had several close friends in the orchestra, including Briece Mochrie. He had last seen her on the Friday afternoon during the recording session with the orchestra.'

'I believe there was a considerable amount of social mingling with the orchestra members, so you must have known her quite well personally, Mr Kirkbridge?' I repeated.

His eyes flickered, before he shifted slightly in his seat. The faintest flush swept over his features. *You old goat, you fancied her.*

'Er, yes. She was very popular, Senior Sergeant,' he acknowledged. He might have been hiding something, but I suspected the chilly demeanour was normal. I pried and probed for as long as I could.

Had he observed an obsessive fan hanging around

the concert hall?

Had Ally herself or anyone else commented on someone taking an unhealthy interest in her movements?

Did she gamble?

A discarded lover who might be responsible for the snatch?

His negative response to all my questions was frustrating. 'And are you a musician, Mr Kirkbridge?'

He eyed me suspiciously. 'I am a classically trained pianist, Ms Prescott, but of course, I am hardly the professional standard of Ms Carpenter.'

'How long have you lived in Australia, sir?'

'I have been here for six years and as you must be aware, I am now an Australian citizen.' If looks could kill, I'd be flat on the floor. Why? It was a perfectly normal question, so what did he have to hide?

We parted on uneasy terms and I made a note for someone in the team check him out, hoping to find some skeletons rattling in his cupboard in the near future. Perhaps Sir James McPherson would be more approachable later in the afternoon.

Tuesday: 8.30pm.

I kicked off my shoes and slumped into my armchair in front of the fire, restless and dissatisfied. I wanted to unwind, but couldn't bring myself to read, watch television or even fire up the oven and make a batch of scones. There's something about kneading the butter through the flour, shaping the dough and the smell of freshly baked food at the end which soothes, but not this time.

Our dogs collapsed on each of my feet. My geriatric cat squeezed herself into the space between my hip and the armrest, and my eyelids drooped as my mind drifted back to the late afternoon interview with Sir James

McPherson.

We arrived at 4.15 when the building which housed the headquarters of the orchestra was all but empty. Somewhere deep in its bowels, a cleaner whistled as he dragged his equipment around. The sound of our footsteps resounded off the walls as we walked along the deserted corridors. I resisted the compulsion to tip-toe.

The incredibly tall Sir James greeted us with English upper-class reserve and the charm of an Antarctic ice berg. I am not a small woman, but the top of my head just reached his armpit. Ben Taylor is tall, but his eyes were level with Sir James's chin.

The conductor ushered us into a comfortable room lined with books and sheet music scattered over a grand piano, which took up most of the space. So he too, was an accomplished musician, as well as a celebrated conductor.

He waved us to upright chairs in front of his desk. 'Well, Detective Senior Sergeant Prescott, I haven't got much time to spare, so what can I do for you?'

Crushing a spurt of anger, which wouldn't have helped my mission, I fired off the same questions we had put to Kirkbridge.

Sir James stared at me, obviously surprised by my confrontational attitude. He folded his lips as though he was going to refuse to answer, and then appeared to think better of it.

'One thing at a time, if you don't mind, Senior Sergeant. Let me see? First question: my relationship with Ms Carpenter is as mentor, conductor, her immediate boss, if you like. She is a brilliant concert pianist who will go far in her profession.'

He paused and I imagined him thinking, *'If she's alive to pursue it.'* He blinked, and made an obviously major effort to focus back on us.

'I'm not privy to her social life. I do know she has several close friends in the orchestra.'

He went on to corroborate what everyone told us, but I sensed he was being deliberately evasive. As we rose to leave, pretending an after-thought, I asked him about his relationship with the pianist. I wasn't surprised to see the familiar red tinge stain his cheeks. Was this another case of an old goat thinking he could get to base with a young chick? Well, a twenty-five year old would seem young to him, though he was only in his late forties.

We'd been searching through parks, paddocks, alleys—everywhere possible—for four days. If the victim of abduction doesn't turn up within the first forty-eight hours, they're probably dead. Sorrow squeezed my heart. Somehow this young woman had touched me personally. Was it the feeling of familiarity I had when I looked at her? I closed my eyes and my mind of all but a prayer. *Please God, keep her safe.*

A sharp crack jerked me back to the present. A piece of burning wood split in the heat and tumbled over the edge of the grate onto the hearth. I got up stiffly and dealt with it. Harry had flown to Sydney to try and obtain family information from his ancient cousin Emily, who was in a nursing home. If he verified our suspicions of who Eloise Carpenter really is, I might be obliged to withdraw from the case.

CHAPTER 20
Hide and Seek

Brie

Tuesday: 7.00pm.

The little rat-shit vehicle I borrowed from a mate felt as small as a sardine tin. A permanently-broke jazz musician, he hated the colour of his car which had been bought for him by his parents. *'It's a girl's car,'* he'd whined. I was grateful; dull bronze meant camouflage. I'd swapped my sleek, black Nissan 360Z drop-head coupé for the little hatchback, because Jess would recognise it. My mate was ecstatic. I told him the same story as when I had asked him to borrow the bug I planted in Jess's kitchen from his parent's security business: I wanted to check whether my latest girlfriend was cheating on me. Now I wish she had. At least she would be safe.

I parked under the Moreton Bay fig tree around thirty metres from her house and out of range of the streetlight. When she left, I was determined to follow. If she had a visitor, I would find out who it was. I picked up my water bottle and took a sip, but I needed to be careful. Sooner or later I would need to dive into someone's hibiscus bush and take a piss. Being chased by a family dog with my cock flapping in the breeze would hardly be cool. A woman stopped nearby to let her dog baptise a gatepost. I shifted impatiently and made a show of glancing at my watch. *Just waiting for my girlfriend to reveal her true colours, madam.*

It had been a hard day, ending with Jess and Michael's five o'clock arrival at the pub. Pamela and I were sitting at a corner table, plotting ways to find Ally. I was just about to confide my budding career as a sleuth when they walked in the door. Jess's expression was thunderous; Michael's cold and remote, putting me immediately on the alert.

Pam bore in straight away. 'What's the matter with you two?'

I knew she was hurt Michael hadn't followed up Friday night at the club with a date, but fucking hell, life had hardly been normal since then.

'What business is it of yours?' snapped Jess. She dumped her handbag on the table, dragged off her coat and slung it over the back of a chair. Michael scowled at her, and then asked us if we wanted a drink.

'Not yet mate, but there's some here for you two,' I replied, realising he hadn't noticed the extra beer and glass of wine on the table. He took his coat off, folded it methodically, put it over the back of his chair and sat down. No one said anything for a moment and then we all started to talk at once.

'Are we having dinner here?'

'What's the matter with—?'

'Anyone want to—'

'How are we going to—?'

It ended in an impasse. A nasty smile hovered at the corner of Michael's mouth. Jess pouted and took a big gulp of wine. Pam glanced nervously at me. It was shaping up to be a fun evening.

'Anyone want to work on the Triple tomorrow?' I asked. Beethoven's Triple Concerto scheduled for a concert in three weeks time. I didn't dare mention Ally.

'Why? We've got plenty of time yet,' Jess objected flatly, 'and in any case, there's no one available to play it.' Her deliberate omission of Ally's name was more shocking than if she'd actually said it.

'No. Well—' I suggested that the music tutor for the orchestra might stand-in.

'Richie? That idiot?' Jess slammed her glass down on the table. 'I wouldn't give him house room. I don't know why you all like him so much because he's a first class prick.' That probably meant he had called her bluff at some time or another.

'I've never had any problem with him,' I remarked mildly, 'but if you don't want him, what about asking Vern? He might be available.' Vern was a pianist who occasionally practiced with members of the orchestra.

Michael baited Jess. 'Well, does milady approve of the fair Vern?' he asked, running his hand through his long hair, pretending to be precious. Pam and I swapped apprehensive glances. Jess swelled visibly, a flush of rage suffused her face and her eyes blazed.

'Fuck off, Michael! If you can't say anything constructive, shut up. And I don't give a stuff about the Beethoven's Triple Concerto.'

'Come on, Jess! He was only joking,' said Pamela, always the peacemaker. Jess took a huge gulp of wine, which went down the wrong way, then proceeded to snort it all over the table. We jumped up, pulling out handkerchiefs; Pamela grabbed a handful of tissues out of her bag. People nearby turned around to enjoy the show.

'Listen, I'm going. I can't be bothered sitting here, I've got a date tonight.' Jess jumped to her feet, brushed the remnants of wine droplets from her sweater and skirt, snatched up her belongings and stormed off toward the exit. We watched her go in an awkward silence.

'Well,' said Pamela after a moment, scrunching up wine-sodden tissues, 'I wonder what set her off?'

I had recognised Jess's fleeting, satisfied smirk. She didn't want to be there with us and chucking a tantie was a good way of making her exit. Everything had gone exactly the way she wanted it.

'I heard her on her mobile bollocking someone this afternoon. She wasn't happy, that's for sure,' I reported.

'What did she say?' Pam asked, curiously. Michael looked at me through narrowed eyes, but said nothing.

'I don't know, I didn't hear enough, but she was furious.'

Michael snorted and jumped to his feet. 'Jess always thinks she knows best. Anyway, who cares?' He picked up his coat and shrugged into it.

'You're going too? You've only just got here.'

'Don't feel like it, mate. My round next time, okay?'

We made eye contact, his cold and hostile. I felt as though a horse had kicked me. In the last couple of minutes something disturbing had surfaced, but I didn't understand why. Yet.

As Pamela gathered up our glasses and headed for the bar, I thought about Michael's reaction when I mentioned Jess's angry phone call. Could it have been to him? Or *about* him? It was then I phoned my mate and arranged to exchange cars for the night.

Deep inside, my knot of cold fear grew. I wriggled around trying to get comfortable. My feet tangled with the pedals as I attempted to stretch. On impulse, I opened the glove box and fossicked amongst the collection of receipts and empty sweet papers. Then I got lucky; there was one toffee left. I took it out, carefully unpeeled what remained of the wrapping and picked some fluff off the sweet before popping it in my mouth. Tucking my coat tighter around me, I leaned my head against the door pillar and sucked, prepared to wait as long as it took for something to happen.

Fear for Ally's safety constantly flared, sending shockwaves of fright through my body. I leaned my head back against the door pillar and thought about what had attracted me to Ally, but couldn't come up with anything major. It was mainly the small things I could remember, like the way she moved, cleaning, cooking—I could and had watched her sewing, the economical movement of her hands. But most of all, what turned me on was her kindness to everyone, young and old.

A week ago, I hoped we'd have a passionate affair. There was no point in commitment. In a few months time, Ally would be in Canada to do a concert tour, and I would finish my contract with the Pacific Symphony and go to Europe. We might hear of each other through the grapevine and maybe come across each other sometime. If we were both unattached, we might have dinner and end up in bed. Who am I kidding? I'd make sure we went to bed.

Or she would have a bearded husband who'd be wearing a baby in a sling and Jesus sandals...shit. And maybe in a few days, a week or a month, *I'll be standing by her grave.*

I guess I "do" terror after all.

At the age of fifteen, I was introduced to the delights of sex by the seventeen-year-old daughter of our neighbour, employed as a junior roustabout by my farmer father. The sheep shearing season lasted for several weeks, so my extensive tuition in the wool bins after dark was highly successful and a godsend to the skinny, pimply kid I was at the time. Since then, I had pretty much gotten whatever I wanted from women, so being put in my place by Ally was, when I recovered from the shock of being stymied, a refreshing challenge.

Now, a vision of the future without her stretched before me. I wanted to roar with anguish, to punch something, or someone to assuage the feeling of helplessness. If I could get the bastards who'd taken her, I'd tear them apart with my bare hands.

The back door of Jess's cottage opened, and I could see her walking to the garage in the beam cast by the sensor light mounted on the corner of the house. I started the car and gently revved the motor, keeping the lights off. She drove around the side of the house and out onto the road. I kept my head down as she roared past, heading for the city. I put the lights on, did a U-turn, and followed cautiously.

Trying to keep a car-length or two back from her small Honda was tricky in the evening traffic. We headed onto the freeway and drove for a good ten minutes before Jess turned off.

The road got steeper and narrower as we reached the foothills of the mountains. The number of vehicles had decreased. I was worried she'd get suspicious about the same car lurking at the rear, so dropped back until I was about fifty metres behind as we climbed into the range. A car coming toward me had its lights on high beam, forcing me to slow down until I almost stopped. When my eyes adjusted to the night again, Jess had disappeared. I panicked and put my foot down, which didn't get me too far in the ancient heap of metal.

It soon became apparent she had turned off somewhere. Homes are hidden all over the mountains, many at the end of narrow lanes where someone can vanish within seconds. I traced my route back to where I almost stopped, turned and drove slowly, peering into the bushes on either side of the road.

If you stare at something for long enough, the object becomes so familiar you could pick it out of a heap, so I had no trouble recognising the tail-lights of Jess's car moving down a long driveway to the left. I switched my headlights off, turned in and crept slowly after her. When she slowed and stopped, I pulled into a space off the driveway, killed the motor, rolled down the driver's side window and waited. A motion-sensor light came on at the house. Jess climbed out of the car, gathered up what looked like an overnight bag and walked toward the front door.

An older, tall, dark-haired man came out onto the verandah. I watched as she ran up the steps and walked into his arms. Down the well-lit hallway behind them a dark-haired woman stood and watched. Was the man her father? Not likely. She hadn't seen or spoken to her parents for years. *Could Ally be here?* I weighed the likelihood of that with the success of walking up and knocking at the front door. *Zilch.* Headlights blazed in my rear-vision mirror.

I didn't have time to duck as a car roared up the driveway. It drew level and the man driving turned his head and looked straight at me. The vicious glare would have cut me in half had it been a saw.

Christ! Get out of here.

As he swept past, I started the motor, threw the little car into reverse, put my foot down and backed up the driveway to the road. I couldn't see to steer properly. My hands jerked on the steering wheel, swinging the car violently. Small branches caught in the side mirror. Leaves showered through the window; a twig raked my cheek.

I risked a glance in the mirror. The other car was turning around fast. I put the headlights on and gunned the tiny motor down the main road. The little car gave an astonished leap and took off.

My heart pounded; blood trickled from the stinging cut on my cheek. For a few minutes there was no sign of a follower, and then lights appeared in the rear-view mirror.

He was rapidly closing the gap.

I crouched over the steering wheel, urging the Suzuki car on. Drivers coming the other way leaned on their horns as they fronted my headlights. The car behind me caught up and settled right on the back bumper, forcing me to take more chances. It swerved and began to draw alongside, until I could see the dark shape of the driver in the side mirror. I did a lightning inventory of what was in the car. Nothing available for a weapon. Can't out-run him. Need to turn off but where?

I slammed back into second gear and squeezed the brakes. My pursuer swept ahead and rounded the next corner. A white letter box indicated a driveway a few metres away. I swung the wheel to the left and turned in, almost side-swiping a guide post. I slid the car into a small clearing behind the trunk of a huge gum tree and switched off the headlights and ignition.

The only sounds were of my own breathing and ticking as the motor cooled. I wound the window almost fully down so I could hear anyone coming and sat perfectly still, listening to the sounds of the night.

So was he Jess's new boyfriend? Maybe he thought I was a bloke stalking her. Well, I was, but not for the reason he might imagine. A minute or two passed and then I heard a vehicle approaching slowly along the main road. Some instinct made me lock the doors, before I slid down as far as possible below the level of the windows.

My hearing became super-tuned, my pulse raced. Minutes passed, but the engine faded. I waited a minute or two longer, but as I began to sit up, I heard it coming back.

I raised my head a fraction and peered out. The driver paused at the entrance to the driveway, then turned in and stopped, idling quietly. I flattened myself along the front seat. The floor smelled of joggers, rubber mats and discarded Macca's French fries. A stinking paper wrap rustled under my foot. The beam of a powerful torch swept the bush, passed over the trunk of the gum tree...hovered...came back, swept higher, scanned again ...moved further on over the bushes to my right...then flashed along the driveway.

An owl flew low overhead, momentarily caught in the light. The driver flashed the torch around for a few more moments and then turned it off. I heard the car door close; the engine rev and the car back out onto the road to move slowly away.

I stayed where I was, counting until I reached five minutes. Then I sat up and breathed freely again.

Shit, that was close.

My throbbing cheek reminded me I was walking wounded. I took my handkerchief out of my pocket and started to wipe the cut, peering into the rear vision mirror.

A hand came through the window and grabbed me by the throat.

My lungs strained to suck air as I struggled desperately to find the button to power the window up.

No button.

Fuck! This car had a wind-up handle.

A blast of hot breath blew into my face; I snorted in Aramis.

His eyes burned into mine as he leaned closer to get leverage.

His hand slipped, releasing the pressure on my windpipe not a second too soon. He fought for a better grip as I punched wildly at his face. The window was almost up.

He grunted and tried to bite my hand before I could

rip it away.

I shoved him hard, trying to break his hold on my throat.

He squeezed harder.

I got my hand up again and lashed out, trying for his nose.

He jerked backwards, letting me go.

I held my throat with one hand, started the motor with the other as I fought for air.

He lunged again and caught me by the shirt collar.

I wound the window back against his arm, rammed the car into gear and slammed my foot onto the accelerator. It shot forward, dragging him with it.

The car scraped the side of the tree, jouncing the steering wheel out of my hands.

I grabbed it again.

He screamed and cursed, struggling to keep his feet.

As the car gathered momentum, I wound the window down and released his arm.

He dropped to the road.

I gunned the motor, raced along the driveway to the front of a house, hurled the car around the forecourt, bounced it over flower beds, flattening rosebushes and narrowly avoiding the fountain.

My lungs whistled as I struggled to breath. Driving like a maniac, I passed the gum tree, the headlights catching my attacker on his knees at the side of the driveway.

Roaring out onto the main road, I swung down the mountain, trembling with exhaustion and fear. *What the hell had Jess gotten into?*

CHAPTER 21
Painting by Rote

James

Tuesday: midnight.

Eloise had fallen asleep on the settee. I sat in the armchair opposite staring into the fire, reflecting how one's life can completely change in the time it takes to speak a few words. Flames flickered in the grate. A log occasionally disintegrated amid a small shower of sparks, pretty much mirroring our spirits. The music of Bach played quietly in the background, but I found no comfort in it. The ticking clock on the mantelpiece measured our time to wait for the phone call.

Pictures flicked through my mind like images from an old film—the night I first met Eloise in a pub full of shouting students, her very shyness attracting my attention after she fell over my feet, instant heat springing between us as our eyes met. Springtime, lying beneath a tree, deep in an English woodland, my head in Eloise's lap as she traced my face with her delicate fingers, tickling my throat and chest, sliding inside my jeans under cover of the surrounding foliage. The memory of her warm, satiny skin seeps into my nostrils. The smell of wildflowers, the feel of the woollen rug beneath our bare legs...

I harden, remembering our passion, opening her shirt,

sliding her bra up to stroke and lave her rosy nipples, to bury my face in her hot, full breasts. Eloise performing sentry duty—'Someone's coming, James, quick!'—and we'd curl into a ball, like pythons, wrapping ourselves in her shirt to hide her nakedness, kissing until hasty footsteps signalled an embarrassed retreat, giggling at our duplicity. I doubt I would be agile enough to avoid detection now. My well-regimented life has been swept away as though it never existed; my facade of self-containment has collapsed. How did she feel about me after thinking I callously abandoned her all those years ago? Did she want me now? And if so, how would I cope if she left again, this time of her own accord?

The pain of losing her has remained with me all this time. Could I handle it better now I'm middle-aged? I looked at her, imagining her beautiful mouth pressing against mine, our tongues twining together. I have only to move a metre and take her in my arms again. God, how I'd loved Eloise.

I forced my thoughts in another direction, one of equal doubt. How will Ally feel when she finds out I'm her father? Despite my initially ambivalent feelings, I'm beginning to come to terms with my fatherhood. I knew Susan Prescott and her young colleague thought me a cold, unfeeling bastard during our interview earlier today. Behind my public facade is a mass of good old-fashioned guilt and desperate—yes, a father's fear. I know I appeared to be an old fool who fancied his chances with a woman young enough to be his daughter. At one time they'd have been right.

Now Pamela Miller knows I'm Ally's father I couldn't see the point in hiding my relationship to Ally, but Eloise swore both of us to silence. She feels the least number of people who know the easier it would be to keep the fact of the ransom demand secret. She's right. Pamela, offered to scrape as much money together as she could. Of course, I wouldn't accept, but we promised to ask for help if needed.

The shrill ring of the telephone sent my heart rate into orbit and started the dog barking.

I froze.

Eloise's eyes flew open. She sat upright in one fluid movement, threw off the travel rug and leaped to her feet. 'Answer it!' Her hand hovered above the mobile phone which had arrived in the mail that afternoon. Ashen-faced, eyes wild in the firelight and despite her small stature, she resembled a warrior woman. She spoke slowly, as if I was one of the bewildered and of course, I was. 'James, you have. To. Answer. It.'

My heart pounded. Fear churned my stomach. She nodded encouragement and quickly reached out to touch my hand. I took a deep breath, picked up the phone and pressed the "talk" button.

'Yes, is Ally safe? I want to speak to her.'

The familiar voice rasped back into our lives. 'She's alive for the moment and that's all you need to know. Have you got the money?'

Eloise' eyes met mine, willing me to remain calm. I took a deep breath. 'I've got a hundred and eighty thousand in cash and nine hundred thousand coming within three days. I need more time to get the re—'

'Shut up and listen carefully, because I'm only going to say this once,' he snapped. 'This is how you're gunna do it. The hundred and eighty thousand is to be put in a bag which will be at your letter box by one o'clock this morning. A little something will be waiting for you inside it as a sample of what could happen if you don't follow instructions. Right? Do you understand?'

'Yes.'

'Good, because you'll be watched. You are going to

register yourself with eBay, using the names, Hamlet88 and Frisbee88. By tomorrow morning there'll be two hundred items posted and the item numbers will be on a list tucked in with your present. The current ones have been on the site for several days and each auction is due to finish on Saturday. Some are Buy Now. That's only the start. As you buy them, there'll be more posted and more numbers will arrive in the mail box. Don't think you can watch it either, because then you'll get something you really don't want. Right?'

'Yes.'

'Now, each item has its starting price listed and that'll be the least amount you have to pay for each transaction. You follow?'

'Yes.'

My hand trembled as I scribbled the aliases under which I had to bid, on the back of an envelope. I hoped I would be able to read it later. Eloise's jerky breathing was interfering with my concentration. Out of the corner of my eyes, I saw her press trembling hands to her stomach. *Christ, don't throw up now, El.* The voice continued. 'Don't pay way over the starting price unless other bidders join in, because if you pay too much, it'll be suspicious. But one thing you have to do is make sure you win every item. Your girlie's life depends on it and you better believe it! Right?'

'Yes, I understand.'

'Don't think you can find me through eBay, because the items are up for auction under different vendor names. All payments will be direct deposit in cash, into especially set up bank accounts. You can't put a trace on them, because they're going to be closed minutes after the money shows up. *No PayPal, no cheques.* Each transaction will go through and you leave positive feedback all along the way. The only difference is you'll never get anything you buy. Just follow the instructions bit by bit, like painting by rote. All right?'

'Yes. How long is this going to take?'

'As long as it needs to. And get more cash out because you'll be making a lot of deposits at your letter box. Remember, your daughter's life depends on you carrying out the instructions and not telling the cops.' He disconnected.

Eloise looked at me, white-faced, as she sank onto the settee. I poured a dram of whisky, but her hands shook violently as I helped her hold the glass. She gulped, choked and started coughing. I took it away, gave her my handkerchief then sat beside her, rubbing her back. I wanted to smash the kidnapper's face in, run over him with the car—anything.

I slowly recounted the instructions we had been given, adding more to the paper as we recalled it. 'The bidding ends on Saturday,' I reminded her.

'Does that mean we get Ally back then?' Eloise asked, her eyes alight with hope.

False expectations wouldn't help either of us. 'There are no guarantees.'

She listened to me intently, the handkerchief obscuring the lower half of her face. Her mass of hair had dropped out of its coil and flopped onto her shoulders. I stroked it away from her neck and she collapsed against my chest. A wave of desperation and love swept through me, my arms automatically enfolding her as though we had never been apart. Tremors coursed through her body.

'James, it didn't seem real until now. It's like we're in a stupid...movie or something...and what are they going to send us as a present this time?'

Remembering the hank of bloodied hair, the first sample, I tried to sound re-assuring. 'It's all right, we'll get through this, I promise you.'

The letter box is half a kilometre from the house. At 12.30am, I prepared to set out on foot, not wanting to draw attention to the expedition. My household staff would be justifiably curious if they saw me uncharacteristically tramping around in the early hours of the morning. As I shrugged into my outdoor coat, Eloise grabbed hers.

'James, I'm coming with you!' she announced briskly, as she thrust her arm into a sleeve.

The dog jumped to his feet. A midnight adventure! Things were looking up. 'Eloise, you should stay here,' I protested weakly. She glared at me, tossed some used tissues into the wastepaper basket and then grabbed an extra handful which she thrust into her pocket.

'If you expect for one minute you're going to do this alone you've got another think coming!' she replied, as she picked up the dog lead and a torch from my desk.

'You're exhausted; you should stay here and rest.'

'Rubbish, I'm coming. This is not something you should be doing on your own. It's dangerous. They might be out there!' she said, bending down to clip the lead to the dog's collar.

'My dear, I couldn't be safer. I'm the money tree, remember?' I replied dryly. She snorted and headed for the door, towed along by Benji.

I was glad to have their company, but I wasn't about to let her open the so-called present. Picking up my briefcase, I ushered her out to the foyer, collecting the key to the letterbox from the hooks beside my study door. At the bottom of the steps, I wrapped her small fingers in my own and thrust both our hands into the pocket of my coat, warm, comforting; too much so.

The leaves on the trees beside the drive rustled in a gentle night breeze. Stars blazed in the Milky Way giving dim natural light, augmented by the torch. An owl hooted nearby. By mutual consent, we didn't speak. The only sound was our footsteps and Benji's nails clicking on the tarmac as he panted along in front. My back cringed as though in the sights of a sniper's rifle. Somewhere someone was watching, probably through nightglasses.

We reached the front gate after about twenty minutes and confronted the ugly metal castle, which my landlords obviously thought stylish. It had all the charm of a striking snake. I shone the torch onto the canvas sack folded at the base of the pole. A rope was tied around the neck. When Eloise let Benji's lead drop, he went to the other side of the pillar and promptly lifted his leg. Eloise fumbled with the lock on the back door of the castle.

'Wait! Eloise, I'll do that, I've got the key,' I said hastily, grabbing at her hand. 'We don't know what's in there.'

'Hurry *up,* James.'

She thrust her hands into her coat pockets. I switched on the torch, tucked it under my chin and opened the case. For a few moments, Eloise watched me scoop up the bundles of notes with clumsy hands before bending down to hold the neck of the sack open. It took only a minute or two to finish the job and tie the rope tightly.

'Hold this— '

I handed the torch to Eloise, fished the key to the castle out of my pocket and proceeded to turn the lock. A small golden gift box encircled with red ribbon tied in a huge bow, was in the cavity. My heart sank. Eloise looked on, fearfully. What next?

'We're not going to open it until we get back to the house,' I announced, putting it quickly into the briefcase. I could hardly bear to touch it. She nodded slowly.

I padlocked the castle and we headed along the driveway with the dog bringing up the rear, trailing his lead behind him.

Something tugged at my mind as we walked, about the key and the padlock, but the harder I tried to remember, the faster it skittered away. It'll come to you.

It was all we could do not to run as we neared the house. I put the case on the desk and opened it. The golden swirls on the cardboard sparkled in the light reflecting the flame from the fire. I slowly untied the ribbon and lifted the lid off. Inside was a tiny parcel. I took a deep breath and peeled back the tissue paper.

A second before Eloise screamed, I recognised one of the elaborate gold and garnet earrings which the members of the orchestra had given Ally on her birthday.

It was still attached to a piece of bloodied earlobe.

CHAPTER 22
Illusions

Ally

Wednesday: before dawn.

The sand is hot, but in the shadow of the Wild Pony, it's cool and damp. I can hear the waves slashing the beach below us. Smell the salt air ... why didn't I let Briece make love to me before? Coward...wasting time...

Ooh, that's so good...his hands are stroking, kneading gently, pressing in all the right places, sliding up...and down ...and around ...the sun forms a halo around his head.

Heat slithers through my body, flooding my senses. My breath comes in short gasps.

He is leaning over me, cupping my breasts. I can smell sweat. He must have been running.

My nipples harden as he tweaks and soothes, then his hands slowly slide over my stomach, slip between my legs, which part to allow him access to my innermost parts.

My body writhes with hot pleasure.
I try to look up at him, but cannot open my eyes.
He moves around me..
Cool air wafts over my hot, bare breasts.
I can feel his weight pressing on me.
I try to reach for him, but my arms are lifeless.
He scoops up my breasts, presses them together and suckles first one nipple then the other. His tongue slides around,

licking my breasts all over, then back to my nipples to feast greedily. A long way off, someone is moaning.

Oh hurry, hurry...I want you...I've waited too long.

My head lashes from side to side, as I thrust my hips into his erection, urging him to take me, now...now!

I can feel his hot knob ramming against my crotch as he tries to thrust past the leg of my panties.

No! Wait—wait—it hurts!

I struggle, but his body is pressing me into the wet sand.

Wait! This is all wrong, it shouldn't be like this!

I try to push him away, but my arms are scattered on the sand like washed-up seaweed.

A strangled sound forces its way out of my throat.

He giggles. He giggles?

'What the hell do you think you're doing? Get off her!' A woman's voice cuts across the moment.

Help me...help me.

He stops moving; I feel the muscles of his body stiffen. He heaves himself off me. My swollen breasts are hot and wet.

I try desperately to open my eyes, but I can't. I try again. Bright flitters of light pierce my eyes, then flash past to illuminate a muscular man with the face of an angel, smooth olive skin, curly black hair and huge dark eyes, who is looking down at me, smirking as he zips up his jeans.

I know him. Scarpia.

The Cow stands beside him, face suffused with rage, the light from the torch she carries flashes off the walls.

'Don't touch her, she's vermin,' she snarls. Hatred turns her eyes to volcanic, black stones.

I can't stay awake any longer.

Blessed darkness.

CHAPTER 23
The Numbers Game

Eloise

Wednesday: 4.00am.

Ally's screams send me hurtling along the pathway to the side of the house. A man and a woman are tearing at her clothes. I leap onto the back of the man, plunging my hands into his hair, pulling as hard as I can. He roars, bucks me off and turns. It's Georgie! Her face is swollen and green. Patches of skin fall around me like confetti. I scream and bat at the bits with my fists. The smell of death closes over me and I vomit mightily. I can't stop even when my intestines start to come out of my mouth, great gobs of blood and pus spilling over the ground...the parts coming up are those of a cow...

'Eloise, Wake up, you're having a nightmare!'

The light from coffee table lamp blinded me.

'Let me go! Ally. I've got to save her—'

'No, no, it's me, James. It's all right, it's all right, you're safe.'

I could hear and feel his heart beating against my cheek. He held me tightly until I recovered enough to recount the details of my nightmare. After I stopped gasping and snorting into his sweater, I realised I had fallen asleep in the study.

My heart pounded against his broad chest; the male smell of him filled my nostrils. Memories swept through my mind of his hot flesh pressing mine, our bodies locked together, gasping with passion as we brought each other to frenzied climax. Without thinking, I pressed closer. He rocked me for a moment, before holding me away from him to gaze into my face, his expression inscrutable.

'Do you feel as though you can stay here while I get you a cup of something from the kitchen?'

I was embarrassed. Had I shown my burgeoning feelings for him? But I was scared witless and not staying upstairs on my own. 'No, no! I'm coming too.'

'No, Eloise. Lie back, it's cold out in the kitchen. I'll only be a few minutes.'

After James had opened the gold-wrapped box, I fainted and when I came to, found myself on the sofa. We'd tried to talk our predicament through, but the heat from the fire and the comfort of the sofa had lulled me to sleep. Had he sat in his chair since then, watching over me?

Perspiration trickled down my throat as I pulled myself into a sitting position, so stressed I could hardly breathe. I pulled my sweater off; the room was suffocatingly hot.

Where was James? My heart leapt with fear, but before I panicked, he returned carrying a large tray which he placed on the coffee table.

'Are you feeling a bit better?' He handed me wet facecloth to wipe my face and hands and a handtowel to dry off. Two cups of steaming coffee stood on the side table.

'Yes, thank you.' I smiled shakily, and slowly smoothed the warm, wet, cloth over my hot cheeks. 'I seem to have lost control completely.'

'It's hardly surprising. I couldn't imagine how it

must feel to have a child kidnapped before this, now I'm beginning to understand. The stress is horrendous for you.' He handed me a cup of coffee which I sipped gratefully.

I sighed. 'Sometimes I don't know how I can bear a second more of it. I want to scream and yell and break things. When are you going to start with—'

'I got the item numbers. This morning I'll set up the account and see what's what.'

'I want to do it with you.'

'Well, yes, you can, if it doesn't upset you too much.' He looked at me doubtfully. 'We won't be receiving anything though, thank God.'

Inexplicably, the last time I heard from Ally, jumped into my mind.

Mum, would you please send me the green dress with the pleats? It's hanging in the wardrobe under something else.

'Yes, I'll get it in the mail tomorrow.'

'Thanks millions, mum. Talk to you soon!'

Was that to be the last conversation I would have with my daughter? About a dress? No. It couldn't be... terrifying images chased through my mind, threatening to overwhelm me. Before I could let go again, James put his cup down and took my hands in his. 'Tell me about Ally as a baby.'

'What?' For a moment, I couldn't work out what he was saying.

'Ally, Eloise. What she was like when she was a baby. Tell me about her. Please.'

Was he hoping to distract me? Delighted that at last he was expressing interest, I reached for the holdall which I brought with me, opened the side pocket and took out the folders of photographs.

He gazed wistfully at images of Ally as a baby and

later, playing with the animals, wearing her pet rats on her shoulder like epaulets, clowning with friends, receiving awards for her music. Regret for what might have been swept through me again. The unthinkable forced its way to the forefront of my mind, in spite of my efforts to quell it. *She may never know her father.*

After he looked at the photos, it was as though at last we had touched common ground through our daughter, as though our lives had finally intersected. Perhaps we would establish a friendship, but more than that I didn't dare hope for, though my heart was sending me signals that it would like to take up from where it had been left, twenty-six years ago.

The night sky was giving way to daylight, the huge house silent, almost menacing, when we went to the kitchen. In spite of him turning the lights on as we walked through the long, high-ceilinged hallway, I felt as though demons lurked in the shadows as I passed.

The cold, black and white kitchen was an uncomfortable place to be, a sharp contrast to my homely cottage with its shabby cupboards and dog-scuffed doors. I dismissed an involuntary image of James, enormous in my small house. In spite of his caring behaviour, I had no reason to believe he might want to embark on a relationship with me after Ally was found. If…don't even think it. But my wayward thoughts persisted. The man I had loved and hated all these years was actually standing only a metre away. *This is Ally's dad, father of my child. Surreal.*

Ever competent and talented, basically James hadn't changed. But what of his inner self? The musician and incongruously, the businessman? He was never soft, but somewhere there lurked a sweet core, a willingness to care for those weaker than himself. And he was trying to save Ally.

My mind almost flipped out again. I had to know.

'Where did you put the...?' Golden box.

'Um...' He was unable to prevent the merest flicker of his eyes toward the freezer. He saw me shudder. 'I know how you feel, but there was nothing else I could do with it because,' he paused, 'it's evidence.'

'I think this is getting too dangerous and we should tell the police. I know Georgie could have been killed for some other reason than to do with us, but I can't help feeling it's not a coincidence.' My leg muscles clenched so tight with tension that my knees literally jiggled under the table.

It was James's turn to disagree. 'We have to keep quiet. It was my idea to go to them before, but since this... gift box, I realise you were right. If we keep quiet, they will continue to trust us. Maybe they won't touch her again.' He hesitated and then continued, 'at least they didn't cut off one of her fingers.'

I choked. Coffee sprayed all over the table, coming out of my mouth, nose, and running back into my throat. Tears poured down my face. James leapt to his feet, grabbing a tea towel with which he proceeded to mop up. I couldn't stop coughing as I tried to suck oxygen.

'I didn't mean to upset you, Eloise. Oh *damn!*'

Gradually getting control of myself, I flopped back on the chair. 'I hadn't thought of that, but you're right. At least it wasn't that.' My voice wobbled.

Of all the terrible things they could do to Ally, maiming her hands would surely be the worst, apart from killing her. For a moment he looked uncertain and then he reached out to touch my hand.

'Eloise, I think you should come and stay here with me at the house, at least until this is all over. Will you do that? No one knows I'm Ally's father, so the media won't find you here. Believe me, if you stay where you are, they will hunt you down and hound you and Pam.'

He looked at me, anxiously.

Poor Pam. I felt guilty leaving her to deal with the media when it got out she was a friend of Ally. She didn't need the hassle of having shrieking journalists and rampant photographers following her every move. Nor did I. 'You'll regret it if you don't,' I told myself and accepted, crossing mental fingers that Pam wouldn't feel abandoned.

We went up to James' bedroom where I lay down to rest, while James gathered some fresh clothes and headed for the shower. The doona's comforting softness envelop my tired muscles.

My daughter. *Mutilated.* Please God, they'd drugged her when they cut off the lobe of her ear. Or was she fully conscious? No, stop it! Think positively. Plastic surgery can do anything now. *Oh God, no.*

I forced my thoughts to Masters Island. Georgie, my best friend was dead, murdered. But who hated her enough to kill her? She drank too much sometimes and occasionally was very abrupt, which upset some people. What could she have possibly done to get stabbed? Was this related to Ally's kidnapping? Had she told someone who Ally's father was? Was that person afraid she would connect him or her with it?

James, Pam and I talked over everything which had happened since Ally disappeared. We women feared they would treat her badly, perhaps not feed her properly, but James assured us they wouldn't want to damage the merchandise. I thought what they'd done so far was more than enough. Perhaps they didn't care, because they planned to—*don't go there.*

He emerged from the bathroom, fully dressed. I climbed wearily off the bed. 'There are clean towels there for you, Eloise. Can you manage on your own for a short time now? I want to go and set up this account.'

The corners of his mouth turned down with distaste.

I could tell from his expression that he was champing at the bit to get on with it. As I heard myself answer "fine" the incongruity of the answer struck me. We humans fall over, hit our heads and have blood pouring out, or we trip, land flat on our faces and feel we'll never get up again—but still say "Fine, thank you," when asked if we're all right.

'Come to the study as soon as you're ready. I'm cancelling a couple of appointments so I don't have to leave here. James looked at me, thoughtfully. 'You need a car and I'd like to get you one so you can be independent.'

I was astonished. 'I have a perfectly good car at home!'

'I know you do, but you need a car to get around in while you're up here. You're reliant on Pam or myself for transport. Let me hire one for you, Eloise, please?' He gave me one of his rare smiles, so like Ally's.

'All right,' I capitulated, 'but only a jam tin on cotton reels, thank you.'

His lips twitched as he punched some numbers into the phone, spoke for a few minutes, hung up and then turned back to me.

'I don't think for a minute they expect to get three million out of us, Eloise. Using eBay is an easy way to get maybe a few hundred thousand at the outside, because it's essentially a quick "get in, get out" exercise and amateurish. But keeps us busy and in a constant state of panic. As far as I can see, it's the only explanation for such a bizarre way of getting extra money.' The muscles in his jaw clenched. He was keeping himself tightly under control, but the strain showed around his eyes and mouth.

Downstairs, the dog barked. The housekeeper, Mrs Fox, had arrived.

'A Lexus will be delivered at 9am,' said James, as he went to the door.

'A Lexus? That's hardly a little car, James!' I protested.

He looked at me in surprise. 'You need something decent to drive.' An understatement indeed. 'Right. And I'll get started with this stuff, then we had better eat something.'

I must have made a small sound, because he looked down at me sternly. 'You have to eat, Eloise. You aren't helping anyone, least of all Ally if you don't keep healthy.'

He visibly braced himself and picked up the list, mouth tight, eyes bleak. Greatly daring, I reached behind him, my right breast brushing his arm as I rubbed the small of his back with slow circular strokes. He looked up again, startled.

'You used to do that when I was stressed over exams. It always calmed me,' he said quietly. We looked at each other for a long moment. A flash of tangled limbs and heat, slid into my mind. I could see the pulse at the base of his throat throbbing; he drew in a sharp breath. 'When this is over and Ally is safe, we'll go away and have time together,' he said, thrusting his hand into his pocket to jingle his keys and coin.

Suddenly, his eyes narrowed. 'My God, it has to be someone who's been here!'

I gazed at him, speechless.

'I'm stupid. I knew there was something I was missing. The letter box key is always kept on the hook where you saw me get it last night. Either someone broke in or it was a tradesman who was here.'

His face twisted.

'Maybe a member of the orchestra, or it could even be one of my friends.'

CHAPTER 24
Doing Coffee

Detective Senior Sergeant Susan Prescott.

Wednesday: 11.00am.

My nose ran, my throat felt raw and I was cranky. The media were battering the front of Headquarters down, begging for information. What we didn't give them, they invented. My husband, Harry, had arrived back from Sydney and the information he brought with him was causing a great deal of angst. I lurked in my corner of the room all morning, thinking and snivelling into tissues, while Evan conducted the early briefing. Occasionally a member of my team would poke his or her head in the door, start to speak, take one look at my thunderous expression and promptly vanish.

We had checked out the credentials and backgrounds of all the members of the orchestra, the directors and three administrative staff. I was disappointed to discover there was nothing sinister in the lives of any of them, including Sir James McPherson who had been pestering the Commissioner daily, wanting to know what we were doing and why we hadn't found Ally Carpenter. I would love to have wrapped my hands around the conductor's throat and squeezed until his eyes popped out. We're doing our best, for heaven's sake!

The detective from the CIB in Townsville who answered my enquiry about the artist, Georgie Hird, rang back at 11am. They had interviewed a friend of Georgie Hird and Eloise who was house-sitting Eloise's cottage. Irritation oozed down the line. 'She acted as though she knew nothing, but I'm not convinced, ma'am,' he said.

'How can I help you, then?' I sucked my teeth and twirled my pen in my fingers, wishing he would get on with it.

'I need everything Eloise Carpenter knows about Georgie Hird. Could you assign someone to interview her for us?'

I agreed to do it myself.

'Ms Hird died as a result of a long, thin piece of metal. There was a half-finished sweater in a basket in her bedroom, so it seems likely a knitting needle was driven through her heart. One steel number 11 is missing and a single thrust was all it took,' he said, and then expanded on the details.

'The forensic report advised she died instantly, there was little blood, but bruise marks on her arms where someone held her tightly. There are abrasions on her body, so we figure she was murdered in the house, carried to the cliff edge and thrown onto the rocks. She'd not been immersed in the sea and not had sexual intercourse prior to her death.' Then he added a detail which only the killer would know.

After we finished speaking, I sat and turned the case over in my mind. It appeared too much of a coincidence for Ally Carpenter's godmother to be murdered while the girl was missing. However, on the face of it, a connection between Ally Carpenter's abduction and the murder of the artist seemed far-fetched. Reason suggested Ally's abduction was sexual, and the presence of the woman at the nightclub couldn't preclude that.

It would be easy to leave her body in the bush outside

the city, and large freezers have been known to make handy receptacles for inconvenient truths. Perhaps it was wishful thinking, but I had a feeling she was still alive. In the meantime, I agreed to question Eloise Carpenter about Georgie Hird.

I picked up the telephone and rang Ms Carpenter's mobile, which she answered on the second ring. I regretted not having news to give her, but she didn't seem surprised. Fleetingly, I wondered why not and then plunged into the reason for the call.

'Ms Carpenter, Townsville CIB has been in touch with me regarding Miss Hird's murder. I would like to ask you some questions if you feel up to it.' There was a moment of silence, during which I grabbed a clean tissue and dabbed my dribbling nose.

'Yes, I'll be happy to give you any information I can… but I don't know if there's much I can tell you,' she replied.

'Perhaps it might be better if I met you somewhere and we talk, Ms Carpenter?'

It would be a good excuse to get myself out of the building, leave behind the pests such as the "James" heavyweights from the Pacific Orchestra and the screaming media pack.

We arranged to meet at a small coffee shop, not far from Pamela Miller's flat.

I got waylaid several times in the effort to escape headquarters, having fought off Evan's well-meaning efforts to come with me and ignored Ben Taylor's hopeful glance as I swept by. I was going to pick Eloise Carpenter's brains and felt I could do better on my own.

It was a fine, autumn day and the air was crisp with the promise of a cold winter. As we sat in the trendy little café opposite a park, making small talk while we waited for our lattés to arrive, I looked closely at Eloise.

Her face had taken on a translucent appearance, accentuating her exhaustion. Her eyelids were heavy and red-rimmed; her eyes told of tearful nights.

We confessed to watching our weight, but then decided to throw caution to the wind and have caramel-cream cakes. For a very short time it was possible to forget the reason why we were there, but then reality kicked in.

'Okay, Senior Sergeant, let's get it over with,' said Eloise, as she scooped a spoonful of froth from the top of her coffee and licked the spoon.

'First of all, how are you holding up? And have you changed your mind about the police liaison officer visiting?' I asked, after we had taken the first sip of our coffee and bite of cake.

Her eyes widened. 'No, thank you. I have Pam and my friends to help me. The orchestra administration has been very good to me and there are other friends I can call on. The doctor has given me some sleeping tablets in case I need them.' Her expression said she wouldn't take them in a pink fit.

'Okay. Well, let me know if we can help you in any way, won't you?' I smiled reassuringly at her. 'Are you staying at your goddaughter's place for awhile?'

'Er, no. I'm going to stay with a friend.' She blushed and kept her eyes on her latté, carefully breaking up the froth with her teaspoon. *Oh yeah?*

'You're not going to stay in Ally's house?'

'No, I couldn't bear it. Pam and I went over, but it was too awful with Ally not there. I just couldn't stay and certainly not on my own.' Her mouth wobbled, as she stirred her coffee vigorously, splashing droplets over the rim of the cup. 'All the time I was there, I expected to hear her come through the door, and I could smell her clothes on the bed, the bathroom—everywhere in that house, I could feel my daughter's—' she faltered, searching for the right word, 'essence.'

She looked at me, mother to mother. 'It was like when she was a baby, you know? Their scent. I used to wonder how sheep knew their own lamb in a flock of hundreds, but once I had my baby I understood.'

'Oh yes. I know exactly what you mean.' I nodded slowly, remembering the birth of my twin daughters. The personal aroma of your children never leaves the archives of a mother's memory. *Pity the other memories of my first marriage wouldn't disappear.*

Time to return to business. 'I'll need your phone number and new address if you're moving location, then.' I clicked my biro and waited expectantly. She looked embarrassed. 'You have my mobile number, Senior Sergeant,' she pointed out, our personal moment now scotch mist.

'I do, but I also need to know where you're staying,' I said gently. 'In case we need to collect you to identify Ally,' was my unspoken thought.

'Look, I'd rather not say.' She squirmed. 'Isn't it enough you have my mobile number?'

'We'll leave it for now,' I replied. I could have insisted, but I needed her co-operation. The list of questions which my colleague in Townsville requested lay by my plate. 'All right, now if you don't mind, I would like to ask you some questions about Miss Hird. Was she ever married or did she have children?'

'No, Georgie was a strange woman in a lot of ways. She was a lovely person—yes, I know everyone says that about a friend, she wouldn't have been my closest friend if she wasn't—but she was also the most self-contained person I have ever known.' Eloise gazed into her mind's eye, oblivious to my presence as she remembered her relationship with Georgie Hird.

'She loved Ally and Pam.' She smiled. 'They were more like sisters than friends, you know. Most of the time Pam was at home with me because Rosalind, her mother, had to work nights to make ends meet.'

'I see. Did Ms Hird have any relatives?'

'Her mother and father died quite a few years ago, they were in the French Resistance during the war. Georgie inherited an enormous amount of money when they passed. She used to talk about some cousins in France, but apart from them, she was the most—alone—person I have ever met with regard to family. We were both alone, Mrs Prescott, because I had no-one either, so she became my sister and Ally's aunt.' Eloise's face crumpled and she fumbled for a handkerchief.

I waited until she had recovered and then asked, 'Do you know if she had a man friend?'

'Yes, she did, but I didn't know his name. Ros and I were sure the creep was married. He came and went on a boat, but I don't know if he actually owned it. He used to moor it well away from the jetty. But I never saw him. No wait, I did see him once!'

She paused for a moment, looking anxious. 'You need to understand. Georgie was a very private person when her love life concerned someone she knew she shouldn't be seeing. If it was above board, she was quite open and flounced around introducing him to everyone. She was one of those "larger than life characters," you know? But if he was a married man, and much as I loved her I do have to admit she wasn't selective, she wouldn't even tell me who she was seeing. As if I'd tell anyone.' The expression in her eyes told of her hurt.

I waited patiently, saying nothing, waiting for her to finish wiping them with a man-sized handkerchief. 'Georgie would tell us when an "illegal" man was coming to stay, so we wouldn't phone or visit while he was there. I know this one used to come to the island and I think she saw him in Brisbane as well as Townsville when she had an exhibition showing, but whether he was actually associated with it, I couldn't say. Georgie exhibited all over Australia and overseas, so she could have met him anywhere, for that matter.'

She took a long pull at her latté. I nodded encouragingly.

'But I did see him close-up, one night about a year ago.' She paused and gazed into her mind's eye.

'And?'

'His back was to me. He's tall and broad-shouldered with dark hair, but I couldn't see his face or hear his voice. I'd gone over there to take some eggs to Georgie and she must have forgotten to tell me he was coming. Perhaps it was unexpected. Anyway, as I walked up to the back door I saw them sitting at the kitchen table. He stood up while I was watching.'

'Did they see you?'

'No, I ducked back.' She smiled. 'I didn't want to intrude and anyway I couldn't see much. Clean window panes weren't important to Georgie.'

I scribbled my notes, before she got the guilts over spying on them. 'How long had the affair been going on, Ms Carpenter. Do you know?'

'I think eighteen months, perhaps two years. We were quite surprised it lasted as long as it did.'

'Why was that?' I asked.

'Well, Townsville's about sixteen hours from Brisbane by road, if that's where he lives, and then you have to get the boat to and from the island, so it can't have been that easy to keep it going. Of course they could have flown each way if he had a friend with a small plane,' she explained uneasily, 'but I suspect he mostly came by boat.'

'So, in all that time you and Mrs Miller never found

out his name or anything else about him?'

'No.' She wriggled. 'As I said, Georgie could be very close-mouthed about the affairs she shouldn't have been having. In twenty-six years she's probably had at least— oh, heavens—fifteen, maybe twenty love affairs that I know of.'

'On average, how long would you say Ms Hird's relationships lasted?'

'Well, it varied. At least one was for several years and then she found out he had been living with his wife all along. Most only lasted a few months.'

'Why did Ms Hird never marry?'

Eloise grinned. 'She maintained she never wanted to be tied down. She always said that since she liked to paint at three in the morning a husband would be more of an encumbrance than a comfort.' Her face lit up as she smiled at the memory.

'Can you think of a reason why anyone might murder Ms Hird?' I asked, watching her closely.

'No, I can't.' Eloise looked me right in the eyes. 'There's no reason I know of as to why she would be murdered.'

Oh yes you do.

'Has Rosalind Miller been interviewed?' she asked me quickly, before looking down at her empty coffee cup. I leaned forward and steepled my hands.

'Yes, Townsville CIB questioned her, but she didn't mention seeing Ms Hird's latest lover. '

She eyed me warily. 'Rosalind lived on the mainland. It's unlikely she would have seen him.'

'Did you ever see the boat and its name?' I asked.

'I saw it on several occasions at night when I was walking my dog along the cliff near the house. It's a big white one, and no, it's never been close enough to shore to see the name.' So he, or his employer are pretty well-heeled.

'Did Ms Hird have an agent?'

'She did at one time, but they fell out. Georgie did all her own business in recent years.'

'Do you know why? What was the agent's name?' I asked. This sounded promising.

'It was a woman, but it was a long time ago and I can't remember her name. It would probably be among Georgie's papers. Something about her not doing the right thing.'

My Townsville counterpart had divulged other information. Georgie Hird had not forgotten her pseudo family in her will. Ally inherited her cottage and most of its contents, Pamela Miller her jewellery. Jessica Rallison would receive several paintings, of which there were copious numbers left to the local branch of the RSPCA. Eloise and Rosalind Miller were to share her cash and considerable investments. Eloise inherited the current dog as well. I hoped Georgie Hird had made this arrangement with her previously, but I suspected there would always be room for one more animal in Eloise's home.

I had every intention of asking her to come to the station, so we could interview her in depth and have her sign a statement. 'Would you like another cup of coffee?' I suggested, hoping to keep her relaxed.

For a moment, it looked as though she would accept, but suddenly she glanced over my shoulder and stiffened. As I turned to see what had attracted her attention, she jumped up from her seat. 'I'm sorry, Mrs Prescott, I've just seen someone I know. Are you finished?' she asked distractedly, gathering up her handbag.

'Er, yes, but I need your—'Eloise bolted out the door, '—address.'

Left with my mouth open and feeling foolish, I stood

up and hurried to the front of the café, but there was no sign of her. Cursing myself for being sluggish on the uptake, I returned to the table and stuffed my notes into my briefcase, picked up my handbag and left the café.

At least I had obtained more information for Townsville CIB. No one could hide that well for over eighteen months. The crew of the island ferry, trawlers, pleasure boats, and fishermen moored off the island. Someone, somewhere, knew the man's name and where he had come from. I would catch up with Eloise Carpenter again very shortly.

As I walked to my car, depression descended again. My cold raged and I was about to override all my principles, the code I followed throughout my law enforcement career. I was going to conceal something which, if discovered, could actually compromise the case and get me severely reprimanded.

If my husband's final investigations yielded what we suspected, then I had just been having coffee with my sister-in-law.

CHAPTER 25

On The Mountain

Eloise

Wednesday: 12.15am.

I pushed the car through the traffic as fast as I dared, slipping through amber lights, dodging jay-walking pedestrians and zipping recklessly past delivery vans. Three cars ahead, the small nondescript, silver something-or-other ploughed on.

I enjoyed having coffee with the always professional Senior Sergeant. Apart from when she was asking questions about Georgie and a possible lover, she was friendly and chatty. It was time out from fear, sort of. Under other circumstances we could have been friends, but she is a policewoman. She's so good at making people want to spill their innermost secrets that I almost blurted out the truth about Ally's abduction. But she would take charge. It's her job and Ally's already in terrible danger.

Susan Prescott's mouth dropped open as I bolted from the café. I was sure I had seen Georgie's lover drive past going toward the city. I had forgotten to mention the man's square, bullish head. His image was fresh in my mind because I'd just been talking about him, and of course I saw him from only a few feet away the night he visited Georgie, but I would stake my life on it being him.

We crossed the William Jolly Bridge and set course for the northern suburbs. Mine was the third car back, but the cars in front of me peeled off at the next lights, so the small Mazda sedan was right in front of me. I could just see the odd shape of the driver's head and the top half of his female passenger's. She kept turning toward him; occasionally he would turn to look at her. Had he ever seen me with Georgie on the island? I know there were photos of us together in her house, so he might recognise me. I was determined not to let that creature get away without discovering his lair. Whether or not he was somehow connected to Georgie's death, I had to know what he was doing in Brisbane. And so help me God I would somehow have him killed, if he was the one who had taken Ally. James would find a way.

I reached over to the back seat and grabbed my new sun hat, clapped it on my head, fumbled in my handbag for my sunglasses, then tipped the car's sun visor down hoping it would hide me. My shoulders were hunched and stiff with tension, my hands locked in a death-grip on the steering-wheel.

The car phone rang, almost causing me to jump out of my skin. I had never been in a vehicle which had one as part of the normal equipment. My caller was James. Despite the fact that it's illegal to talk on the phone whilst driving, I had to take a chance on the police catching me.

His voice was a cheep which broke up as I passed through mobile dead spots.

'Eloise? Where are you? I...ring you at Pam's place... no answer...where...coming back...'

Keeping my eyes on the car ahead, I screamed back, trying to talk like a ventriloquist so no one would see my lips moving and know I was on the phone.

'I'm following a man I think is Georgie's lover! '

'Whaaaat? I can't...you!'

'I thought I saw Georgie's lover.' My voice wobbled perilously.' You know, my friend who was murdered?'

His voice finally came through, loud and clear, nearly blasting my ears off. 'Where was he?'

'In the West End. This morning I met Detective Senior Sergeant Prescott at a café just down from Pam's place. She asked me all sorts of questions about Georgie.'

I struggled to concentrate as tears welled up in my eyes. No matter what, I had to keep the other car in sight. Another driver cut in ahead of me. The small silver sedan sped up. Has he realised he's being followed?

'Go on!' James shouted into the momentary pause, as I slowed behind the car in front.

'She asked me if I knew anything about Georgie. Who she was sleeping with or who might have it in for her,' I explained. The silver car was pulling far ahead. We were passing through an outer suburb and I swerved to miss a pedestrian who turned to give me the evil eye. In a burst of frustration and rage, I actually gave him the forks.

We cleared the tiny local shopping centre and the car in front turned off into a side road. I was immediately behind the silver vehicle again. Would he realise he was being followed? And if he did, then what would I do? As I drove, I filled James in on what had transpired in the café and when I told him I had almost confided in the Senior Sergeant, he was adamant and exhorted me not to give in.

The reception started breaking up as we reached the foothills.

'What's he doing now?' asked James.

'Nothing, just driving...I'm still a few cars behind him. How did the eBay buying go?'

'Well,' he replied dryly, 'I could shower you with diamond rings, priceless paintings which aren't at all our taste.'

'Uh oh, he's turning off and stopping! I'll have to keep going!'

'El!...Eloise...wa—' I'd lost James's voice for good this time.

I swept past the silver sedan, peering at my quarry out of the corner of my eye as I drew level with his car window, then flicked my eyes to the left and back to the front as he turned his head to glance at me. I caught a fleeting glimpse of him and his passenger's face as I drove. He was wearing sunglasses and looked reasonably innocuous, but I would recognise him again. His passenger certainly would know me, but the Lexus' tinted windows may well have obstructed her view. I drove steadily into the mountains, not daring to turn around, sick at heart and ready to collapse.

Then I almost "blew it." Suddenly the little car appeared, only a few hundred metres behind me. My legs started to shake again; my heart pounded. He had to know I was following him or was he simply moving over to let my car pass? The Lexus was faster than the Mazda; maybe he was a courteous driver. A mad snort of laughter burst out of me, but my hands trembled on the wheel as I realised my immediate predicament. Had the hunter become the hunted?

I drove on, looking for somewhere to turn off and hide. In the movies the heroine escapes or finds a place to park in the city when she needs it. I didn't have the nerve to duck down a driveway. What if the owners were at home? I could always pretend I was lost, but if the place I chose belonged to him, the outcome didn't bear thinking about.

I might have to drive the long way home across the mountain range, around the big dam and through pro-

bling all over and sick with despair.

The passenger in the silver Mazda had been one of my dearest friends for twenty-five years: Pam's mother, Rosalind, who was supposed to be minding my cottage and animals on Masters Island.

CHAPTER 26
A Wedge Between Friends

Pamela

Wednesday: 9.00am.

I stepped out of the lift and paused. Unusually, the place was deserted near the dressing rooms. I tried not to run as I navigated the silent corridors leading to the concert hall, my feet echoing around the building. The clanking of a cleaner's buckets in the ladies loo reassured me a little as I passed, but suddenly the thought occurred that maybe rehearsal was being held somewhere else. The usual noises were not coming from the auditorium, but when I arrived on stage, the orchestra was seated.

My fellow musicians eyed me uneasily as I threaded my way between music stands and chairs to my designated place. The normal racket of eighty chattering, laughing people getting ready for rehearsal, was absent. There were no jokes, no betting on the coming weekend's football outcomes or, ominously, gossip. Even the two most placid of men, Bob and Hans, emitted an aura of quiet agitation.

Jess's appearance shocked me. She's so beautiful that when she comes into a room, men point their noses in the air like gun-dogs and snap to attention. But now her eyes were huge smudges in her pale face and her hair was knotted untidily, with strands flopping around her shoulders. Sensing my gaze, she looked up, but gave me no acknowledgement. Her eyelids flickered, and then she stared at her score without expression. I remembered the fear in her voice when I told her about Georgie's death and felt uneasy.

Brie appeared to be lost in thought. Lines of tiredness and worry etched his face, making him appear older than his twenty-eight years. He turned his head to speak to someone and I was shocked by the dark marks on his throat and a cut on his cheekbone. Had he been in a fight? Or were they the signs of enthusiastic sex? Surely not. *But had he been lying to us all along?*

I felt as though I was under siege. The television channels were full of the news of Ally's disappearance. Early last night, Aunt Eloise phoned to say she was staying with James. Ally's agent phoned, as did her accountant, who pretty much only crawls out of the woodwork around taxation time, and just about every friend she's ever made. Skype ran hot with calls from overseas as conductors, musicians and ex-boyfriends phoned or wanted to chat. My email had to be emptied several times and my snail mailbox bulged with cards. Friends ringing the doorbell day and night have contributed to the manager of the units where I live complaining about the other tenant's privacy being compromised. 'Your lease is up next month, Miss Miller. We might have to consider our options,' he rumbled spitefully. My eyelids twitched with exhaustion. I'm not good at keeping secrets, and "worry" has morphed from hobby to habit.

Sir James McPherson lurked at the piano talking to James Kirkbridge and John, the orchestra manager. Their faces looked haggard under the brilliant stage lighting. I sensed someone behind me and flicked a glance over my shoulder. Michael was crowding my personal space. Something alien glinted in his eyes, but then it was gone.

He turned away, every line of his body saying, *'Shuttered. Don't pry.'* I felt as though I had climbed down a ladder and unexpectedly found a rung missing. Embarrassed, I turned back to my music.

Because Sir James was fart-arsing around talking to some of my colleagues, I allowed my mind to drift, inevitably, to the past.

After we graduated from the Conservatorium, Ally and Jess's careers surged ahead. Fortunately my CDs are good sellers; old ladies in nursing homes are particularly partial to them I am told. 'So cheerful, dear' one wrote, but solo performances drive me insane. My nerves get so shot before a concert, the stage-hands leave a bucket next to the entrance just for me, Puking Pam. But as part of a large orchestra, I adore my career.

Would I be completely fulfilled if I had someone to love and who loved me? All my life, I've sensed an empty space beside me, with no understanding of why it should be so. The part of me which feels missing returns strongly in times of stress. Bobby, my imaginary childhood friend, filled a gap which even Ally was unable to do. Sometimes I still manage to summon him up from wherever he is domiciled while my back is turned. *Am I such a desperate that I have to rely on a phantom? So alone that even as an adult, I revert to a childhood imaginary friend.*

Most of the men I date are either divorced, getting over a relationship or commitment-phobic, and almost all shorter than I am. It's no joke being 183cm and nor are the "funnies" people make about it.

Brie dated me a couple of times after we met, but when Jess joined the orchestra he lost interest. At first I was hurt, but to be honest, hadn't seriously believed anything would eventuate from our three or four casual dates.

I rarely saw either Jess or Brie socially during their relationship. I think they only got out of bed to go to work, but as fast as it began, the affair burnt itself out. He was the one to break it off and I couldn't help feeling just a little bit pleased. Yeah, I'm a vengeful hag. I saw him first, Jess. Not that that made any difference in the long run.

The percussionist Michael Whitby joined the orchestra from the Melbourne Symphony. My friendship with him appeared to be progressing well, when Guess Who loomed on the horizon? Overnight, he scudded out of my orbit into Jessica's. Once again I felt abandoned, bereft and unattractive. Damn, stop whining, Pam. Get over it.

Now, Jess has found someone else while keeping Michael dancing on her g-string. 'I'm keeping him to myself, Pammie,' she confided, 'but this time it's the real thing!'

Each time the phone rang my heart jumped, but every call broke my heart. I had lost my friend, the only sister I would ever have. We were born on the same day, in the same hospital, Ally ten minutes or so after me. I try not to visualise the desolate years ahead, the birthdays we might never share, the bridal and baby showers we may never throw for each other if the worst has happened to Ally. Fear for her safety threatens to send me spiralling into a mass of pain from which there might be no escape.

'Miss Miller? Are we to have the pleasure of your company, or are you planning on just being a pretty face?'

I jumped, sending my music score flying and kicking my instrument case across the floor. Sir James stood on the podium with his hands on his hips, glaring down at me, his baton clasped firmly in his left hand, sticking out at a mad angle like the tail of an animal. The orchestra waited with breathless anticipation for him to tear me to pieces. Embarrassed, I squatted and dragged my case back beside me, scrambling to pick up the sheets of music scattered around my feet.

'Er, I'm sorry, Sir James, won't be a moment.'

'That's all right, Miss Miller.' He flashed a savage smile. 'We'll wait. After all, we have nothing better to do today.'

Somehow I got back onto my chair without causing any more trouble, picked up my flute and waited for his cue. I was startled when he glanced at me sympathetically before looking down at his score and raising his arms. I gathered myself, grateful for the glorious, comforting music of Bach.

Wednesday: 4.30pm.

By four o'clock we were all shattered; nobody wanted to linger. The stairs echoed with the sounds of racing feet, the lift shot up and down like a demented bathescope. Musicians burned rubber in their haste to get out of the underground car park.

Sighing, I picked up my gear and turned to leave. Jess, Michael and Brie were standing by the door waiting for me. Michael was reading something on a small piece of paper, but I sensed it was an excuse to avoid eye contact with us. As I walked slowly toward them my eyes met those of Jess and then skipped to Brie. A vibe passed between us, a feeling all was not as it seemed.

Suspicion had driven a wedge through our friendship the size of a Mac truck.

CHAPTER 27

A Precarious Position

Brie

Wednesday: 7.30pm.

A brisk breeze swayed the branches of tree under which I parked. I kept the window halfway down and listened to the sounds and smells of people living—a radio playing just inside the window in front of which I had parked and nearby, someone cooking.

A few dogs walked their owners around the block. People were still trickling home from work and some obviously leaving for a night out. Further along the street, a woman screeched with laughter and a car door slammed, followed by the purr of a very expensive motor. I ducked down as it sped past.

Light from the street lamp made it dangerous to lurk any closer to Jess's house. A drive-by observation had revealed no more than a soft glow inside from the skirting-board light which would be on in the hallway. When she went out, it would be a good chance to collect the bug I stuck on the underside of her kitchen table.

I wriggled around, trying to stretch my legs. Rehearsals had been fucking terrible. We made stupid mistake after even stupider ones, which sent Sir James into a rage, and were all glad to finish the rehearsal. Pam, Jess, Michael and I headed gratefully for our vehicles, barely stopping to talk. In order to find out whether she was going to be home, I asked Jess if she wanted to go for a drink after work, but she declined and archly informed me she had a date. Assuming an expression of mild regret, I wished her good night. Michael dived into his vehicle and took off, sour-faced, with a squeal of tires. Obviously he was not the one she was going out with.

I wondered about the type of relationship Jess had with the people living on the mountain, particularly the bloke who nearly throttled me. Was he the new boyfriend? She had a sister, but the older couple couldn't have been her parents. She hated them and would never have kissed her father. There was nothing to suggest those people had anything to do with Ally's disappearance and I felt foolish now, stalking Jess. Out of the corner of my eye, I had seen Pam's expression when she spotted the bruises on my throat. A couple of friends in the orchestra saw them too and teased me about my sex life. No one realised they were finger marks and guessed I had been attacked, so for once, my randy reputation came in handy.

Fear and helplessness were driving me crazy. I was trying hard to have faith in the police, but I bet they didn't know any more than I did. If I had arrived at the club sooner, if I had looked harder, if I ... but she was taken before I even got there.

If I found anything to suggest Jess had something to do with Ally's disappearance, I would tell Detective Senior Sergeant Prescott. I've never hit a woman in my life, but if Jess was involved, I wanted to kill her. I might have to settle for scaring the living shit out of her.

Enough. Time was slipping by. I started the motor, drove quietly to the dead-end, did a U-turn and stopped in front of the house. My plan was to walk up and knock as though I was expecting her to answer. If she wasn't there I would use the spare key, which I found forgotten in a drawer. With any luck, she'd not changed the locks.

The street was deserted. Next door was listening to something on TV in which sirens played a significant part. Their dog barked, unheard in his kennel on the other side of the fence. Jess's verandah boasted a canvas blind which was at half-mast on the western side. A small shoe rack placed to one side of the door held sandals and a pair of joggers.

No one answered my knock.

I glanced over my shoulder as a man came out of a house across the street and got into his car. My hands shook a little as I put the key into the lock, turned it then twisted the knob and pushed it open. Technically, I was not breaking in, but I knew I had no right to be there.

The dim night light above the skirting board illuminated the length of the hall all the way to the back of the house. I slipped inside.

My senses tingled.

Nothing stirred.

Something felt wrong.

For a moment, I couldn't work out what it was, then I realised—Jess always left music on when she was out, but there was only silence. A sliver of fear shivered its way into my gut.

I moved slowly forward, glancing into each room, wincing as a floorboard creaked.

A figure stood against the far wall of the spare bedroom. My heart leapt and I held my breath. Then I remembered Jess's dressmaking dummy. I leaned against the wall, sucking air as I waited to recover my nerve. The wind had picked up outside, rattling the canvas blind. I jumped as it bounced hard against the verandah railing.

Someone sighed, so faintly that for a moment I thought I'd imagined it. The sound came again, a slight sob. I stopped in my tracks, listening and then edged forward. Was Jess still there? Perhaps she was in bed with the new boyfriend. If they came out of the bedroom, how could I possibly explain why I was in the house? And how the hell could I get out again without getting the crap beaten out of me?

I was about to turn around and sneak out, then realised a keening sound was coming from the direction of the kitchen. I edged forward, trying not to let the floorboards creak and stopped in the doorway. A coppery stench permeated the air and made me gag. I tried not to breathe. Her electric kettle shone in the glow from the pilot light on the stove; the clock ticked loudly.

The sighing sound came again, low down. I switched the light on and scanned the room.

Nothing. I moved forward, skirting around the side of the table.

My foot touched something.

Jess was lying in front of the stove, blood flowing in rivulets from her stomach, pooling massively around her. Stunned, I dropped to my knees. 'My God, Jess, what's happened?' I asked, stupidly. Her glazed eyes stared dully back at me, her hands clamped over her stomach and blood-soaked white t-shirt. She shifted lightly; blood welled up over her fingers. Her mouth opened.

'Jess, don't try to talk. Just stay still.'

Something to wad it with. Where did she keep her tea towels? I couldn't think straight. 'I'll get an ambulance, hold on!' I begged her.

Every second counted. I wrestled my mobile phone off my belt and half-rose to dial. She flapped a weak hand on my arm. 'Brie...stop...listen...' Her bloodied hand scrabbled at my sleeve. I dropped to my knees again and leaned over her, trying to hear what she was saying. '...meant to be a joke...Ally...teach her a lesson...they...I didn't know they...meant to hurt her... '

She gasped and began to choke. Blood welled out of her mouth; she plucked at my arm.

'Don't try to talk! I'll just—'stop the bleeding. My hands shook violently. I ripped my jacket off, threw it aside then dragged my t-shirt over my head, rolled it into a ball and wadded it against the wound in her stomach. Blood saturated it in seconds. I reefed a handkerchief out of my pocket and tried to wipe her chin and neck. Weakly, she batted my hands away. More blood bubbled up. She started to speak again and I could only just make out the words.

'But they wanted revenge...the money, too...but I didn't know why...too late.'

A great flow of blood streamed out, her body rippled and her soul left her eyes. I stared down at her in horror. She couldn't be dead. I had placed my hands in the CPR position in the middle of her chest when I sensed movement behind me. I started to turn; help had arrived.

'Thank God. Phone an— '

Something crashed into my head.

I was lying on a large, bumpy, soft pillow. My skull threatened to split open, my nostrils filled with the stench of blood. I opened my eyes slowly, cringing in the light. Jess's dead face was inches from mine, her dark eyes blank.

Christ, she's gone. Who would...? I braced myself on her body, pushed up and back onto my knees and then tumbled on my arse. My chest was smeared with blood, my jeans and hair soaked. Blood splattered my face, up my nose and in my mouth. My head felt as though it would explode any moment, while my stomach considered whether to hurl where I stood or allow me a moment to get to the laundry.

I struggled to stand, but my feet slipped in the huge pool. I grabbed the table, levered myself up and skittered to the sink. Seemingly everything I'd eaten in the last twenty four hours came up. I was trembling, sweating and icy with shock. My head ached; breathing was a struggle. A row of clean glasses were upside down on the shelf above the sink. My hand shook so badly I only just managed to grab one and turn on the tap, taking several tries to get it aligned underneath the stream of water.

My teeth chattered on the rim of the glass. I rinsed my mouth and spat into the mess, letting the water flow, trying to flush the vomit down the drain. It wasn't going fast enough. I grabbed a serving ladle out of the utensil caddy and stirred. Whoever hit me over the head must have killed Jess, someone who had been in there all along, waiting for her to die, and I walked straight in, stupidly, innocently.

I turned the tap on harder, dodging the splashes as the water gushed, then pulled a tea towel from the drying rack to wipe my face. I had to ring the cops, but as I staggered over and slumped into a chair on the far side of the kitchen table, it began to dawn on me I was in a precarious position. How was I going to convince them, or anyone, I hadn't killed Jess?

I ran my hand carefully across the back of my throbbing head, into the sticky mass on my scalp. A lump was forming rapidly. The only sound was the clock ticking. Incredibly, just twelve minutes had passed since I got out of the car.

Remembering what I came for, I took a tea towel and wiped my hand before furniture-surfing weakly around the table, bending down and peering underneath. The top of my head felt as though it was coming off. I almost pitched face first onto the floor; my vision danced.

I could just see the device. Some belated instinct for self-preservation prompted me to wrap the tea towel around my hand before I touched it. After a couple of wrenches, it came unstuck and was stuffed into my pocket. I was freezing; bouts of shivering set in. I got up and wobbled over to my jacket and picked it up, trying not to fall face first onto the floor.

Jess. Beautiful, quixotic, all that talent gone. It was unbelievable...terrifying. No matter what she had done, she didn't deserve this. 'Shit, now I'll have to ring the police,' I muttered aloud, as I began to shrug myself awkwardly into the jacket.

'Oh no, Brie, you're not ringing anyone,' a familiar voice said quietly. I jumped and spun around.

She stood in the doorway, staring at me, narrow-eyed, her face as cold as winter.

Pam.

CHAPTER 28
Damage Control

Pamela

Wednesday: 8.26pm.

It was a stand-off. We each waited for the other to make the first move. He stood there, half-dressed, holding a white red-splattered t-shirt, blood smeared all over his chest, up to his throat and splashed around his ashen face. His skin shone luminous in the light, eyes dazed with hair sticking up, all gelled with blood. The stench of it filled the kitchen; nausea rose in my throat. Looking for air, I realised all the blinds were down and the curtains drawn.

Jess was lying on the floor, one arm flopped by her side, the other across her stomach. I could see something horrible poking through her blood-soaked clothes. Her face was half-turned away, eyes blank. No one was home anymore.

My heart beat faster. Would he turn on me now? I looked back at Brie, my lips so stiff I could hardly form the words. 'Why did you kill her?'

He stared at me as though I was speaking a foreign language. 'What?'

'Why did you kill her?' I couldn't seem to get through to him.

He was silent for a moment and then shook his head.

'I might ask you the same thing!' he muttered. 'Why did you kill her—and hit me?'

'I didn't kill her. And what do you mean, hit you? I just walked in here now and found you like this.' I gestured to the floor. 'Jess dead, and you covered in blood. What am I supposed to think?'

Don't look at Jess...you can't help her now and you are in danger too...keep your eyes on Brie. Get ready to fight or run.

Fear and perspiration warred to be number one. My ability to placate Brie could save my own life. So, if he was going to ring the cops was it a double bluff?

I wouldn't have thought Brie could turn paler, but he did. His legs visibly wobbled. Clutching the table for support, he lowered himself onto the chair and buried his head in his hands. I looked around the room; there was nothing close to hand to defend myself with.

'How did you get in here' he asked.

'The front door was half-open,' I replied.

'But I closed it after—' he paused, '—I came in.'

I had more important things on my mind. 'Where's the knife?'

'*What* knife?'

'The one you stabbed her with of course,' I snarled.

He was dazed, barely functioning and appeared harmless enough. I stepped forward, bent and glanced under the table; nothing. I braced myself to search the area around Jess. No knife. The cutlery drawer was pulled out, but there was nothing which looked remotely like a murder weapon in there. A wooden kitchen-knife block stood on the counter, but none were missing.

'Answer me, Brie! *Where is it?*' I was ready to bolt for the front door.

He looked up, his lips moving soundlessly. I stepped to the sink, and picked up the glass on the draining board to pour him some water, but the stench of vomit coming from the drain hit me like a wave. Trying not to breathe, I filled the glass and handed it to him. He swallowed it in a couple of gulps and took a deep breath.

'I don't know about a knife. Pam, I swear to you, I didn't touch her. I came around to talk to her and I found her…dying. I tried to help and then someone hit me.'

A likely tale, but when he put his head down on his hands again, I saw blood oozing from a sticky wound on the back of his skull. Instinct told me he wasn't a cold-blooded killer, but what about a crime of passion? Their relationship ended quite a while ago and now he was mad about Ally, but Jess possessed a talent for taunting men into rage. Could there have been an argument which ended in murder? And if Brie hadn't killed Jess, was it the new boyfriend? Or an ex-boyfriend? My thoughts flew to Michael.

The killer should be well and truly gone, but what if he was still around? I listened carefully, trying to pick up the vibe of the house but couldn't sense any other presence. If someone had been there, he could have sneaked out while we were talking. I had to make a decision.

'Right. What have you touched?'

'I don't know. I can't think …' Brie shook himself, as though coming up for air and pushed himself upright. 'Pam, I must call the police. We have to call the police.'

'No. No. You're not ringing the police! *If you do, Ally will be killed!*'

His mouth opened in astonishment, but I cut him off before he could speak. 'Believe me, it's true. Now, shut up and pay attention. What-have-you-touched?' I enunciated, trying to get his attention.

He gestured to the sink area. 'The bench, taps, the sink, table, chair, the drawer. What do *you* know about

Ally's disappearance, Pam?' His eyes gleamed with suspicion.

'I'll tell you later, there's no time now.' I swept to the sink, placed the hem of my skirt over the handle of the drawer where I knew Jess kept her dishcloths and rubber gloves, opened it and pulled on a pair of green ones. Then I picked out a cloth, wet it, squirted on some dishwashing liquid and began to scrub the sink, taps and surrounds, the drawer handle and all the places I suspected had our fingerprints on them.

'We've got to get out of here. Get your things together, while I finish this. We'll talk when we get back to your place.' I whisked to the table and wiped around the edges and top, which bore the marks of his blood-soaked hands.

He picked up his t-shirt and a bloodied tea-towel, scrunched them into a ball and started to shrug into his jacket again, his face pinched with pain. I felt no sympathy for him. I needed to prevent him calling the police and that meant recounting what had really happened, and the reason why Ally had disappeared. But first we had to get out of there. Fast.

Keep going, don't stop whatever you do! Don't look at Jess.

When I was satisfied that the chair was thoroughly wiped, I grabbed a garbage bag out of the cupboard, threw the tea towel, dishcloths, glass, ladle and fork into it, then held the top open for Brie to add his t-shirt. I looked at his feet.

'Go over there,' I jerked my head at the laundry door, 'take your joggers off and hand them to me. Keep your socks on and don't step in the blood.' My voice cracked on the last word.

He removed his joggers without argument. I squatted and wiped the floor where he left footprints going to the sink, then threw his things into the bag, ripped off the rubber gloves, put them in and twisted the top tightly closed.

'Now, we're walking out of here, calmly and quietly. Be careful where you step. If we see someone watching or walking their dog or whatever when we get outside, we'll stand for a moment at the front door, pretend we've just arrived and knock on it. Right?'

He nodded, as he pulled the sides of his coat together and zipped it up to his chin. I looked at him closely. Please God, he wouldn't blow it now, but he seemed to have recovered a little and appeared to be willing, for the moment, to let me run the show. I fished in my bra for a tissue and used it to polish the light switch after we turned it off.

The dim bulb on the hall skirting-board prevented us bumping into anything on the way out. Jess had heavy blinds installed in every room of the house to prevent the creep next door looking at her, so it was unlikely anyone could have seen the kitchen light from outside.

I opened the front door with the tissue in the palm of my hand, then we stepped onto the tiny verandah. Before we closed the door behind us, I wiped both the inside and outside knobs again. As we turned to leave, I almost knocked over a low rack holding a pair of Jess's sandals. Next door's dog barked and we braced ourselves to go through the pantomime of just arriving, but the TV inside their house continued to blare. I tucked the garbage bag under my arm.

'Where's your car?'

Brie nodded at a small nondescript sedan parked at the front of the house.

'That's not yours.'

'I borrowed it from a mate. But Pam, I don't know if I can drive home.' He touched the back of his head. I looked at him suspiciously. 'I needed to get something from the house while Jess was out, so as I had a key and—the key! Where—'

His eyes darted around in panic, before he slapped his pocket and pulled out a key, letting out an audible sigh of relief. I realised I had been holding my breath. Resisting the impulse to sag to the ground and scream, I tugged his arm.

'Now, get back to your car, Brie, and follow me. I know somewhere near here where it won't attract attention. We'll leave it for the night and go to your place and then I'll jog back for it in the morning. Be careful. So help me God, if you get picked up by the cops I really will kill you!' I snarled.

He shrugged and didn't answer, just folded himself awkwardly into the ridiculous little car and slowly followed me to a quiet street, where he parked and locked it up. The short journey back to his flat was uneventful, but nevertheless I breathed a sigh of relief when it was over and we were safely inside.

'I've got to clean up, Pam. How about you pour yourself a drink?' he said, gesturing to the liquor cabinet.

I had other things on my mind. 'Have you washed the clothes you wore yesterday?'

He looked at me, puzzled. 'No. They're still in the heap.'

'Okay. Listen carefully. Make sure you change into yesterday's clothes after you've showered. Spray these—' I gestured toward the bloodied gear he still wore, '—with stain remover. Soak them in it and put them into the washing machine immediately. Everything— socks, underdaks, shirt and jeans. Do two cycles and then put them into the dryer. When they're finished, take them out and put them back on. Wear them every day, wash and dry the undies overnight. *Do not* put them into the washing pile. Put your joggers into the machine after your clothes. If the worst happens and the cops ask you for the things you were wearing tonight, then give them yesterday's. Are you following me?'

Brie stared at me, rabbit-in-the-headlights, while he worked it out, then nodded carefully and tottered toward his bedroom.

Grabbing a full bottle of Scotch, I stalked into the kitchen, got two large glasses, sloshed it in neat, followed it up with ice and took a huge gulp. Then I picked up the bag containing the utensils, towel, and t-shirt, resolving to put it in my car first thing in the morning. The t-shirt would go in the wash and I would figure out what to do with the rest.

Suddenly my legs gave way. I flopped into a chair, barely managing to put the glass down. Liquor slopped onto the surface of the table. Tremors started in my arms and worked their way through my body. I gasped and shuddered, as tears poured from my eyes. Jess. Jess dead.

Grief and fear overwhelmed me. I stuffed my icy hands between my knees and rocked backward and forward, weeping for I don't know how long. Then Brie wrapped his arms around me and held me tightly to his broad chest. We wept for Jess, for Ally and for the peril we were in. Finally, we managed to pull ourselves together. I wiped my eyes and took another big swig of whisky.

'Careful, you'll get sloshed,' cautioned Brie. He declined the shot I poured for him and went to the fridge from which he took a cordial. He didn't look much better, though some of his colour had returned. Hospital wasn't an option because of what had happened. His hands shook as he drank the sweet liquid and handed me a towel to wipe my eyes. A couple of mouthfuls were all it took for the whisky to fire through my stomach.

'Are those yesterday's clothes you have on?'

'Yeah,' he replied quietly. He was exhausted and probably suffering from mild concussion. He shouldn't have driven even a short distance, but there had been no option.

We needed to re-group. 'Now, tell me everything. And don't leave anything out!'

He started with the outcome of his visit to the police station on Saturday afternoon, right up until that moment. Amazed, I listened as he described his stunt with the recorder and the wild ride through the mountains, the fight with the stranger resulting in the bruises to his throat, culminating with finding Jess and being hit over the head.

When he finished he leaned back in his chair, limp with exhaustion. I stared at him wordlessly. Undoubtedly, he had alerted the kidnappers to the fact that he was nosing around, and now Ally would be in even greater danger than before. Fear made me lash out at him.

'You fucking idiot! Who do you think you are, Bruce-fucking-Willis? What else have you stuffed up?' I shouted. 'You could have been killed. Someone must have been still in the house to hit you over the head!' I was about to hit him myself.

'Keep your voice down,' he hissed. 'I thought I saw someone in the spare bedroom, but it was only Jess's dressmaker dummy.'

'Jess sold that dummy on eBay a month or more ago,' I advised him, very, very quietly.

We made eye contact, silently acknowledging who had hit Brie over the head and why. 'Where's the tape?' I asked, finally. He fossicked around in his addled brain, remembered where it was and walked unsteadily down the hallway. A few minutes later, he returned with the recorder which he put on the table, then sat down and tried to pour another cordial. His hands trembled so badly, I took the bottle and did it for him.

'I'm surprised he didn't kill me too,' Brie said, after he gulped a mouthful.

'That's easy. You're meant to take the blame for her death!'

'So who could have killed Jess?'

'How the fuck should I know?' I snapped, exhausted.

After a moment's silence, he smiled weakly and apologised. 'I'm sorry, Pam. We're too stressed to cope, that's all. What about this thing, then?'

We looked at the little machine; the moment of truth was at hand. Brie flicked a switch and Jess's voice came through. We couldn't make out much. She talked about her work and inconsequential things, but we did hear the most important bits.

'...no, I don't Angel...why not?' There was silence for a moment, as she listened to what the person on the other end of the phone was saying, then: 'No! You can't, you told me it was a...money? *No, not Ally!*'

Her voice broke up into static. Now we had the nickname of her boyfriend, or girlfriend. So Jess's words bore out Brie's version of what she said to him before she died. We let it run for a while, but the recording broke up into static.

'I hoped it might work better than that,' Brie said, dejectedly.

'It doesn't matter, at least we know she was involved with someone, knew about Ally's kidnapping and after what she told you...' I paused.

Jess sounded concerned for Ally. Were the kidnappers getting edgy? At least it appeared she was still alive and I knew her parents were working hard on amassing the ransom.

Brie's movements were slow, his eyes slightly unfocused, but he had more colour in his face.

'So, what do you know about Ally being kidnapped? I think you had better tell me everything too, Pam. I'm grateful for what you did at Jess's, but I still think we should have called the police. If they find out we were there and destroyed evidence the shit's going to fly, all over me. It's not too late to call now.'

'Hang on a sec, we need coffee. I'm getting tipsy.' I got up and went to put the electric kettle on. I needed to fill him in on the real reason for the kidnapping which tied in with Jess's words on the tape. I didn't dare think of his last comment about destroying the evidence. I wasn't at all sure that move had been wise, but it was done. There was no going back. A thought nagged at the back of my mind. Something I had forgotten...

Then I realised what it was.

Brie's taupe-coloured handkerchief was lying by Jess's head, but I had neglected to put it in the garbage bag.

CHAPTER 29
Re-grouping

Wednesday: 9.30pm.

They met at the house on the mountain, faces tense. The operation could be in danger of falling apart. The father was defensive and resentful, because he couldn't condemn the son for committing the same crime of which he, himself, was guilty. They hadn't planned on murder yet, but hey—shit happens.

If the artist hadn't pushed him, he wouldn't have done it. For twenty months he had kept her sweet, while the arrangements were made for grabbing the girl. A good fuck and she would do anything for him. Georgie needed a lover, was only too happy to take one when the opportunity arose and he was an expert in bed. She wasn't beautiful, but with her arresting looks, it hadn't been a hardship. He needed only to keep it up, literally and figuratively, when his employer made fishing trips to Masters Island, or on the occasions when Georgie met him in the city. He would meet with her just often enough to maintain a relationship and to keep her happy.

Several times he had gone to her house quite openly. He was confident no one would remember him among the hundreds of tourists who caught the ferry to the island in summer. When she brought her paintings to Brisbane, they could meet without fear of them being observed. She had accepted everything he said without question, until Monday night.

The cops could never connect him with the murder. He had been at the island legitimately since Saturday afternoon, one of many yachtsmen anchored off the island. His boss spent the evening with friends in the bar of the local hotel, and had not realised his captain was away from the yacht. The crew were drinking on the other side of the island.

It was a shock when Georgie confronted him, but he hadn't wasted any time. She liked to knit. He'd snatched up one of her steel needles and driven it into her heart, before she had time to understand what was happening. In the second before she died, her accusing gaze told him she realised he was indeed responsible for Ally Carpenter's disappearance.

He dragged her to the back door of her house, turned the light out and picked her up in a fireman's lift. With the Carpenter woman gone, there was no one to witness it. Just before he threw her over the cliff, he identified the perfect means of further terrorising the girl's parents into cooperating, without damaging the "golden goose." He took the fishing knife from the pouch on his belt and cut off Georgie's earlobe, which he put in the freezer of the bar fridge in his cabin on the yacht. It was a simple matter to insert Ally Carpenter's earring into the dead flesh when he arrived in Brisbane. His face creased with pleasure, as he pictured the mother's face when she saw that particular offering.

Another lonely, middle-aged woman, Rosalind Miller had been only too eager to make acquaintance with the dark-haired attractive man in the mainland supermarket, ten days ago. She had fallen into his hands like an overripe mango, a bonus when she confided her friendship with the Carpenters. A few honeyed words to the trusting woman and he found out everything about the mother, and how the police investigation was progressing.

His wife was enthusiastic. 'Keep in with her so we can find out what's going on.'

Just as well his wife was not quite so keen on sex any more. He had his doubts about keeping June and Georgie satisfied, but it worked out just fine. It wasn't until he actually killed Georgie, he realised he had grown fond of her. But she signed her own death warrant by questioning him about whether he had told anyone the identity of the girl's father. In spite of his denials, she accused him of being involved.

He wasn't sure it had been a good idea to invite Ros to fly down to Brisbane for a romantic interlude so soon after Georgie's death, and he wondered briefly about the woman who had driven behind them up the mountain. But she had vanished, so he must have been mistaken in suspecting she was following them. 'Coincidences do actually happen,' he assured himself.

They had another bad moment when someone followed Jess into the property on the mountain a couple of nights ago. He had taken Angel to task for chasing and assaulting the driver.

'What did you do that for? Now he's going to wonder what was so important that you had to attack him. You could have fucked up the whole operation if he'd gone to the cops!'

'How was I to know? Anyway he had no business coming in here,' his son replied, truculently.

'He probably just came to the wrong address. I would have re-directed him and he'd have gone off, none the wiser. But no, you had to be the big hero.'

But as far as they knew, there had been no repercussions. The driver might have good reason for not going to the cops, such as he'd been spying on them, or maybe the bloke thought he had stirred up an irate householder and wasn't going to make an issue of the it.

They just needed to sit tight. Almost a million dollars had poured in already. They had made the second phone call and Ally Carpenter's father agreed to everything they asked, more money drops and keeping on with eBay. The family laughed, as he mimicked the father's strained tones. It was good to keep him on the run and busy, because there wouldn't be much danger of them going to the cops.

Everything appeared to be going to plan, but now they had a situation on their hands: the murder of the violinist. He struggled to contain his anger and fear. This latest hiccup might blow their plans wide open.

'She found out why we really snatched the girl. She threatened me,' Angel growled, his eyes glittering.

Even the father felt a moment of unease; his eldest child was dangerously unpredictable. The stepmother watched impassively. Her own father, the fourth member of the group, cracked his knuckles and turned his head away. His favourite possession, his shotgun, stood propped by his side.

Her husband continued to scold his son. 'You could have brought her here again. We would have talked her around, reminded her it was her own idea to begin with and we were only helping her to ruin the Carpenter girl's career. Doing her a favour. You didn't have to go off half-cocked and kill her, you stupid bastard!'

He jumped to his feet and began to pace, his mouth tight and angry. He should have bashed the kid more often when he was little. The boy had always been violent and whereas that was occasionally handy, this time it was a liability. Mind you, when they got rid of the pianist, Angel would do it, no worries, but for now he had to be kept under control. That meant calming him down. In spite of everything, he loved his son, and you didn't cry over spilt milk. You got on with the job.

He rested a hand on his son's shoulder. 'Okay, okay, it's done. Now we have to decide what to do. You're sure you left no fingerprints? No traces of anything?'

The son shook his head, tossed off the remains of his drink and slammed the glass down on the table beside him, wincing from the pain in his arm. The flesh was deeply bruised when the intruder crushed it in the window of the car.

His stepmother leaned forward anxiously. 'What about the knife? Where is it? You should have got rid of it!'

He didn't answer, just smiled, bent to the battered backpack resting on the floor beside his chair and undid the buckles. Slowly he retrieved something bundled in bloodied material, which he unwrapped with care. The fishing knife lay wickedly in its bed of lilac-coloured towelling, its eight-inch blade and soft rubber grip smeared heavily with congealed blood. The sharp tang of it filled their nostrils. The father didn't want to look too closely at something grisly, which remained caught on a serrated point.

'Whose towel? It was one of Jess's?' He wanted to be sure.

'Yep, but they'll never know it's missing.' The son smiled pitilessly. A memory of Jess, wrapped in it, flashed across his mind, all the sweeter for the last time he had seen her. He licked his lips as he re-wrapped his favourite knife and handed the bundle to his stepmother. He knew she would do a perfect job.

'We'll clean it up and keep it for next time, darling,' she smiled. Her short, black hair gleamed in the firelight and her eyes glowed with love as she looked at her stepson. She had removed the theatrical cheek pads and discarded the nondescript wig before she left for the mountains. Ally Carpenter would have had trouble recognising her as the masked woman who accompanied "Scarpia" on his bi-daily visits.

They would hold their hostage until the last possible moment while they milked her father for everything they could. A couple more days and they'd get rid of the girl, but for now the money was flowing in smoothly. The wife needed to wreak her revenge and the son had plans for her, pre-death.

There were really no problems, apart from the murder of the violinist. All they had to do was keep their heads down and not attract attention to themselves. Satisfied, they listened as the woman turned on the taps in the laundry.

'We'll have a cup of tea when you've finished with that!' called the father, as he switched on the television. The three men settled down to watch the soccer, having re-assured each other nothing could connect them with either crime, as long as they held their nerve.

CHAPTER 30

Dark Aura

Ally

Thursday: dawn.

At first light, the little room takes on a surreal glow and it's possible to pretend each day might be the one they let me go. They've warned my father against calling in the police or they'll send him bits of me. Will my fingers be next? They would love the chance to ruin my career and my life. My terror of that is so great, I can't allow myself to dwell on it.

Pain stabs through me if I try to take more than shallow breaths. I think my ribs might be broken. My face is so sore I can hardly bear to touch it. My left eye is feeling better. I can open it a little bit now.

I try to remember every single note of music I've ever learned, but even Schubert's glorious Litany cannot calm me.

God, please keep the police hunting for me.

'What if mum can't get to my father, or he thinks it's a scam and won't pay? Perhaps he doesn't believe I exist. Could she get DNA done on my hair and blood in time to convince him to save me?

My mind scuds willy-nilly, seeking ways I might escape, but who am I kidding? My body aches. I force myself to roll over, reach out and break my fall to the floor, as the stretcher tips me out. It's only centimetres, but feels like falling through forty feet. I struggle onto my knees, bracing my hand against the wall. 'You can do it...come on, Ally.'

Was that someone talking? Where? I struggle up, totter to the window and squint through the grill but see nothing different. Am I hallucinating now? Outside, everything is still the same, acres of lawn and distant trees. I press my face gently against the metal, wincing as I try to get an angle view. There is no other building in sight, no one to signal to and no one can see me.

Nausea again. Crush it. I grab the window sill with both hands. Bloody arms are shaking. They didn't speak or acknowledge me in any way last night. The woman leaned through the door and dumped a sandwich on the floor, while he stood in the entrance. The silence is more frightening than his taunts. It's as though there's nothing more to say.

The seal on the water bottle's not broken and I can't feel a pin hole anywhere on it. I twist the top open and take a cautious sip. The wind is rushing across the top of the building, making a piece of tin clatter somewhere. My mind flips around, unable to let go of the obvious. What reason, other than money, could there be for someone to kidnap me and hold my father to ransom? Spite? Revenge for a business defeat? Jealousy? Maybe it is just about the money.

They're here again. It's too early in the day. The door opens, the woman stoops and places a packet on the floor. The expression in her eyes is like a leopard stalking its prey, daring me to run so she can bring me down, sink her teeth into my neck and tear out my life.

Scarpia stands between us, assessing me through the eye sockets of his balaclava, knowing me. I was drugged when he attempted to have sex with me, but I know what I felt. The shame of my body's betrayal crawls through me.

He won't touch me while she's close by, but there's no comfort in that. We make eye contact. Dark energy emanates from him; there's something he wants me to understand. I don't want to know what he's done now.

I can't bear this, day after day. Will they ever let me go? No.

I've seen his face.

I need to hide inside myself in this naked room, an unlikely sanctuary most times, but one which they invade at will.

CHAPTER 31

Dubiety

Brie

Thursday: 2.00am.

I woke up and couldn't get settled again. Images of Jess's staring eyes catapulted me from one scenario to the next on a searing round trip in limbo, with Armageddon along for the ride. The smell of death flared in my nostrils making me inhale carefully, trying to ignore the nausea swirling in my stomach. I dropped off to sleep again, but only minutes seemed to pass before I jerked awake, heart pounding as I fought sweat-soaked sheets. At 3.30am, I crawled out of bed and staggered to the kitchen to make coffee and find some panadol for my aching head.

I couldn't believe only eight hours had passed since Jess died. It was unlikely she had been found, but fear rippled through and around me. Would anyone remember seeing the old hatchback parked down the road? It still had to be collected. *Christ almighty, how are we going to get out of this?*

Images of happier times jostled memories of the night before, Jess laughing up at me in a park—she loved luxury picnics with wine and strawberries—a flash of her sitting beside me in a cinema, hiding her face in my shoulder when the murderer took another victim. Oh, God.

Last, Jess the brilliant violinist sending notes glittering from her bow to standing ovations. Another picture popped into my mind; Jess puce with rage and disappointment, after I broke off our relationship. 'Oh, Jess, I'm so sorry.'

A moan preceded a muffled curse from the third bedroom. My hand jerked, splashing hot liquid over the bench. It was a moment before I remembered that Pam had stayed for what was left of the night.

The bedside lamp clicked on, followed by rustling noises. I made another cup and carried it to the door of the room. She was lying flat on her back, struggling to get the bed clothes untangled, knickers well and truly on display. One boob had flopped out of her bra. I moved a discreet distance away.

'Pam? Pam?'

'Whaaat? Oh, Brie. Uh, what's happening?'

'Can't sleep. Worrying about Ally, thinking about Jess.'

I took my time returning. She sat up in bed, fully covered, gazing at me with haunted, dark-ringed eyes. Her hair stood on end and she looked like I felt, deranged. Sweet, loyal Pam, so damn talented and laid back, cutting her CDs, playing with the orchestra and so afflicted by stage fright she might never achieve her full potential. 'It's not fair,' I thought, savagely. For a moment, I wondered, with regret, what might have happened had I not been side-tracked by Jess. Would Pam and I have—but then I met Ally and no other woman meant a romantic damn.

'Here,' I held out the cup. ' I heard you thrashing around. I can't sleep so I thought some practice might help.'

'I'll get dressed and join you,' she announced.

'Righto.'

I wandered to the music room, stood the mugs on a

shelf and turned on the light. Pam shuffled in as I was fingering a few notes on the piano, a work I was currently composing, swooped on her coffee, took a great gulp and grimaced.

'Ouch! Too hot!' She put it back on the shelf and plopped into a chair. 'I kept having nightmares. How's your head?'

'Still aching, but not as bad now I'm up. God only knows where we go from here. There's not much we can do except sit tight.'

'You know the police are going to want to talk to us, don't you?'

I wriggled uneasily. 'Yep. But since you cleaned everything...'

Pam's words tumbled over each other. 'I'm not infallible, Brie. Like, I think I got it all, but who knows?'

'Now you tell me?'

'Brie, if we're cornered, all we can do is tell the truth, but I hope it won't come to that. Whatever happens, we don't tell them about Ally. Got it? And I told you about her father in strictest confidence.'

'Yeah, I got it.'

'And don't let on you know who he is! You know why Aunt Eloise and James need to keep it a secret.'

'You mean, you and Aunt—Ms Carpenter—want us to keep it secret,' I snapped. 'You know I think telling the police is the best thing to do!'

She cast me a liverish glance and then narrowed her eyes. 'Ally's life depends on us keeping quiet.'

'Yeah, and for how long? Until the kidnappers—' I must have been shouting, because Pam started shushing me—' get three million dollars? And just how much time do you think that's going to take? What will happen to Ally after that?'

'Brie, calm down, for God's sake.' She patted my

arm. 'It won't help.'

The cops would be interviewing Ally's mother and they would soon find out for themselves, but there was one more thing to be said. 'Pam, I know I owe you for tonight. You believed in me and you put yourself on the line. You could get into serious trouble on account of my blundering.'

She smiled. 'Brie, what are friends for?' Then she looked at me, eyes narrowed and assessing. 'You're in love with Ally, aren't you?'

'Yes. But I don't know how she feels. We were going to…uh…talk about it after we'd been to the club.' I raised my eyes to Pam's face. 'And now she might not be…'

The sentence which neither of us wanted to finish, hung in the air. 'She will be safe, Brie. Hold that thought. Now, how about we keep ourselves occupied?'

I got up and lifted my instrument out of its case. Pam moved to the piano stool and began to play an accompaniment to Saint-Saens 'Cello Concerto No 1,' I joined in and we tried to stave off our mutual demons.

Thursday: 10.30am.

Hammering on my front door brought me upright, disorientated and trembling with fatigue. The police?

'Coming!' I croaked, swinging my jean-clad legs to the floor. I squinted at the clock, hung-over from lack of sleep. The events of the previous night flooded back and fear joined the churning in my stomach.

'Brie! Hey mate, are you there?'

Michael. What the fuck was he doing here? I went to open up. He surged over the doorstep, looking unnervingly cheerful, clutching a pile of music and a large paper bag of something greasy. I could smell doughnuts.

'Geez, you look shite!' he announced, dumping his

armful on the kitchen table. 'Coffee on?'

'Nah, jug'll boil in a minute though.'

I trailed after him and propped myself against the bench watching as he grabbed the milk from the fridge, got mugs out of the cupboard and spooned coffee from the jar I'd left open in the early hours. He babbled away about nothing in particular as we waited for the jug to boil, and then made it himself.

'Do you know where Jess is?' he asked, as he turned to hand me a steaming mug. 'I rang her before I left home, but there was no answer.' So that's it. You want to make sure she's not here with me.

'No, I don't.'

Just then, Pam sauntered into the kitchen, dishevelled and sleepy. 'I smell coffee,' she moaned piteously, nose twitching. Michael's eyes widened; I could see the wheels turning.

'Pam stayed the night in the spare room,' I announced forcefully. She blushed and turned away. 'We were practising and got on the piss. She couldn't drive home.'

He looked at me doubtfully, then at Pam who was rooting with apparent unconcern in the cupboard for a clean mug. Shrugging, he went on to talk about the music he'd brought over, jazz promised to me for the Friday night quartet.

Cat created a diversion by leaping onto the counter looking for her breakfast. I opened the fridge and rummaged for her food, hoping Michael wouldn't mention Jess again, but of course, he did. 'So, when did you last see Jess? I tried to ring her. Do you think she's away with that new boyfriend of hers?'

I wasn't aware that he knew he'd been made redundant. Judging by his expression, he wasn't best pleased by the situation.

'Or she could have gone to the shops?' Michael continued, as he poured hot water into the mug, which Pam held out like a begging bowl.

'What do you know about her new boyfriend, Michael?' she asked, casually.

'Not much. I saw him a couple of days ago, but I didn't realise she was sleeping with him while she was still with me, 'he said, angrily. 'He's an Italian-looking type. Kept looking around to see if anyone was eyeing her up.'

If what I suspected was true, the bloke didn't want to be seen with her.

'He looked familiar somehow.' Michael took a deep draught of coffee, glaring at the floor.

'Where were they when you saw them?' I asked, as I put Cat's food down, fussing over her, trying not to betray too much interest in the answer.

'Outside that new pub in Wellington Point the night of the cricket awards. They got into a black Audi.'

Michael played cricket with one of the suburban clubs. Pam and I looked at each other. The boyfriend must have had his work cut out to keep a low profile, because Jess hadn't been the sort of woman content to stay at home eating takeaway pizza too often.

It was about then there was more hammering on the front door accompanied by a chorus of voices. Pam rolled her eyes and Michael brightened visibly. Two of my sisters had arrived.

As I went to open it, I thought Pam's designs on Michael were doomed. He and Lara, my liveliest sister, had always fancied each other, even throughout his dalliance with Jess. From the anticipatory gleam in his eye, I realised they were both single at the moment. I wasn't happy about it. Michael was a little too fond of the weed and I suspected he used stronger stuff on occasions.

The girls tumbled over the threshold, chattering and

exclaiming as they realised who was there. Pam's face fell when she saw Lara, who trilled a beeline for Michael. Karen wanted to know who in the orchestra had died?

For a split second, Pam and I froze. She threw me a warning glance, before edging behind the girls. Michael hadn't heard her question, but as Lara talked I could see he was being brought up to date. 'There was a brief announcement on the 10 o'clock news this morning that a member of the Pacific Orchestra was found dead,' she turned, and informed us all. 'We thought it was Ally for a moment, but then the announcer said "violinist."'

'What do you mean? When was this?' I asked, trying to look shocked. Behind their backs, Pam rolled her eyes.

'Do you mean you don't know?'

'Of course I don't know!' I snapped. They gaped at me in astonishment. Even I could hear the bite in my tone. 'Sorry. I was just surprised,' I lied.

'They didn't give a name, just said a violinist with the orchestra was found dead this morning.'

Karen obviously thought I was a bad-tempered drongo. So what else was new? Michael's worried expression seemed unconvincing. Did he know more than he let on? I wondered how serious his affair with Jess had been. Did he actively resent her for dumping him? How well did I really know Michael? It's said there's a murderer somewhere deep inside all of us. Her dying confession could have been guilt, but her murder nothing to do with Ally's kidnapping. Was jealousy the motive for Jess's murder?

'We haven't heard the early news this morning.' Pam stopped abruptly, realising what her words implied. My sister's eyes bored into her and then swivelled accusingly at me.

'I thought you were keen on—' Lara bit her lip, as she stopped herself saying Ally's name.

'Trust *you* lot to jump to conclusions and it's not

what you think. Pam and I were practising last night and it got so late she stayed in Jake's room,' I assured them, referring to my flatmate who was spending six months with the Melbourne Symphony. Their faces cleared and the moment of awkwardness passed.

'Do you girls want coffee and doughnuts?' I asked, heading for the electric jug, anxious to divert attention from everything.

The sun promised a great winter day, but the black vibes enveloping me turned it to dust. The chattering of my sisters and friends faded, thoughts swirled around my head like mice in a wheel and settled on Michael. Undoubtedly, Jess had given him a key to her cottage. Perhaps he called later and found her dead? Or had he been there earlier, masquerading as the dressmaker's dummy in her bedroom after stabbing her and hitting me over the head?

By now, the police crime scene people would know there was a steady procession in and out of her cottage the previous night. The cops would question everyone today, including Ally's parents.

It was only a matter of time before they got to us.

CHAPTER 32

Shredding the Witnesses

Detective Senior Sergeant Susan Prescott

Thursday: 7.30am.

Six days since Ally Carpenter's abduction and the media was screaming for police blood. We had eliminated a lot of possibilities, but so far the only positive note was that her body had not turned up—yet.

I was stunned to hear the news that Jessica Rallison, first violinist with the Pacific Orchestra, had been found murdered. Apparently her manager arrived at her house for a breakfast meeting and, unable to rouse her, panicked and called the police. When they broke in she was found on the kitchen floor, stabbed to death.

I asked Evan if they knew when it might have happened.

'Last night,' he replied. 'Apparently she was talking to her manager about six o'clock and said she was going out to dinner with a friend. It's a nasty one, Susan.'

'Does he know who the friend was?" I croaked, 'and where are you?'

' I'm at the scene now. Are you coming now?'

'Depending on the traffic, I'll see you shortly.'

'I'm not going anywhere.' Evan loved a good murder to get his teeth into and this looked a real doozy.

I turned the car toward the West End. The bad-tempered, morning traffic was heavy as usual, so it was like wading through treacle to get to the cul-de-sac where Jessica Rallison lived. The way things were going, the Scenes Of Crime Officers—SOCO—would be there long before I was.

A police car was parked outside, ensuring I had no trouble finding the address. It was fronted by a group of women, several of whom were in dressing-gowns and fluffy slippers. One was enjoying a cup of coffee in a thermal mug. A few small children, an assortment of dogs and a huge marmalade cat made up the contingent excitedly awaiting developments.

I found a park close to the action and poked my ID under the nose of the teenage constable guarding the front gate, who immediately snapped from "here comes a nosy member of the public" stoicism to deference.

Jessica's cottage was a style of small, originally cheap home popular in the 1900s, and which were now trendy among the so-called glitterati. The tiny verandah held no pot plants, chairs or table, only a shoe rack holding a pair of untidy, white sandals. 'A prickly, lonely girl,' was how I described Jessica to the team, after the unproductive interview Evan and I conducted with her late on Monday afternoon. *Jessica, Jessica, what did you know that you weren't telling? Has it cost you your life?* I checked in with the uniformed constable who was guarding the front door, keeping the crime scene log.

A tall, square van pulled into the slot held vacant for them outside the gate. The street audience rustled with anticipation as the forensic team climbed out, carted their cases to the lawn and proceeded to kit themselves in jump suits.

'Morning, Susan, another nasty one, then,' said pathologist John Lynch, referring to a gruesome murder we had been investigating for the past couple of weeks.

'I believe this one's a musician of some sort. Have you been inside?'

'No, just arrived. I interviewed her on Monday in connection with Ally Carpenter's disappearance.'

'Any news on her yet?'

'No, no leads, but this throws up some very interesting questions,' I replied, trying hard not to burst into a paroxysm of coughing. My face felt like a puffer fish about to explode.

He clucked sympathetically, picked up his case and winked. 'Nasty cold you've got there.'

'I'll come in and have a gander,' I said, accepting a pair of overshoes. Leaving me spluttering, he trundled hastily inside, followed by his overalled, masked troops. They looked like blue Ghostbusters.

Evan detached himself from the crowd where he joined 'uniform' in soliciting statements. 'Nothing to report. We've sent her manager home. The bloke's in shock, but he's coming in to make a statement later today.'

'My—' I sneezed so loudly that everyone outside turned to look and someone sniggered. I dabbed delicately at my raw nostrils with a handful of tissues. 'Sorry, I can't help it.'

We discussed our strategy, Evan at a safe distance, after which he left to organise a doorknock of the surrounding houses.

The next door neighbour arrived full of information and pushed his way into the conversation between one of the constables and a woman carrying a small child on her hip. 'He gives me the creeps' Jessica had told me, shivering. He was also the reason she installed extra heavy blinds to prevent him peering through the windows. Her killer must have been delighted. If the neighbour had worked out that he was a suspect, he showed no sign of it from his demeanour. We might well wipe the sanctimonious expression off his face by hauling him into the station for questioning.

I smiled viciously, as I donned a pair of latex gloves, identified myself to the officer keeping the log and stepped into the hallway. The overpowering stench of blood and faeces ensured I maintained shallow breathing.

Jessica lay beside the kitchen table like a broken porcelain doll, her thick black hair glued in a pool of blood, her half-closed eyes opaque and arms resting by her sides.

'Bled to death. Rigor mortis has set in, so she's been gone at least three hours, but probably closer to ten or twelve judging by her eyes,' John announced laconically, as he squatted outside the perimeter of the blood. 'Someone grabbed her recently,' he added, as I squinted at the smudge marks on her upper arms. Faint bruises showed on her mouth and cheeks.

'Looks like he held his hand over her mouth while he did the deed, or else an accomplice did.' John turned to his carry-case of specimen jars. 'No apparent defence wounds, so either he was incredibly quick or she knew her attacker. Likely both.' He secured plastic evidence bags over her hands and secured the openings at her wrists to retain any skin or hair samples which Jessica may have gotten from her killer.

A wave of sorrow for life lost made me want to cry. *'No, I'm feeling fragile because of this cold...'*

As I sidled around the side of the room toward the back door, the light from the window highlighted smear marks on the table. Someone had wiped the edge. Something lay on the floor, a piece of material. I bent down and peered closely. It was a blood-soaked handkerchief. Interesting.

It would be hours, if not the following day, before

we could gain full access to the house. Jessica's body wouldn't be moved for some time. The initial tests, body temperature and an external examination of her fully-clothed corpse would be carried out where she lay. The house would be torn apart for blood stains and other evidence. Fingerprints would be taken. Her computer, her correspondence, diary—not a skerrick would be missed or a single aspect of her life left untouched.

Media vans were pulling into the street as I stepped out onto the verandah and was checked out on the crime scene log. I wondered who tipped them off, hoping it was one of the neighbours and not a member of my team. Turning my face away, I picked up pace, dived into my car and scooted out of there.

Townsville CIB was understandably astonished when I rang to give them the news of the latest tragedy.

'Holy shit!' breathed my opposite number, 'We only just started on Georgie Hird's murder and another one connected to your missing woman gets knocked off. Hardly a coincidence, is it? What are you doing to them?' He snickered loudly, then proceeded to update me on the investigation into Ms Hird's death, and advised me of Rosalind Miller's absence. 'We let her go down to Brisbane because she had business there.'

'Wasn't she supposed to be minding Eloise Carpenter's place?'

'Apparently the postmistress has organised someone else to do it. And the media's swarming all over the island. Seems they've picked up on the connection between the Carpenter's and Georgie Hird.' It was only a matter of time before they discovered that.

Making a note to check with Pamela Miller on her mother's visit to Brisbane, I brought him up to date on what little we knew of Jessica's life. I didn't envy him having to perform the unenviable job of telling her parents that they no longer had a daughter. After we'd finished speaking, I sat for a few minutes imagining how the mother would feel. I knew if it were one of my daughters, I would never recover. I gave myself a mental shake and walked over to Ben Taylor's desk.

'Benjamin? What are you working on at the moment?'

'The pharmacy burglary, ma'am.'

'Okay. Anything pending?'

'No, ma'am.'

'You can come with me and help alert the management of the Pacific Orchestra to the fact that they're going to be advertising for another violinist. We need to find out if any of them knew who Jessica Rallison was going out with last night.'

I stuffed an unopened packet of tissues into my bag and grabbed a bag of cough lozenges. On our way out, I gave a list of names to a hotshot young detective with instructions to find out everything about the people on it, fast, or I would make sure he played Santa at the next police family Christmas party.

All in all, it was sometime before we finally arrived at the orchestra HQ. The manager of the Pacific showed no sign of being overjoyed by our visit. He drew himself up to protest, but soon changed his tune when we told him why we were there.

'No! My God, how? ' He was flabbergasted. 'How *did* it happen?'

After I supplied the bare facts, his face turned ashen and he sat down abruptly. A frightened secretary rushed to pour him a glass of water and advised the directors were in the boardroom. I thought we had better get to them quickly, in case the whole building heard the news before they did.

The PA to the Chairman, a stalwart old biddy, tried

to prevent us crashing the meeting, but when we flashed ID she backed off, sucking her teeth.

The array of directors around the highly polished table looked like a gang of well-fed crooks from a gangster movie. Empty cups and the remains of scones, jam and cream littered the centre. The Chairman raised his eyebrows in a "what is this all about, we're busy" way, and waited for me to state our business. I took petty pleasure in giving him the silent treatment from just inside the doorway. Finally, he rose with half-hearted courtesy and strutted over to block any further progress into the room.

'Yeeees, er—?' he drawled, running a hand through his sparse amount of hair, he flexed his meaty shoulders as though for battle.

'We have some bad news, Mr Greenway...' I didn't beat about the bush.

He turned green and withered, Louie the Fly to my squirt of Mortein. His fellow directors, seeing their colleague at the point of collapse, lurched to their feet and surged toward us. Ben shooed them back to the table; I positioned myself where I could gauge individual reaction to the news.

'Ladies and gentlemen, Jessica Rallison was found dead in her home this morning.' I waited for the horrified buzz to die down. 'She was murdered, but when or by whom we do not know as yet. I'm sorry.'

They were so shocked they forgot to try intimidating us. More than two hours passed, before we got all the staff statements sorted out. If anyone knew who Jessica's date was for the previous evening, they weren't telling. Some members of the orchestra were having a theory session downstairs. Her close friends were understandably devastated. Michael Whitby looked furtive. What did he have to hide? Note to self: check him out.

Pamela Miller, who looked as though she hadn't slept for days, buried her face in Briece Mochrie's shoulder and wept. I couldn't think what puzzled me about Mochrie, who looked tired and unwell, but it would come to me. Catching my sceptical glance, he volunteered the information that he had a migraine. 'Join the club, mate,' I thought, wryly. Ally Carpenter's abduction was probably getting to him, but I felt there was something more.

'Ma'am, you really shouldn't be here,' said Ben, as we left the building. 'You should go home to bed.'

Tell me about it! 'I can't, but thank you for your concern. Now let's get back and see what we've got here.'

I flopped into the car and closed my eyes. Uncharitably, I wished Jessica Rallison could have at least waited to be murdered until I recovered from my cold.

SOCO phoned through the preliminary report just before five o'clock.

'Susan, I've got some more information for you to go on with,' announced John Lynch. 'Going on room and body temperature, it appears she was probably killed between 6 and 10 pm last night. There's no a blood stain or signs of a struggle in the other rooms. No defence wounds on her hands and nothing under her fingernails. Everything would indicate she was killed in the kitchen. The woman was excessively tidy and house proud, which was helpful.

He took a deep breath. 'Someone placed his hand over her mouth, probably to stop her screaming for help while she died. She was stabbed with a serrated-edged knife. Cause of death was a severed renal artery and she would have bled out in ten to fifteen minutes. There was a carving knife and a number of other sharp knives in the cutlery drawer which we've taken for testing, but it's likely her killer brought the murder weapon and then took it away. The angle of the wound indicated he, or she, was standing facing her, so a right-handed slash. As you saw at the scene, she had recently been held firmly by the upper arms as well and we have got fingerprints, but as yet, no match.'

He paused again, as someone with him asked a question. Paper rustled and some murmuring ensued before he continued.

'Path results will show if there are toxic substances in her body or possible drug-use, though there was no indication of it. No evidence of rape, but she'd had recent sexual activity. Semen present was collected for future DNA comparison, and she was eight weeks pregnant.'

He paused for a moment to let the news sink in. My mind skittered around this new development. Had she confronted the father, Michael Whitby perhaps? Or Briece Mochrie? Was it the motive for the murder or was the killing connected to Ally Carpenter's abduction? *God, let us get to Ally before it's too late.*

'A man's handkerchief was lying beside her head, covered in blood and a man's partial shoe-print near the body with another superimposed over it, indicating someone stepped on the first print. It's smudged, but we should be able to match it when you find the right jogger. We're chasing up the brand-name. There were also skid marks in the blood, which someone attempted to wipe up. So, evidence that at least two people were present in the house. Now we get to the really interesting part. The Polilight showed someone wiped the sink and draining board, the kitchen benches, table and chair. Either that person or the other party vomited into the sink, so it and the drains yielded good samples for DNA.'

I tried not to think about that.

'Someone wiped the light switches, door knobs and anywhere there was a possibility of fingerprints. But—'

I could hear the smile of satisfaction in his normally laconic voice—' when we turned the kitchen table upside down, we found the remains of some blue-tack. It's evident a business-card sized object was stuck there very recently. Looks like she might have had a listener. Excuse me—' I heard him sip some liquid, no doubt his favourite, cold "cat's pee weak" black tea.

'Her personal letters and diary have been bagged up. You can have them shortly. There's another diary in her bedroom, which has a couple of entries in it. Must have lost the main one at some time and bought another. We've finished with it.'

I managed a thank you before a coughing fit overtook me.

'Susan, you should be at home. Let that lazy bugger Evan takeover. The state you're in, you're not going to be much use to the investigation.'

Reluctantly, I agreed and we signed off with his promise to fax the report over.

Five o'clock. My colleagues were shrugging themselves into their jackets, laughing and making plans to go to the pub. Evan stuck his head in the door. 'For chrissakes, Susan, get home. You look like something the cat dragged in and then rejected!'

'Thanks a lot, my friend.' My sarcasm didn't quite come off, because I sneezed all over my papers and had to fumble for the tissue box.

He shook his head sympathetically. 'Go, just go. The investigation will still be here in the morning. Have a rum and a good night's sleep. I'll let you know if anything breaks.'

I picked up my briefcase and handbag and dragged my coat on. I couldn't wait to get home, have a hot bath, and while I was steaming in there, I would figure out just how to tackle Jessica Rallison's colleagues and friends. We would start with Eloise Carpenter and then tackle Pamela Miller and Briece Mochrie again.

If they didn't start spilling their secrets, I'd shred the buggers, bit by bit.

CHAPTER 33
The Weakest Link

Detective Senior Sergeant Susan Prescott

Friday: 8.00am.

The media were waiting for me on the front steps of police headquarters, screaming questions. I ducked as a microphone boom brushed the top of my head.

'Have you got a suspect?'

'Senior Sergeant Prescott, why was Jessica Rallison murdered?'

'Is this connected to Ally Carpenter's disappearance?'

'Is someone out to get the orchestra? '

'No comment! A statement will be issued this morning,' I croaked, cursing my decision to park on the street instead of in the car park.

'Over here, Susie!' A camera flashed in my face.

A clutch of brawny young constables dived into the fray to rescue me. I reached the CIB in a fine rage, slammed my briefcase down, hurled my shoulder-bag onto the chair and cast a vicious glance over the front page of the newspaper. The Carpenter case, with the Jessica Rallison murder as a likely add-on, had become a drama of epic proportions. 'Mystery of the Missing Musician,'and, 'Violent Death of a Violinist' were favourite, trite, headlines.

A knock came at the door. My immediate superior, DI Bruce Peterson stood in front of me, looking anxious. 'Susan—' He hesitated. As an experienced husband, he was adept at identifying the signs of a crabby female on the loose. 'Getting to you are they?'

'The whole case is getting to me!' I moaned, tamping down guilt at not having told him of my possible family connection to the Carpenters. Hopefully, research done by one of my team would confirm it or otherwise before I needed to confess. If the worst happened, the dilemma would be taken to the superintendent and I would probably be out of the case.

He waved a sheaf of papers. 'We're ready for briefing, if you are? I'll sit-in this morning.'

We made our way to the Major Incident room. The team hitched their chairs closer. Taking a deep breath, I updated the details of the SOCO reports and then called for the results of team research. 'Right, so what have we got this morning?' I looked wearily at Ben Taylor, as I plucked tissues out of a box on the desk beside me.

'We did the house-to-house, but no one saw anything on Wednesday night, or if they did, they weren't saying. I obtained a list of recent visitors to the house, ma'am.' He read it out. Pamela Miller, Ally and a few I recognised as members of the orchestra.

'Men.' He flicked the page of his notebook over and licked his lips. 'A tall, dark-haired man visited a couple of days ago, late in the afternoon and stayed for about twenty minutes. The informant couldn't pin down the day, but swears it was this week.' He paused to consult his notes. 'The description matches Briece Mochrie. A fair-haired man has been a frequent visitor, but not recently. He matches the description of Michael Whitby.'

There was something more exciting to impart. 'The woman directly across the road at number 88, a Mrs

Annie George, observed a new male caller, stocky, thick black hair, swarthy complexion. She didn't get a good look at his face because he always arrived and left in the dark.' The new boyfriend?

'Get her in to help with an identikit, Ben. Let me know if she comes up with something helpful. SOCO has fingerprints, but no match. Now, what have you got on Eloise Carpenter, Adam?'

The tall, lanky detective got to his feet, flipping open his notebook. 'Ma'am. Eloise Carpenter, born Eloise McFadden in Dubbo, 19th February, 1961... '

As he described Eloise's early family life, I realised she was indeed Harry's half-sister, born three years before him. Ally Carpenter was my niece! Now was the time to admit my relationship.

'There is no record of a marriage either in the UK or here and she changed her name by deed poll just before settling on Masters Island,' he finished. Who was Eloise hiding from?

'Ma'am? '

I pulled myself together. 'Thank you, Adam. So we have nothing to indicate who Ally Carpenter's father was?'

'No, ma'am.'

Was Ally's father the key to this? He was supposed to be dead, but I was sure Eloise had lied. And if so, did he know she was missing? We didn't know his name, but could what we thought to be a predator snatch actually be a kidnapping for ransom? I had previously dismissed it, because at that stage there was nothing to suggest any of the family were rich enough to make it worth anyone's while to commit such a dangerous crime. I needed to shake Eloise down for the truth.

Her tone became apprehensive when I phoned for an appointment, but she couldn't refuse. After all, I am "the police." At first she asked me to meet her in another coffee shop and when I refused, she offered to come to headquarters, but I insisted on going to her. I could have demanded she come to the station, but felt I would get more out of her in informal surroundings. Reluctantly, she gave me the address of the friend with whom she was staying. Not wanting any surprises, I decided to front her there and then.

'Ms Carpenter, is Ally's father still alive? And are you with him now?'

There was a long silence, during which I could hear her breath coming faster.

'Eloise!' It was an order.

She cracked and admitted she was staying with him. The upmarket address in Brookfield sent a jolt of excitement through me, followed by a surge of anger. God only knew how much time had been lost because the people involved had pissed around while we wasted time conducting a fruitless search.

We turned into the imposing entrance to the secluded property, sped along the tree-lined driveway and stopped at the bottom of the steps leading to the front door. I could see a cluster of outbuildings amongst the trees a few hundred metres away; it was apparent we were in the presence of serious money.

'Kidnapping for ransom,' Evan announced thoughtfully.

'Hm. It's looking more likely now I've seen this. If I'm right, the girl might be still alive. Maybe. Let's see if we can shake them out of their tree.'

Parents of kidnapped children will pay every cent they can get their hands on and lie 'til the cows come home, after being advised in no uncertain terms that their child will be killed if the police are brought in. If this was indeed the case we were up against it.

Eloise Carpenter opened the majestic door accompanied by a border collie holding a squashed plastic milk bottle in its jaws. She was dressed conservatively in dark slacks, a crisp blouse and a black cardigan trimmed with black and gold buttons. Her feelings were unsuccessfully disguised by what she may have hoped was an impassive expression. If what we suspected was the case, I almost felt sorry for her. Who could say what I would do if our situation was reversed?

'Good afternoon, Ms Carpenter.'

I smiled and held out my hand as I reached the entrance. She took it with obvious reluctance, released it quickly and invited us inside. A faint aroma of furniture polish lingered in the air. Pale sunlight streamed through a leadlight window at the far end of the hall leading out of the foyer, spraying a rainbow of coloured shards onto a gallery of paintings. We might have lingered, but Eloise opened a door and motioned us into one of the most beautiful rooms I have ever seen.

Massive, bay windows over-looking the garden were framed by emerald, full-length curtains. Comfortable high-backed armchairs nestled around an imposing stone fireplace in which a fire crackled comfortably. Bookcases jostled for position alongside more paintings, backdrops for the gleaming black, grand piano. Piles of music cluttered an elegant Queen Anne style desk and incongruously, a tiny pink plastic garbage bin filled with pencils perched somewhat precariously on one end of the keyboard.

'Crikey, not exactly on his uppers, is he?' Evan muttered through motionless lips. I smiled grimly; this was getting more interesting by the minute. Eloise walked across to the nearest armchair, bent down and spoke quietly.

Ally Carpenter's father stood up and turned to face us.

Evan gasped; my jaw dropped. 'No wonder you've been hounding the Commissioner day and night, wanting to know what we're up to,' I thought drily, watching him for signs of weakness now that we had tracked him to his lair. Apart from a little strain around his eyes, there was none. Clearly used to ruling the roost, he stepped forward, playing the grand host to perfection. 'Sergeants, won't you take a seat?'

We were ushered courteously into armchairs and the couple sat side by side on the sofa opposite. The 'vibe,' which swirled like demon smoke around them, was familiar: desperation. They didn't touch or even glance at each other, but they were choreographed in emotional and mental synchronisation.

So, that was how things were. They were required to co-operate with a murder investigation, but paying a ransom to kidnappers isn't illegal. Anyone can give money away, but *hiding* a kidnapping is a crime, though one could never convince terrorised parents of that. A jury either, I suspect.

Evan took out his notebook. I tried to rattle them by allowing the silence to lengthen, but this time it didn't work. Reluctantly, I spoke first. 'Thank you for agreeing to meet with us this afternoon. As you know, Jessica Rallison has been murdered and I would like to ask you a few questions.'

They nodded agreement.

'Sir, and Ms Carpenter, are you aware of anyone who might have borne a grudge against Jessica?

Eloise scrunched a dainty handkerchief in one hand and reached to touch her partner, James, with the other.

'No.'

'Are you absolutely sure?' I knew Eloise had been close to Jessica. I had also heard a great deal about the young woman's penchant for rubbing people up the wrong way.

He glanced protectively at Eloise, 'She wouldn't know, Ms Prescott.'

Eloise pressed the handkerchief to her mouth and peered over it, eyes brimming. I stripped my voice of any semblance of sympathy. 'That's not strictly true, is it? From what we have been told, Jessica Rallison was a girl with problems. Pamela Miller, Briece Mochrie and you, Ms Carpenter, have all told us that Jessica and Ally fell out approximately eighteen months ago while they were still in London. Getting back to Ally's disappearance, we also have reason to believe Jessica was upset because Mochrie broke off their relationship, then turned his attention to your daughter. Would you like to comment?'

'I'm sorry. I only know what I've already told you, Senior Sergeant.'

I eyed her thoughtfully. 'Are you aware of anyone who might want to harm Jessica within or outside the orchestra?'

'No, I really don't and Ally didn't say anything to me other than Jess was angry with her.'

Her face creased in anxious lines. James put his arm around her, squeezed her shoulder and spoke sternly. 'And as I've said previously, Senior Sergeant Prescott, no. Ally would have told me if she had, I'm sure. We don't tolerate bullying, and we act to diffuse any acrimony between members of the orchestra before it gets out of hand. However, the members of the orchestra are all professional musicians and so far we've never had cause to intervene in any dispute.' he added.

'Uhuh.' I made a note. 'Do you know anything about Jessica's personal life? If she had a new boyfriend, for example?'

They appeared genuinely puzzled. 'No, we don't know a lot about Jess's recent love life. But I understand from Pam that Jess is, or was, having a relationship with Michael Whitby,' said Eloise. The tremor in her voice belied her appearance of calm.

Evan rustled his notebook as he turned the page. 'Sir, is there anyone you can think of who might want to harm you—either through business or social dealings?'

Ally's father passed his free hand over his brow in a weary gesture. I watched his face for any sign of subterfuge. 'Senior Sergeant, Ms Prescott, if I knew of anyone at all who might have taken Ally or killed Jess, I would tell you immediately.' He looked me straight in the eyes, but couldn't hide the slight suggestion of tightening around his mouth.

'We covered this before in our previous interview, but I want you to think very carefully before you answer. Just how well did you know Jessica?'

He gaped at me, flushing. 'I resent what you seem to be implying, Senior Sergeant. I only knew Ms Rallison as a musician with the Pacific Symphony Orchestra. I met her socially on occasions, but had no dealings with her on a personal level!' he barked.

We sat in silence for a long moment, before I answered in measured tones. 'I was not suggesting anything to the contrary, sir. What I really want to know, is if you think Georgie Hird and Jessica Rallison's murders were connected in any way to Ally's disappearance?'

They made eye contact; Eloise took up the mantle of spokesperson.

'We wondered about that ourselves, Ms Prescott, but we can't see any connection other than they were friends. As you know, Georgie was Ally's godmother.'

She thrust her handkerchief into her face. Her man put his arm around her and glared at me, ready to "fight ze bull," who was currently, myself. I waited for her to pull herself together. 'I have to ask you both for an account of your movements on Wednesday evening between six and eight o'clock.'

'We dined here at about seven. Mrs Fox, my housekeeper can vouch for the time, and we didn't leave the house that night.'

It was highly unlikely this pair had anything at all to do with Jessica's murder, but I sense there was more to it than they were prepared to reveal. Time to try another tack. 'Have you heard from anyone in connection with Ally's disappearance?'

I almost missed the merest imperceptible movement toward each other and then Eloise deliberately relaxed her shoulders and assumed an expression of bewilderment.

'Oh no, Senior Sergeant, should we have? We're count—' her voice broke, and she tried again. 'Counting on you to find her!'

He enfolded her small hand tightly in one of his huge ones and leaned forward as though about to stand up. 'We know nothing.'

As far as he was concerned, the interview was finished. I sat tight, thinking rapidly. It was time to shake them up. Repressing an almost uncontrollable urge to choke the living shit out of them, I spoke forcefully. 'Ms Carpenter, sir. In cases of kidnapping, particularly for ransom, it's a very foolhardy thing for family members not to contact the police, regardless of what threats are made. If anyone contacts you, or has contacted you in this regard, you would be well advised to tell us everything you know.'

Stark fear flashed across Eloise's face, then vanished as swiftly as it had come. She frowned. 'That isn't an issue here, Senior Sergeant.'

You know a damn sight more than you're telling, my girl.

I left the kidnapping caution to ferment in their minds for the moment. 'Perhaps you've had time to think about this now. Are you sure Ally or any of her friends, such as Jessica or Pamela, didn't become involved with a religious sect while they were overseas? One whose members might think that abducting Ally is a good way to make money?'

Again her mother denied Ally was involved with a religious group. I made eye contact with Eloise first and then with James. 'Have you received a ransom demand?'

'No, Senior Sergeant,' they replied calmly, but not quite in unison. Their lack of reaction betrayed them.

'You know, we would treat any information you could give us with the utmost confidentiality? I'll ask you again, have you received any communication from Ally's abductors?'

'We know nothing, Senior Sergeant,' Eloise answered firmly. Nothing, my arse.

'Have you been in touch with Briece Mochrie or Michael Whitby within the last 24 hours?'

The merest hesitation ensued before they gave an emphatic denial.

'Does Ally know you are her father?' I asked James. I had pushed about as far as I could without actually taking them in for questioning.

They glanced at each other, before Eloise said quietly, 'No, Ms Prescott.'

Ally's reaction might be quite a surprise for them when she discovers who he is, I thought.

'Well, that's all for the moment, thank you.' I nodded abruptly, got to my feet and wandered in a deceptively aimless manner over to the paintings.

'You have some wonderful art work here, sir. Did you bring any of them from England?' I asked. 'A Turner, if I'm not mistaken?' I positioned myself to check it in the light streaming through the window.

'Oh, yes, James has beautiful taste,' Eloise enthused. As she glanced up at the wall, I recognised my husband's face in her features. I wanted to put my arms around her, to beg her to tell me what was happening.

'Is Mrs Fox available, sir?' Evan's voice cut across my wayward emotions, effectively snapping me away from thoughts of consanguinity between Eloise and Harry.

'Follow me, Sergeant.'

I waited until they vanished, then slipped into the foyer to run my hand over the nearest painting and the next, then the one opposite. Further along the wall there were two spaces. Paintings had been removed. Were the originals being cleaned, or were they in a vault somewhere for safe keeping? Hidden away on an estate, staff at his beck and call, there was no reason not to keep his treasures where he could enjoy them—unless something catastrophic had occurred and money had to be raised in a hurry.

The dog came to lean against my legs, the squashed plastic bottle still between his grinning lips. I bent and stroked him. 'Fine watchdog you are.' Voices heralded Evan's return from his interview with the housekeeper.

As we drove away, I glanced back, but the couple had gone to ground in their fortress.

'Well, that was something else,' laughed Evan, as he drove a leisurely pace down the long, bitumen driveway.

'What do you mean?'

'You certainly know how to upset the resident lord and his lady. You went from being Senior Sergeant to Ms Prescott and back again in about three different moves.'

'Too bad. What did the estimable Mrs Fox have to say?' I asked, clawing through my shoulder bag for cough lozenges and fresh tissues.

'She confirms their story, but I didn't expect anything less. Tell me about the paintings.'

'At least seven are prints. There are two empty spaces where small ones have been removed. If they're not in a vault or being cleaned, there could be another explanation and that is, he's sold the most valuable ones and substituted prints. Could he off-load them in a couple of days? Art's not my forte.'

'Sure,' said Evan, as he turned the car onto the main road.

'Kidnapping is an emotional crime. It only works if there's someone who cares enough to pay, and he's the perfect target. I think someone's holding the girl for ransom and he's liquidating some of his assets. Depending on how much has been demanded, but even he would have to hustle to get huge amounts of cash together in a day or two. We'll check his bank accounts. The art blokes can approach their informants and find out what the go is. If that's the case...'

'That sort of bloke always has expensive cars. Wonder if he's sold them? I'll check when we get back. Pity if he's got something special.'

'You men are all the same. Bloody cars,' I teased grimly.

He frowned and straightened in his seat. Clearly he had something else on his mind.

'Come on, what is it?'

'Dunno. It'll come to me. In the meantime, we should get the staff checked, although that would have been done before they were hired.'

I flipped my mobile open and contacted a member of the team. 'Put someone onto digging into the bank accounts of this person.' I gave the details then looked at Evan. 'I have something to tell you, but I'm asking you to keep it to yourself for the time being at least.'

He stared ahead, eyes narrowed, as I told him about my family connection to Eloise. When I finished, he was silent for a moment, then said, 'Okay, Susan, you'll know if it's going to get in the way of the case.'

'Thanks, mate. Now we'll pick the weakest link and take him apart.' I replied.

'Him?'

'Briece Mochrie. He's knows a damn sight more than he's letting on. ' I stuffed two cough lozenges in my mouth, and trumpeted savagely into a handful of tissues.

CHAPTER 34

The Sound of Silence

Ally

Friday: late morning.

Breakfast was two bananas and a bottle of water. Are they about to let me go? Or is my real ordeal beginning? If they get the money and leave me here, I could starve to death. No one will know where to look for me. There's got to be a way to save myself. Think. I can barely move and my chest hurts. Perspiration reeks under my armpits and my breath stinks. But I'm still alive.

I've lost count of the days I've been here. I hear a car coming and going sometimes. I'm relying for company on people who might kill me. Am I expected to go mad? No. They couldn't care less what I do or feel.

They're not speaking to me now, but he watches me like a snake waiting to strike. The taunting was scary, but icy silence is terrifying. I punched him on the arm yesterday, but he just swept me aside as he left the room. A violent reaction would be better than nothing. Perhaps Brie will kill him for me. 'For God's sake, Ally, get a grip on yourself.' Brie couldn't bring himself to kill anything bigger than a cockroach.' The sound of my voice is startling in the silence.

My skin crawls with shame, as I remember my body responding, unfolding like a flower to Scarpia's mouth and hands. Deep down I acknowledge he is a skilful... lover. Even now, remembering, heat rises within my secret places. I hate myself. I want to hide under a blanket for the rest of my life.

'Leave her alone. She's vermin...' That hurt.

I know something dreadful has happened, but what? Have they kidnapped someone else? No, they couldn't cope with two...but perhaps there's more in their gang than I thought. I have flashes on and off, of the night they grabbed me from the disco. My impression is there were four, maybe five of them. God, I'm hungry. Has everyone forgotten me? Are the police looking for me? Do they even know where to start?

Why did mum lie about something so desperately important to me? She watched me longing for a father my whole life and still lied. It's my life, for God's sake, and I'll never forgive her.

Insidious thoughts invade like skeletal fingers, probing endlessly into the innermost recesses of my mind. What if my father doesn't care enough about me to pay the ransom? What if he doesn't care enough about mum to do it? Perhaps I'm an embarrassment and he's pretending not to be my father or maybe he doesn't even believe I'm his daughter? What really happened before I was born? He might have left her for another woman. Or even another man.

I can't show these monsters how frightened I am. The shame of being grateful to them for letting me live will brand me forever. Sometimes I feel a vibe coming from somewhere. Is someone praying for me? Is anyone even thinking of me?

I had a new dream last night. A child I used to sit next to in primary school was standing, staring at me with huge round eyes. I couldn't prevent myself shrinking from him. Suddenly, we were in a circus tent and all around the outside of the ring, but inside beside the canvas, was a waterway where clowns jumped in and out of boats. When the child realised I couldn't get to the boats, he smiled, and then his face disintegrated into a gelatinous mess.

'Hurry up, Ally, I've been waiting for you!' he called, in a high, piping voice. One of the clowns shoved me and I woke up, drawing painful gasps as my lungs expanded against my battered ribs. Perspiration broke out all over my body; shudders of fear shook my body. Davy died on his tenth birthday, after his drunken father beat him to death.

Was the dream an omen?

CHAPTER 35
In The Frame

Detective Senior Sergeant Susan Prescott

Friday: noon.

A row with Harry blew up this morning, shocking me with its intensity. Having returned to Police Headquarters after a frustrating interview with Ally Carpenter's parents, I was wolfing a sandwich and scribbling notes, when my telephone rang.

'Harry, we've been through this! Please! You must stay away from her until we've found her daughter,' I pleaded, cursing my impulsive phone call advising him of the result of our investigation into Eloise' background. If only I had kept my mouth shut.

'But she'll need family around at a time like this!'

'Harry, she may not know you exist and it's the worst possible time for her to cope with it.'

'Worst possible time for you, you mean!' he snapped. Normally a comparatively placid man, he turned cranky when his back ached.

'No. Yes, for both of us. If you compromise my investigation, I'll be forced to take steps.'

'It's all about you, isn't it? Always you and your job, Susan, so when am I going to be considered first for once?'

A young constable came into view, brandishing a

sheaf of reports. I nodded to him and held out a hand. He bounded across to my desk to pass them to me, but we failed to connect and the papers went flying all over the floor.

'Oh, *bugger!*' Frustration ripped through me. I wanted to scream. The constable scrabbled around trying to collect them, as Harry snarled in my ear:

'You're not even interested enough to listen to me! Why I bothered even going to Sydney to talk to—'

'Oh stop it, Harry. I'm trying to work and talk to you at the same time. Can we leave this until tonight? *Please?*'

Silence reigned for a couple of seconds.

'All right, Susan, have it your way as usual, but don't be surprised if I'm not here when you get home.'

He slammed the receiver down in my ear and my spirits sank. I understood his eagerness to talk to Eloise, but this was a kidnapping and murder investigation. It wasn't the first time he threatened to walk out on me, but so far he's only retreated as far as his office behind the house where his secretary, who was besotted with him and who hated my guts, would cosset him with cups of tea and cream cakes. And I don't give a monkey's—stop it, you silly cow, focus on the case.

The papers were piled neatly back on my desk. I nodded my thanks to the constable who whipped out of the room, no doubt to spread the word about his senior sergeant having a "domestic."

I skimmed the autopsy and crime scene report on Jessica Rallison in order to précis it in my mind:

'...died between six and eight o'clock Wednesday night... four right-handed knife thrusts. Actual cause of death, perforation of the renal artery. Stomach contents, remains of ham sandwich, but nothing else. No match for the fingerprints found all over the house. Pregnancy, as reported earlier.'

I put the papers into the file, reflecting that in spite of our computers, we seem to generate more paperwork than we did back when I was a recruit. I rested my head on one hand and reached for tissues with the other to blow my already tender nose, trying to thrust personal issues out of my mind. Ally Carpenter's parents could close ranks as tightly as they liked, but the pieces were slotting into place.

Retrieving Jessica's front door key from the pocket in the front of the file, I got to my feet, stuffed more clean tissues into my cavernous black shoulder bag and picked up my coat.

'Ben, what are you working on right now?' I asked, as I marched up to his desk.

'Just finished the bank job in—' He named the recent hold-up where a couple of intrepid tellers had downed the robber, a strapping fifteen-year old kid and sat on him until the police arrived. His mother was threatening to sue the tellers. 'My Garrett is a good boy,' she screeched to the media, who were thoroughly over-excited by it all. I well remembered the vicious, experienced young face snarling into mine, as we took him into custody. 'Okay. I'm going to Jessica Rallison's house. You can come with me.'

DC Taylor's eyes lit up, as he saved his work and bounced to his feet like a dog let off a chain. Evan trundled up, papers under his left armpit and plastic bag of exhibits in hand. 'Off to the scene of crime, Susan? I'm about to go through the neighbour statements. The solicitor has sent details of Rallison's will. She left Pamela Miller all her musical instruments and Eloise Carpenter her CDs and royalties. The sister gets everything else, including her house and car. She'd not included her parents, or Ally Carpenter.'

The parents being left out was understandable, but

I hadn't realised how far relations had deteriorated between Jessica and Ally. Everything I knew and had subsequently learned about the violinist hadn't endeared her to me, but I felt sorrow and anger when my shocked Townsville colleague reported that Jessica's mother, when advised of her daughter's death, said coldly, 'I've never liked my daughter, Detective,' and shut the front door in his face.

Friday: 1.30pm.

The cottage already wore an abandoned air. The houses nearby averted their shuttered, upmarket eyes like people at an elegant cocktail party confronted by a particularly bumptious member of the hoi polloi. Most of the residents were at work. A lone dog trotted by, peed on the gate and went on his way. Overhead, a 747 sped on its majestic way to possible exotic climes. Life would go on without the beautiful violinist.

We unlocked the front door and stepped into the airless house. The smell of putrefying body fluids, mingling with a faint aroma of magnolia made breathing undesirable.

I shivered. Jessica's spirit had well and truly left. 'For God's sake, let's open some windows!'

I flicked the light switch just inside the front door, and we leapt to the task with enthusiasm, gratefully sucking in the fresh air. Where to start? Officers from Scenes of Crime would have examined every inch of the place, but we put our latex gloves on anyway. A fleeting memory of something to do with gloves wisped into my mind, but was gone before I could grasp it.

'See if you can find anything significant in there. You know what to look for.'

I left Ben in Jessica's office and wandered through

the house, trying to get a better understanding of the victim's personality. Questions raced through my mind as I stood in her bedroom. Powder from fingerprinting coated the sills, door handles, jambs and personal belongings. Bed linen and pillows were tumbled around, exposing a luxuriously-appointed mattress. Cupboard doors gaped and clothes were piled haphazardly onto a padded window seat. Pots of eye shadow and mascara wands were jumbled together with compacts, liquid bases and bottles of perfume on the dressing-table, a nice mess for her sister to sort out.

Moving on, I investigated the black and white bathroom, noting the top of the cistern resting against the wall. Forensics inventory of bathroom contents' skimmed through my mind:

'One pair of men's underpants (a Mother Lode of DNA) a comb, toothbrush, cake of soap and one damp face flannel. Lots of bath lotion and shampoo, and three towels, two of which were white and one lilac. In the linen press, two pale blue, two bright red, two black—and one lilac? It didn't fit. If they found the missing towel in the house it would have been itemised in the report. Jessica's murderer would have had to wipe off either sweat or blood, or both, and, if the murder wasn't premeditated, find something in which to wrap the knife. A towel would have come in handy. I glanced down the list. No mention of a knife obviously missing from the kitchen, and I had seen a set sticking out of a wooden block when we were interviewing her previously. The knife could be an accessory, like a dog-stud belt or wristband.

Her nightie and dressing gown hung from a hook behind the door. I fingered the terry-towelling robe and dipped my fingers into the pockets. Empty, of course. A faint scent of magnolia clung to its fibres. As I stepped into the hallway, Ben came out of her office and handed me a leather-bound diary, burgundy cover smeared with finger-print dusting powder.

'SOCO's taken the computer in for analysis. There's a couple of postcards from her sister and some bills from local traders left. This would be the replacement diary, fingerprinted by SOCO. Nothing much in it though, ma'am. Bookings for teaching jobs and private tutoring, concerts with the orchestra, rehearsal times, that sort of thing. No social dates. I thought she was this hot-shot violinist, CDs and everything, but there didn't seem to be much going on with her career. There's the date pencilled in for Wednesday night.'

He handed the book to me. He was right, the contents were sparse. A notation in a margin about Wednesday night, 'A. Dinner 7.30 pm' Initial A? as in the report and corroborated by Miller and Mochrie. Hm...

'Ready to tackle the kitchen?'

'Not quite, ma'am, I'll be a few minutes more.'

He bustled off and I stepped into the kitchen, skirting the blackened mess on the floor, making a note to contact the scenes-of-crime cleaners. No loved ones should have to see this.

It was difficult to absorb the mind of the woman who had lived in the house. The kitchen was immaculately appointed with everything of very good quality, sharp-angled and rigid. What was it about your life, Jessica, which made you so obsessive? So neat, so controlling. Obviously, she didn't cook much. Some herbs and spices, sugar, but not even a packet of flour or any of the ingredients one would expect in what I considered a 'normal' household. The refrigerator contained a litre of skim milk, half a dozen eggs, olive oil spread, some low fat cheese, a jar of patê, several bottles of wine, mineral water, half a loaf of bread and some fruit.

My gaze roamed across the cupboards, over the chairs

toward the laundry, then back. A vase of flowers decorated a bench in the corner of the kitchen. They should have been wilting in the airless house. I stepped over and ran my fingers slowly down the petals, skimming over the realistic resin water-droplets and artificial petals. I thought Jessica had been the sort of woman who would have fresh hot-house blooms and lots of them, heavily scented and richly coloured. Strange. Perhaps she was allergic to pollen? Note to self, ask Pamela Miller.

I turned to the cupboard beside the sink and opened it. Cutlery in the drawer, further down, medicines, headache tablets, sticking plaster, vitamin capsules. On the bottom shelf, gladwrap, a roll of foil, tea towels, dish cloths, folded neatly. Who irons tea towels these days? And an unopened packet of rubber gloves.

I had closed the drawer and turned toward the laundry when it struck me. Gloves. A flash of Jessica Rallison pulling on a brand new pair of green rubber gloves on the day we arrived at the back door to interview her. The cellophane packet was lying on the bench and she had stuffed it in the waste bin while we were talking to her. I swung back, opened the cupboard under the sink and peered inside. The garbage bin was there, empty from the administrations of SOCO, along with numerous cleaning agents, a scrubbing brush, dust pan and brush. So where were the rubber gloves I had seen her wearing? Even Jessica was unlikely to have thrown them out after only a day or two's use. I tramped into the laundry and ratted through the cupboards. There was no sign of them, so I pulled out my mobile and dialled.

'John? Susan Prescott...yes, I'm sure you are busy. Look, I'm at Rallison's house. Did your team bag up a pair of quite new green rubber gloves? Okay, I'll wait.'

The key was on the inside of the back door. Holding the phone to my ear, I unlocked it and the outer screen door to step into the back yard. Like the front patch of garden, it was immaculate. A line of small shrubs stood to attention on each side of the cement pathway leading to an elderly Hills Hoist. I could hear background voices in the pathology laboratory, as John spoke to his staff, so I used the time to wander to the garage, where a spade, hoe and rake nestled next to a small lawn-mower. A well finger-printed, and powdered blue Honda Jazz was waiting forlornly for a mistress who would never again climb in, sling her handbag into the passenger seat and start the motor. There was no evidence of an animal or bird sharing her life.

John came back on the line. 'Susan, no green rubber gloves were found at the scene, only a pair in an unopened package in the bottom kitchen drawer. We left them there. Is there a problem?'

'Maybe. I'll get back to you and thanks for checking for me.'

I trotted back into the house, locked the back doors and went straight to the sink. An interesting idea was starting to form in my mind. The violinist's hands were tiny and slender. Her gloves were too small to fit the average man, who probably wouldn't think of using them anyway. I checked the towel racks. No dishcloth there or in the laundry, no tea towels either, but it had been wiped with something. In my opinion, a female cleaned up the crime scene, then left the crime scene with the gloves and cloths.

So, was she protecting someone else or herself? So, find the woman who wore the gloves, the man with whom her friends said she planned to dine on the night she died, the people who obviously visited Jess the same night, and the father of her baby. A piece of cake!

I sighed. Pamela Miller and Eloise Carpenter, both of whose hands were small could be in the frame. Briece

Mochrie had large hands, ditto Michael Whitby, and were either of them the father of her baby? Or was it the new boyfriend mentioned by Eloise? The one with whom she replaced Whitby. Had he killed her because she was pregnant? Or had Whitby because he was jealous?

I went to join Ben in searching through the music room, opened my mobile and punched in Evan Taylor's number.

'Evan...? Yes, I'm fine thanks. We're almost finished here. We found a couple of things, but I'll fill you in when I get back. I know damn well Mochrie's hiding information. Put out a call to locate him and after we've interviewed him, I want him under surveillance.'

I paused, thinking fast.

'Round up three of the team to follow Pamela Miller and Michael Whitby. Make sure whoever you send hasn't been seen by either of them. They're not to let Miller and Whitby out of their sight...no, don't pick them up ...I want to know where they go and who they talk to. I'll sort the overtime. And Evan, ask Bruce Patterson to get an order from Superintendent Greaves to apply for phone surveillance. We need to get it authorised and set up before Mochrie gets a chance to ring anybody after we finish with him.'

CHAPTER 36

Just Routine

Brie

Friday: 4.00pm.

'You knew her didn't you luv?' Mrs Schubel roared. With arms like Christmas hams, she heaved the biggest schnapper I've ever seen out of the freezer and slapped it down on the marble-topped bench with a resounding thwack. Its dead eyes and those of its relatives reminded me a little too vividly of Wednesday night.

'*Sssh!* Sandra, he was going out with her! They used to come in here all the time, remember?' the girl on the till hissed. Her eyes flickered warningly in my direction. The line of women waiting to be served craned their necks and rustled expectantly. Rage built inside me.

'Ah, yes, she did enjoy a nice piece of fish. I was forgettin', sorry luv. So you must be pretty upset about her being murdered and all, then?' Mrs Schubel shouted happily, not to be denied her moment in the sun. A collective gasp swept through the shop.

'Yes. We're all sorry.' I snarled, politely. Shit. Why the fuck did I come in here?

'Are you in the orchestra, darling?' A little wizened up woman, ninety and "not-out," peered up at me brightly, faded eyes sparkling with pleasure.

'Yes, I am.'

I took out my wallet, as Mrs Schubel's laconic husband slowly parcelled my order.

'What do you play then, love?' asked granny, standing on tip-toe to hear my reply.

'The cello.'

'The *what?*' she screeched, presenting me with her left ear, the better to hear.

'The *cello!*' I bellowed.

She smiled and nodded. 'It's yellow!' she informed the assembled populace.

My tightly wrapped bundle of fish was dumped into a plastic bag and handed over. As I paid and turned to leave, a couple of teenage girls waiting their turn to be served fluttered their eyelashes and burst into muffled giggles.

The thought of going into the butcher shop, with fresh cuts of meat in the display cabinet, had hardly been an option under the circumstances, but I needed to get some fresh food for myself and Cat. I felt safe in the record mart because it was too crowded for anyone to connect me with the photos of Ally or Jess in the daily paper, but coming in here had been a big mistake.

My mood didn't get any better when I reached my car and caught the eye of a uniformed cop standing beside the front bumper. Having spent the last two days waiting for them to interview me about Jess, I wasn't best pleased to see him turn away and start talking into his mobile, but he didn't make any move to approach me.

I unlocked the car, slung the parcel of fish onto the back seat amongst the bags of fruit, milk, bread, tins of cat food and toilet rolls, got in and gunned the motor. As I pulled into the stream of traffic, I glanced at the rear-vision mirror.

He was still talking. We made eye contact; I broke first.

After I had driven about a block, a patrol car fell in behind me. I hadn't heard from Pam since the previous morning and debated whether to drive to her place for a council of war or return home. It would take ten minutes to get there and all I really wanted was to practice for the night's gig at the club, obsess over Ally and figure out how to get out of the mess we were in. Thinking of the fish, I sighed and took the next turn left, followed by a dedicated constabulary.

I swung into my street and the patrol car turned away. It wasn't a surprise to find Detective Senior Sergeant Prescott and an off-sider parked outside the entrance to my block of units. The unmarked silver Ford sprouting a radio aerial out of its roof was a dead giveaway. I realised that if I hadn't returned to my flat, the cop in the patrol car would have pulled me over and ordered me home or taken me in to the police station.

I watched out of the corner of my eye as the attractive lady cop climbed out, hitching the strap of a large, black, leather bag over her shoulder. The young bloke who interviewed us at orchestra administration got out of the driver's side. They walked up to the entrance of my parking bay and stood, waiting patiently for me to acknowledge their presence. I left the bags in the car and turned, adopting a mask of indifference, but my heart started to beat faster. This was it.

'Mr Mochrie, you might remember Detective Constable Ben Taylor? We would like to talk to you about the murder of Jessica Rallison.'

The young bloke flashed his card and they waited, obviously expecting me to either run for it or gather up my groceries.

'Of course, Ms Prescott, if I can help I will.'

I scooped everything into the green bags, dragged them out and led the procession to the front door where

I put the shopping on the ground and opened the door in ominous silence. Cat, who ran to greet me, reared back and fled down the short hallway ahead of us as I lugged the stuff inside. 'She doesn't like strangers much,' I muttered, dumping the bags onto the kitchen bench. 'Would you like some coffee?'

'No thank you, Mr Mochrie, we only need to ask you a few questions. Just routine.'

Playing for time and composure, I made them wait while I stuffed the perishables into the refrigerator, before inviting them into the lounge room. Cat, disappointed, sat down and licked her furry, well-padded arse.

Crunch time had arrived.

Detective Senior Sergeant Susan Prescott

Friday: 4.30pm.

It was a typical bachelor flat, but I was surprised to see it was tidier than most I visited, until I spotted the overflowing garbage bin through the window by the back door, indicating frenzied activity had recently taken place. Briece Mochrie's demeanour was icy, and judging by his darting glances sideways, he was desperate to get to the telephone. Ben sat on a straight-backed leather chair, took out his notebook and waited with pencil poised. Mochrie swept a pile of sheet music from a stool and perched. I took up residence on the sofa.

We allowed the seconds to tick away before launching into the interview. Mochrie's glorious good looks had waned since he had come to the station to identify Ally Carpenter on the CCTV footage; a rooster with his plumage plucked. Finally, I took out a notebook and plunged right in.

'Mr Mochrie, did you kill Jessica Rallison?'

His face whitened and he almost leapt off his chair. 'No! No. Of course not.'

'Where were you on Wednesday night, between five and midnight?'

I could see the wheels turning as his mind squirreled frantically. 'I was with Pamela Miller. We had dinner, and then spent some time watching TV.'

He was game, but he wasn't much of an actor. His reply was too hasty, and his relief at getting the information across without making a mistake, too obvious.

'What was on TV at the time you were watching?'

'Er...the...we watched Send in the Dogs, then one of those airline programmes where everybody shouts at the booking staff.'

'I think you should consider your answer very carefully, Mr Mochrie.' He zeroed in on me, flaring his nostrils, narrowing his eyes and looking thoroughly dangerous. As a sexual turn-on it was spectacular. *Oh no, my lad, I'm immune to the likes of you!* Well, I hoped I was.

'Ah...I don't think it was the airline one, actually. I think we switched to ABC 1's film."

He obviously wasn't aware that the movie on ABC 1 had been cancelled on Tuesday in favour of a political bun-fight. I knew, because Harry had been waiting to see it and been pretty cranky when they changed the program.

I made a note and changed tack. 'How well did you know Jessica? Apart from when you had the relationship with her?'

Mochrie took his time, carefully orchestrating his answer. 'We went out for a couple of months and broke up in March. I saw her as a friend, with Ally,' His voice wavered ever so slightly when he mentioned Ally, then returned to normal. 'Pamela and Michael Whitby as well, but I told you this last time you asked.'

'Do you know if Jessica had been having a relationship with anyone recently?'

'She was having a relationship with Michael, but I heard she was slee—seeing someone else at the same time. I don't know who.'

After probing some more I sat quietly, attempting to re-build a stressful silence. I had no intention of telling him about Jessica's pregnancy. The less information he could give his friends, the better. We couldn't expect the DNA results for some time, but with any luck I could shock the chief protagonists into admissions. A surprise for Mr Whitby? Or, if he was lying, Mr Mochrie.

His gaze zeroed in on Ben, who was scribbling in his notebook. I watched the expressions flitting across his gorgeous face.

Did you murder her? Did you find her dead or dying? Call it woman's intuition or ESP, he knew more than he was letting on. 'Mr Mochrie, you do realise that tampering with evidence at a crime scene is punishable by law?'

'Yes, of course. I watch The Bill, Ms Prescott,' he replied, uneasily.

I would have taken it further with him, but I wanted to get Whitby first and let Mochrie dig himself in deep. I contemplated our surroundings to gain an impression of his background. Dozens of music text books, composer's biographies and some crime, interspersed with photos of mum and dad. There was a large one which included a brother and three pretty young women who were obviously his sisters, standing side by side, nursing armfuls of cats. A warm, close family. Strange. There were none of Ally, whom we had been assured he was mad about.

'Mr Mochrie, may I use your bathroom, please?'

The unexpected request jolted him for a moment, but his innate good manners rose to the occasion. He pointed along the hallway then sat down to re-focus on Ben, who began subjecting him to a barrage of routine questions: when had he last seen or spoken to Jessica, enemies she may have made and relationships in the orchestra. The repetitious nature of these would annoy him, but we needed see if he kept his story straight. I trotted along the passageway, glancing into the various rooms as I passed. Spare room, bed made up, but not well. Someone had slept there recently by the looks of it. Who?

Next one, music room—ah, and then the master bedroom. The cover on the huge bed was pulled up roughly. Several pairs of shoes and a pair of joggers lay scattered on the floor; a heap of jeans and t-shirts strewn over a chair. A pile of books, some of which had pieces of paper marking the pages, were on the floor by the bed. He was a reader, not a poser. Photos of Ally Carpenter covered the dresser. In the largest one, Mochrie was wrapped around her, Uluru in the background. Pain twisted my heart, surprising me in its intensity. Now I knew her relationship to our family, desperation gripped. We had to find her. Fast.

I shot into the bathroom, had a quick pee—not being one to waste an opportunity—flushed, washed my hands and was back in the lounge room, hopefully before our host twigged what I was up to. I had, however, taken a lightning glance into his bathroom cabinet in which there nothing exciting, aftershave, toothpaste. No condoms, but there was no time to rifle the bedside drawers.

They looked up as I walked in. 'Have you finished, Ben?'

'Yes, ma'am.'

Settling myself down again, I treated Mochrie to a long stare, before smiling companionably at him. 'Do you know Ally Carpenter's mother, Mr Mochrie?'

'I've never met her, 'he replied easily. 'I was away when the orchestra held its Meet The Family night.'

'Do you miss Ally?' I asked, curious to see how he reacted. He was silent for a moment, jaw clenched, eyes downcast, before answering quietly.

'Of course I do, er, Senior Sergeant. She's with me day and night.'

'We've interviewed both of her parents,' I said, in what I hoped was a reassuring manner. 'Have you met her father?'

'Ally's father died before she was born!' he announced indignantly.

'I can assure you, Mr Mochrie, we've not been talking to a ghost,' I said. 'Who told you he was dead?'

'It's common knowledge, Ms Prescott. All her friends know that.' Mochrie leapt to his feet and stalked to the window where he stood with his back to the room, hands thrust into the pockets of his jeans, shoulders in shut-out mode. Over-acting. He knows the father's alive. I glanced questioningly at Ben, who raised his eyebrows in silent response, then concentrated on his notes, all in copybook Pitman's shorthand.

'Crikey,' I breathed. 'We've got a young genius here no less.'

He beamed at me proudly, knowing I was marking time. 'Taught myself, ma'am.'

'Really? How fast are you?' I asked, glancing at Briece's uncompromising back.

'One hundred and fifty words per minute, ma'am,' Ben followed my gaze, smirking as we watched Mochrie fuming. It was only a matter of time before smoke emerged from his elegant ears.

'Well, when you get tired of the police, you can work up to court stenographer,' I joked lightly, hastily smothering my smile as Mochrie turned to glare at us. Petulant are we? Not used to being ignored, even for half a minute!

I rose to my feet, Ben following suit. The street and telephone surveillance teams should now be in place at this flat and also Pamela Miller's. Michael Whitby would be waiting for us back at the station.

I nodded to Ben, who opened his briefcase and whipped out a large evidence bag. 'Now, Mr Mochrie, I would like the clothes and shoes which you were wearing Wednesday night, thank you. I'll give you a receipt for them.'

His eyes widened and he went through the nostril-flaring routine again. For a moment, I thought he was going to protest, but he shrugged and led the way to the main bedroom. There he selected an obviously unwashed pair of jeans and t-shirt from the pile on the chair, swiped a leather coat off a hanger on the back of the door and dropped them all into the bag.

I took a receipt book out of my handbag and began to list the items. 'Underpants too, and vest, if you wear one.'

He looked at me as if I were mad. I doubt anyone had asked him that since he was ten years old, but he rooted around in the pile of clothes on the chair, fished out a pair of black under-daks and dropped them into the bag. Ben secured it and produced a smaller one, into which he invited Mochrie to put the joggers he maintained he had been wearing the night of the murder.

On impulse, I held the receipt book out to him and asked him to sign his name. He shot me a look of surprise, but did so obediently—with his left hand. Jessica's killer, according to forensics, was right-handed. I tore the receipt out, handed it to him without comment as I closed the book and put it into my shoulder bag. As soon as we reached the car I would call for someone to collect the contents of Mochrie's garbage bin before it was emptied. He preceded us silently through the hall, oozing desperation for us to leave. The door was half-closed before we turned to go down the steps.

The expression on his face fell as I swung around:

'By the way, you won't mind coming to police headquarters tomorrow morning to have a sample of your fingerprints and DNA taken, will you Mr Mochrie?'

CHAPTER 37

Machinations of A Ferret

Detective Senior Sergeant Susan Prescott

Friday: 5.30pm.

Michael Whitby was not overjoyed to be questioned at CIB Headquarters. I had not personally interviewed him at any stage in the case and his sulky expression didn't inspire any desire in me to do so. He refused to make eye contact as he was ushered into an interview room, along with his legal representation. 'Forensics have the gear he reckons he wore Wednesday night and fingerprints done, Susan,' Evan announced, striding briskly ahead of me. I skipped to catch up as he wheeled through the door of the interview room intent on catching his prey.

Whitby sat quietly beside his older, world-weary solicitor, a marked contrast between the legal and the arrogant, bearded drummer. So-rr-ee, percussionist. Evan started the tape, introduced the session and logged the time before settling beside me. We read Whitby his rights, reiterating that he was there for questioning, but not under arrest. 'My client understands that, Sergeant,' said the solicitor.

'What have you got to tell us, Michael?' asked Evan, in a deceptively mild manner. Whitby exchanged stares with us and looked down his long slim nose. His solicitor half-closed his eyes and waited us out, a game in which he was well-versed. Our quarry shuffled his feet, frowned, cleared his throat and looked irritable. I made eye contact briefly with the solicitor, who raised his eyebrows.

I had my sarcasm ready to weigh in, when Whitby cracked. 'I haven't done anything wrong. If you haven't got anything on me, then you have to let me go. Isn't that right?' he asked his brief, who nodded reassurance.

'We're wondering what you can to tell us, Michael. We may call you, Michael?' I asked, icily.

'It wouldn't do any good if I objected, would it?' he snapped, hauling himself upright in his chair.

'Did you kill Jessica Rallison?'

He didn't turn a hair 'No.'

'Were you there when she was killed, or after she died?'

He leaned back in the chair and cast his small, round eyes to the ceiling, a picture of long-suffering forbearance. He reminded me of a particularly well-nourished ferret.

'Of course I wasn't there.' He crimped his lips as though trying not to smile.

I could feel Evan's anger smouldering in his voice. 'Michael, you would be well advised to take this seriously. It is a murder investigation, you are in police custody and we don't have to release you for twenty-four hours. You had a recent relationship with Ms Rallison and we need to question you about that.'

His eyes widened. 'I have a concert to play!'

'Well, you might need to cancel unless you can give a suitably substantiated explanation of where you were on Wednesday night, between 6 and 10 p.m.'

He glanced at his solicitor, who leaned over and whispered in his ear. We waited patiently. I hoped we could match his DNA to something to take that smirk off his supercilious face.

'I was home in bed, Senior Sergeant, with someone.'

Evan made a note. 'Name?'

'She's married.' I was damned if I could see why any woman would risk her marriage with this foul little creature.

'Name?' Evan persisted.

'I'm protecting the lady's good name.' Whitby sneered piously.

'She has a good name, then?' I asked.

His eyes narrowed and he whipped around to the solicitor. 'Do I have to put up with this? Is it legal?' he asked angrily.

'I'm afraid it is, Michael. You need to give the lady's name. And if she can support your alibi then you have nothing to worry about.' He looked at me for confirmation. 'It will be kept confidential, Senior Sergeant?'

'If Michael can have his whereabouts confirmed during the time frame given to us by forensics, then the lady's husband doesn't need to know.'

Whitby shrugged and gave me a name, which I recognised as that of a harpist with the Pacific Symphony.

'When your story has been corroborated you will be free to go if we find no other evidence against you. For the time being, you will be returned to the holding cell.'

He was sitting there looking precious. I stood up, pressed the buzzer under the table and waited until a uniformed officer came to escort him back to the cells. As Whitby headed for the door, I stopped him in his tracks:

'Oh, by the way, Mr Whitby, Jessica Rallison was pregnant. If the DNA sample you gave us earlier matches that of the foetus, we'll be having another little chat.'

It was 7.30pm by the time we got back to Whitby,

who showed signs of deterioration. He slumped in his chair, scraped his fingers through now unkempt hair, attempted to realign the creases in his trousers and then spoiled the effect by-jittering and swinging his feet around. He looked like John the Baptist on Speed.

I didn't have time to stuff around with his theatrics, so I let him have it. The results of the DNA tests wouldn't be available for some time, but given the spate of TV shows where results of DNA tests are obligingly produced in ten minutes, I hoped he would swallow it.

'Michael, you admitted you had an affair with Jessica Rallison, so will it be a surprise if your DNA matches that of her baby?'

He froze, eyes wide with shock. We waited impassively, but were yearning to grab him by the throat and choke the living shit out of him. He coughed, looked anxiously at the duty solicitor and threw his hands out in a helpless gesture.

'It couldn't be. I never...'

'Don't come the raw prawn with me, mate. Do you want to get home? I can't imagine for one minute you would want to stay in the cells for the night. So, let's have the truth, Michael,' Evan asked wearily.

'E r...no.' He licked his lips nervously, pulled a grubby handkerchief out of his pocket and wrapped it around his shaking fingers.

I leaned forward and looked him straight in the eye. 'Michael, I think it's time you told us everything you know about her private life. If you had nothing to do with her death, then there'll be no evidence against you. Will there?' SOCO hadn't found anything in Whitby's house to link him with the crime, damn it!

Whitby leaned over and whispered into the ear of the solicitor who requested time with his client. We rose, signed off the interview and walked a short way along the passageway, where we stopped and leaned against the wall.

'You know this idiot's a "user," Evan commented matter-of-factly, jerking his head in the general direction of Whitby, as he flipped through the Rallison folder. 'Keep him without it long enough and we might get something useful out of him—'

Before he could continue, the door opened. The duty solicitor poked his head out and said something to the constable on guard who in turn signalled to us. We signed in again; Whitby sat back, blinking nervously.

'Michael will tell you what you want to know, Senior Sergeant.'

We waited with less than bated breath.

'Jess helped set up Ally Carpenter's kidnapping,' he stated baldly.

I felt as though the top of my head was lifting off. At last, the truth, I hoped. 'You had better tell us everything. Ally Carpenter's life could depend on it!' Please God, she was still alive and hanging in there.

Whitby talked rapidly, his words jerky and sometimes incoherent, he verbally sketched the deterioration of the relationship between Ally Carpenter and Jess Rallison.

'Jess thought her career was sliding and was jealous of Ally's success, but I don't think she was getting less work. Ally was becoming well-known and because she has a better agent, she was getting to be in demand. Then Brie dumped Jess and went after Ally. After that she sort of dumped me. I don't know the name of Jess's new boyfriend or who the other people involved are.' His mouth turned down at the corners. I hoped he wouldn't start crying.

'How can I be sure you aren't making this up because you're angry at being two-timed, Michael?' Bad cop.

He snapped his head up and fixed me with his version of a death stare. It didn't impress me; he should have taken lessons from Mochrie.

'I wouldn't tell you if I didn't know about it.'

'So how did you get into the act?' I asked, sarcastically.

For the benefit of our suspect, Evan shot me a calming glance. 'He's trying to answer, Sarge. It's very painful for him.' Good cop.

'I wasn't under any illusion I was first choice. Jess was a woman who always had to have a man in tow. I was keen and she is—was—beautiful.' His face twisted as he picked up the glass of water on the table beside him, took a huge gulp, almost choked and coughed into his handkerchief. *For chrissakes, get on with it. We haven't got time for you to die now.*

'A short time ago, she met someone else but continued to see both of us. But she swore she wasn't sleeping with him. And I'll repeat this,' he flashed a glance between us, 'I don't know his name. She was very secretive, always giggling into her mobile, but she said it was only a joke 'they' were playing on Ally to spoil her career and as revenge because of Brie.'

'When did she tell you this?'

'A few days after Ally disappeared.'

I was furious. 'Was Briece Mochrie involved?'

'I don't know for sure, but I'll bet he knew what she was doing.' Whitby's eyes glittered spitefully.

'Why would you say that?'

He shrugged.

'This would be a good way to divert attention from yourself. How do I know you're not lying?'

'Because I'm not!' He looked shifty and wriggled in his chair.

'Tell me exactly what else Jessica said to you,' Evan asked in his best avuncular manner. Whitby shot him a grateful look; they always fall for it.

'A few days ago she confided to me it was all out of hand, but she still wouldn't say who was behind it, even though she was pretty scared. And that's all I know.' He clamped his lips tightly shut.

'So why didn't you report it, Michael? You knew a crime had been committed. We've searched for Ally for a week now and you didn't tell us? It's called withholding evidence, concealing a crime, aiding and abetting—'

Allowing the words to hang in the air was an oldie but a goodie. 'Jess said they would get us both if we went to the police and I believed her,' he blurted.

I leaned back and stared at him thoughtfully. They? It fit with the CCTV footage from the nightclub. 'Now come on, we're running out of time here. Who else was involved, Michael?'

'I told you, I don't know. She didn't say and I never asked.'

'Did you go to her house the night she died?'

He shook his head. I could have killed him there and then. Evan shot me a warning glance and leaned forward.

'Aloud, for the tape please, Michael.'

With ill-grace, he denied being there. Then someone peered inside the door and whispered something to the uniformed constable. We were needed elsewhere.

'Release Whitby,' I snapped to the Duty Sergeant as we emerged from the room, 'but put him under surveillance,' to Evan.

CHAPTER 38
Unwanted Goods

Eloise

Saturday: 7.00am.

The sight of my friend Rosalind sitting in the car beside the man whom I knew to be Georgie's lover, maybe murderer, chased through my mind until I became exhausted. James reiterated the notion that she probably didn't know anything about Ally's kidnapping. His reasoning nearly drove me bats. 'Calm down, El. You're assuming something which has no basis in fact.'
'But, James, he killed Georgie!' I wailed.

'You don't know that, and remember, if he was seeing Georgie on the island, he could well have been having it off with Rosalind on the mainland. Lots of men sleep with two women at the same time. And no, I've never done that!'

He smiled briefly, before continuing. 'They would not necessarily know about each other's involvement, and Georgie could even have been killed by a tourist trying to rob the house. No doubt the police will find out.'

'I hope you're right,' I sniffled, heartbroken by the slaying of the woman who had been the sister of my heart.

I *had* woken up with a sense of hope that Ally would

survive this.

'You had a fucking terrible night and so did I,' he said, running his hand distractedly through his hair. My heart ached at the strain in his face. I longed to touch, to comfort, but would he welcome such a move? Nothing he had said led me to believe he wanted to be touched affectionately.

'Did you? Well, today I've made up my mind to be positive. No more crying. We can't let Jess's murder—' that terrible word—'deflect us from ensuring Ally's safety.'

'That might have nothing to do with Ally. Jess could have been killed by a jealous lover. But she was frightened about something to do with Georgie's murder, remember? When Pam told her about it on the phone.'

'Yes. Yes, I do. But with Ally still missing, her ear and the eBay stuff…' I could hardly bear to voice my thoughts on that subject. I took a careful sip of hot coffee.

'Well…' He left it at that. James could actually meet their demands, but if he hadn't been very wealthy or responsibly inclined, Ally wouldn't have been worth kidnapping in the first place.

He announced he was going back to his computer and he would see me at breakfast. It was all too much to cope with. I put my empty cup on the bedside cabinet and stumbled off to the bathroom before I gave in to my mood and stayed in bed for the rest of the day with the bedclothes pulled over my head.

Saturday: noon.

I had been trying to keep occupied by arranging flowers in the massive Spode vase in the vestibule while James was crouched over his computer. I needed another jug of water from the kitchen. Mrs Fox was standing on the far side of the room with her back to me, putting china into a high cupboard. The radio played her favourite country music and concealed my approach. Before I spoke, she reached awkwardly into the top shelf and her arm scraped the side of her head. Her hair lifted. In the moment before she tweaked it straight, I saw gleaming black tresses peeping out from under the dull, brown mop.

I couldn't believe it. Quietly, I backed away from the door and almost ran back to the study. I could hardly wait to tell James.

'Really? Sure you weren't mistaken?'

'I'm not. She really does have thick, black hair underneath the wig. There doesn't seem to be any reason why she would try to disguise a head of healthy hair with nondescript fake hair. It doesn't make sense!'

'Does she know you saw it?'

'She had her back to me and the radio was on so she didn't hear me. I got out of there and came straight in here.'

I sensed his mind working at lightning speed; the expression on his face could have been carved in stone. 'I'd not thought...Eloise, next time you see her, whatever you do, don't let on that you know she's wearing a wig. There's something strange here. Let me think about it for a while.'

'What is it? Just tell me.'

He took me by the hand and guided me into the chair beside his. 'Trust me, we'll discuss it as soon as I find out a few things. If you can't treat Mrs Fox normally, stay away from her. Somehow I feel it's vital she doesn't realise you know she's wearing a wig.' His eyes bored into mine, his expression grim.

'You must tell me what you're on about. I'm part of this and I need to know.'

'All right, but I'm trusting you to hold it together. Promise, El?'

My heart beat faster. Mrs Fox had always seemed so mild and pleasant. In the light of what James was implying, I felt as though a kitten had tried to rip my throat out.

'We've gone into this before. The ransom demands, the letter box messages and money drops. How did the kidnappers get hold of the key? It has to be someone I know—a friend, a member of the orchestra or my household staff. I thought of them at the start, but it didn't occur to me they would be so bold. If it's them...'

'But Mrs Fox? She's such a quiet, modest woman. And her father? That old man! I know he's a surly old thing, but surely...'

'Ssssh. We can't jump to conclusions, but we always knew it had to be someone who knew me well. If Mrs Fox and her father are in it, that probably means Angelo is involved as well. They've had constant access to the keys.' He thought for a moment. 'Georgie and Rosalind were definitely the only ones you told?'

'No one else knew, not even my doctor. I didn't put your name on Ally's birth certificate and my family's all gone. Who's Angelo?'

'My chauffeur and handyman. He drove you here Sunday.' I shivered, remembering his cold gaze in the rear vision mirror.

James stared into space for a few minutes and then reached for the telephone.

'I wouldn't think the old man and Angelo could plan an operation like this, but Mrs Fox is another story. I'm getting someone to re-investigate the staff. My solicitor had a check on them and their references, but it was purely for employment purposes. One thing's certain though, they don't have criminal records. At least, they didn't when they came here.'

As he gave the details of his employees to the person at the other end of the phone, I glanced around the now familiar room, noting with surprise that a small landscape now occupied the space where his parents' photo had been. I was surprised not to have noticed the change, but reflected that the past had become unimportant in the scheme of things. The present was all that mattered.

As he laid the receiver back into its cradle, a deep, inner impulse made me enfold his hand in both of mine and hold it against my breasts. The response was swift and warm. He turned his head and looked straight into my eyes, sending a hot flush creeping up my neck, into my face. An electrical charge sizzled through my body. My breasts tingled; warmth spread between my legs.

'Go for it' urged a voice, deep in my heart.

'I need you so much, James,' I whispered, my heart pounding nervously. He slowly untangled his hand from mine and gently traced my face with his finger, then slid his hand down my throat to enclose my breast. My heart galloped as he bent over me and crushed his hot mouth to mine. His tongue slicked over my lips, then plunged inside. I heard myself whimper with excitement. The male smell of him invaded my senses.

He hauled me to my feet and crushed me against his powerful chest with one arm, pulling my hair out of its knot with the other. Heat flared between us like a living entity. We strained closer as I savoured the rock-hard length of his erection. Thrusting my hands under his sweater, I wrenched his shirt out of his waistband and slid my fingers over his hot, smooth skin. His powerful muscles flexed as I touched; his fingers raked the full length of my hair and settled around my bottom.

He slipped his muscular thigh between my legs and

I rubbed myself against him. We staggered across the room, collapsed onto the sofa and tore each other's shirts open. My bra disappeared. He drew my breasts up between his huge hands, then ran his tongue over first one, then the other, before drawing my nipples up into his mouth, sliding his tongue around the tips.

I was on fire.

He slid his hand inside my slacks to cup me through my panties, as we murmured incoherently against each other's mouths.

'God El, I wasn't sure you...'

'You must have known...I've got to...'

A resounding clang came from the kitchen, startling us into awareness of our situation.

'Come on!' James helped me up and we hastily arranged our clothing. He grabbed my hand and we went for the door, peering out into the foyer to make sure the coast was clear. We tried not to make a sound as we scurried up the stairs and barged into his bedroom. He turned the key in the lock and we fell on the bed, tearing at each other.

He ripped my panties off; I broke the zipper on his jeans.

It was as though we had never been apart.

Saturday: 4.30pm.

Rosalind rang, full of information about her new lover and to tell me she had been in Brisbane for a few days, although she reassured me my animals were being looked after. It wasn't hard to keep my responses muted because I could barely speak to her. What was she playing at? Was she complicit in Georgie's murder? Was she involved in Ally's kidnapping? I knew I had to maintain control of my temper, but a few encouraging noises and she was well away.

Firstly, she swore me to secrecy. It seemed he was separated, but didn't want to give his ex-wife ammunition to get more money out of him. I duly promised not to tell anyone and reassured, she rattled on. His name, she confided, was Tomaso Esposito, he was fifty-two and he lived at the Gold Coast. By the time she finally calmed down, I had far too much information. According to Ros, Tommy, in spite of his age, was a first class stallion.

'Eloise, I'm so excited, I never thought in a million years I would actually meet an eligible man at my age. They always want the young ones, don't they, but not Tommy!'

She bubbled over with details of her exciting, fabulous love life, eager to share her happiness with me for a further twenty minutes or so, after which I went to tell James all about it.

James re-assured me. 'Well, firstly, it would appear she hasn't a clue he was Georgie's lover. You said Rosalind hadn't seen him with her. She's not going to be happy for too long if it turns out he murdered Georgie. And secondly, we don't have any reason to suppose she's told anyone about me or that this character is involved in any way with Ally's abduction. From what you've told me about your long friendship, it's most unlikely Rosalind would be a party to anything which would hurt Ally. And Georgie might still have been killed by someone robbing the house.'

He wrote Tommy Esposito's name on a piece of paper and reached for the phone to send a minion on the hunt. That done, he turned and wrapped his arms around me, resting his cheek on the top of my head.

The few experiences of sex I had, paled beside the passion we shared during our afternoon of love-making.

I tightened my arms around his waist and burrowed into his body, drawing comfort from the heat of his swift response and from his male smell. He ran his hand over my head and combed his fingers through the long strands of my wild, loose hair.

'You do believe Ally's going to be all right, don't you?'

He kissed me. 'As sure as I can be. We have to be positive, to believe there's no reason to do anything to her as long as they're getting the money and once it's all over they'll let her go.' It was a lifeline. If James said it, then it had to be right, but...

'Or kill her,' my mind persisted. 'Yes, *that's—*' No. Shut up. Oh, please, please...God, if you're really there...

For a split second, I see myself standing over a supine form, saying, 'Yes, that's my daughter...' No. Shut up, Eloise, don't even think it. I thrust the terrible image aside and clutched at James's words like a drowning ant to a piece of straw. 'And then?'

'He put me away from him and looked down into my eyes. 'Eloise, I have something to ask you. When we get Ally back, would you come and live with me? I want you so badly, El and don't want to lose you again.'

Could I give up my home, my job? My hard-won independence? My mind grabbed at thoughts, discarding them and moving on in a wild dance of indecision. I had a second chance to be with the one man I've always loved and now we knew who was really to blame for our separation. There was no decision to make, but something needed to be explained before I committed myself.

'I've been on my own a long time, James. I would be a loving partner, yes, but I'm not a dependent person now.'

'I wouldn't expect you to be otherwise. Could you be

happy in this house?'

'This place is big, but it's pretty full of your collection of music and art. There isn't much room to move.'

He looked thoughtful. 'I can have boxes of stuff shifted over to the storerooms above the garages. Old Bob can move them tomorrow, and then you can see where you want to put your things if we decide to remain here. That is, if you'll come and be with me?'

'James, I want to be with you so much, but I can't think of anything except Ally's safety right now.'

'Of course, but will you come and live with me?' he persisted.

The thought of losing him again was untenable. 'Yes, of course I will,' I answered, discarding practical considerations.

His face lit up as he enveloped me in his arms. Passion flared again, before he gently and regretfully held me away from him. Our eyes met, promises silently made.

'This time we're going to make it, darling. Don't worry, we'll sort it all out, and Ally will come home to us. Hold the thought close to you. Now, I'm going to do a little reconnoitring. Take the dog for a walk.'

He placed his fingers over my mouth as I started to protest. 'I'll be careful.'

My emotions swirled as he called the dog and they headed out the back door. If James suspicion proved right and his staff were involved ... but if they weren't, we would be no worse off. He had nothing to lose by investigating. I just hoped he wouldn't run into trouble because if he did, I had nowhere to turn except to the police. What would happen to Ally then? And I'd be on my own forever.

The rest of my life stretched before me, bleak and lonely, the great hole left by the loss of my child...I pulled myself away from destructive thoughts. *Eloise, for God's sake, stop it. You're not helping yourself or anyone else like this. Think about your future with James. You've loved him for twenty-six years, and now you're going to get your wish. Be thankful for that, at least. And keep telling yourself that Ally will come home safely.'*

My heart beat faster as I watched James and his dog set off toward the distant garages and accommodation block, where Mrs Fox, her father and the chauffeur lived. With its imposing façade and clock-tower attic, it seemed an excellent place to store unwanted goods.

CHAPTER 39
As Dusk Falls

Ally

Saturday: sunset.

A stranger told me I am going to die tonight.
Ice chips of fear trickle through my veins.
Minutes race as seconds; if I hold my breath, will it keep me alive longer?
No.
Please...I have so much to do yet, a career that's only just started and so many plans for my future.
I want to have a family one day, but now I'm being pushed out of the world before I've even lived.
The wooden floor feels like concrete beneath my knees. I wrap my arms around my body.
So cold. So scared.
My imagination forces the knife into my body—my stomach—my chest. Please, God, let it be a gun.
They've drugged my water for days. I could drink it all at once so I won't know anything when it happens, but what if I get a final chance to run? Some small part of me is still hoping something will happen.
What did I do to deserve this? Deep down, I think I always knew I could never escape. The woman's hatred grows stronger every day. It's not all about the money, but what? They won't tell. They're too happy for me to

beg.

God, please, someone find me before it's too late.

I brace myself against the bleak timber wall and peer out into blackness.

The power of life and death.

Terror is giving way to rage.

How dare they decide how long I am to live?

CHAPTER 40
A Bit Of A Glitch

James

Saturday: 5.45pm.

A slight breeze stirred the leaves in the trees. The traffic on the main road murmured in the distance. A few early stars pierced the celestial canopy as the sun began its descent behind the hill, but still providing light for a walk in the garden.

Demanding the keys to the tower storeroom would allow me access to the immediate vicinity of the staff quarters. Despite the kidnapper's threats, I intended to call the police when I satisfied myself there was good reason. Things had gone too far. Detective Senior Sergeant Susan Prescott's warning about the consequences of not informing the police if we were in trouble kept returning to my mind. I had allowed the earlobe, along with a lock of Ally's bloodied hair, to deter my intentions, preventing Eloise from calling the police after the first ransom demand and the phone calls since then.

My stupidity rankled. How could I overlook my staff's access to the keys and to myself? It gave them a perfect opportunity, though currently a motive—apart from money—escaped me. I tried to comfort myself with the age-old assurance—surely people we know just don't do things like that. It wasn't working. Eloise's return had clouded my judgment. My solitary life had made me complacent. Since Helen's death, my emotions skimmed only the surface of my heart.

I walked slowly. Rage fought for control and I reminded myself to keep a sense of proportion. I needed proof of more than Mrs. Fox's wig. There are many reasons why women wear them, but Eloise maintained Mrs Fox had beautiful natural hair.

Eloise. Her warmth, the incredible beauty of our lovemaking threatened to distract me further, but I needed my wits about me for the coming encounter. Fear for my daughter warred for first place with my love for her mother.

Benji hurled himself enthusiastically after the ball which I threw for him as I watched for signs of life. The staff residence, a medium-sized cottage adjoined to the workshop and garages, formed an L-shape. Two storerooms resided atop the structure.

I continued to let my gaze wander, seemingly aimlessly, skimming the windows, swinging across to the now defunct orchard and vegetable gardens at the far side of the compound, where lights showed behind the curtains of the staff cottage.

Inside Staff Quarters: 5.45pm.

They were pleased with themselves. The woman sipped her wine appreciatively between mouthfuls of food. The family munched on slices of roast lamb, gravy and mint sauce, crisp, roasted potatoes, pumpkin and onion with glistening, freshly-picked green peas on the side, washed down with Fourex. Pavlova would follow.

The stepson looked forward to an evening of clubbing, the grandfather, fixated on 'The Bill', chewed as fast as he could. The woman would attend her weekly card night. They left nothing to chance and would stick to their normal routine. The girl's parents were so terrified that they wouldn't—*couldn't*—tell the cops. The primary reason for the kidnapping was about to play out, the money a welcome bonus. The Carpenter girl waited upstairs ready to be killed by Angelo after he arrived home from his night out.

It was a happy family party, until they heard the dog barking.

At first they took no notice, but as the barking grew louder, they realised his master would be close by. Three pairs of eyes met. The woman rose quickly, went to the window and peered around the side of the curtain. 'He's on his way here!' She glanced wildly at her father, then at her stepson who pushed his plate aside and leapt to his feet.

'I'll head him off,' he hissed, spun for the door, wrenched it open and barely avoided slamming it behind him.

The old man coughed nervously and spat into a pot plant. 'Keepin' her here under 'is nose was always a mistake. I told *him* that,' he snarled, staring truculently at his daughter.

She snatched up her glass of wine from which she proceeded to take angry sips between sentences. 'No, it wasn't! Where else could we operate without anyone knowing about it? He's never come over here in all the time we've been working for him, so why now?'

Her father poured a cup of tea with a palsied hand, the pot shaking ominously, splashing droplets of hot liquid onto the tablecloth. Parkinson's Disease had him in its rapacious grasp, but he could still function. His daughter made no attempt to help him. Her eyes flickered to the shotgun leaning against the kitchen cupboard and across to the door.

'Calm down. It's just a bit 'uva glitch! No need to get yer knickers in a twist. He probably just wants to talk to Angelo about the cars. There's no chance he knows she's up there,' her father re-assured. He glanced at the ceiling, then leaned forward and blew on his scalding tea before taking a long slurp of his beer.

'Do you really think it's about the cars?' she asked.

'Christ only knows, but the lad'll divert him.'

She spared her succulent dinner a regretful glance and pushed her plate away. She opened the refrigerator and took out a brightly painted plate on which stood a glistening Pavlova, complete with strawberries on top, slathered in cream and dusted with icing sugar. Her father's eyes focused greedily. 'You're not a bad cook, June,' he conceded. 'Not a patch on what yer mum was, but not bad for all that.'

His daughter cut a piece of Pavlova, eased it onto a plate and set it in front of him with rather more force than strictly necessary. The base of the meringue split, scattering sugary crumbs over the tablecloth.

'Hurry up, dad. I'm going out shortly, so get a move on. You haven't even finished your main course yet,' she snapped.

Her father curled his hand possessively around the plate, guarding what was left of his meringue. 'Oi! You didn't hafta break it, luv!'

CHAPTER 41
A Just Reward

James

Saturday: 6.22pm.

As I neared the entrance to the workshop, Angelo burst out of the front door of the flat. I stopped and waited for him to approach. I've never thought about him personally one way or another, but Eloise maintains he is a cold, evil man. As far as I was concerned, he did his job and was civil, which was all I required.

My business agent advertised for staff just before I leased the residence the previous year, interviewed many applicants on my behalf and reported himself dissatisfied with most. Then Mrs Fox offered herself as package deal with her father and stepson as cook/housekeeper, chauffeur/ handyman and gardener. They produced impeccable references which were verified by a previous employer in Sydney. Only too glad to have my staff problems solved, I instructed the agent to hire them.

But as I watched Angelo come toward me, zipping up his black leather jacket against the cool night air, I understood why Eloise was uneasy in his presence. His dark eyes focused on me without expression; his muscular body appeared poised for combat. He stopped about a metre away, adopting a deferential pose. 'Ah, Sir, I'm glad you're over here because old Bob wants me to talk to you about a new bore.'

I was taken aback 'A bore? That's for the owners of this place to decide. Can't Bob discuss this with me in the morning? Where is he?'

Angelo does not normally take an interest in anything other than maintaining the cars, driving me or my guests if required or doing mechanical repairs around the place.

'He's not well tonight, so I offered to come and talk to you instead.'

'I see. Nothing serious?'

He shook his head and appeared about to expand on it, but I cut him short.

'I came to check out the space in the tower storeroom. Where's the key?'

'We don't have one, sir. There aren't any in the flat or the workshops.'

He avoided eye contact. Behind me, Benji whined. I glanced down. The dog was looking up at the tower. Something was out of kilter in the shadowed window. I glanced casually up at the tower then without pausing, turned my head to scan the trees surrounding us. I allowed my gaze to casually drift across to the staff quarters and back to Angelo. The dog moved closer and barked. Angelo picked up the slimy ball and threw it awkwardly in the opposite direction to the buildings. Benji glanced after it, but resumed his surveillance of the building. I bent down quickly, grabbed his collar and shook him gently. 'Be quiet!' We needed to get back to the house, fast, before the dog gave my game away.

'I want a full scale hunt for the storeroom keys, otherwise we'll have to get a locksmith in on Monday. I'll ring you in the morning. Goodnight to you.' I nodded briskly and turned to leave. Angelo returned my salutation with due deference, but underneath the veneer of good manners he appeared shaken. Damn.

I maintained a steady pace back to the house, trying not to bolt. My mind bounced around ways of discovering what was different about that window. Mrs Fox had advised us she and her stepson were going out for the evening. Bob would be watching television and would turn the sound up because he refused to wear a hearing aid.

My first thought was to ring the police, but if I called them out on a goose chase I would lose my efficient staff and probably get sued as well. But what if they had taken Ally? What if the police stormed in and it started a siege? She might be killed in crossfire. Had I watched too many American movies?

The bad news was a hundred metres between the outer buildings and the back of the house. The good news was the number of shrubs and small trees giving cover. I tried to re-assure myself the police wouldn't dream of jeopardising Ally's safety. Perhaps I could lure the staff out of the flat while the police rescued Ally, if indeed she was there. But if that were the case, they would have someone guarding her.

I felt as though I had stepped into a war zone.

When I got back to the house, Eloise was working in the kitchen. 'What happened? Did you find anything?' she asked, nervously clutching my sleeve.

'There's something needs checking out. It won't take long and then I'll tell you all about it.' I kissed the top of her head, bolted for the study and snatched my binoculars off the shelf. Two huge urns maintained sentinel each side of the front steps, perfect for my purpose. Steadying my elbows on the ledge around one, I aimed the binoculars at the tower and twirled the focus until it came into sharp relief.

Shock arced through me. *A grill on the inside of the window?* It had not been there when I inspected the property before taking up the lease. I carefully adjusted the focus. Definitely a security grill and even allowing for the failing light, the glass shone black. Tinted?

Something moved.

I squinted into the lens, trying to make the image sharper. Was Angelo keeping a girlfriend up there? Or was it Ally? My mind whirled through various impractical plans, then rejecting them almost immediately.

'James? Where are you? *James?*' Eloise came up behind me, a note of panic creeping into her voice. I stood up and gently propelled her back inside, where I recounted my suspicions. She wanted to dash over there immediately, but I talked her out of confronting the family, laying out my reasons for taking precautions. As I had expected, it wasn't easy.

Having calmed Eloise down, I telephoned the staff quarters and called off the search for the key, advising Mrs Fox I had changed my mind and explaining that my cartons could stay in the upstairs rooms at the main house.

The relief in her voice terrified me. While Eloise bobbed around in agitation, I located the key to a locked room where the owner of the house kept personal property. In the event of fire or water damage, he had shown me the blueprints of the buildings. A few minutes of examination and I saw the possibility of a plan.

The first part was to find out if there actually was someone, a woman, in the tower room, and the first opportunity to reconnoitre would be that night. Mrs Fox and Angelo planned to go out and Bob was, to all intents and purposes, out of the equation. Everything hinged on keeping the trio lulled into a false sense of security.

I'm pretty fit for my age, but young muscles could carry it out faster and I knew just the lad for the job. As

I picked up my mobile to call Briece Mochrie, I reflected grimly that since my parents ousted Eloise twenty-six years ago, no one has gotten the better of me until now.

Things were about to change.

STAFF quarters.

June was in a frenzy of fear, but Angelo reassured her. 'He wanted to look in the tower. Needs a place to store some of his stuff, but I said we didn't have keys to it. He said we gotta hunt for them tomorrow. He's gone back to the house, but we've got to ring dad. We could be in deep shit. Bastard dog started whining at the tower! I'll knock the fucking thing off too if I get a chance.' He balled his right hand and punched it into the palm of the left, face twisting with rage.

'I'll call Tommy,' his stepmother announced. 'He's down at the yacht club checking on the boat.'

Angelo took a deep breath, sidled to the window and peered around the edge of the heavily-lined curtain. The old man resumed eating, as June talked to her husband 'Yes, we'll sit tight. Go ahead as arranged? Of course ... that late? Well, we were going to do it tonight anyway, so there's no reason to change anything is there? It won't matter what he does about the keys after that.'

She glanced at her father and stepson, biting her lip as she shifted from one foot to the other. The ticking of the wall clock echoed the thudding of their nervous hearts. Angelo smiled and fingered the pristine blade of his knife. The old man chewed slowly, trying not to let his teeth clack. He didn't want to miss out on anything.

'All right then, around midnight. I'll remind Angelo to leave the gate open to the back road.' June hung up and turned to face them. 'Right, we stick with the plan. You can still go out, Angelo, but make sure you're back before midnight. I'm going to cards, but I'll be back in more than enough time. Dad, you just carry on as normal. For two pins if it wasn't that I want to be there, I'd get you to finish her off now, but he wants to be back here for it too, in case of trouble. Says it's safer to stick with what we arranged.'

She jerked her head in the direction of the house. 'They spent the afternoon in bed, so they'll be sleeping together tonight. That'll keep them out of the way.' She laughed. 'Your father'll get rid of the body. By morning there'll be no trace of her upstairs. We'll keep working here for awhile and then resign, as planned. I'll enjoy organising the food for her wake. Stop that!' she added irritably, as Angelo flicked the edge of the blade over and over, against the ball of his thumb.

Reluctantly, he put the knife on the table and smiled. He expected to have a little fun as a suitable reward for his diligence. He just hoped they would give him enough time to finish what he began the day his stepmother copped him with Ally. He would have been into her, given a few more minutes. Now there was a second chance. The fact she'd be drugged like last time was neither here nor there. He would prefer she fought him because it was more fun and appealed to his need for power, but it didn't matter in the long run. He remembered the feel of her full, rounded breasts in his mouth and her lush, soft body beneath him. His fingers twitched with the urge to pleasure himself.

Just then, the phone rang. They glanced apprehensively at each other. June picked it up. 'Hello...oh I see, yes. Very good, sir.' She put the receiver down, relief easing the harsh lines between her brows and around her mouth. 'He's changed his mind about finding the key. Going to keep his stuff over at the house.' She stood silently for a moment, looking at each of them in turn, her dark eyes burning with a deep, agonising pain, carefully nurtured for thirteen long years.

'Remember, I'm going to see her before you do it, Angelo. She knows she's going to be killed tonight. Tommy told her this morning, but she has to know why. Ally Carpenter is going to pay for what she did. *And that's my just reward.*'

CHAPTER 42

Confessions and Collectibles

Detective Senior Sergeant Susan Prescott

Saturday: 8.00am.

We're running out of time. Fear held me tightly in its grip. I pulled into the underground car park, grabbed my briefcase and hurried to the lift, arriving as it was about to bear a brace of stalwart constabulary to the upper levels. A 'Morning, ma'am' chorus erupted as I stepped in and smiled briskly. We all gazed at the floor indicator. The muffled snickers behind me suggested that I had interrupted a dirty joke.

My team were gravitating toward the white boards at the far end of the room while I shed my coat and poured what passed for a coffee. When we started collating reports, other CIB members would gravitate to our end of the campsite to listen in.

'Ma'am, we're ready.' I grabbed my notebook and sat on the edge of a table, trying not to fidget. Inspector Bruce Peterson came and sat beside me. My neck muscles felt as though they had been tightened with screws. Briefly, I closed my eyes and willed strong vibes to Ally Carpenter. *Hang in there, Ally. Don't let go.*

'Ben, what have you got?' asked Evan.

'Sarge, there's nothing significant in Jessica Rallison's email history, but her phone records show that during this previous fortnight she made one hundred and sixty three calls to a pre-paid mobile. On the landline, there were twenty-five to Michael Whitby, sixteen business calls, thirty to friends and one to Ally Carpenter at seven pm last Friday.

Setting up Ally? Maybe. I remembered the description of Jessica's mother's reaction when advised of her daughter's murder by CIB Townsville. Oh, Jessica, you were such an unhappy, unloved girl. Would the sister care enough to come and sort out the house and collect the car or get professional packers to do it? Jessica must have known about the pregnancy. Perhaps the father wasn't in a position to be embroiled in a scandal and killed her to prevent it...

My attention snapped back to the present. 'Nothing from Briece Mochrie's clothes as yet. Len?'

' No, but Mochrie had his DNA taken this morning, Sarge.'

'Good, now—'

'Excuse me a moment. Evan, surveillance on Miller and Mochrie. Anything yet?' I asked.

'No, there's been no action, ma'am.'

'Leave it in place until tomorrow morning. We'll re-assess then.'

'A neighbour of Rallison's rang in to report seeing a small, bronze hatchback parked under the trees Tuesday night last week. Her dog pissed on the wheel. A man was slumped down in the front seat, but she couldn't see his face. Of course she didn't get the number.'

Collectively, we rolled our eyes. That sense of urgency niggled me again.

'Okay. Cody?' Evan waited for the next report.

'Townsville police rang this morning and advised they have identified Georgie Hird's lover as Tommy Esposito, aged 58, one hundred and eighty centimetres, dark hair, skippers a yacht for—' He named a prominent Townsville businessman. 'The suspect has,' Cody walked to the white board and proceeded to pin up a computerised photo, 'this distinguishable feature.'

We examined the dark-haired, dark-eyed man, with swarthy skin and head so square it looked like a box with a face painted on it and a black wig on top.

'He's wanted for questioning into Georgie Hird's murder, but has disappeared. The only link we have so far to connect him to this case is that Hird was Eloise Carpenter's best friend and godmother to Ally. The post mistress stated Esposito had been seen walking on the cliffs with Miss Hird at dusk on at least one previous occasion.'

A detective constable came into the room waving a fax printout. 'Following on your inquiry, ma'am, early this week, Ally Carpenter's father started selling his art collection and cars, a Gull-wing Mercedes and an E-type Jaguar.'

My spirits picked up. 'Sir, looks as though we might have a break-through!' DI Bruce Peterson smiled like a shark.

The detective continued. 'There've been large amounts of cash going out of his accounts during the last week. He visited his deposit box in the bank's vault four times and obtained a substantial line of credit. He paid the money he got from the auto and art sales into his account, but then started spending it again.'

'Maybe he just wanted to get rid of his collection and move in a different direction? Or perhaps he's broke,' one of the team speculated. I didn't believe it. I picked up my now cold, half-empty cup of coffee, stood up and glanced in enquiry at my superior.

'Carry on Susan. Let me know what you want. I can arrange for extra bodies from uniform.'

'Okay, let's work on strategy. We're going with Ally Carpenter being kidnapped for ransom and it looks as though her father is amassing a lump sum to pay to the kidnappers. If so, we need to know when and where the drop is going to be made and who's making it. They obviously haven't done it yet or the girl would have been released, or...' I paused.

We all knew what "or" might mean. One of the junior members of the team piped up. 'Ma'am, what about Briece Mochrie for the drop? He's Ally Carpenter's boyfriend and he's bound to know the father's alive by now. May have known all along.'

'You're right. We'll keep him under surveillance. If he has a coughing fit, I want to know.'

Open discussion started; ideas flew thick and fast. I excused myself and headed for the restroom. On the way back, I was waylaid by an Inspector from Fraud. As we conversed, I overheard something which didn't immediately ring a bell.

'I couldn't believe it. There was this totally insignificant painting going for thousands of dollars on eBay last night. No one in their right mind would pay that much for it and that's not all. There's been stuff sold in fine china, jewellery—you name it, this dude's buying it. And for stupid prices! Either he's a total wanker, he's opening a shop or he knows something I don't. I tell you, it's fucking insane, mate!'

I stopped talking and turned around. Two young detective constables were sitting at their computers having a slag session. EBay...

'Susan?' The DI looked at me, puzzled.

'I'm sorry, Alan, you were saying?' I apologised. We concluded our conversation, then I scooted back to my troops.

It was going to be a long day.

Saturday: 7.00pm.

The news was bad.

'They've lost Briece Mochrie, Susan. One moment he was buying groceries and then he took a call on his mobile and disappeared. His car's gone from the car park. An all-points bulletin's been sent out to pick him up,' said Evan. Fear for Ally ripped through me; I forced my mind to concentrate.

'Bloody hell! What was he doing at the supermarket? He had a carload of groceries yesterday afternoon before we interviewed him, so how come he was back there tonight? And how long ago did they lose him?'

'Around fifteen minutes ago. Somebody took their eye off the ball and they've been running around like headless chooks ever since,' he thundered, as he bolted for the lift, followed by three of our team.

'He's deliberately given surveillance the slip. They'd better find him again or I'll put them all on traffic duty,' I snarled.

The eBay wanker. Why would someone buy rubbish art, jewellery and cars on eBay for outlandish prices? Wealthy people were canny with their money.

It hit me like as stab in the ribs with a knitting needle. Could it be possible that some of the ransom was being paid via eBay? Anonymous, discreet, it was a place where accounts could be opened and closed in short spaces of time, but amateurish. A way of keeping frantic parents occupied or very clever indeed? As long as money seemingly changed hands without problems, there would be no reason for anyone to suspect what was happening. If it hadn't been for a young constable who just happened to know his collectibles market...gotcha!

I dialed Evan's mobile. 'Evan? Is Pamela Miller still at home?'

'Yes, she's there,' he shouted against the roar of the surrounding traffic.

'Get someone to go in and check it out. Make some excuse. Ditto, Whitby.'

'It's already done, Susan.'

'Good. Where are you?' I asked.

He told me.

'I'm joining you out there.'

'Best not yet, until we get a fix on Mochrie. I'll let you know the minute we have a sighting. Sit tight.'

'Remember, just follow and don't lose him.' My heart pounded. My inner voice screamed 'Hurry hurry.'

'Yes, Susan, *I know.*'

He signed off quickly, before I could hound him any further. 'Probably the whole damn orchestra's in on this,' I thought bitterly, but then I remembered a slight hesitation as Eloise denied talking to Briece Mochrie recently and it all slotted into place.

I snatched up my bag and coat, phoning Evan back as I ran.

'I think I know where he's going! Where are you now?'

I shot into the lift, tucked the mobile between my neck and shoulder and stabbed frantically at the button for the car park. Evan's voice was faint, but the salient details got through. I talked fast, arranging to meet on the street that ran along the rear of James's property and advising Evan not to use sirens.

Hurry! hurry!

I threw my belongings into the car, hurled myself behind the wheel and drove off, struggling to fasten the seat belt as I wove in and out of the traffic.

CHAPTER 43

Armageddon

Saturday: 7.30pm.

Angelo turned the engine off and coasted quietly through the back gate, thoughtfully opened by his stepmother for his father to gain entrance later that night. He was not going to miss out on playtime with Ally Carpenter. He was looking forward to it and June wouldn't stop him this time. It would be great fun slaughtering Ally while he was fucking her, pleasure which had been denied him when he was forced to kill Jess.

His father, the expert strategist, had hand-picked her for the "in" saying Pam Miller was no use, as she had no axe to grind with Ally. Using his exceptionally good-looks and charm to ensure an affair with Jess, stirring her festering jealousy to plant the suggestion in her mind to play a joke on Ally.

But when he arrived at her house on Wednesday night she had been hysterical, having realised they had used her jealousy for their own purposes and that kidnapping the Carpenter girl was not a prank after all. She had grabbed her mobile and tried to dial Triple 0. He smiled, remembering the terror in her eyes, the whimpering when she realised he was wasn't going to bash her—just gut her like a fish. He padded past the windows of the lounge room, his joggers soundless on the concrete. That old goat, Bob, would be slumped asleep on the sofa, drooling into the cushions with his loaded shotgun beside him. 'Got it in case of home invasion,' he explained.

Angelo paused as he rounded the side of the building, licking his lips, studying the landscape like a wolf on the hunt testing the air for rivals to its prey. Nothing moved. Re-assured, he walked to the door leading to the tower, quietly opened it and slunk up the creaky stairs, well prepared with torch, gag and knife.

Saturday: 7.40pm.

James and Brie set out, carrying an extension ladder between them, using the light blazing from the main house as a guide until their eyes became accustomed to the dark.

A gentle breeze stirred the leaves of the branches like wind chimes, overhanging the pathway; the silky fronds flicked their cheeks. In the distance a dog howled, telling the night air of abandonment. An owl hooted and launched itself from a branch which arched overhead, a great feathered kite gliding on its hunt for prey. Small animals scurried for cover.

The outline of the access door at the end the building was just visible. Shadows cast by the surrounding trees made it hard to judge the height, as they struggled to lean the top of the ladder against the wall. It clattered and bounced on the timber before the ends wedged safely under the slats. The noise echoed around the countryside. They held their breath, waiting for someone to burst out of the flat.

Nothing happened.

'You got everything?' asked James, softly.

'Yep. Jemmy, torch and screwdriver.'

'Remember, we only need to look inside. Any sign of someone being held, get back the way you came and I'll text Eloise to ring the police regardless of what the bastards threatened. If I'm mistaken and there's no one, or only a girlfriend of Angelo's, come down by the stairs. The old man's still in the flat. He's quite deaf, but we've got to hurry.'

'Ms Carpenter won't come after us, will she?' asked Brie.

'No, I made her promise she'd stay at the house. If anything does happen, I want her safely out of it.'

Brie nodded, stuffed the torch into his shirt and tucked the iron bar in his belt where it swung awkwardly over his hip like a medieval sword. Cursing, he hitched it around against his back and checked his mobile was on vibrate.

'Okay. I'll text you if it's clear.'

James held the ladder while Brie climbed to the top, braced against the wall and began to work on the rusty bolt on the access door. He dragged the jemmy out of his belt, hooked it under the end and wrenched. The bolt squeaked as he jerked backward and forward, then shot back with a sound like a gun shot. He remained motionless, waiting for a response from the staff quarters. When there was no reaction he opened the door.

The cavity between the rafters and the roof loomed black and menacing. Some ten metres ahead, according to the building plan, a narrow, metre-long ladder would be bolted to the wall of the tower room, giving access to its ceiling. Brie turned his face to the side, trying not to suck air as he waited for the first blast of mouse stink to disperse.

'I'll start now,' James called up to him softly. Brie nodded, took the torch out of his shirt and switched it on, aiming into the blackness ahead. Beady eyes glowed and then vanished. He tried not to think about interrupting a carpet snake in the middle of a hunting expedition.

Scrambling across rafters whilst holding the light was not a normal activity for a classical musician, but he was young and fit. Fresh air wafted through the open access door behind him. Sweat trickled down his face, his hands stung from the rough splintered edges of the rafters and his knees burned. He crawled as fast as he could toward the ladder leading to the tower roof, where the atmosphere was thick with the stench of decay.

June Esposito's friends would have been horrified if they realised what kind of entertainment the apparently kindly, middle-aged housekeeper and card fanatic was planning for later that night. She was known and much admired as the Demon Queen of Five Hundred, the envy of the fanatical card club with whom she spent three evenings a week.

She had switched the ring-tone of her mobile phone to vibrate in order not to disturb the game but, absorbed in the current hand, she hadn't felt the text message arriving: changed mnd cmg home ar 10 min.

Her eyes gleamed with excitement, spectacles glinting in the firelight as she contemplated a perfect hand: King, Queen, Ace, Joker and a run of Diamonds. How lucky could you be? They were only playing for dollar coins, but it didn't matter. She had almost a million dollars already.

James slipped into the shadows and worked his way slowly along the side of the building, a tyre lever tightly in his right hand, a torch in his left. A figure came around the side of the house and disappeared quickly through the door at the bottom of the stairs leading to the storeroom overhead. James halted, hardly daring to breathe. It moved so fast that he had almost missed it. He took a deep breath and tightened his grip on the weapon.

He started forward, only to duck down beside a large, wooden keg filled with flowers as a car slid through the back gate and stopped behind the house. The headlights went out and a car door clunked, followed by the crunch of footsteps on the gravel. A flash of colour from the television, a short burst of sound and a neatly-dressed man with something strange on his head stepped into the house, closing the front door behind him. James sent a text warning Brie of the arrival and waited to make sure the stranger stayed inside.

Brie crouched beside the bottom of the short ladder which led to the access door above the tower room ceiling. A scream came from somewhere underneath, high and urgent like the cry of a small animal. His heart pounded, rage surged through him. A woman was in danger.

He jammed the torch between his shoulder and neck and reached to shove hard against the access door. At first it didn't give, then creaked inward. Another blast of foetid air hit him. Ignoring it, he stuffed the torch back in his shirt, scrambled up the ladder, squeezed through the aperture and fell in a heap next to the manhole in the ceiling of the tower room.

Underneath the ceiling a man laughed, followed by the sound of a fist thudding into flesh. A woman shouted and another bark of laughter followed. James's plan flew out of Brie's mind; he didn't feel the vibration of his mobile phone as the text message arrived.

A large box covered half the manhole. He yanked it away, over-balanced and fell back. The edges of the rafters bit into his spine. A thin shriek came from the room below. He dragged himself up and lunged forward, scrambling for a handle on the cover. Wresting the screwdriver out of his pocket, he dug it into the crack at the edge of the cover fighting for leverage, hooked it under the timber and wrenched the hatch up. In one fluid motion he flipped it back and dropped feet-first into the gap.

His legs crumpled as he crashed to the floor, his right ankle twisting. For an instance he was winded, but oblivious to pain, he pushed himself up in one swift movement. It was then he realised he had left the jemmy in the ceiling. A huge torch lay on the floor, its beam lighting up a man who was crouched over something against the wall. For a second they stared at each other in shock, before the other bared his teeth like a wild animal and leapt.

Brie dodged, his assailant sailed past to land on his knees. The man scrambled for something on the floor, then sprang up and lunged back at him.

A blade flashed.

Brie leapt aside again and kicked out, catching his adversary on the thigh but lost his balance and toppled over, upending a metal stretcher.

A muffled scream came from underneath.

As he tried to get to his feet, his assailant leapt on him. They rolled across the room, gouging, punching and clawing.

Brie was fighting for his life.

As James reached the entrance door leading to the stairs, he heard the high-pitched squeal come from somewhere directly above, followed by a man's laugh.

He paused for a moment, listening. A muffled shout came, followed by a crash and sounds of a fight. He stumbled up the stairs, tripped on the top step and went down on one knee, trying to keep a grip on the tyre lever. The torch rolled out of his other hand and bounced. He groped on the floor and found it just in time to turn the beam onto a man hurtling up the stairs behind him, face twisted with menace.

Using the lever and torch like epées, James kept the new arrival at bay. His assailant's arms threshed wildly, as he tried to get close enough to attack. James smacked the metal tyre lever into his face. With a muffled howl, the man fell down the stairs, cannoning into another halfway up.

As both men rolled to the bottom, James turned back to the door, dropped the torch and tried to wrench it open.

It was locked.

He thrust the tyre lever into the crack between the jamb and the edge, jerking it from side to side, trying to spring the door open.

The wood cracked.

The sounds inside the room escalated, as bodies crashed into the walls and hit the floor.

The door started to give way, then suddenly crashed outward, almost knocking him off balance. He leapt aside, then dived into the dimly-lit room, slipped and fell heavily onto his side. A torch on the floor spun around, its beam flashing in turn on the up-turned stretcher, a porta potti lying on its side and the legs of the combatants. Locked in mortal combat, the struggling figures staggered and lurched to the centre of the room.

As James tried to get to his feet, the world exploded with a deafening roar, and he was showered with blood.

CHAPTER 44
After Dark

Detective Senior Sergeant Susan Prescott

Saturday: 7.55pm.

Something smashed in the buildings beyond the perimeter of the estate. The night was split asunder by the blast from a shotgun. For a shocked moment, the countryside forgot to breathe.

'Go, go!' I shouted.

Evan and Ben ran, followed by two of our team with guns drawn. I raced beside them, trying to keep the beam of light from my torch on uneven ground. The target looked a hundred miles away.

We grouped outside the entrance to the building, waiting to see if anyone came out.

Nothing happened.

We started up the stairs, flattening ourselves against the walls. The stench of gun powder, fresh blood and faeces was overwhelming.

Nothing stirred.

'Someone turn a light on!' screamed one of my team from the top of the stairs. Evan fumbled around until he found the switch on the wall outside the door. Light flooded the room, revealing bodies strewn on the floor, with two men standing, dazed, one holding a shotgun. The team shouted, 'Drop it! Get down! Down! On your face! Hands behind your backs!'

'Jees-us, get an ambulance!' Ben's voice cracked with panic.

I sent out the call and squeezed through the doorway into a small room. Three dishevelled, blood-spattered men knelt on the floor. One was an old, grey-haired man, the other square-headed Tommy Esposito. The third prisoner was Ally Carpenter's father, whom they released on my identification.

Two blood-splattered bodies lay in a heap in the corner of the room amid debris leaking from an upturned porta-potti. Sheets of blood-spattered and what was probably urine-soaked newspaper were scattered on the floor. My team whipped out surgical gloves and pulled them on. An officer carefully picked up the shotgun, put the safety catch on and bagged it.

I looked at the bodies. The one sprawled on top had been shot in the back at point blank range. Amid the bloodied mess, I could see backbone and ribs. A broken torch stuck halfway out of what looked like lumps of meat on the floor.

A groan came from underneath a stretcher which was tipped against the wall. For a split second everything stopped.

James got there first and assisted by one of my team to turn it upright. A young woman was lashed on top, legs spread-eagled, her face bruised and smeared with blood, long hair tangled and wet. She moaned again, deep in her throat. Blood had seeped through the gag in her mouth. Her camisole top was rolled to her waist, exposing bloodied breasts.

Ally Carpenter.

I skidded over and struggled to undo the gag. James knelt, trying to untie the cords binding her icy limbs. Ben thrust him aside and cut the ropes. Her eyes opened, rolled and closed without focusing. Her arms and legs flopped uselessly.

Shocked? Drugged? Probably both.

Her ashen-faced father slid down the wall to sit beside her and stroke her face. As I wrapped my coat around her, I noticed he was using his shirt as a sling. I moved to check it, but he shook his head emphatically. Turning my attention to the carnage, I recognized Briece Mochrie lying partially obscured by the shotgun victim. His features were almost unrecognisable, a slice in the side of his neck, blood oozing from his throat. Oozing—

'Mochrie's alive! Where's the ambulance for God's sake? Quick, apply pressure.' I scrabbled in my coat pocket for a handkerchief, a scarf, anything.

My team rushed to pull the top body away. 'Where's the fucking ambulance, for Chrissake's?' someone yelled.

Sirens blasted their way through the night, surging closer as I listened. 'Almost here,' I yelled. Evan, calm amid the chaos, held both hands over the wound in Mochrie's throat, blood trickling through his fingers.

A woman screamed above the hullaballoo. Eloise barged her way in and paused a moment to gaze in horror at the bloodbath. Seeing James sitting by Ally, she shrieked and threw herself at them. He leapt up and caught her in mid-air with one arm as she slipped, almost crash-landing on her daughter.

'It's all right! El! She's alive!' he shouted.

I couldn't hear myself think. The sirens stopped outside the building and I stepped out of the room onto the landing. Red, white and blue lights both from emergency vehicles flashed insanely around the staircase. A gang of paramedics thundered up the stairs and promptly jammed themselves in the doorway. The smallest, a woman, squeezed through and followed a pointed finger to Mochrie. One stopped, briefly, to examine the dead man.

Within what seemed like only minutes they stretchered the cellist out of the room wrapped in a foil blanket, his face covered by an oxygen mask. A tube snaked from his arm to a bag carried by a paramedic. His head appeared scalped. Two medics attended Ally, while James occupied himself with preventing Eloise grabbing her daughter.

It was finally over, with one man killed and another so badly wounded he might not survive.

CHAPTER 45
Aftermath

Detective Senior Sergeant Susan Prescott

Sunday: 10.00am.

I arrived at the hospital, battled my way through the swarm of media and scooted behind a trolley load of flowers. James joined me as I took my place with the group of people waiting at the lifts. We called first at the ward where Eloise, suffering from shock and exhaustion, had been kept overnight,

'Mrs Prescott, please, will you wait while we see Ally?' she begged.

I explained that I was visiting in my official capacity and they would have to be patient while I saw their daughter alone. We helped her into a wheelchair and parked it outside Ally's room. The forthcoming interview between parents and daughter would be interesting.

Ally Carpenter leaned back against her pillows, gazing out of the window across the city to the mountains. My heart turned over. Her face was battered and bruised, lips puffy and still seeping blood. Her eyes were blackened and swollen; one was weeping. As I watched, she dabbed at it with a wad of soft dressing. A chunk of hair had been cut from the side of her head. A cradle kept blanket pressure off her legs. She turned her head when I closed the door and watched without curiosity, as I pulled a chair over to the bed and sat down.

'I thought I'd never live to see the mountains again,' she croaked, sizing me up out of her good eye, after I introduced myself.

'I must admit I didn't think you would either and I'm extremely relieved you're safe. Do you feel up to talking to me?'

'Yes.' She stared at me. 'I know you! I just know you somehow. I couldn't believe...anyone was...searching for...me and then one night...I felt someone was looking out for me,' she said slowly. 'Was it you?'

'I was very concerned for you,' I replied carefully. 'What night was that?'

She frowned. 'I can't remember. The days and nights rolled together. But I felt something, that someone had said a prayer. Does that sound quite mad?'

'No. It doesn't, and yes I prayed for you and sent you vibes.'

She grimaced as she tried to smile, and then reached for a glass of water on the trolley. Her nightgown fell open at the neck to reveal thick dressings over what the doctors had advised were cuts and bites on her throat and breasts.

'Thank you. Brie? Where is he? They said he was all right now. Does that mean he's been hurt?' she asked fearfully, as she put the glass down having only taken an awkward sip.

'He was badly injured and the doctors needed to operate. He's in ICU, but he's doing well. We didn't save you, by the way. He did.'

'Oh, my gosh.' She made a feeble attempt to push the bed covers back.

'No, stay in bed, Ally. You can see him when you're both up to it.'

She flopped weakly back onto the pillows and I gently drew the bedclothes over her again. 'Can you tell me what happened? Don't worry if you can't remember everything. The main details are important, the rest can wait. Just take it slowly and if your mouth is too sore, we can leave it until later.'

She filled in the events of the past week and was quite calm until I had to tell her of Jessica Rallison's murder. The news of Georgie Hird's death was even harder.

Then she asked about the kidnapping. 'They said my father is rich. Was that the only reason?'

'Primarily no, but they were determined to get everything they could. Do you remember one summer on Masters Island when you were twelve?'

Her eyes widened.

'You and a group of children, including Pamela Miller, goaded a boy called Steven Henderson into climbing Wild Pony Rock. He fell and was badly injured.'

'But he recovered!' Her eyes filled with tears. 'He was in hospital for awhile, but he got better, didn't he?'

'Yes, he did, but when he turned sixteen he committed suicide.'

'No. Surely not.' She looked horrified.

I took her hand in mine. 'Apparently, Steven was always a mentally fragile child and an unstable teenager. I won't pretend the accident didn't have a bearing on that. He needed to wear a calliper permanently on his leg from the injuries he received on the rock, but it wasn't the only factor. He was brutally tormented at school and his parents' divorce was extremely traumatic for him. His mother blamed you for his disability, which she insists was the only reason he committed suicide. She was unable to accept that her son had mental problems long before the accident, and that his parent's behaviour contributed to his troubles. In consequence, he didn't receive the psychiatric care which may well have saved him.'

'It was the day of the Teddy Bear's picnic to raise money for the community hall,' said Ally, sadly. 'We'd eaten and the adults told us to go off and play. We didn't go far at first, but we ended up on the beach at Wild Pony Rock. We had all been told to stay away from it, but,' her mouth twisted with self disgust. 'we didn't listen. We started daring each other to climb it and then I picked on Steven—' Tears rolled down her cheeks. 'And I—he—'

'Ally, you were a child.'

'That doesn't excuse what I did. I was twelve and should have known better. Pam tried to stop me, but of course, I wouldn't listen.'

I wrapped my arm around her shoulders and squeezed gently. 'Who else knew about it, Ally?'

'Everyone who was there, all of the people who live on the island. I got into terrible trouble, we all did, and the police gave me a good talking to. Mum—' words appeared to fail her.

'We're satisfied we have the whole story now,' I said, mentally wincing.

June Esposito arrived home as her husband and father were being loaded into the police van. We watched in amazement as the woman collapsed into screaming meltdown. Deprived of her opportunity to wreak revenge on Ally, the discovery that her stepson Angelo, with whom she was totally besotted, had been blasted to death with the shotgun by her panicked father, sent her over the edge of sanity.

Beyond caution, she couldn't tell us about the plan fast enough, after which it took four burly police officers to hold her for the paramedics to plunge a sedative injection into her buttock. Her shrieked invectives faded as the ambulance bore her away.

At the station, June Esposito's father, Robert Fox,

filled us in on the details. Tommy Esposito hid behind the time-honoured, 'No comment.'

'She's right. I was to blame for Steven being crippled,' Ally said, tears rolling down her cheeks. 'I've had nightmares about it for years. I'll never forgive myself. And Georgie and Jess are dead because of what I did.'

'Tommy Esposito killed Georgie. Angelo was Jess's new boyfriend and he murdered her. We haven't got the full story yet, but enough to know the basics.' I didn't think Ally needed then to hear how her friend died or that she had been pregnant.

'Angelo?'

'Yes, he was the one who attacked you last night.'

'Scarpia. That's what I called him.' She shuddered and pulled the sheet tighter against her chest.

'Scarpia?'

'Yes, from the opera, Tosca.' She went on to explain that Scarpia, the evil agent of police raped Tosca, the heroine. He was a brute and they all died in the end. I wasn't sure I was best pleased about the analogy of the police behaving so badly, but my concerns were more immediate.

'Did Angelo rape you, Ally?' I asked.

'No, but he would have if Brie hadn't got in and saved me.'

Relieved, I told her what we knew so far, including Jessica's collusion in her kidnapping.

'Jessica pointed you out to the Esposito's in Traynor's that night.'

'I didn't realise she hated me enough to actually do that. We weren't getting along while we lived in the UK, you know, but I thought we were friends again.'

'Did you tell Jessica about Steven's accident sometime?'

'Yes, Pam, Jess and I talked about it one night in

London when we were getting stuck into the wine.'

I recounted the rest of the events as matter-of-factly as possible. 'Tommy Esposito married Steven's mother, June, after her divorce. It was her idea to kidnap you and make their fortune. Tommy was having an affair with Ms Hird and one night when she had too much to drink, she told him your father's name. June Esposito saw the advertisement for household staff which your father placed in Brisbane Courier Mail and came up with the idea for herself, Angelo and her father, Robert, to apply. Tommy obtained false employment records for them and they presented themselves as a package deal. Actually, they were very lucky to get taken on as a group, but as is so often the case, the devil looks after his own.'

I paused. If Ally showed signs of being too tired I would stop, but she appeared to be holding up.

'After Tommy killed Ms Hird because she realised he was involved in your kidnapping, he made a play for Mrs Miller, your mum's friend. Of course, he knew it was the perfect opportunity for him to find out what your parents and the police were doing. She didn't know he was anything but what he presented himself to be, a new lover.'

I didn't tell her they sent Georgie's ear with Ally's earring in it gift-wrapped to her parents. She would find out soon enough about that.

'They were never going to let me go. A man with a weird-shaped head, told me I was going to die.'

Tommy Esposito. Nice. Tears welled up and her mouth wobbled, but she continued stoically. 'Then Scarpia came up there last night, and forced me to kiss his—ugh. I kept trying to fight and turn my face away, but he gagged me and punched me a lot.' She looked at me, shame-faced. I knew the doctors had taken scrapings from inside her mouth to test for Hep B or venereal disease. *Dear God, please let it be negative.*

'I should have fought harder.'

'You wouldn't have stood a chance with him if you had,' I said bracingly, an image of Jessica's murdered body flashing into my mind.

'He was about to r-rape me,' she repeated.

I stood up, leaned over the bed, gently clasped her fragile, trembling body in my arms and explained why Angelo could never hurt her again.

'But why me? Why should I be alive and three people dead? First Steven, then Georgie and Jess, all gone because of me.'

'They're not dead because of you, Ally. Each one of them made a decision for which he or she was responsible. What is going to be the hard part for you is making sense of what happened.'

We shared a moment of understanding before I gave her more news. 'Your parents are out there waiting to come in. Are you ready to meet your father?' I heard the whole story from James the night before.

She nodded nervously.

'I'll go out and send them in. Talk to you later.' But as I turned to leave the room, someone knocked softly on the door. Ally sat up straight, smoothed her hair back from her face and took a deep breath.

'Come in.'

CHAPTER 46

Recriminations

Ally

One week later.

The nightmares are drowning me. Scarpia dances around Wild Pony Rock, my father and mother are urging him on. Stevie lies smashed on the ground. The waves close over him and wash him out to sea. Georgie is urging Brie to throw me off Wild Pony Rock. I'm left standing helpless on the beach, paralysed by fear. Brie is standing smirking at Scarpia

He turns on me, savagely. 'Well, you wanted to fuck him, didn't you?'

I wake up, screaming, bringing Pam stumbling into my room to comfort, a nursemaid's duty, a sister's caring. And the shock of finding out my father's name ... of all the men in the world, why should he turn out to be my father? My gut crawls with shame as I recall how his good looks affected me when we first met. I knew it was mutual, but thank God I met Brie before either of us made a move.

My almost-intimacy with Angelo makes a relationship now with Brie churn my stomach. Mum keeps trying to talk to me, but I can't face her yet. She came to my hospital room in a wheelchair, looking pale and drawn, her leg wrapped in bandages from the knee down. Apparently, she was injured when she threw herself at me in that horrible room.

My father was with her. I took one look at him and felt as though the top of my head was coming off. His shoulder and arm were supported in a sling. Their hopeful smiles vanished as they saw my expression. I can still hear myself screeching, spewing shock and betrayal like a river of acid.

'You? You're my *father?* How could you do this to me? You were supposed to be my friend. Why didn't you tell me who you were?'

The instant I paused for breath was not long enough for either of them to get a word in.

'So after all these years you want me to be glad you're here? Well, *woop-de-doo!*' I shouted, tears pouring down my face and into my mouth, almost choking me. 'And where were you when I needed you? Did you even care that you abandoned me?'

The kind policewoman stood open-mouthed by the door. Mum came out of her shocked trance. 'Ally, darling, I can explain—'

'Explain? What is there to explain, for God's sake?' I shrieked. 'Where were you when I was a little girl? When I watched all the other kids' fathers at sports days and being there on Parent and Teacher night? And were you in the front row at my first concert being p-p-proud of me? *Of course not.*'

I turned on him so viciously that he actually stepped back. 'And where were you when I made my first recording? Cheering me on? I think not! Too busy making millions!'

Mum finally managed to interrupt. 'Ally, Ally, James didn't know about you. *I never told him.*'

She wheeled herself over to the bed, stood up and tried to put her arms around me, but I pushed her away.

She stumbled and would have fallen if he hadn't caught her up with his good arm and helped her back into the chair. He attempted to intervene, but my venom stopped him in his tracks.

'What do you mean, *you didn't tell him?* There was no such person as Robert Parker, was there?'

Her stricken expression told the story.

'So, you didn't tell him I even existed?' I had to get it right.

Her face whitened. 'No, I didn't tell him about you, Ally. It's not James's fault. He only found out when you went missing a week ago. And yes, I lied. I couldn't tell you about my past. I just—*couldn't.*'

She reached out to me with shaking hands, but I shrank away. The policewoman started to leave, but when mum shot her a desperate look she remained, standing against the wall. Mum wheeled herself forward and put her hand on my shoulder. 'James was furious with me when he found out. It's a long story Ally, and you have every right to know it.'

I shook her hand off and flicked him a glance out of the corner of my eye. When he opened his mouth to speak, I cut him off again. 'I'm twenty-five. You had plenty of time to let him know I existed and to tell me the truth. I can't deal with this now. You want absolution from me for all the years I had no father? Well, it's not going to happen. You knew where he was all along, but even when I joined the Pacific you didn't tell me. And you must have known he was involved with the orchestra.'

I burst into tears, hiding from the flurry of appalled activity around me. The detective must have sent them away, because next moment she enfolded me in her arms and rocked me like a child. I roared even louder. Then I felt a prick in my arm and realised the nurse had given me a sedative.

'Do you feel a little better now?' Detective Senior Sergeant Prescott asked a few minutes later, as she dried my eyes with a damp face cloth.

'Yes, thank you. I don't want to speak to mum yet. I can't get my head around him being my father. She said he was an accountant. She even had a photo of a man she said was my father. My whole life is a lie.'

She handed me a glass of water. 'It's been a shock, but you'll eventually remember the good times, that your mum loved you and was trying to protect you,' she said firmly, possibly feeling that a little less melodrama from me would be an excellent thing.

Then she told me about the week they'd spent while the police had been searching for me.

' Your parents have had a terrible time believing you might be returned to them in pieces, if at all. Your father worked out the plan to reconnoitre the premises with Briece Mochrie. If no one was being held there, they would leave quietly. If they discovered someone imprisoned, he planned to call us. But when Briece heard you scream, he jumped through the manhole and tackled Angelo. Your father fought off the other two men with a tyre lever.'

The image it conjured up felt preposterous. That self-contained, sophisticated man whacking someone with a tyre lever?

'You've been through an ordeal which would send most people off their heads and make no mistake about it, you won't have an overnight recovery,' she finished.

'Post-traumatic stress? I asked drowsily, leaning forward as she took some pillows away and encouraged me to lie down.

'And survivor's guilt, but if you work with it rather than against it and let yourself be helped, then you'll recover. You're a strong girl and you've got an advantage that many don't.'

'What do you mean?'

'You have a loving family, friends and you're well-liked by your colleagues—'

She reached for the card on a gaily wrapped package sitting on the table nearby and read it to me. *"Hang in there! Splash some of this around! Love from Jacq xx"*

'For me?'

'Yes, your friend wants to make you feel better and let you know she's going to be there for you.'

'I only have mum though, there's no other family.' I was feeling very sorry for myself.

She hesitated. 'Your mum doesn't even know this yet. In the course of our investigations we discovered that your mum is my husband's half-sister. I'm your Aunt Susan.'

My eyes flew open. 'But mum doesn't have any brothers or sisters.'

'Her mother, your grandmother, had my husband Harry, by her second husband. Eloise was her daughter from her *first* marriage. My twin daughters, Marli and Brittany, are your cousins.'

CHAPTER 47
Closure

Detective Senior Sergeant Susan Prescott

They buried Angelo Esposito in the far corner of the cemetery, surrounded by hosts of wing-spanned angels, fading plastic flowers and weathered photos of the departed. A line of majestic gum trees stood sentinel, protecting the resting place of his tortured soul. A gentle breeze wafted from the paddocks beyond, where newborn lambs would frolic in the spring. In the distance, a backhoe lay in wait, ready to trundle over to bury the young life forever.

His distraught mother was helped to the graveside by stony-faced sisters. Their father stood a couple of metres away between two detectives, an unyielding, handcuffed figure. Elderly relatives, traditionally black-garbed and wearing head scarves, gathered behind the immediate family and hesitantly recited the Lord's Prayer, lagging two words behind the priest. A ragged "Amen" finalised the proceedings and the coffin was slowly lowered into the green-draped hole. The mourners each sprinkled a handful of soil into the grave before they turned to leave.

I lingered after the group departed, watching as two brawny, overall-clad council workers piled the floral tributes a short distance away and then moved the backhoe into position to fill the cavity. I felt a morbid fascination in watching the emotionless performance of their duties. Did they give a care to the person they would be burying under the earth? They stopped to light cigarettes, inhale deeply and flick the matches on top of the casket. One of them made a joke and my question was answered.

A cold wind blew across the cemetery. Drawing my coat tightly around me, I looked one last time upon the lonely site. How many victims bore the smudge marks of that young man's passing through their lives? We would probably never know. Great sadness swept through me when I had looked on his beautiful, dead face. He could have done anything, achieved any goals he set himself. So why and how had his life gone so wrong? But when I remembered the cruel mouth and venom of Tommy Esposito, it all made sense.

CHAPTER 48

Promises

Ally

Brie made a rapid recovery and returned to his flat just a few days after I was rescued. He couldn't drive because his throat, arm and shoulder were still bandaged, so Pam brought him to my house and told him to phone her when he was ready to return home.

'Come in, Brie and sit down. You look terrible,' I said, trying to keep my voice light and airy. He followed me to the lounge room where, white with pain and exhaustion, he eased himself onto the settee. I hastened to make coffee while I gathered my thoughts. 'Would you like something to eat? Pam made some scones and there's jam and cream somewhere—' I babbled, as I opened the refrigerator door.

'No thank you, Ally. We need to talk. Please come and sit down,' he requested.

'I haven't thanked you for rescuing me. I want you to know I'm very grateful,' I said, setting the steaming cups on the coffee table. My appreciation for him saving my life sounded trite and shallow; I felt dirty, full of sorrow and terribly guilty because I couldn't respond as he wanted.

'Ally, I'd protect you with my life.'

'You already did, 'I replied, taking the chair opposite him. He looked at me silently, gorgeous blue eyes showing his hurt at my aloof demeanour. I realised something about him was different, but couldn't think what it was.

'What is it, Ally? I realise you don't want me to tell you how I feel, but last week was the worst fucking time of my life, thinking you might be dea—' words appeared to fail him. He put his coffee mug down and leaned back on the settee. 'What happened? Did that bastard actually rape you?'

'No, he didn't. He assaulted me.'

'It wouldn't matter to me if he did, because—no, I didn't mean that how it sounded, Ally. I meant I love you no matter what happened. I didn't mean—'

I rescued him from his stumbling sincerity. 'I know what you intended to say, Brie, but no, he did not rape me. He didn't get the chance, thanks to you.'

Brie's expression eased and then to my astonishment, his eyes filled with tears. He dashed them away with his good hand.

Yearning to respond but unable to commit myself verbally, I forced myself to move over beside him. He wrapped his arm around me and I rested my head against his chest. His heart beat strong and fast against my cheek and my aversion to being touched eased somewhat. 'Calm down. This is Brie, your friend,' said my inner voice. 'He would never hurt you.' 'Brie, I know how you feel and if I hadn't been, kidnapped and everything, I would have...slept with you. I really feel for you, but too much has happened all at once. I need space to get my head around everything. Can you understand that?'

'Yes, I do, Ally. I think we all need to recover from it, none more so than yourself. But promise me we'll get together when we've both had time to get over this? We'll take it slowly and see how it goes.' He gently kissed my mouth.

'I promise.' I was grateful for the reprieve.

He smiled briefly and we went on to talk of other things. I realised then that the boy who had romanced me had been replaced by a mature man who loved me enough to allow me to heal at my own pace. I didn't see him again before his mother and sisters bore him off to recuperate on their family property.

Apart from an awkward hello at both Georgie's and Jess's funerals, I still hadn't spoken to my mother. Two thoughts kept recurring: What if something had happened to her before she finally got around to telling me who he was? Would she have ever given me the information if I hadn't been in such danger? We buried Georgie in the Masters Island cemetery on the hillside overlooking the ocean. Early winter-morning mist enveloped the island but by ten o'clock it dispersed, leaving a cold, sunny day.

The sun turned the whitecaps to tinsel; mica chips in the granite headstones sparkled like the diamonds Georgie loved. The smell of salt spray filled our nostrils as sea gulls screamed overhead and swooped across the headland. I carefully avoided looking at Wild Pony Rock rearing up against the horizon. The media gathered in the distance, ducking as the birds dive-bombed them. I gazed at the flower-laden casket, mum's wreath uppermost. Guilt seared through me. Susan was adamant that Georgie was a victim of her own weakness, alcohol, and bore responsibility for her actions. If she hadn't blurted mum's secret, she would be still alive and I wouldn't have been kidnapped. It works both ways, Ally. Intellectually I understood, but my capacity to cope with everything that had happened was diminished.

A couple of days later, we trooped into church in Brisbane and took our places for Jess's funeral. Brie sat next to Pam. Her mother, Aunt Rosalind, horrified and unnecessarily ashamed when she discovered she had been dating Georgie's boyfriend and murderer, sat on the other side of me at the far end of the pew. Susan and Harry, my mother's previously unknown brother and sister-in-law, sat between Brie and mum. My parents tried to talk to me, but I could only shake my head. Friends from our school days and university mingled with our colleagues in the orchestra. Anxious to demonstrate their importance, the directors shuffled into the pew in front of the musicians. Jess's sister and some geriatric relatives attended. Her parents did not come and no plans were made for a wake. After the service, the congregation made courteous noises and fled to their cars.

The orchestra management arranged for Pam and me to take six weeks leave of absence. Detective Sergeant Taylor and Susan jumped Pam through hoops, threatening to charge her for interfering with a crime scene. Brie was reluctantly let off the hook after he handed over the recorder which he planted under Jess's kitchen table. Michael, convicted of concealing a crime, received a suspended sentence.

Just before I left the country, James persuaded me to lunch with him. To begin with I felt awkward, finding it hard to get my head around the fact that, for the first time in my life I was actually sitting opposite my dad. He waved my grateful thanks for his intervention away with enviable panache and then talked about the orchestra, my career plans and his life. We cautiously avoided the subject uppermost in both our minds, but eventually he took a deep breath, looked me in the eye and grinned sheepishly.

'I fancied you for all of five minutes when you joined us.'

'Ditto, also for all of five minutes! Perhaps we instinctively recognised the similarities between us, because now it's obvious we're father and daughter. I don't know why it wasn't spotted before,' I replied, my reward the relief which passed over his face.

He reached across the table and took my hand. 'Ally, I'm proud to be your dad.' He hesitated a moment, then plunged into the controversial. 'Eloise is not to blame entirely. She knows she handled it wrongly and I want to fill you in on our history. Will you let me do that?'

I toyed with the stem of my wine glass, glancing around at the crowded restaurant. 'I need to know. I do love mum, but I just don't understand what happened or why she lied to me all my life. Can we get out of here?'

'Of course,' he replied, signalling for the bill. As we walked through the Botanical Gardens, James told me about their romance in 1983 and its aftermath.

'Are your parents still alive?' I asked, shocked by the duplicity which had destroyed their relationship and left me fatherless.

'No.'

I took his hand. 'It's a bit late to call you "dad" but if I ever get married will you march me down the aisle?'

CHAPTER 49

Coming Home

Ally

Pam and I took leave and flew to the South Island of New Zealand. I felt lost, violated; dark corners and alleyways were terrifying traps. Pam had a cousin there who owned a huge tract of land near Te Anau where we could be undisturbed but not get lost.

Amid the clear, cold air, we hiked the mountains and picnicked on rocky outlooks, attempting to come to terms with Georgie and Jess's deaths and my part in it. Counselling was offered before we left Australia, but at the time, escape seemed more attractive. All I wanted to do was breathe freely again, to learn to cope with the panic attacks, which seized me when least expected.

'Whichever way you look at it, Pam, I'm to blame for Steven's death,' I said one night. 'Why would you be responsible for his suicide years after what happened at Wild Pony Rock?'

'Because I forced him into climbing the rock. Being injured was obviously the beginning of his troubles. Imagine having to face the rest of your life limping because some stupid, bullying idiot made you climb a rock?'

'While you're busy castigating yourself and harking back to the bullying, said stupid idiot was only twelve years old at the time. And I was there too. I should have stopped you, so I'm to blame too.' It was very noble of her, but we both knew no one could have stopped me.

Pam tried another tack. 'Just suppose I was to injure you in some way now while you're twenty five and when you're fifty you kill yourself because of it. At what point after that should I stop feeling responsible for what you've done?'

I opened my mouth to protest, but she held up her hand to silence me.

'Are you your brother's keeper for the rest of my life? No. Same as Jess was responsible for her actions in what she did to you.'

There wasn't much I could say to that, so I had to let the subject go. Somehow I would have to find a way to forgive myself.

Pam was equally pragmatic about my mother. 'Now you know what happened between your parents, you have to suck it up about being fatherless. Okay, so Aunt Eloise lied to you and sure it was wrong and you were deprived, but Ally, we've just finished talking about your mistakes and how imperfect you are. Your mum is human and she did what she thought was best at the time.'

'But keeping it up for so damned long. How could she?' I whined.

'Ever wondered where you get your bull-headedness from, you daft bugger? Take a look in the mirror.' She took a slurp of wine. 'And another thing for you to get through your thick skull, Aunt Eloise raised you all on her own and made sure you got a good education. She went to work all hours to make sure you had the best of what she could afford, and accepted all those stray animals you brought home and she looked after your pet rats while you were away at college.' She paused to fix me with a death stare. 'And Ally, while you're complaining about your mum lying to you, you might remember that she loves you unconditionally.'

That fixed me right enough. Susan discovered that Jess and Julia had been sexually abused by their father, which explained Jess's reticence about her family. I had been blessed with a loving mother and safe home. No wonder my snivelling grated on Jess and prompted her to teach me a lesson. I would miss her for the rest of my life. I would feel guilty for the rest of my life.

Occasionally Pam and I both imbibed too much "Chateau cardboard" and collapsed into helpless drunken giggles or floods of tears. We still had to give evidence at the trial of Tommy Esposito and the old man. June Esposito was incarcerated in a psychiatric hospital, unlikely to stand trial.

Crazed images streaked through my dreams, sending bizarre messages of menace. June Esposito bent over me, tugging at my throat, pulling at my fingers. Steven plucked at her sleeve crying, 'Kill her, mummy, kill her.'

I awoke sobbing and totally out of control, to be comforted by Pam who had her own demons to conquer.

'I'll never forget seeing Brie standing there, covered in blood, Ally. At first I thought he had killed Jess, but I had to take a chance on him. I mean, this was Brie.'

'I couldn't see him murdering her. There's not a nasty bone in his body and besides, he's mad about animals,' I said, though what that had to do with absolving him of anything, I didn't know. 'He adores his cat. Took her home with him to the farm.'

Pam finished reading a text on her mobile and looked up, grinning. That was Jacq Mabardi with some "gossip" for us. Guess what? Michael might have survived with admin after the suspended sentence, but he was caught dealing drugs and thrown out of the orchestra. Then he ran off with Nia, the harpist who joined us just before you—' Pam couldn't continue. Uncharitably, we roared with laughter.

We stand on a rocky outcrop watching a waterfall plummet in a great cascade to a rock pool, far below. Two wild deer step out of the bush on the other side of the ravine and watch us for a few minutes before stepping delicately back amongst the trees. I suck a deep breath into my lungs, savouring the sounds and smells of this glorious place.

'You know something? I'm ready to go home. What happened to all of us will never go away, but we're going to be fine.'

'Yep! Let's get back to Te Anau.' Pam answered, grinning. It's hard to believe I'm actually punching in my father's mobile number to let him know we're coming home.

The flight home can't pass quickly enough, but finally we grab our bags and rush through the fast lane in Customs. Totally hyped, Pam dives into the driver's seat of our hire car and barges into the Brisbane afternoon traffic.

One thing I've learned from what's happened. Do not waste time in life or hang on to regrets and petty squabbles. Treasure the people who love you, and make the most of life while you can. I know Brie wants to see me. He'll try to take things slowly, but I'm going to get him naked so fast his head'll spin.

'Shift your bums!' I bellow at slower drivers, as we fight our way into the city.

Pam crouches over the wheel like a racing greyhound. 'Hey, did you hear the one about the traffic cop who spun out of control on point duty?'

'Do tell!'

'His control spun out and wrapped around his truncheon!'

'Ha ha!' I sneer happily, 'very funny.'

'It would be if you saw the size of his truncheon' she roars. We pull into a space at the front of her block of flats, laughing helplessly at our stupid joke as we bundle her backpack out of the boot.

'Bye, see you next week at the wedding!' she calls, as she scampers up the steps into the building.

'Yo.' I am still laughing as I reach the freeway and head out of the city.

James broke his lease on the estate where I was imprisoned, bought a farm outside a small country town and moved there with mum. It's dusk by the time I arrive. The two younger dogs race the car along the driveway, their joyous barks alerting the house to my arrival. I scramble out of the car and reach the top step just as mum flings open the front door. Behind her looms James.

'I'm home for the wedding!' I throw myself into her arms and nearly squeeze her to death. 'Mum, I'm sorry. I just couldn't come to terms–'

'I'm sorry too, darling, Please forgive me.'

I reach out to my father, who steps forward and wraps us both in his more than adequate wing span. My heart is so full, the darkness is briefly conquered. For now, happiness is paramount. *Just think, this time next week you'll be Mr and Mrs James Kirkbridge!'*

Glossary of Australian Terms

Chooks...chickens.

Wharfie.....................................waterside worker.

Galah............a mad clown of a grey and pink parrot who doesn't mind making a fool of itself.

Drongo..stupid person.

Louie the Fly........................a well-known and long-running Australian TV advertisement for fly-spray.

Chateau Cardboard............................a silver foil bladder of wine with a tap in the bottom, inside a cardboard box; invented by Australians and used with much enthusiasm, particularly at barbecues and wild parties.

Ninety not out.........cricket term indicating a person is doing well/healthy for their age.

On the piss.................getting stuck into the wine, a drinking session

DISCLAIMER: Masters Island is as much a figment of the imagination as Brigadoon! The characters in this novel are too mad to be real!

Acknowledgements

I wish to thank my patient reviewers from The Next Big Writer workshop site, without whom NAKED ROOM would not exist. JL Campbell, sonny, Jessica Chambers, kyla, Verity Farrell, Carolyn Kuzcek, Caroline Kellems, Bob Keen, Patti, Susan Etheridge, Mike 2439, Keith Campbell, Isabel IV, Nathan B. Childs and Sol Nasisi, your site rocks!

And thank you to my dear friends Sergeant Cary Bensted, Pam Cairncross, Margaret van Blommenstein, Andrea March, and Robin Dunn for your kind encouragement and time in reading this manuscript.

Author's Bio

Diana Hockley lives in a southeast Queensland country town, surrounded by her husband, Andrew, two cats and six pet rats. She is a dedicated reader, community volunteer, and presenter of a weekly classical program on community radio. She and her husband once owned and operated the famous Mouse Circus which travelled and performed throughout Queensland and northern New South Wales for ten years. They also bred Scottish Highland cattle. She has three adult children and three grandchildren.

She has had articles and short stories accepted and published in a variety of magazines, among them, Mezzo Magazine USA, Honestly Woman (Australia) the Highlander, Austin Times and Austin UK, Australian Women's Weekly, It's A Rats World, Solaris UK, Literary Journal of University of Michigan USA, Foliate Oak, children's website Billabong. In 2006, she was awarded Scenic Rim Art Festival prizes for poetry and fiction in 2006.

Her next crime novel, The Celibate Mouse, featuring Detective Senior Sergeant Susan Prescott, will be published in 2011

Sample chapter of Diana Hockley's next Susan Prescott novel, The Celibate Mouse

CHAPTER 1
A Little Unpleasantness at the Sheep Dog Trials.

Susan Prescott

Saturday: noon.

There was no mistaking the crack of a high-powered rifle.

Jack Harlow, the final competitor in the sheepdog trials was shot in front of an audience of twenty-five hundred people, two trial judges, three sheep and his border collie, Stephen. He went down like a pole-axed steer, slamming into the gate at the last holding pen. The sheep seized the opportunity to escape, bolted across his body, leaped the dog and took to their trotters.

Susan Prescott watched, aghast. Perspiration prickled up her spine, then down her arms to her finger tips. Marli buried her face in the front of her mother's sweater.

Pandemonium erupted, shattering a moment frozen in shock. At first, people believed that a vehicle had backfired behind the grandstand. Rumours circled the arena at lightning speed. A wave of conflicting information, punctuated by cries of disbelief, spread to where they sat. A young woman seated a couple of levels below the mother and daughter turned and shouted, 'I thought he had a heart attack, but they said Jack's been shot!'

White-faced, Marli pulled away and wiped her eyes. 'Aren't you going to go down there, Mum?'

'Certainly not! I'm on stress leave, remember? The local police will handle it,' replied Susan. *I can't handle this, it's too soon.* Officiating, over another crime scene, even temporarily would shatter her fragile composure.

The overcast, sullen day got worse. A woman, whom she later discovered to be Harlow's wife, Penelope, was walking back from the food kiosk. A group of agitated people rushed up to encircle her. A moment later she dropped her takeaway meal and attempted to scramble, screaming, over the fence into the arena.

She got stuck. Bystanders pushed and pulled until she landed in a heap on the other side. Clouds of dust rose as she got to her feet and staggered across the grass to be met by a flustered official waving a clipboard in the air. The mob around the victim parted for a moment and Susan glimpsed someone folding a coat, presumably to put under Harlow's head. *No, you mustn't do that!*

His dog was hauled away from the inert body, the sound of its howls heartbreaking. Distressed, she fumbled for a tissue. A man jumped the fence, rushed over, picked up the animal and headed for the exit gate. One of the judges carefully removed the coat from under the victim's head and commenced CPR.

'Did you hear that, Fran? Who on earth would want to shoot Jack?' called a woman sitting on the seat below Susan and Marli.

'Half the fucking town, I'd say,' a man sitting nearby muttered. Sniggers of agreement rippled through the surrounding spectators.

The recipient of the query glanced around the stand, presumably hoping to pass on the information to anyone who might be appreciative. Catching Susan's eye, she quivered with curiosity. 'Do you know the Harlows?'

'No, we're only visitors here,' Susan replied, taking deep breaths to quell the imminent threat of nausea.

Disappointed, the woman turned away to join in a nearby huddle of excited onlookers.

The action in the ring stepped up, as someone with more common sense than the rest began to manage the situation. The mob of people around the victim parted and a coat was placed over Harlow's head. His widow flapped around in the centre of the group, while a woman tried to comfort her. Men circled, speaking furtively into mobile phones, staring at the ground. An official from the sheepdog association organised another dog to round up the three sheep cavorting across the trial bridge.

'How they're going to get any sense out of this lot I don't know, but I'm damned sure not going to be amongst them,' Susan muttered, watching the children caught up in the drama. Several small boys had taken advantage of the lull in proceedings to kick a soccer ball back and forth on the far side of the arena. A patch of sunlight suddenly pierced the clouds, lighting the scene in the centre of the arena like a surreal theatrical production.

When the report and inevitable phone video footage was aired on the early evening television newscast, those with ghoulish tendencies would be kicking themselves for not making an effort to attend. The final of the championship sheep dog trials had never been so exciting.

Susan caste her gaze across the grounds. The victim had dropped like a stone, indicating a possible direct hit in the head or heart. He'd fallen to his right, so she knew the shooter might be somewhere in the vicinity of the announcer's box. The five-metre tower at the side of the arena looked like an excellent place to pick off a target, but was a risky proposition.

Heads bobbed inside as she weighed up the likelihood of it being the source of the shot. 'Not up there, unless it was a conspiracy; unlikely.'

Cars lined the fence on both sides of the pillars which supported the small announcer's box. The sniper could have fired from inside one, or crouched between them— 'Maybe from the hillside? No, too exposed,' she muttered. A long distance shot would require a telescopic sight which could reflect the light and draw attention. He or she was long gone, unless the rifle was stowed while the perpetrator mingled with the crowds.

Her police training warred with an overpowering urge to escape, to avoid any involvement. Private fear won hands down, coupled with the necessity to keep sixteen year old Marli from experiencing the aftermath of violent death.

A vivid memory of scolding a woman for fleeing the scene of a particularly gruesome scene sprang into her mind. 'If you ever get to walk in my shoes, officer, then you'll understand how I feel,' the woman had retorted. Now she, a Detective Senior Sergeant, recently Acting Inspector, was intent on emulating her. It was not an auspicious start to their country stay.

Marli and Susan had arrived on to stay in Emsburg shortly before lunch. Marli's twin, Brittany, had chosen to live in Sydney with their stepfather, Harry, and his new partner. In an effort to assuage her daughter's loneliness, she had allowed Marli to arrange to buy a puppy from a breeder of Border Collies. They had stopped at the local showground to collect it, but the woman was competing in the trials when they arrived, so they had found seats in the grandstand to watch the competition.

Never having attended a sheepdog trial, Susan had been interested but confused about what was happening. The farmer sitting beside them, leaning a little closer to Susan than strictly necessary, explained the procedure sotto voce, like a commentator at a billiards tournament.

'The man and dog are a partnership, see? They have to drive three sheep through the gates, over the bridge, then into that pen.' He pointed to the one near the exit to the arena, 'They have fifteen minutes to do it before the hooter sounds. The handler has to keep walking between the points without stopping or backtracking. He can signal or whistle the dog, but nothing else. We can't clap until he's closed the gate at the last pen, otherwise the sheep'll most likely take off and they could lose points.'

Susan watched as the canine half of the team cast a swathe around three recalcitrant sheep on the far side of the arena and turned them toward the next obstacle, whereupon they bolted in different directions. Undaunted, the dog streaked, a black wraith, around the arena and patiently gathered them together again. Amid much stamping of feet and defiant glares, the sheep were herded reluctantly into the last pen, whereupon the dramatic conclusion to the life of Jack Harlow had taken place.

The championship competition having been blown to smithereens, the farmer abandoned the women, with a regretful glance at Susan accompanied by a muttered apology, to join a group in the stands below.

Ashen-faced, Marli sat rigidly, hands tightly clasping the neck of the tote bag which carried everything she considered necessities of life and to which she appeared permanently connected.

'Come on, Marli, it's time we left.' Once they had collected and paid for the pup, Susan intended to leave the area immediately and go to the farm where they were going to house-sit their relative's property, five minutes outside the country town.

Trying to hurry her daughter along, Susan grabbed the tote bag, stuffed Marli's iPod and hat inside and thrust it back into her hands. A police uniform moved into the centre of the crowd around the victim as they started down the steps to the exit gate. Almost immediately, an announcement came over the tannoy, ordering everyone to remain on the grounds until further notice.

The crowd moaned collectively. Loud protests broke out, as people tried to control fractious children. Nearby, a newborn baby bawled and what appeared to be it's toddler sibling set up a sympathetic wailing. A tired-looking young woman grabbed the child by the arm and jounced the pushchair down the steps making the baby screech even louder as they left the stands.

A man stood up, cupped his hands around his mouth and roared his displeasure to the officials. A couple of small girls, giggling hysterically, jostled through the crowd, almost knocking Marli off her feet.

Unable to censure them without revealing herself as the "police," Susan ducked her head and pushed through the crowd, towing Marli behind, hoping any observers would think they were heading for the restrooms.

Within a couple of minutes they arrived at the back of the grandstand in the competitors' camping area, where Susan propped herself against a fence post and waited for Marli to locate the breeder. Happy, hairy faces beamed at her from behind mesh dog boxes; tails swished enthusiastically. Resisting the impulse to "sweet-talk" to the fur- faces, she hoped the promise of five hundred dollars would outweigh the woman's curiosity about what had occurred in the arena and she would be waiting for her young customer.

James Kirkbridge, her brother-in-law, had already delivered the Prescott dogs to a neighbouring farm, before he and his wife, Eloise, had flown from Brisbane to the UK on urgent family business. The animals would be delivered to the farm later that afternoon.

The sun vanished behind the clouds again underscoring the day's disaster; a chill wind rose from nowhere. Susan was struggling into her coat when Marli arrived back at the car, clutching a curly-coated, squirming black and white bundle with beguiling blue eyes. Colour blossomed in the girl's cheeks again as she smiled and nuzzled the pup, thoughts of the drama in the ring briefly forgotten in the excitement of the moment.

Susan paused, battling a modicum of guilt and wavering about returning to the arena. 'Darling, I need to check out what's going on. Don't worry, I'll be right back, I promise. Wait for me here. Okay?'

'Mum, for God's sake, I'm almost seventeen, not seven! I'll be here, okay?'

Susan eyed her daughter's stormy expression and hastened to ward off a "teenage moment. 'I'm sorry, I didn't mean to treat you like a child.'

Marli shrugged, giving off an air of nonchalance, though the expression in her eyes retained the shock of what she had witnessed.

Susan left her struggling to hold the over-excited pup, walked to the corner of the grandstand and peered at the action. The centre of the ring resembled a kicked ant heap, as agitated officials and competitors buzzed around bumping into each other. High-pitched screams, like the squeaks of a mouse, came from the centre of the melee.

Any decision she might have made to join in the action was irrelevant when an ambulance trundled through a side gate onto the grounds, closely followed by a blue and white- checked patrol car. A movement on the town-side of the grounds revealed the arrival of a media van. Anxiety shot through her. The last thing she needed was anyone from the press to spot her. She slunk back to Marli.

'Come on, let's get out of here!'

Doubling back and then dodging behind trees and advertising hoardings as they passed gaps in the buildings ensured no one saw them, as did the circuitous route through the competitor's caravans and motor homes. They reached the car park without being prevented from leaving, much to Detective Senior Sergeant Susan Prescott's relief.

She knew that if she lost her hard-won control, her stress leave would be blown before it had even begun, and the counselling she had received after Detective Constable Danny Grey's death barely three months previously, would be all for nothing.